I0551900

OUTSHINE

HOUSE OF OAK BOOK FIVE

NICHOLE VAN

Fiorenza Publishing

Outshine © 2017 by Nichole Van Valkenburgh
Cover design © Nichole Van Valkenburgh
Interior design © Nichole Van Valkenburgh

Published by Fiorenza Publishing
Print Edition v1.0

ISBN: 978-0-9968936-4-0

Outshine is a work of fiction. Names, characters, places and incidents are the products of the author's imagination or are used fictitiously. Any resemblance to actual events, locales or persons, living or dead, is entirely coincidental.

To my readers,
For tirelessly begging to know Daniel Ashton's story.
This one is for you.

To Dave,
You know how much I love your spreadsheets.

Prologue

THE BLUE DRAWING ROOM
KINNINGSLEY, THE SEAT OF VISCOUNT LINWOOD
HEREFORDSHIRE, ENGLAND
NOVEMBER 12, 1826

You are wrong, Daniel—"

"No! I'm not. It's the only correct explanation, Jasmine. You just said so yourself."

Daniel Ashton paced before an enormous paned window, hands shaking, breathing serrated. All of him jagged shattered pieces.

He refused to meet the gaze of the petite, dark-haired woman standing across the room, arms hugging her upper torso.

It was already bad enough to *feel* the weight of Jasmine Linwood's pity. He had no desire to actually witness the tears quietly slipping down her cheeks.

"I know this is difficult . . ." she began, her tone placating, as if he were a little brother she was about to reproach.

That Daniel considered himself to *be* her honorary younger brother was beside the point.

"No! Scaling a cliff is difficult. Running a marathon is difficult. *This*"—he paused his pacing to point a shaking finger at her—"t-this is a living hell I refuse to accept!"

"Daniel"—a hiccupping sob—"s-sometimes the logical answer isn't the correct one—"

"No!" he roared, finger still pointing, still shaking. "You m-might be a mystic, but that doesn't mean you understand everything going on here. You *cannot* t-take this from me—"

He gasped out the last words, spinning around to face the window. Emotions choked, acrid and burning in his throat.

Hope. He had to cling to hope. Because without hope, only madness and despair existed.

Daniel was used to living in shadows. But this time . . . this time was different. If he couldn't fix this . . . the darkness would never leave, never lift. Boundless in its breadth. Fathomless in its depth.

Some wounds were too deep to ever heal. The best he could hope for was an uneasy coexistence.

Breathe in and out. One day at a time.

Unbidden, his eyes darted to a wooden box resting on a table beside the window. The box that had become his constant companion. Not for itself, but for what it contained.

Promise you will keep it for me. Don't forget.

Guilt crushed his chest in a destructive vise.

How could he have done this?

Daniel kept secrets and solved problems for the most powerful men in the world. He was considered by some to *be* one of those powerful men.

He *would* fix his mistake, correct his wrong.

"Daniel, p-please—"

"No!" Lungs heaving. "'Til the day I die, I will *never* stop fighting for this!"

Silence.

His razored breathing echoed through the room, mingling with Jasmine's quiet weeping behind him.

He would never agree with her.

He *had* to have absolution.

There was no other way.

And then . . .

Between one heartbeat and the next, something . . . changed.

The entire world hushed. Motionless.

The very air portent-laden.

Years of spy work had Daniel's senses instantly screaming *Danger!*

He stilled and turned, meeting her watery, wide-eyed gaze.

He shook his head. "Something is wro—"

Abruptly, Jasmine flinched, as if hit by an unseen force. She screamed—pain-filled agony—arching backwards, mouth an 'O' of horror and anguish.

Daniel lunged for her, catching her convulsing form an instant before she hit the floor.

"Jas!"

Her entire body jerked in a seizure, eyes rolled to the back of her head,

"Jasmine!"

Then, he heard it.

A deep rumble from far away, drawing nearer.

Like a steam locomotive. Or a vast mining explosion. Or an airplane during takeoff.

The sound reverberated. A sonic boom?

No! It was a—

The windows rattled. The floor shook. Items danced across tabletops. Chandeliers swayed.

Daniel clutched Jasmine's convulsing body to him, pulling them both to the middle of the room, barely dodging a vase toppling to the floor.

He had experienced earthquakes before. One on a rare family trip to Disneyland as a child. He and his sister, Kit, had clung to the motel bed as the TV rattled and car alarms blared.

All long before the time portal in Duir Cottage had forever altered the trajectory of his life.

The rumble turned into a roar. A jet engine of sound.

Daniel tensed, ready to crawl underneath the large grand piano for protection. He held Jasmine closer, her body still twitching—

The shaking abruptly stopped.

Both the earth's and Jasmine's.

He cradled her suddenly limp form in his arms.

Chest heaving, he noted the cries of servants, the frenzied barking of dogs. Timothy, Lord Linwood desperately calling for his wife.

"Timothy . . ." Jasmine moaned, face deathly pale.

"Timothy is coming, Jas." Daniel brushed hair off her face. "We'll get you help."

Abruptly, her eyes flared open.

"No!" She clutched his coat.

"Jas?!"

"The portal!" Her terrified blue gaze met his. Voice agitated. "Daniel . . . something has happened to the time portal!"

Chapter 1

No one expected a ruddy fishwife screeching at drunken sailors on London's south docks to be a venerated Peer of the Realm.

And that was the one (and only) beauty of Fanny McCusker.

She was the perfect alter-ego for a spy.

Which allowed Mrs. McCusker—a.k.a. Daniel Ashton, Lord Whitmoor—to shriek insults with impunity at his quarry . . . a merchant ship's captain smoking a pipe across the street.

"Cap'n, yer mum's so daft she climbed a glass wall to see what was on the other side," Daniel shouted at the man.

Nothing like a 'yo momma' smack down, Regency-era style.

Captain Adams turned his head.

With her broad girth, penetrating voice, smattering of facial hair and complete lack of social filters, Fanny McCusker was expert at extracting information in the most obnoxious way possible.

The wise ran when they saw her coming.

"What did you just say about me mum?" the captain snarled, taking a step Daniel's way.

Captain Adams was many things . . . *wise*, thankfully, was not one of them.

"Yer mum's teeth are so yellow, God said, 'Let there be light,' and yer mum just opened her mouth," Daniel jeered.

"Shut yer trap, woman!"

"Make me!"

Captain Adams lunged toward Daniel.

Bingo.

Daniel hitched up his boned corset, clapped a hand on his bonnet and took off for a side alley, Captain Adams hot on his heels. Reaching the back of the alleyway, Daniel ducked into a recessed area where his right-hand man, Garvis, waited.

Captain Adams rounded the corner, only to stutter to a stop, eyes huge as he stared down the two barrels of Garvis' pistols.

" 'ave a seat 'ere, Cap'n." Daniel kicked a stool in the man's direction. "I just wants to 'ave a wee chat."

Captain Adams, however, had not risen to his levels of infamy by backing down from a fight.

"I gots nothing to say to you, woman," the man sneered, raking his eyes over Daniel, clearly weighing his chances at out maneuvering the two of them.

Daniel chuckled. It was not an amused sound. "I wouldn't do it. I suggest 'ee sit, Cap'n."

Today would be Fanny McCusker's grand finale—one last appearance before Daniel retired. God-willing.

After nearly ten years in the Home Office serving the Crown, the persona of Daniel Ashton had evolved into the legendary public figure of Lord Whitmoor, renowned for his daring feats—a man somewhere between Robinson Crusoe and Ivanhoe.

The captain hesitated.

"You're trying me patience." Daniel's voice was deceptively calm. "Shall I have me man shoot yer right or yer left kneecap first?"

Without blinking, Garvis shifted one gun to point directly at Captain Adams' knees. Daniel and Garvis had their routine down—not so much good cop/bad cop, as bad cop/even worse cop.

Captain Adams was not . . . *un*impressed. He licked his lips.

Over the years, Daniel's exploits and extraordinary methods of gathering information for the Crown had made him the subject of newspaper rumors, broadsheet cartoons, ballads, a dreadful threepenny opera and as of late—

"How do you know I won't whitmoor ya?" the captain asked.

—a verb.

Daniel filed that under 'Signs It Was Time to Retire'—when the general populace considered your name so synonymous with secrets and unexpected clandestine behavior that you became a part of speech. Bow out when his career had hit its zenith, so to speak.

Over the years, Daniel's assignments from the Crown had consumed an absurd amount of time and energy. Something he saw as both a pro and a con.

A con because it left him with less time to pursue personal matters. Specifically finally fixing his terrible mistake of two years ago and resolving the problem of the time portal.

A pro because his attempts to solve those two problems had met brick wall after brick wall. Currently, he was at an impasse without a way forward or back. His espionage work provided a welcome distraction from the bleak darkness of his thoughts.

A rogue blast of anguished guilt shot through his chest, instantly tightening his breathing.

What *was* he going to do now? He had to solve this problem and leave behind these two *years* of self-loathing and pain and torment—

Don't go there!

Focus, Daniel.

Garvis fired a warning shot, splintering rock and wood next to Captain Adam's right knee.

~ 11 ~

The man flinched and yelped. Daniel flowed into action.

He seized the captain's arm and twisted it around between the man's shoulder blades, expertly applying pressure that almost dislocated the captain's shoulder, causing excruciating pain.

Captain Adams collapsed to his knees, roaring in agony.

"Or maybe Fanny 'ere will whitmoor you instead," Garvis drawled.

Daniel bent the captain's arm further. " 'ere now, Cap'n. Let's 'ave a wee chat, shall we? Start by explainin' how large sums of newly-minted money ended up in wine casks aboard yer ship."

Without waiting for a reply, Daniel applied more pressure and, between the captain's screams, elicited the information he needed.

Mind distracted, he eked another couple hours of living, avoiding the guilt that threatened to crush him into dust.

Chapter 2

A HACKNEY CAB
LONDON, ENGLAND
AN HOUR LATER ON JULY 24, 1828

She should not have come.

She should have stayed at home, safe in the shell of her anonymity. Remaining as she had always been—the background wallpaper against which others lived their lives.

Pride was one of the seven deadly sins for good reason and, at this moment, Fossi Lovejoy was far too guilty of it.

But . . .

She had traveled one hundred and twenty-four point nine miles already. 'Twould be cowardice to not see the thing through when only two point four miles remained of her journey.

And Fossi Lovejoy was many things at the moment—furious, outraged, indignant—but cowardly was not one of them.

Righteous anger had a way of fortifying one's spine, she had discovered. Lord Whitmoor could *not* be allowed to steal from her.

The hackney cab rocked along the crowded London street for another half a block and then suddenly lurched to a stop, throwing Fossi forward, knocking her knees against the opposite bench.

A quick glance out the window showed that two enormous wagons—one filled with wine casks, the other with wooden crates of hissing geese—had managed to tangle their wheels. Naturally, the drivers felt the need to expound upon the other's stupidity, family heritage and reproductive habits at colorful length.

Heavens. London is certainly proving educational.

Fossi sat back on the seat, twisting her gloved hands. Wondering for the fifty-third time since breaking her fast at the Boar and Rose Inn if pride and outrage justified her transgressions.

Mentally, she cataloged her sins over the last three days.

First was the lie she told her father. She was not, in fact, visiting an ailing schoolfriend of her mother's in Bath. The good Reverend Josiah Lovejoy erroneously assumed the elderly woman was paying for Fossi's travel expenses.

Which led to her second transgression—Fossi was a genteel lady traveling alone without a chaperone. Her pitiful savings only supplied enough money for one person's transportation, not two. Bringing a companion had been out of the question.

Not that Fossi needed a chaperone. Her reputation, such as it was, could hardly suffer from this trip. A lowering thought, but nonetheless true. Her financial status (poor), age (thirty-two this past summer) and education (far more expansive than sensible) already ensured her spinsterhood.

No person in England was more *un*marriageable than a plain, aging, poor, *clever* woman.

It was impossible for her chances of matrimony to sink any lower. A black mark on her honor would simply be another shovelful of dirt on an otherwise deeply buried dream.

Granted, that knowledge had been scant comfort on the overnight mail coach when trying to sleep between a farmer's wife who reeked of onions and a sweaty businessman whose hands had a distressing tendency to wander where they shouldn't.

Then there was the vanity and pride of wishing to protect her work from Lord Whitmoor's exploitation, which had been the catalyst for this journey in the first place.

The cab lurched to life, moving slowly through the crushing traffic. A fruit monger argued with a flower girl. A weathered old woman played a hurdy-gurdy hanging from her neck. A street sweeper held up carriages while he cleared the road of manure and filth so his patrons could cross on (relatively) clean ground.

London was different and yet exactly what Fossi had always expected.

Loud. Noisy. Chaotic.

A sea of humanity.

But in all her imaginings of London, she had never considered the smells.

Coal smoke, rotting garbage and mildew. The stink of stagnant water and cattle stockyard and unwashed bodies. The last smell, in particular, seemed ground into the hackney itself. Not to mention the floor of the cab which Fossi found disturbingly sticky.

She glanced for the sixty-first time at the magazine clipping clutched in her gloved right hand.

It had appeared in *Scriptis Mathematicis*, the foremost scholarly publication for the Society of Mathematicians—a society to which Fossi belonged. Or rather a *man* named Foster Lovejoy belonged.

Women were not welcome within the Society, naturally.

Fossi could not afford a subscription to *Scriptis Mathematicis* but instead relied on friends within the mathematical community to forward copies to her.

This particular notice in last month's journal had instantly captured her attention. The clipping showed a complex mathematical equation and then ended with the words:

> *One who knows the solution to this equation should present himself and the solution to Ashton House in Mayfair, London.*

Fossi chewed on her cheek.

The fact of the clipping was nothing out of the ordinary—others entreated the Society for answers to mathematical questions with shocking frequency.

It was the *what* of the clipping that made Fossi's blood stir in righteous indignation.

The equation displayed was *hers*. A creative idea she had scribbled in her notebook one night several months ago.

She had talked to no one about it, shown it to no one. But there it was nonetheless—distinctly recognizable parts of it published in *Scriptis Mathematicis* for all the world to see.

Why had Lord Whitmoor taken her theorem? Of all the secrets in Britain, why had he chosen to pilfer hers?

Well . . . she assumed Lord Whitmoor had taken them. Or at the very least ordered the pilfering done.

Thanks to newspaper reports, everyone in Britain knew who resided at Ashton House, particularly after the events of last April when Mr. Daniel Ashton had miraculously foiled an assassination attempt on the king. Mr. Ashton had been gravely wounded as a result, adding to his aura of power and mystique.

In gratitude for his service to the Crown, Mr. Ashton had been elevated to Baron Whitmoor. The society broadsheets had been rapturous about the new Lord Whitmoor—the elegance of his person, the intelligence of his parliamentary speeches, the largess of his fortune. It was said debutantes swooned when he passed them at Almack's.

The man had become a *verb*, for heaven's sake.

The news rags, of course, loved depicting him. Lord Whitmoor regularly appeared in the political cartoons of Mr. Cruikshank. The Lord Whitmoor of those drawings was an autocratic figure, meticulously dressed in the latest fashion, staring down the opposition with icy eyes. In one memorable sketch, Lord Whitmoor rises with collected superiority from the hatch of a large wooden horse, surprising disheveled Trojan soldiers who look remarkably like his political opponents.

The cartoon, of course, was the very definition of being 'whitmoored'—an unexpected act which caught one by surprise and changed the outcome of events.

Daniel Ashton, Lord Whitmoor was a master of secrets and surprises.

But why had he concerned himself with *her* secrets? *Had* he deliberately stolen her theorems? And if so, why spy on Fossi Lovejoy?

Whitmoored, indeed.

Fossi had no previous experience with the upper echelons of the aristocracy. While her mother was yet alive, they had on occasion called upon Sir Peter Nobly, a local baronet of some (self-declared) importance. He had enjoyed practicing his schoolroom Italian with her mother, and she had enjoyed speaking the language of her maternal grandparents. That was the beginning and end of Fossi's interactions with the peerage.

But her father had ensured she was well-educated in the vagrancies of the aristocracy. The depths of their depravity. The heights of their pride. The loftiness of their self-regard.

To say that Daniel Ashton, Lord Whitmoor, was out of her sphere of social interaction was a gross understatement.

Fossi had no delusions as to her own importance. Life had never allowed her such luxury.

Lord Whitmoor would see himself as a shining star to her pathetic grain of sand.

She knew herself to be completely invisible. Brown hair, brown eyes, a height that was neither too high nor too low, a figure that ran neither too lean nor too plump . . . though a friend of her mother's had once remarked that Fossi's complexion was quite fine.

Externally, Fossi was utterly forgettable.

But inside . . . oh, inside she was color. Vibrant reds and oranges and blues. Poppies and bluebells. A blistering summer sunset after a glistening rain.

A pity her inside had never made itself known upon her outside.

Lord Whitmoor would view her as a chafing bit of grit, one to be hastily dispatched.

But—here she gripped the magazine clipping more firmly—she couldn't let this pass. Even a tiny speck of sand, when correctly placed, could make itself felt. And if she had to stubbornly scrape at Lord Whitmoor until he explained his actions to her . . .

Well, she was prepared to be an irritant.

Chapter 3

ASHTON HOUSE, MAYFAIR
LONDON, ENGLAND
A WHILE LATER ON JULY 24, 1828

Fossi tapped her booted foot, watching as the bustle of the inner city gave way to the wider streets and calmer atmosphere of, what she could only assume, was Mayfair. Elegant people in elegant clothing walked elegantly down streets which were . . . elegant, of course.

Fossi had landed in one of the fairy tales she told her nieces and nephews. Only she was certainly no Cinderella and fairy tale dreams were a luxury she had relinquished long ago.

Her muscles felt stretched thin, taut and jumpy. She found herself humming an Italian aria . . . one of doom and despair.

It was more than just nerves, this restless energy. Since receiving the clipping and deciding on this course of action, her emotions had gone topsy-turvy and she hadn't a clue how to right them.

The hackney finally creaked to a stop in front of an imposing town house—three stories of marble columns topped by a large pediment.

She paid the cab driver after a brief haggle over current versus historical values of the shilling and how that related to hackney cab fares—the man was not amused and drove off with frightening alacrity.

Fossi waited for one of those elegant couples to pass her before facing the looming front steps.

Purposefully, she reached into her reticule and swapped the magazine clipping for a smaller piece of thick white paper. Armed as much as she could be, she sucked in a deep breath, straightened her shoulders and marched up the stairs, rapping the knocker with a firm hand.

A decidedly top-lofty butler opened the door and peered along his prominent nose at her. He raked her up and down with a dismissive sniff.

"The servants' entrance is around the left, opposite the mews."

The door slammed in her face.

Right.

She had hardly come this far—braving onions, wandering male hands and outrageous cab fares—to be kept out by a condescending butler.

Gritting her teeth, Fossi rapped again.

Mr. Top-Lofty opened the door, scowl deepening.

"I am here to see Lord Whitmoor," Fossi said in her most educated accent. She swept past the man into the cavernous entrance hall.

Fossi might be poor, but her mother—God rest her soul—had insisted she behave like a lady. Not that her mother would have approved of Fossi barging into a gentleman's home unannounced but, oh bother, she was determined—

"His lordship is not at home to visitors, madam." Mr. Top-Lofty's scowl morphed into a full-on glower.

His unspoken words being, *His lordship is not at home to visitors such as yourself.*

Perseverance, Fossi.

"I have endured the travel of one hundred twenty-seven point three miles—nearly two hundred thirty-five thousand wheel rotations—not to mention the consistent friction between the forward momentum of the carriage and the counter up-down propulsion of rutted roads resulting in a nearly constant jarring war of forces—" Fossi stopped. The butler's eyebrows had merged with his hairline. *Focus.* "Basically, I am a person of great patience, sir. I am happy to wait in this vestibule until his lordship *is* at home to visitors such as myself."

Fossi knew something that perhaps eluded Lord Whitmoor in his gilded palace—when you had so little in life, you defended the few things that *were* yours with ferocious tenacity.

No aristocrat would take her theorems from her. Not even the infamous Lord Whitmoor.

Fossi extended the slip of paper to the butler. "My card for his lordship."

Mr. Top-Lofty took the calling card she had prepared before leaving home and turned it over, reading what was written on the opposite side.

The man froze, eyebrows still standing at attention. She had wrested his interest, at least.

Mr. Top-Lofty raised his head, mouth drawn down. "It will be some hours yet before his Lordship returns."

"As I said, sir, I am prepared to wait. This chair here will suit my needs." Fossi gestured toward an ornate side chair flanking an equally ornate side table just inside the front door.

The butler's expression froze. "Lord Whitmoor will *not* be amused by your waiting in his entryway, Miss Lovejoy."

Fossi was quite sure that was code for *Mr. Top-Lofty* would not be amused by her waiting in *his* entryway.

She took two steps to the side and sat down on one of the chairs. "I do not particularly care what Lord Whitmoor thinks."

She fixed him with her best school-marm look. When one was a spinster, one had to use the weapons at one's disposal.

Before the day was out, Lord Whitmoor would rue trying to steal from her.

Given how Mr. Top-Lofty's lips twitched, she thought he might actually agree with her on that point.

A TOWNHOUSE NEAR PICCADILLY
LONDON, ENGLAND
AROUND THE SAME TIME ON JULY 24, 1828

DANIEL STOOD TAPPING a top hat against his leg in the well-appointed front parlor of Mr. Edward Stewart, Esquire. Garvis leaned against the mantel, face grim and threatening.

After his questioning of Captain Adams, Daniel had stopped by one of his halfway houses and shed the trappings of Fanny McCusker. He was now attired as Lord Whitmoor from the shoulders of his meticulously brushed coat to the bottom of his glossy, champagne-shined Hessian boots.

Unlike Mrs. McCusker, Lord Whitmoor exuded wealth and power wrapped in unemotional ruthlessness. A man of legendary exploits who had the ear of the King himself and excelled in 'whitmooring' the unsuspecting.

Lord Whitmoor was someone to be feared.

And given what Daniel now knew about Mr. Stewart's nightly visits to the Royal Mint, courtesy of Captain Adams, the man had every reason to be terrified.

Which explained why Mr. Stewart was on his knees, begging for clemency.

It was an unfortunate pose for many reasons, the least of which being the unobstructed view it afforded of the man's sparsely-populated hairline.

"My wife, my young son . . . what will become of them?" Mr. Stewart darted terrified glances between Daniel and Garvis. "Have mercy."

Daniel merely raised an unimpressed eyebrow. Lord Whitmoor was not known for his mercy.

Garvis cracked his knuckles to emphasize the point.

Edward Stewart blanched.

Daniel tugged on his left coat cuff, face an impassive mask. "I am not the originator of your punishment, Mr. Stewart. I am merely its executioner." The man flinched at the word, as Daniel intended. "You should have considered the matter *before* deciding to embezzle funds from the Crown."

Perspiration glistened on the top of Mr. Stewart's bald head. "I had no choice. Creditors were on our doorstep day and night. My poor wife couldn't sleep."

"Insomnia is hardly justification for theft, Mr. Stewart."

Garvis cracked another knuckle, giving his not-smile smile.

Mr. Stewart whimpered.

Daniel repressed a sigh. When had he tired of playing the persona of Lord Whitmoor?

He longed for simplicity. For the rolling Gloucestershire hills and Whitmoor House lit with the first rays of sunrise as he galloped up the gravel drive.

The vision . . . *hurt.* A visceral pang.

Daniel had taken Whitmoor as his title, but the name had already long been associated with him due to his large estate, Whitmoor House.

How he ached for his home.

Though not as it was currently. Right now, the thought of returning was so unbearable—

Guilt punched through him, blinding in force.

No! Don't go there.

He pulled his thoughts back from the brink of that abyss.

Two years he had been trying to right his wrong only to be thwarted at every turn. He *had* to find the man he sought and together they would fix the mistake Daniel had made.

It was almost impossibly ironic . . . the master of espionage himself unable to solve a personal problem of this magnitude.

If only! If only he hadn't done what he had—

Daniel brutally pushed aside his bleak thoughts.

Distract yourself.

"P-please," Mr. Stewart blubbered. "My family will be cast out!"

"That is not my problem." Tone utterly frigid.

Assuming Edward Stewart's wife wasn't involved in her husband's clandestine activities, Daniel would secretly ensure the woman and her son came to no harm. But her husband didn't know that.

"You cannot be so heartless."

Daniel fixed him with a look that clearly communicated that he could and would be *exactly* that.

Not so much heartless as stone-cold.

He was Whitmoor, after all. His reputation and verb-ish designation had not risen from fluff and hearsay.

"I suggest packing a few things, Mr. Stewart." Daniel checked his pocket watch. "Your stay in Newgate Prison promises to be a lengthy one."

ASHTON HOUSE, MAYFAIR
LONDON, ENGLAND
LATE AFTERNOON ON JULY 24, 1828

FOSSI SHIFTED HER feet again in the front hallway. The chair had been comfortable enough for the first four hours, but a slow burning sensation had started on her outer right thigh about an hour ago.

Her stomach growled. Unfortunately, she had not thought to pack any food when she left the inn. She had prepared for a straight-forward frontal attack, not a drawn out siege.

Was this prolonged wait part of Lord Whitmoor's psychological game when dealing with lesser mortals?

Well, she was no stranger to hardship.

Fossi studied the space again. A side table flanked by two chairs. Another small table across the way. An urn on a pedestal. Three paintings (two of hunting dogs, one ocean scene, all three uninspired). Patterned, baroque wallpaper. An imposing staircase sweeping up to the receiving rooms on the second floor.

And footmen. Thirteen of them at last count. They passed through the hallway with startling regularity, dapper in their green and gold livery. It was only when the sixth one passed that Fossi had realized—

They were all the same height. Every last one.

And now, thirteen footmen later, she was stumped.

What sort of man hired human beings in matched sets of thirteen?

Why thirteen? Were footmen better as a prime number?

A sound to the right of the staircase drew Fossi's attention. A figure emerged from a back room, carrying a bucket of water around the corner.

Ah.

She had been wrong.

Make that fourteen footmen.

She shifted her poor leg again, trying to get comfortable.

Lord Whitmoor could have fifty-one footmen of precisely seventy-two inches in height for all she cared.

She would still be here, laying siege to his entry hall, waiting for her chance to speak to him.

AN HOUR LATER, the front door heaved open.

The abrupt noise jerked Fossi awake, her head whipping to attention.

Heavens. Had she fallen asleep then?

A large man swept inside, his back to her.

She stared at his broad shoulders and dark head as he set down his walking stick and doffed his top hat, placing it on the table opposite her. He then proceeded to pull off his gloves.

"Collins!" The man's voice boomed through the large hall. He craned his neck looking up the grand staircase.

Surely this was Lord Whitmoor himself, correct?

Only a lord could enter a house with so much . . . presence.

Fossi clenched her hands around the reticule and bonnet in her lap.

A smell tickled her nose. What was it? Unwashed bodies? Excrement?

Fossi took a deeper breath. And promptly gagged.

Definitely all that and more.

For not the first time, she pondered the irony of taking her deepest breaths when the air was at its foulest.

Wherever this man had been, it had *not* been a pleasant place.

It seemed an ironic analogy for her current situation—confronting a glittering lord who reeked of decay and filth.

She fumbled for her handkerchief, pressing it over her mouth and nose.

"Collins!" The man called again, muttering something under his breath. Was there a fly buzzing above his head?

The man turned and promptly froze.

Impossibly blue eyes met hers with chilling force.

Fossi instantly straightened her spine and stood up, the energy of his gaze drawing her to her feet. She slowly lowered her handkerchief, breathing in shallow breaths.

He stared with intense stillness, eyebrows drawn down, dark brown hair shot with strands of gray at the temple. He was clearly older than her, though not by much—a powerful man in the prime of his life.

It was definitely Lord Whitmoor himself. She hadn't known until that very moment how thoroughly broadsheet cartoons captured their subjects. Spot on, in this instance.

More to the point, she had vastly underestimated his potency.

Lord Whitmoor was somehow worse and yet more than her imaginings. In all her mental ramblings, she had pictured a man like Sir Peter Nobly—corpulent, indolent and foppish. A condescending fool she could mentally mock and bring down to size.

But as she watched him continue to tug off his gloves with meticulous precision before tossing them on the table with his hat, she sensed that Lord Whitmoor was many things . . . but a fool was clearly not one of them.

They stared at each other for a long moment.

What was the social protocol when confronted with the lord of the manor after laying siege to his entryway? Did she speak first? Or should she wait—

"For you, my lord." Mr. Top-Lofty suddenly appeared at Lord

Whitmoor's elbow, saving her from mishap. He extended a silver platter toward his employer.

Goodness! Her card was upon the platter, like a petition presented to the king.

Her heart triple-skipped and the moisture in her mouth instantly fled.

Lord Whitmoor moved his attention from Fossi and picked up her card from the platter.

Mr. Top-Lofty—Collins, she supposed—shot a quick glance at her.

Fossi held her breath.

Lord Whitmoor studied the front and then flipped the card over. He read what was there, all of him going impossibly still.

This was it. This was the moment.

Would his lordship grant her an audience?

Fossi took a half-step forward, intent on pressing her case should Lord Whitmoor decline to see her. He would have to call on a pair of those matching footmen to toss her out if he refused to hear—

Collins' glance turned from polite to quelling.

Know your place, Miss, it sternly said.

Lord Whitmoor's shoulders sagged, almost like a sigh of relief.

"Did Mr. Lovejoy say how I could reach him?" Lord Whitmoor tapped the card. "I see no return address here."

Mister Lovejoy?

Fossi froze.

Collins blinked. He looked at his employer. Then to Fossi. Back to Lord Whitmoor.

Collins cleared his voice. "The, uh . . . person in question . . . has been waiting for you, my lord."

"Excellent! The man was wise to wait. Good work, Collins." Lord Whitmoor clapped his butler on the shoulder.

Something that felt distinctly like hysterical laughter bubbled in the back of Fossi's throat. Or perhaps it was a rising sob. Oddly enough, it was difficult to tell the difference—

"I assume you put Mr. Lovejoy in the library?" Lord Whitmoor nodded in approval, not waiting for a response. "I've been to Newgate, as I am sure my odor informed you. Let me change my attire and then show Mr. Lovejoy up to my study immediately."

Fossi was unsure if she should feel elated at being granted an audience or appalled at Lord Whitmoor's instant assumptions.

"Yes, my lord." Collins spared another glance for Fossi.

The butler opened his mouth to say something additional, but Lord Whitmoor was already moving toward the stairs, his back turned to them all.

"Oh and give this . . . whoever she is—" Lord Whitmoor flicked a hand toward Fossi behind him. "—a tuppence and send her on her way. I do not believe we have any staffing needs at the moment."

Lord Whitmoor bounded up the stairs, Fossi's card still gripped in his hand.

Collins raised his eyebrows in her direction.

"Well—" The butler rocked back on his heels. "—your day just became decidedly more interesting, now didn't it?"

Chapter 4

Daniel climbed the two flights of stairs to his bed chamber, calling for his valet.

His pulse pounded and hope swelled, a balloon in his chest.

At long last!

He had *finally* found the man he had been searching for!

He studied the calling card again as he tugged at his neckcloth with one hand. The bold, hand-written script leapt off the paper.

Foster Lovejoy
Member
Society of Mathematicians

An odd name to be sure, but who was he to judge?

He flipped the card over and examined the line of numbers and symbols scrawled across its surface.

Hallelujah!

The author of that blasted theorem had taken the bait.

Relief swamped him.

Daniel had a path now. He could move forward. Finding Mr. Love-joy was the first step toward redemption. The guilt lurking at the periphery of his thoughts abated, deciding for now not to pounce.

Better yet, without the weight of his duties to the Home Office, he could devote all his energy to correcting his terrible mistake. His hands shook with anticipation as he carefully set the card on his private writing desk.

His valet arrived with a nod and proceeded to help Daniel shrug out of his coat, the sour smells of prison flooding through the room. Newgate was a cesspool and the scent lingered for days. Pity Daniel didn't have time for a bath, but surely Mr. Lovejoy would be understanding.

Daniel enjoyed most aspects of living in the nineteenth century as opposed to the twenty-first, the century of his birth. He had, after all, deliberately chosen to live in this time period. It suited him, even when it took months to do something that a smart phone with an internet connection could accomplish in mere moments.

But every now and again, a life-altering crisis arose that nothing in nineteenth century could solve. Antibiotics to cure an illness. A car or airplane to quickly move between two points. Or, in this particular case, a computer to crunch mathematical data.

Daniel didn't have a computer, obviously. More to the point, he also couldn't *access* a computer which was the irony of the situation.

If he could access a computer, he wouldn't actually have need of one.

Lacking a computer, he had resorted to tracking down the next best thing—a mathematical genius.

The post in *Scriptis Mathematicis* had been a last-ditch effort to flush out a particular mathematical mind he knew to be living at this time. Given his intended path, Daniel was relatively confident he hadn't altered history by publishing what he had.

Besides, desperate times and all that . . .

Daniel pulled on clean trousers and shrugged into a freshly laundered shirt. Then, he donned a pin-striped waistcoat, buttoning it up.

In the twenty-first century, the theorem was called Fourier's Nemesis—a stark innovation on a Fourier Series, a branch of calculus that studied waves and frequency. Jean-Baptiste Fourier, the mind behind his namesake theory, had published his groundbreaking work on heat and wave theory only a few years ago in 1822.

From Daniel's coursework in engineering at the University of Gloucestershire (Class of 2015), he remembered studying Fourier, as well as Fourier's Nemesis. The originator of Fourier's Nemesis had long been heralded as an anonymous mathematical genius of astounding talent.

Scouring current 1828 scientific periodicals had yielded nothing. Whoever the mathematician was, he kept a low profile. So Daniel had resorted to publishing his own notice.

Daniel lifted his chin, allowing his valet to tie a well-starched neckcloth.

To his credit, Daniel was smart enough to not publish the *entirety* of Fourier's Nemesis. He had merely printed salient parts of it—the critical bits, so to speak. A taunt, of sorts. Hopefully enough to goad its author out of hiding.

And, thank heavens, he had finally uncovered the man.

Nearly two years ago, an earthquake had rocked the western portion of Great Britain. A smaller earthquake by the world's standards, to be sure. Probably no more than a six on the Richter Scale. But it had altered something—the portal's position? a critical axis? an unknown object?—*something* which had caused the time portal in the cellar of Duir Cottage to stop functioning.

As the Keeper of the time portal, Jasmine, Lady Linwood had been profoundly affected by the portal's breakdown, initially collapsing utterly, floating in and out of delirium for days. Jasmine had recovered from the worst of the attack after two weeks. Not fully, but enough to function as long as she had extra rest. However, she was not whole, not as she had been.

The broken portal also prevented Daniel from communicating or visiting friends and relatives in other time periods, particularly his sister, Kit, living two hundred years in the future.

The time portal needed to be repaired.

But how? The portal was a physical manifestation of a metaphysical world, a space so complex it defied logic.

His valet held up a tailcoat. Daniel slid his arms into the sleeves and pulled the jacket into place.

Jasmine's explanation of the portal was a mix of mysticism and practicality, much like the lady herself.

Past and Future formed an eternal Present. Time was not a river, but a vast ocean where the lives of every person who had lived, or would ever live, existed simultaneously as concentric circles rippling its surface . . . as if each life were a stone dropped into the water by some mystical unseen hand. According to Jasmine, these rings usually oscillated in synchronized harmony. Up and down, every life breathing together as one.

The earthquake had disrupted this harmonious oscillation, turning the cosmic ocean into a discordant sea of choppy waves. Instead of humming with harmonic power, the portal buzzed with dissonance, harsh and unsettling.

Worst of all, the earthquake and subsequent breakdown of the portal came at a critical moment for Daniel. He had made a catastrophic error—a mistake that *had* to be rectified. But he had to restore the portal before he could move on to righting the wrong he had done.

Daniel was trapped. Unable to move forward or back, quite literally.

He needed a solution. As the portal was essentially a wormhole in Time, mathematics should provide that. He just needed a genius mind attuned to wave theory.

Hence the advertisement in *Scriptis Mathematicis*.

Daniel surveyed his reflection, tugging on his waistcoat as his valet brushed stray lint from the superfine coat. A hint of Newgate still lingered, but it would have to do.

Nodding his thanks, Daniel retrieved Mr. Lovejoy's card and took to the stairs, retreating down a flight to his study, giddy with anticipation.

He looked at the back of the calling card again as he entered the room.

No, it truly was there—Fourier's Nemesis staring back at him in its full glory, clearly and precisely written in bold handwriting.

Footsteps along the hallway announced Collins' arrival before the rap on his door.

"Come."

The door opened. Daniel set the card on his desktop and turned to greet Mr. Lovejoy, a congenial smile on his lips.

Collins blocked the doorway only momentarily.

"Miss Foster Lovejoy to see you, my lord."

Collins moved aside.

The drab woman who had been in his foyer earlier passed into the room.

Collins bowed with what might have been a restrained smirk on his lips and shut the door behind himself.

Only then did his butler's words register.

Miss Foster Lovejoy.

Shock blasted through Daniel's excitement with stunning force, his welcoming words instantly swallowed up in shock, freezing his expression.

This was Foster Lovejoy? The greatest mathematical mind alive? A poor, unremarkable woman who loitered in noblemen's vestibules?

The woman before him was . . . shabby. A gray mouse of a person, gripping a gray reticule and equally gray bonnet that had obviously seen better days.

Daniel blinked, trying to remember the last time anything had caught him so off-guard. A pirate's ship off the coast of Le Havre? Lady Sharpton's garrulous attempts at flirtation during her husband's funeral?

Miss Lovejoy had utterly whitmoored him.

The irony.

Surprise could be the only explanation for his first words.

"*You* are Foster Lovejoy?"

The woman's spine stiffened.

"I am, my lord." Her voice was soft and cultured, gentle and more refined than he would have expected.

She clutched the bonnet ribbons in her hands more tightly, nearly strangling the shapeless thing. Which, to Daniel's purview, could only be counted as a service to humanity.

"But . . . but you are a *woman*." An accusation.

"Yes, my lord." Tone so very dry. "I have been female for quite some time now."

Of all the possible ways Daniel had considered this scenario playing out—if and when he managed to locate the author of Fourier's Nemesis—he had never once considered that the person he sought would be a woman.

Shame barreled in behind his shock and surprise.

Of *anyone* alive in 1828, Daniel Ashton should understand the capabilities of women. Were she here, his sister would have his hide for the sexist slip.

For not the first time, he wondered if he hadn't gone too native in his living of nineteenth century life.

Years of working in espionage had Daniel instantly cataloging Foster Lovejoy—brown eyes and equally brown hair pulled into a tight bun, average height and figure. That said, her oval face itself was regular of feature and not wholly unattractive, calling to mind a Renaissance Madonna. Though without the provenance of angelic hosts and gilded framework, the impact was lost. Her simple gray pelisse did not help the impression, the garment being a solid eight years out of fashion and had obviously been turned and skillfully patched many times over.

In short, she was the sort of woman society was least kind to—poor, unmarried and well-educated. A person he would pass on the street a thousand times without remembering her existence, assuming her to be a lady's companion or housekeeper. Or if he found her in his entryway, for example, would suppose she was looking for work as such.

She would make a perfect spy, truth be told.

Was she truly the author of Fourier's Nemesis, in the end?

There was a fire in her, he supposed. She faced him with her chin raised, determination evident in the way she clutched her bonnet and reticule, in the rigidity of her shoulders. The action highlighted the elegant curve of her jaw, the patrician cut of her nose.

Hmmm. Perhaps more Joan of Arc than a Madonna.

"You may have five hundred and thirty one cartouches on the wallpaper in your entrance hall and fourteen footmen of precisely all the same height—which truly is a disturbing requirement of employment, if I may editorialize—but I will not be cowed," she said into the silence. "I am here to protect that which is rightfully mine."

A long pause ensued during which Daniel struggled to piece together her sentence.

"And what would you protect?" he asked.

"My theorems. My ideas. You have stolen them, Lord Whitmoor. I wish to know how and why you did so and then taunted me with them. And, more to the point, I wish you to cease."

Foster Lovejoy, it appeared, had come prepared for battle.

FOSSI STARED DOWN the haughty nobleman before her, shoring up her courage.

Su coraggio! She mentally pleaded in Italian. *You can do this, Foster Lovejoy.*

Lord Whitmoor was every bit as intimidating in his study as he had been in his entryway.

Fortunately, a change of clothing had at least tamed the stench of prison and curtailed the flies.

He was dressed in clothing that spoke of extravagant wealth without being overtly ostentatious—brushed blue superfine coat a shade deeper than his blue eyes, brown trousers and waistcoat with gold buttons, immaculate white cravat. He was taller than average, though not to excess.

Fossi had the instant impression that Lord Whitmoor did *nothing* to excess. He appeared lean and . . . hard.

Unyielding.

He wore power like others wore fragrance—a subconscious essence which permeated every space he inhabited.

It wasn't arrogance, his power. Arrogance implied a sense of insecurity. The arrogant felt compelled to prove themselves.

Fossi was quite sure Lord Whitmoor had nothing to prove.

She supposed most women would misunderstand this power and call it handsomeness instead. But there they would be wrong.

Lord Whitmoor's face was composed of too many sharp

edges—brow ridge, cheekbones, jawline—to be considered classically symmetrical. His attraction lay in the force of his personality rather than harmonious external beauty.

Case in point—his blue eyes peered into her with chilling force.

Fossi swallowed, regretting yet again the reckless pride that had brought her to this juncture. What had made her think that bravado and righteous ire would be sufficient to win the day against the might of Lord Whitmoor?

Lord Whitmoor reached behind him and plucked her calling card from his desktop.

"*Your* ideas, Miss Lovejoy . . ." He paused, stared at her equation, shook his head and then fixed her with that steely gaze again, brandishing the card at her. "You claim to be the author of this theorem?"

"Yes, my lord." Reflexively, she tightened her grip on her reticule and bonnet, calming their quaking. His eyes darted to her gloved fingers.

Lord Whitmoor would miss nothing.

"I am not sure I believe your claims, Miss Lovejoy." He tapped her calling card against his leg. "Are you certain the theorem is yours and not lifted from another's work? I need a mathematician, not an impostor."

Fossi felt her cheeks flush with righteous indignation.

He stared her down for another moment. It was a truly effective gaze. Fortunately, she had spent the whole of her life receiving such looks from her father. Which was ironic, as her father detested aristocrats as a general rule and would be appalled to be compared to one.

"You may believe what you will, my lord." She notched her chin higher and sternly told her quivering knees to be still. "But belief alone will not stop Truth from being true. I *am* the author of this theorem."

"Indeed." Lord Whitmoor pursed his mouth, as if perplexed.

But something told her the move was calculated. He *let* her see that emotion.

Lord Whitmoor, she was quite sure, considered the world to be a giant chessboard and, like a pawn chain or queen's gambit, emotion was one of many strategies he employed when moving pieces.

The insight itself surprised her. Given his successes, Lord Whitmoor should not have been an easy man to understand. So how could she so quickly read him?

She chose to counter his disdain with a reasoned approach.

"Obviously, I anticipated the need to prove my claim, my lord. You are hardly the first man to see my gender as a negation of my abilities as a mathematician." Was it her imagination or did Lord Whitmoor flinch slightly at those words? "I therefore took the time to bring along a sample of my notes regarding Monsieur Fourier's Series and the research that resulted in my counter to his arguments."

Fossi opened her reticule and pulled out the small packet of papers she had prepared. When going into battle, she believed in anticipating every possible enemy action.

She took two steps toward him and extended the documents, hating that her hand still trembled slightly.

Lord Whitmoor paused a moment and then took the papers, studying them.

Silence hung as he read—the sounds of London traffic a muted hum beyond the light-filled window.

While his head was bowed over her notes, Fossi stole a glance around the room. The space appeared . . . lived in. Books with well-creased bindings lined the wall to her right. A table rested before the bookcases, a telescope, mechanical brass fittings and scribbled papers strewn across its surface. Lord Whitmoor's desk stood straight ahead, imposing and cluttered. A cozy sitting area took up the left half of the space, leather chairs angled toward the gilded fireplace.

After a moment of flipping through papers, Lord Whitmoor handed them back to her, that steel gaze pinning her.

"Your notes are acceptable proof." He paused. Correcting his course after finding it blocked, no doubt. He gestured toward her card. "You belong to the Society of Mathematics? I was unaware they accepted female members."

Ah.

Of course.

"They do not, my lord."

"And yet you accuse *me* of chicanery?"

And there it was. Another calculated move.

Imperial. Demanding. Turning the tables back on her.

Interesting that he had decided not to use charm, which she was confident was another tool in his arsenal. Likely he didn't consider her to be enough of an opponent to warrant a more laborious plan of attack.

The thought . . . burned.

Just once she would like someone to understand that her gender and poverty were not synonymous with ignorance and passivity.

Which probably made her reply sharper than normal.

"Yes, I do accuse you, my lord. You have trespassed into my home, stolen my ideas and then taunted me with them. At least I admit my duplicity in regards to the Society and my gender."

"Admission alone does not exonerate one's guilt."

Grrr.

"You are attempting to muddy the point with logic puzzles, my lord."

"Perhaps. But a sin of *omission* is still a sin."

That shot rankled. "Are you to be my priest then? My judge and jury before God?"

A beat.

"Of course not, Miss Lovejoy." Lord Whitmoor half-perched on the back edge of his desk, humor flaring in his eyes before fading just as quickly. "But your admitted prior behavior does not engender confidence in your future trustworthiness."

Oh!

"If I were a man, Lord Whitmoor, you would have readily accepted my status within the Society of Mathematicians and answer to your theorem as proof of my capabilities. No further questions needed." Against Fossi's better judgment, her voice rose, tone heated.

Emotion would only give Lord Whitmoor ammunition with which to attack her.

She swallowed. *Stay calm.*

"You posted the notice in *Scriptis Mathematicis* to taunt me . . . to draw me out for some reason," she continued. "Now that you have done so and find that I do not fit into the neat boxes with which you label things, you are hardly in a position to cry wolf."

Silence.

His expression retreated.

Had she struck true then?

She had to keep him on the defensive. Press her case. "Furthermore, your outrage over my gender is disingenuous, my lord. How did you learn of this formula's existence without also apprising my sex? Either you are sloppy in your current argumentation or sloppy in your intelligence gathering."

Lord Whitmoor's eyes narrowed. *Finally*, the man decided to view her as a true opponent, not simply a pawn to be brushed aside. Though given the weight of his glacial stare, she wasn't entirely sure this was a positive development.

Lord Whitmoor's face froze, becoming steel. Hard and obdurate. She could practically see ideas flitting through his brain . . . clearly recalibrating his strategy.

He would not make the mistake of underestimating her again.

Su coraggio!

He called to mind an ancient castle Fossi had once visited on a rare trip to Weymouth—stone walls held together by enormous iron brackets. Rigid and unbending. A granite fortress. Impervious and constantly defended against intrusion.

She wondered if his granite-steel extended to his core or if it was instead a sort of armor, a mask. Were Lord Whitmoor's insides like hers? A shell holding all the color in? Like a turtle, keeping all the squishy bits safe from the carelessness of others?

Or was the man stone and steel through to his core?

He cleared his throat. "I am not at liberty to discuss how the information regarding your theorems came into my possession."

Fossi barely stifled an angry huff over his non-answer.

"Forgive me, my lord, if I do not accept such a dismissive explanation." *Show no emotion.* "Is the Crown of England so pressed for excitement that they must resort to pilfering the papers of an unknown female mathematician of small reputation and even smaller circumstances?"

Lord Whitmoor stood and clasped his hands behind his back.

"Perhaps this was a test?" His face remained impassive, giving away nothing now. "Perhaps we needed to measure the depth of your mettle?"

Fossi tilted her head. A test? That made no sense.

Lord Whitmoor was hiding things.

No surprise there.

"The numerical odds are not in your favor, my lord."

"Pardon?"

"I give this interchange only a one in four hundred and sixty-three chance of being a test." Fossi waved a hand, indicating the space between them. "And more to the point, test my mettle to what end?"

"That I *can* answer." He straightened further. "Your mathematical mind is needed. I wish to offer you employment."

It was Fossi's turn for surprise. She blinked.

"Employment?"

"You needn't say the word as if it were tainted, Miss Lovejoy." That faint amusement danced across Lord Whitmoor's face again. "I am prepared to pay handsomely for your services."

"*Pay?*"

"Also not a foul word." Another flash of humor. "Payment and employment are usually joyously welcomed terms."

Lord Whitmoor clearly did not understand her position in the world.

She *was* a lady, despite her poverty. And employment for a lady . . . particularly one with a father such as hers . . . it was simply not done.

No.

It was *impossible*.

"If you have gleaned anything from your espionage efforts, you would know that employment is not something I seek." She nodded her head. "I thank you for your offer, my lord, but I must respectfully decline."

Chapter 5

Miss Lovejoy's words hung in the air between them.

I thank you for your offer, my lord, but I must respectfully decline.

Daniel found himself feeling nearly . . . *flustered.*

Miss Foster Lovejoy unsettled him as no one else had in . . . forever. Was it because so much depended on receiving her help?

She faced him down with quiet poised confidence, asking perceptive questions that he could not answer.

Anger, frustration, fear, outrage . . . *those* were emotions he could work with. But Miss Lovejoy gave him little to latch on to.

Instead, he was left to deal with his own sense of . . . what? Disbelief? Startled bemusement?

Daniel backtracked and regrouped.

Miss Lovejoy had yet to understand that refusing his offer was not an option.

She *would* do this task for him, even if he had to kidnap her and chain her to a desk. Too much depended upon it. Of course, the task would be more pleasant for them both if she helped willingly.

"I can well imagine your concerns, Miss Lovejoy, and my offer of employment to a lady such as yourself is certainly irregular. However, I am faced with a singular problem, and I fear you are the only person who can help me."

It was a calculated move, revealing his desperation while simultaneously appealing to her vanity.

She *was* the only one who could help him, and he was happy to meet whatever demands she would have of him. He would prefer *not* to have to chain her to a desk.

He smiled. It was one of his polite smiles, the one that said, *You can trust me as your friend.*

Miss Lovejoy raised her eyebrows. *I am hardly so easily persuaded.*

"I am sure that a man of your resourcefulness, Lord Whitmoor, will easily find another to take my place. My answer remains the same." She placed her words like cards, fanned before her. Challenging him to up the ante or fold.

Daniel clasped his hands tightly behind his back, mostly to stop from running his fingers through his hair in a most agitated fashion.

Had he considered her terribly plain only a few minutes ago? With her intelligent eyes and classic facial structure, she had a sort of porcelain beauty. Not flashy or ostentatious but steady. She was a woman who would only become more beautiful as she aged, not less.

She regarded him with that same irritating serenity, living out his earlier comparison to a Renaissance Madonna—those unruffled, elegant women who gazed upon painted horrors with calm tranquility. Was she this staid on the inside too? Or was Foster Lovejoy's interior life more chaotic?

"Come, let us stop with this game." He faced her. "You are clearly no naive debutante. You understand the world."

Fire snapped in her eyes, but she remained silent.

"Surely you have a price. I am willing to meet it," he continued.

Miss Lovejoy's brows raised further. "You are quite misinformed in this matter, my lord. Neither my person nor my mind are for hire. And more to the point, you still have not addressed my question regarding your procurement of my theorem research in the first place."

This woman.

He had to give her points for tenacity. But he could hardly tell her the truth—

Well, you see a time portal in Herefordshire has malfunctioned due to an earthquake two years past, and I need a mathematician to reconcile wave mechanics with wormhole theory. I remembered your theorem from my university studies around the year 2012 and voilá, here you are . . .

"I am afraid that my initial explanation is all I am at liberty to give, Miss Lovejoy. But I find your stubborn refusal to help confusing. Everyone has dreams they wish to achieve."

Miss Lovejoy clutched her reticule more tightly. The poor bag was near to being strangled.

Had his question struck true?

"Dreams are a fanciful luxury for the very wealthy and a necessary escape for the very poor." That elegant jawline of hers nudged higher. "I am neither of these things."

Clever. Very clever.

Daniel cleared his throat.

He *admired* her, damn it all.

Hmmmm.

He could be clever, too.

"I think, Miss Lovejoy, that you are . . . afraid." He said the words softly, letting them hang between them.

Given how her brown eyes widened and her breath hitched, she was not entirely unaffected.

"Afraid, my lord?"

Daniel walked slowly toward her, crowding into her space. Not enough to make her bolt, not enough to threaten . . . but sufficient to get her attention.

"Yes. *Afraid*, Miss Lovejoy. A woman with mental gifts such as yours, a woman who has the gumption to pretend to be a man in a man's world . . . well, such a woman has obvious depths of courage and does not give a fig for what the world will say of her."

Miss Lovejoy pursed her lips, clearly uncertain where he was headed with this tactic.

"Thank you?" It was a question.

"You may wish to save your thanks until I am finished, madam."

Daniel continued to walk, circling around her, forcing her to pivot with him if she did not wish to give him her back.

She pivoted.

"I think, Miss Lovejoy," he continued, "you hide behind the mask of your own anonymity, protected by parchment and words. With my request, I am asking you to move into the light, to step in front of the curtain, prepare your lines and become an actor on the giant Stage of Life, as it were. That is why I call you afraid."

"*Oh.*" The exhalation left her in an abrupt rush.

A direct hit.

Daniel pressed his advantage. "You are possessed of courage of mind, Miss Lovejoy. But thus far, this courage has not manifested itself upon your outward life. You hide behind equations and ideas and call that living, but I call that cowardice. Reducing life to analytical musings is nothing more than avoidance."

See? Clever.

"Gracious!" Color flooded her cheeks, brown eyes snapping, chest heaving.

She was mentally preparing to give him a magnificent set-down.

At last. Emotion he could use.

Daniel stopped in front of her again, forcing her to look up, up into his face.

"Within you is a woman of incredible mettle and verve. Someone who wants to seize the reins and take her life to unknown heights." He paused for effect. "When you finally let that woman free, please return to me. That is a woman I wish to know. *That* is a woman who could turn the world on its head."

Those brown eyes continued to snap at him, something fiery and hot blazing just beneath their surface.

Miss Lovejoy was so very . . . alive.

Unwillingly, Daniel found himself intrigued. His little speech had intended to get a rise out of her—which . . . mission accomplished—but perhaps there was more truth than he knew to his words.

What *would* happen if Miss Foster Lovejoy did indeed seize the reins of her own destiny?

Her mouth opened and closed. She swallowed.

And then, just as quickly as it appeared, all that lovely fire drained away. As if she had pulled the plug and allowed it to flow off. Her eyes returned to flat brown and the militant hauteur of her head relaxed.

Daniel felt . . . disappointed.

She took a deep breath.

"Your uninvited assessment of my inner life is duly noted, my lord." Voice prim. Controlled. "As we are clearly at an impasse—you will not answer my questions and I will not agree to your demands—I will trespass no further upon your time. I trust you will cease to pilfer my equations for your own . . . *nefarious* purposes."

"Nefarious, Miss Lovejoy?" Daniel nearly snorted in bemused disbelief.

Did this woman think to dismiss him so easily?

She turned to leave. Paused. And then rotated back to face him, head tilted.

"I fear your game was somewhat off today." Soft brown eyes met his. "You opened with intimidation. You would have done better with respect and charm."

"Pardon?" His head reared back.

She clicked her tongue. "Allow me to clarify. You have attempted to engage me in a sort of chess match, have you not?" She gestured at the space between them. "You are playing some grand contest on a board with players I cannot see, and you wish me to join the game. In this particular salvo, you opened with the equivalent of a Greco-Counter Gambit."

Daniel's mind struggled to follow the chess analogy. How had she grasped the upper-hand again?

She continued, "Such a chess gambit is bold but risky, as it signals contempt for your adversary. It implies that only the loosest of strategy will be needed to win your battle . . . that you can charge in recklessly, overwhelming your opponent with flashy moves and seize the field. I am not interested in such a game and respectfully decline your invitation to play, my lord."

"Well . . ." was all Daniel managed to say.

"You should have trusted my skill as an opponent and gone with something more venerated, like a King's Gambit. Or better yet, dispensed with the games altogether. I prefer to be treated as a person, not merely an obstacle to be beaten." She cocked her head at him. "I would have responded better to respect."

Daniel blinked, words astounded right out of his brain. How had she seen through him so easily?

He swallowed. Regrouped his thoughts. Daniel Ashton had arrived at his station in life by being relentlessly scrappy.

"If I had, would you have said yes?" he asked.

"No," said with matter-of-fact honesty, "but I would have liked you more."

Miss Lovejoy shrugged, giving him a sad smile. She curtsied, precise and proper.

"Good day, my lord."

A FEW MINUTES later, Daniel stood at his study window, watching as Miss Foster Lovejoy waited on the steps below for a hackney cab, her shabby bonnet now atop her head.

Patience, he whispered to the ever-present guilt, eager to blast through him. *We will win her over.*

Miss Foster Lovejoy.

He could scarcely remember the last time someone had caught him so off-guard. He felt positively . . . *nonplussed.* Which, given his career in both business and espionage, was the equivalent of experiencing his own personal earthquake—everything going cattywampus (as a friend from North Carolina used to say).

I prefer to be treated as a person, not merely an obstacle to be beaten.

Far too astute, that observation.

It *was* a sport to him.

How long had he been doing this? Engaging with other human beings as if they were part of a game he was determined to win?

And given the stakes at hand, was it necessarily a bad thing? She *was* an obstacle to be surmounted. His very sanity depended on it.

He twisted his mouth, drumming fingers against a thigh.

Mmmm.

Charm *would* have been a better option. He should have had a tea tray brought up; treated her more like a debutante than a recalcitrant business partner.

Why hadn't he done that? Had she so unmoored him that his very manners failed?

Would you have said yes?

No, but I would have liked you more.

Daniel frowned. He *could* be quite charming when the occasion merited it.

And why should he care what Miss Foster Lovejoy thought of him?

The problem, of course, still remained. Miss Lovejoy was the only one in this current century with the mathematical agility necessary to solve the riddle of the portal.

She didn't know it yet, but their conversation had just begun.

This had only been the first volley of what promised to be a long, pitched battle. 'No' was not an answer he would accept. Not with this. Miss Lovejoy would soon discover exactly how stubborn Lord Whitmoor could be.

Daniel had no doubts as to the eventual outcome. Everyone had their price.

Even Miss Foster Lovejoy.

And if she steadfastly refused to accept payment . . . well, money wasn't the only coercive tool in his arsenal. Chains and a desk still remained an option, though Daniel shied away from the thought.

As he watched her peer up and down the street below, he didn't think that Miss Lovejoy would respond well to such duress.

The door opened. Daniel did not turn around, knowing who had entered.

"Follow her, Garvis." Daniel gestured with his chin toward the lingering Miss Lovejoy. "You are not to lose her. It is critical. Take your notes, as usual."

"Don't I always, W?"

"Yes, but this one is exceptionally important."

He sensed more than saw Garvis bow and exit the room.

Garvis Samuelson had been in his employ for more years than Daniel could easily recollect. Aside from the cheek of calling Daniel a simple letter, W, and being excellent muscle when the situation required it, Garvis had an uncanny ability to blend into the woodwork no matter his locale. A useful trait for a spy.

Garvis would ensure Miss Lovejoy remained found.

The woman in question shifted her feet on the pavement below, craning her neck up at the house next door.

Another knock sounded.

"Come."

Collins entered with his normal polite fastidiousness.

"Shall I have the carriage brought round in an hour, my lord? You are still engaged to attend Lady Haversham's salon, are you not?"

Daniel controlled his involuntary flinch at the thought of Lady Haversham—vivacious, widowed and over ten years his junior . . . every nobleman's dream.

She merely made Daniel feel old.

That did not change the fact that he was committed to attend her intellectual soirée this evening. Lady Haversham fancied herself something of a scholar and attracted the best minds to her salons, particularly mathematicians. It had seemed prudent to attend.

"Yes, Collins. Please have the carriage brought around." Collins nodded and left the room.

Of course, the broadsheets would read more into his attendance, assuming he was looking for a wife who would, in turn, provide him with an heir for his new title. He would be thirty-eight in only a few short months, and he needed an heir, not only because he was Lord Whitmoor.

No, it was decidedly more than that.

Through a twist of fate, Daniel knew himself to be his own eighth great-grandfather. It was a baffling time travel paradox that he was sure sent theoretical physicists into a collective frenzy. But as he hadn't yet faded into nothingness—à la *Back to the Future*—his present course must be the correct answer to the problem.

A hackney cab pulled up to the curb, the driver dismounting to open the door for Miss Lovejoy. She turned her head around as she climbed into the carriage, pausing to survey the front of his town house one final time, bonnet hiding her eyes but framing the elegant oval of her face.

She shook her head. Once. Twice. As if . . . what?

Pivoting, she disappeared inside the cab.

Part of him screamed in horror that she was leaving, that he was *allowing* her to leave. His salvation walking away.

But he was Whitmoor. He had vast reserves of patience to call upon. Garvis would hunt her. Daniel *would* persuade her.

The driver climbed back onto his perch and drove off. A moment later, Garvis swung onto the street from the mews, discreetly shadowing the slow moving carriage.

Daniel watched until the cab disappeared around the corner.

Why had she shaken her head? And more to the point, why did he care?

But the conundrum of Foster Lovejoy would not leave his mind.

Her clever wit haunted him all through the soirée that evening, pinging around his skull as he half-listened to conversation about the East India trade and recent developments in South America.

He found himself thinking about the fleeting fire in Miss Lovejoy's eyes and the graceful curve of her jaw as he attended the theater and danced at Lord Follet's ball.

He considered Miss Lovejoy's keen intelligence as he gave his maiden policy speech as the newest member of the House of Lords. Would she agree that child labor needed to be curtailed?

However, thoughts of Miss Lovejoy turned to desperation a week later as he wandered his enormous townhouse, unable to sleep and clutching a well-worn wooden box to his chest.

Promise you will keep it for me. Don't forget.

Guilt roared through him, turning the edges of his vision black, leaving him gasping for air.

He needed to find redemption.

Miss Foster Lovejoy and her mathematical wizardry *had* to be the source of his salvation.

He would accept no other outcome.

Chapter 6

THE ROAD TO KILMINSTER
DORSET, ENGLAND
JULY 26, 1828

Lord Whitmoor's words would not leave Fossi alone. They rattled around her brain, lurching side-to-side with every jolt and dip of the poorly-sprung mail coach.

Within you is a woman of incredible mettle and verve.

She contemplated this as she bounced a crying toddler on her knee so the exhausted mother to her left could sleep. Did Lord Whitmoor truly think that? Or had he merely been attempting to manipulate her into helping him?

She was inclined to think his words carefully calculated. Lord Whitmoor said and did nothing without first assessing all possible options, and flattery was an effective weapon.

When you finally let that woman free, please return to me.

Well, there was no danger of that. Even *had* she wished to return to Lord Whitmoor—which she didn't, she truly didn't—she had used every farthing of her meager savings for this trip. Another was out of the question.

The child on her lap finally fell asleep, snuggled warm against her chest. Fossi relished the physical comfort of holding him.

Sometimes Fossi thought that was the worst part of being an aging spinster. No one held you. No one touched you. Physical contact was rare.

So Fossi clutched the toddler tight, drank in the measured rise and fall of his breathing, the heavy warmth of him. Mourned, yet again, the children and husband who would never be hers.

That is a woman who could turn the world on its head.

Fossi grimaced at the remembrance.

Flattery, indeed.

Fossi would never be anything more than her current circumstances. Women such as herself had very few options. And were she to lose the love and support of her father and siblings . . . well, that would reduce her options to practically zero.

She didn't need to be a mathematical genius to understand those odds.

But . . . Fossi was an intrinsically honest person. *Too* honest, perhaps, at times. And so, because of this, she held Lord Whitmoor's words up to the mirror of herself, rotating them, looking at them twenty different ways.

Was she merely existing instead of living?

It was an oddly unsettling thought. She had never considered there to be a difference between the two.

Dreams had never been part of her inner landscape. Hope played strongly into dreams, and hope had always been in short supply in her life, particularly over the past sixteen years.

Unbidden, Fossi's throat tightened and her heart plummeted at least a hundred feet.

How odd it was . . . that the pain of her mother's death was ever fresh. The wound that never healed.

Sixteen years without Charlotte Lovejoy's kind voice and gentle persuasion. Sixteen years without the light and laughter of her mother's intelligent mind, whether teaching Fossi the Italian of her maternal grandparents or showing her a new embroidery stitch.

Sixteen years without her best friend.

Remember your name, Foster.

Her mother's last words to her. Fossi had crept to her bedside when the rest of the house had finally fallen into an exhausted sleep. Her mother's face etched with pain in the flickering candlelight. So frail.

"Remember, my Fossi," she whispered. "It's what you were sent here to do— Foster Love Among Us. Never forget."

Fossi blinked furiously, stifling the rawness in her chest as the carriage rocked over a large rut. She looked past the sleeping child in her arms and the child's mother slumped against her shoulder. Beyond the lady's maid who couldn't stop talking to the handsome cooper across from her, out to the countryside creeping along. She bit her lip, trying to swallow back all this . . . feeling.

Such emotion would do her no good.

Lord Whitmoor in his gilded palace risked nothing and asked her for everything. He played with them all, considering her simply one more pawn on his giant chessboard.

The man could take his secrets and games off to another playground.

Her life was fixed. Her father had made that excruciatingly clear over the years.

Just take her involvement with the Society of Mathematicians as an example.

Her eldest brother, Will, had been the first to bring the Society to her attention. Will was brilliant himself and had become a King's Scholar, being granted a scholarship from the Crown to pursue his education. Will had passed that education on to his eager little sister with every school break.

As they grew older, Will continued to help Fossi find an outlet for her mathematical ideas. This led, eventually, to Will putting her in contact with several members of the Society of Mathematicians that he knew from university. Though he now worked as a solicitor in Kilminster near their home, Will continued to act as a liaison between Fossi and the Society.

Fossi's father had caught wind of her involvement with the Society several years ago. After ranting about them for several days, he had (erroneously) assumed that Fossi wanted nothing to do with the Society and had let the matter drop.

As he hadn't technically forbidden Fossi from being involved, she continued to write and interact with members. But should her father find out how deep her involvement was, he would forbid any further contact.

Employment with an aristocrat doing sums? Such unladylike behavior would send Reverend Josiah Lovejoy into an apoplectic fit. Her father would consider her immoral and fallen and disown her, her brothers and sisters following his lead. Once Lord Whitmoor's employ ended, she would be cast out into the world.

The only thing worse than a poor, aging, clever woman was a poor, aging, clever woman *without* familial connections. It was the only place, really, she had left to sink.

And Fossi would prefer *not* to end up in that place before absolutely necessary.

Such were Fossi's thoughts as she finished her journey, transferring at dawn from the mail coach to the stagecoach and then a kind farmer's wagon before alighting at the crossroads before Kilminster. She took her leave with a wave and trudged across the fields, arriving at The Old Vicarage just before dusk.

Her father had purchased The Old Vicarage when her mother yet lived. As its name implied, the building had once been home to the local vicar, but the old church had burned down over a hundred years before, around the time of the Glorious Revolution. A new church and vicarage had been built across town, set picturesquely along the riverbanks. All of which left The Old Vicarage sitting alone next to crumbling, vine-covered ruins and an ancient graveyard.

The building itself suffered from a crisis of identity. Former tenants had added on to its Tudor framework in a jumbled fashion, extending a gable here, adding a room there. The end result, of course, was a building that looked like everything and yet nothing.

Smoke curled from the back chimney and threaded through the drooping branches of an enormous willow planted against the back fence. Two of her nephews wrestled with their dog in the garden—Prudence's boys, which meant her sister was about as well.

"Aunt Foster!" The high-pitched squeal came from the front door. "You're back!"

Two hurtling bodies collided with Fossi on the walk. Two more nieces and a nephew joined in from the front door, Strength's children. Her brother must be here too.

"Rapscallions," she said fondly, rubbing their heads and dragging them all toward the house.

Prudence appeared at the doorway, bouncing another baby in her arms. "You made it home." Prudence handed off the child to Fossi. "It's about time. We expected you at luncheon."

"I am sorry for the delay, Pru." Fossi managed a polite smile, holding the baby close. "Though four coaching horses can roughly pull eight-times their individual strength, that does not correlate to faster travel, unfortunately. Force and speed are not, in the end, interdependent—"

Fossi stopped right there.

Prudence rolled her eyes. "Honestly, Foster, you say the oddest things."

Her sister whirled back into the house.

The other children pushed past Fossi into the entryway. Dimly, she heard Prudence yelling at the kitchen maid, Betsy, to mind the children. Sucking in a fortifying breath, Fossi smiled down at the baby trying to stuff his entire fist in his mouth. Like the rest, he didn't notice or care that her smile was strained.

"Foster!" Her father's voice boomed from the direction of his study. "You will attend me. I have been waiting to dictate my sermon these past few hours."

Home was never perfect, Fossi had long ago decided.

But at least it was home.

THE OLD VICARAGE
KILMINSTER, DORSET
AUGUST 1, 1828

THE NEXT FEW days passed in a blur.

Fossi settled back into her usual routine . . . waiting on her father's needs, transcribing his sermons in her confident hand, assisting Betsy in the house, tending nieces and nephews, ministering to others in their small congregation—Mr. Tally's rheumatism, the birth of Mrs. Brown's tenth child.

And, slowly, her blessed state of numbness returned. Lord Whitmoor's accusations retreated to mere background hum.

Well . . . usually.

Snippets did manage to punch through at the most inopportune moments.

Such as when she sat listening to one of her father's sermons and, instead of thinking upon the parable of the Good Samaritan, Fossi found herself occupied with the steely exterior Lord Whitmoor presented to the world. What would he look like if he was being amiable? *Would* she have been charmed by him?

She spent the better part of a next afternoon quietly singing an Italian ballad that denounced the dangers of roguish men.

Lord Whitmoor crept into her thoughts one evening as she worked on another variation of Monsieur Fourier's Series in her small bedroom. How had Lord Whitmoor known about her work?

She sat back, surveying the small space with its even smaller window, a narrow bed pushed against one wall, her tiny desk against the other. It seemed impossible that someone had stolen into her room and made copies of her notes.

But, clearly, someone had.

Was the spy a person she knew? Or was the agent more covert, entering her room through her little, paned window? She vacillated between feeling horror over her privacy being thus invaded and admiration for the Crown and its espionage abilities.

The next day, as she crossed fields with a basket for Mrs. Brown and her brood, she wondered if Lord Whitmoor thought of her at all after her abrupt departure. There were a great many brilliant mathematicians in England, most of whom would leap at the chance to rub elbows with a man of Lord Whitmoor's consequence. After her little tirade, Lord Whitmoor had probably relegated her to the shelf in his mind reserved for annoying insects and other tiresome things.

The thought left her . . . restless.

Finally, because she was in all things truthful, she admitted that she felt . . . unmoored. Untethered. Lord Whitmoor had shaken things loose and Fossi struggled to set them back to rights.

Nearly a week after her return, Fossi found herself in her father's study, transcribing yet another sermon, forcing down that itchy sense of energy and unrest.

"Will that be all, Father?" Fossi asked, setting down her battered pen and stretching her cramped fingers. Her knees wanted to bounce with agitation.

Her father stirred from his chair, standing to his full height and tugging down his black coat. Though his hair and beard were nearly entirely gray now, Reverend Josiah Lovejoy still projected the vigor of a much younger man, his dark eyes keen and perceptive.

He picked up the sermon she had finished writing out from his dictation, surveying her work. "It will do, daughter. Did Mr. Miller say he would be joining our services today?"

"Yes, Father. He seemed inclined to come when I spoke with him two days ago."

"Excellent. Has he ceased his acquaintance with Sir Peter Nobly?"

Mr. Miller and Sir Peter had long been friends, much to her father's dismay.

"On that point I am unsure, Father."

Her father grunted, his expression a usual mask of malcontent.

Josiah Lovejoy had left the Anglican church when Fossi was still an infant—claiming disillusionment with the fawning secularism in how the clergy interacted with the aristocracy. Her father had found similar minds in the strict teachings of Congregationalists, which led him to establish his own church. Fossi's mother had brought a small monetary settlement into her marriage and between that, tutoring young men and what his parishioners could spare, Reverend Lovejoy kept a roof over their heads and clothing on their backs.

"Well, I shall speak with Mr. Miller about it again." Her father flicked a hand, dismissing her from his study. "I will see you during our evening worship service."

Her father tilted his cheek, a subtle demand for a kiss, which Fossi dutifully placed before bobbing a curtsy and retiring to her own room for a short rest.

But the jittery energy wouldn't let her rest.

Finally, she admitted a single truth. In one thing, Lord Whitmoor was correct.

She needed to demand more from her life.

Not so much dreams, per se, but merely a sense of expanded expectations.

To that end, Fossi pulled out a clean sheet of foolscap from her small writing desk and, picking up her pen, scratched a title—*Things I Wish to Do*. From there, she began to write. Her list of things was reasonable, if somewhat ambitious.

> *Purchase new shoes for my nieces and nephews.*
> *Acquire a new pipe for Father.*
> *Pay for repairs on Faith's cottage.*

At this point, she paused. She supposed the purpose of the list was to note things she wanted to do for *herself*.

To that aim, she added a few more items:

> *Go on a spring picnic.*
> *Ride in a well-sprung carriage, perhaps even a curricle or a high-perch phaeton.*
> *Flirt with a gentleman.*

She paused on that one. *Flirting* with a gentleman presupposed she knew how. Which, clearly, she didn't. She would need to ponder it more.

Attend a ball.
Dance with a gentleman.

The last two items were strictly forbidden under her father's Congregationalist beliefs, but Fossi had learned how to dance from her mother. Surely God did not think there any harm in it?

She continued:

Receive a present for either Christmas or my birthday.
Own a dress that hasn't been turned.

That last point was added in a moment of distress and vanity. It did not matter, in the eternal perspective of things, if her dresses had been unpicked over and over, the fabric painstakingly reversed to present the less worn pattern to the outside. But as she had spent the previous morning reworking yet another gown, Fossi thought it would be so lovely to have something new.

Such a thought, of course, was a terrible combination of greed, pride and envy. *This* was what came of letting such thoughts free.

Granted such thoughts did not stop her from continuing with her list.

Taste a pineapple.
Own a Kashmir shawl.
Found a school for girls.
Meet other members of the Society of Mathematics and be accepted as a woman.
Experience a romantic kiss.
~~Receive a proposal of marria~~

She stopped right there, scratching through the last point.

Wishing for the moon or a unicorn ride were just as likely scenarios as the thought of anyone asking Foster Love Among Us Lovejoy for her hand in marriage.

She frowned, considering.

Now that she looked at it, the last four items on her list fit into that category as well. She scratched through them, too—

~~Found a school for girls.~~
~~Meet other members of the Society of Mathematics and be accepted as a~~
~~woman.~~
~~Experience a romantic kiss.~~
~~Receive a proposal of marria~~

—and wrote the word *Impossible* beside them all.

There was a difference between unlikely things that still seemed within the realm of reality and utterly impossible things that would simply never happen.

When she finished, Fossi studied her list.

Hmmm.

She wasn't sure if her list of *Things I Wish to Do* improved her state of mind or merely highlighted the deficits in her life.

Writing the list was supposed to soothe her sense of unease and agitation. Instead it had amplified it.

This was the problem with *wanting* . . . it was an insatiable appetite.

It was much easier to go through life not wanting at all. One was much less likely to suffer disappointment.

THE OLD VICARAGE
KILMINSTER, DORSET
AUGUST 7, 1828

NEARLY TWO WEEKS after her ill-advised visit to Lord Whitmoor, Fossi found herself helping Betsy prepare herbs in the cold room.

Her sisters' voices drifted in from the front parlor. Prudence, Faith and Charity were there for the afternoon with their children, sewing before attending the evening prayer service. One of the children must have left the door to the hallway open, allowing sounds to drift easily into the cold room off the kitchen.

"It will have to be you, Faith. You are the youngest." That was Charity.

"I do not think my Tom will countenance it," Faith replied.

"Well, it most certainly will not be me." Prudence snorted. "Can you even imagine her living with John and myself? Nattering on about *ratios this* and *equations that?* We should all go mad within a fortnight."

What?

Fossi's blood turned ice-thick.

Surely . . . *surely* they were not discussing . . . *her?*

"She is the oddest creature." Faith laughed. It was not a kind sound. "Has Foster even considered what will become of her once Father dies?"

"Given the way her strange mind works?" Another snort.

"She is already a charity case." Faith again. "None of us can spare the money needed to keep her. I can barely feed and clothe my own children."

"It would be a mercy if someone would hire her as a governess." Charity this time. Most *un*charitably said.

"True, but she is simply too odd for that. Worse, she will never see herself as a burden—"

"Pity we cannot send her to the poorhouse."

"Faith! You are terrible. We would never send Fossi to the poorhouse. How horrible. Besides, imagine what father's parishioners would say to such a thing. No, we will just have to take her in turns and make the best of it."

A hefty sigh. "There is no simple solution to this problem."

Fossi realized that her hands were trembling. Betsy looked over at her with *pitying* eyes. The maid obviously had overheard this conversation before.

"It cannot be me," Faith repeated, voice drifting in. "Tom would be angry and the twins fuss so much already—"

"But Foster could be a help with the twins, no? I think they quite adore her."

"Perhaps, but hired help would be cheaper than feeding and clothing another adult. Particularly one who is so addled."

Fossi felt her breath speed up, harsh and loud in her ears.

The Fossi before London and Lord Whitmoor would have ducked her head down and continued to string lavender, burying the sting of her sisters' words deep beneath her shell.

But the Fossi *after* Lord Whitmoor couldn't do that.

Too many things had been knocked loose, and she didn't know how to contain them anymore. The very walls felt too close.

So with a mumbled excuse to Betsy, Fossi pulled off her apron and darted out of the kitchen, not stopping for a bonnet or gloves, practically running for the fields and a small copse of wood beyond.

A charity case?

Too odd to be a help?

Fossi swiped at her damp cheeks once she reached the soft shade of the trees, her feet automatically taking her along a barely-there path that ended in a small grotto. A trickle of water tumbled down the face of a rock outcropping, landing in a puddle that only the most charitable would call a pool.

She sat on a fallen log beside the small grotto, buried her face in her hands and let it all out . . . all the color and messiness and *living* she kept tight inside. Which was merely a fanciful way of saying she cried her eyes out.

But . . . her sisters were *right*.

She truly *hadn't* thought about what would become of her. She hadn't taken care to ensure she had a definite future. In her narrow world, she had simply assumed that once her father passed, she would continue as she had—caring for her sibling's children, furthering her father's work among his congregation . . .

Never once had she thought her efforts were seen, not as a help, but as a burden.

Oh, the *humiliation* of it . . .

Fossi had long known one simple fact—

She was only as lovable as she was useful.

After all, only pretty or entertaining things were admired and kept simply by virtue of their existence.

In order to be worthy of love—or, barring that, at least esteem—she needed to be useful in some other capacity. Her value as a tool had to equal the effort and cost of her maintenance.

How horrid to discover that nothing could make her . . . more.

Fossi cried until her chest heaved and hiccupped, until her head throbbed and her stomach hurt. Her throat sticky and aching.

Life stretched before her, dense darkness.

Prior to her mother's death, life hadn't seemed so dim. Perhaps it was just the naivety of a teenager. Or, as Fossi liked to think, the gentle positivity of her mother's guiding influence.

Regardless . . . no one besides Will had called her Fossi since.

All the thoughts of the past two weeks tumbled around her.

Unbidden, her mind danced through the Italian verb conjugations her mother had drilled into her—

Fossi, fossimo, fossero . . .

Circling back, as she always did, to her own nickname.

Fossi—wouldst that I had been.

The *congiuntivo imperfetto.* The imperfect subjunctive of *essere* . . . to be . . .

It was a verb form that scarcely existed anymore in English. That subjunctive tense which communicated longing for a past wish or desire.

Fossi, fossi, fosse . . .

Wouldst that I had been . . .

Wouldst that thou had been . . .

Wouldst that he had been . . .

Fossi . . . she heard its meaning every time in her name.

Wouldst that . . . her mother had lived, that Fossi hadn't taken on the care of her siblings instead of marrying (as Prudence and Charity had done), that her oddness and plainness and cleverness hadn't been an equally large deterrent to matrimony.

At least, Lord Whitmoor hadn't been repulsed by those things.

No, he had sought her for her cleverness, for the odd turning of her mind.

Fossi, fossi, fosse . . .

Wouldst that God had granted her a different life. One where her internal existence and outside living could be one and the same.

But such was not her fate.

She stared at the humble puddle with its trickling water until her eyes dried and her hiccups ceased.

Then, she physically washed her face in the cool water and repinned her tumbled hair, while metaphorically locking away all her self-pity and lack of gratitude. Carefully gathering every scattered bit of herself back inside.

And, when she finally felt equal to the challenge of returning to her home and her father and the sisters who did not want her . . . she returned.

Demurely. Decorously. Just as her mother had tutored her to be. Every inch a lady despite her old dress and lacking bonnet and gloves. No shattered running across fields. No odd words at her lips.

She walked up the road and over the three-arched bridge into town, past the new church and its charming vicarage, through the village green, past the Royal George Inn with a fancy carriage in the coaching yard, past the apothecary and haberdasher closing shop for the day, across the road, left at the stone fence . . . down the long lane to The Old Vicarage.

Prudence and Charity met her at the door, Betsy wringing her hands behind them.

Fossi schooled her features into a mask of calm.

"What have you done?" Prudence hissed, voice low.

Not the most auspicious of beginnings.

"Me?" Fossi asked.

"Yes, you!" Charity snatched her arm. "You will send Father to an early grave with escapades like this."

"Pardon?"

"There is no help for it now. Father waits for you in the study."

"Is it true?" Strength, her younger brother, shouldered through the doorway behind Fossi. "The boys came running with the news."

"You'll have to see for yourself." Prudence waved a hand toward their father's study.

"Better not to keep them waiting." Charity nodded, pushing Fossi forward.

What had happened?

Fossi swallowed and walked to her father's study, her siblings at her back, crowding her.

She knocked.

"Come."

Fossi opened the door and walked into the room, Strength at her heels.

Directly ahead, her father stood before the fireplace, hands clasped behind his back, dark eyes drilling into her. He was wearing his most severe black coat which made his graying hair appear nearly white. Her older brother, Will, leaned against the large desk to the right of the door.

Both men bristled with tension.

But it was the other occupant of the room who instantly garnered her entire attention.

Fossi clutched an arm across her waist, as if that alone could keep her astonishment in check.

Why had he come?

"Ah, Miss Lovejoy," Lord Whitmoor said. "How delightful to see you."

He flashed a decidedly charming smile her way. The same kind of smile she imagined a lion gave its prey before consuming it for dinner.

Lord Whitmoor punctuated his remarks with an elegant bow, precise and courteous. It was the perfect gesture with which to greet a debutante but somehow took on a mocking edge when directed at her.

Or, perhaps, that was just her own fragile assessment. She could scarcely recall another instance in her life where she had received such a bow, so naturally it would seem ironic—

Babbling.

She was mentally babbling.

But it was simply so . . . incongruous, the juxtaposition of her father's study and Lord Whitmoor in his fine elegance. He outshone them all. Like an exotic bird suddenly alighting on Reverend Lovejoy's supper table—thrilling, to be sure, but not to be tolerated . . . by either the bird *or* the good Reverend.

"Yes, how delightful to see you, Foster." Reverend Lovejoy's tone made it clear he considered Lord Whitmoor's bow ironic as well.

"And now that you are here, Foster," her father continued, "perhaps you can enlighten us as to why an *aristocrat*"—he practically spat the word—"has descended on my house to call upon you."

Chapter 7

Daniel had gravely miscalculated.

Again.

He had thought to take up Miss Foster Lovejoy's recommendation and use charm this round—another attempt at persuasion before resorting to kidnapping, a length of chain and a sturdy desk.

His aim had clearly misfired given the tension vibrating from the people around him.

Trust Miss Lovejoy to keep him on his toes.

He surveyed the room. Miss Lovejoy was attired in an even older gown than the one she had worn before, its high-waist and faded fabric declaring the dress to be at least a decade past its prime. She clasped her hands across her stomach, dismay written on her face.

And then there were the men. Her two brothers were reflections of her—one older, one younger—with their brown eyes and simple, country dress, though the elder brother appeared to have slightly more sartorial taste than the other. They studied Daniel with wary expressions. In contrast, Reverend Lovejoy vibrated with anger from his shock of gray-white hair to his scuffed shoes.

Garvis had clearly not understood the familial situation when he delivered Daniel his report on Foster Lovejoy's whereabouts. Daniel would have to have words with the man. Peaceful times did not sanction sloppy work, particularly with a mission as critical as this.

"Well, miss? What do you have to say for yourself?" Her father's tone brooked no argument. "Why does this *man*"—here he waved a dismissive hand at Daniel—"wish to speak with you?"

Miss Lovejoy darted those chocolate brown eyes of hers between Daniel and her father, past her brothers and back to Daniel again. Panic flitted across her elegant face, color touching her high cheekbones.

"I-I cannot think that I know, sir," was her marginally garbled reply. "I am as equally surprised as yourself."

She met Daniel's eyes for a fraction of a second, a pleading note in them.

Daniel instantly understood.

Please don't tell them I was in London.

Ah. Of course.

It was obvious the men in her life would never have countenanced her traveling so far alone to answer the summons of an unknown lord.

Unfortunately, her father intercepted her beseeching glance. Daniel suspected little escaped Reverend Lovejoy's notice.

Her father's eyes narrowed, pinning his daughter in place. "What sort of . . . *activities* . . . have you been engaging in, girl?"

The shock of her father's insinuating accusation nearly winded Daniel.

Good heavens!

It took a moment for Miss Lovejoy to follow her father's meaning.

And then color swept her face in a blush of truly magnificent proportions.

"Oh!" She pressed her hands to her cheeks, expression equal parts horror and mortification.

"Father!" The older brother, Mr. Will Lovejoy, rolled his eyes. "You know full well that Fossi has not been engaging in *those* sorts of activities, with or without Lord Whitmoor. The idea is absurd." He shook his head, as if the thought of any man wanting his sister was too ludicrous to countenance.

"Oh," she repeated.

Miss Lovejoy—Fossi, apparently—wrapped her arms around herself again, as if hugging a life-preserver.

Though his mind did snag on her nickname for a moment.

Fossi.

It was . . . cute. How long had it been since he had found anything *cute?*

Her suffering stirred something deep within Daniel, something long buried and forgotten.

"I can assure you, sir," he said, "that Miss Lovejoy's behavior has always been all that is proper and decorous—"

"Pardon, sirrah?" Reverend Lovejoy snapped. "Please describe the nature of your prior interactions with my Foster—"

"Father!" Fossi shot Daniel another distressed, apologetic look.

"Silence, Foster!" Her father whirled on her. "It is just like a parasitic aristocrat to come sniffing around my household—"

"Hear, hear." That was the younger brother. "What could he possibly want with us?"

"Perhaps we should apply to the man himself?" That droll bit was from Will. He still leaned against the edge of his father's desk, arms crossed. "Lord Whitmoor does appear to still be in the room."

He shot Daniel a *'go on'* look.

Well.

How to phrase this?

"Gentleman, I would be honored to explain my presence here. Though, I require your discretion as to the contents of our conversation, as they must remain as secret as possible—"

"I will agree to nothing," Reverend Lovejoy harrumphed. "You will tell us and then we will decide what is to be done."

Daniel's eyebrows shot to his hairline.

Obviously, the good Reverend Lovejoy disliked the aristocracy.

In Daniel's experience, there were two reasons for this attitude. One stemmed from a decidedly American belief in a meritocracy, that each man should be valued based on his own merits and not an accident of birth. Such an opinion was in line with Daniel's own personal worldview. He had, after all, risen to the peerage for precisely those reasons.

But there was another viewpoint which disliked those in positions of power and authority out of resentment and jealousy—the thought being, 'If I can't be the one in charge, then I refuse to support those who are.'

He was unsure where Miss Lovejoy's father fell on the spectrum, but he suspected the latter.

Daniel took in a deep breath. "As you may perhaps know, I work closely with the Crown and Home Office regarding matters of national, shall we say, safety. At the moment, I find myself in need of a mathematician of renowned skill and creative insight. It had come to my attention that Miss Foster Lovejoy of Kilminster, Dorset was such a mathematician—"

"You want Foster to do sums for you?" The younger brother frowned.

"However would the Home Office know about my daughter's predilection toward mathematics?" Josiah Lovejoy fixed Daniel with hard eyes. "Why should the Crown concern itself with my corner of the world?"

Daniel spread his hands wide. "I am in the business of information, sir. 'Twould be compromising were I to share my methodology."

Josiah Lovejoy clearly wasn't buying it. "Does this have something to do with that rotten Society of Mathematics something or other? They came nosing around my Foster a few years ago. I thought I had sent them on their merry way."

Will darted a horrified look at his sister. She returned a quelling stare.

Ah. So the older brother knew.

True to form, Reverend Lovejoy didn't miss their silent exchange. His eyes widened in near apoplectic horror.

"What have you done, you foolish girl?" he hissed.

"Father—" Will began, moving to stand between his father and sister.

"No! You will not defend her, boy." Josiah Lovejoy pushed past his son, towering over his daughter. "What. Have. You. DONE?!"

"Father, don't do this. Not now." Will shot an apologetic look back at Daniel before snagging his father's arm. "I encouraged her, Father. Lord Whitmoor has the right of it. Foster *is* a mathematical genius, and it is a shame to deny the world a glimpse into her brilliance."

"The world?! What does the *world* have to do with any of this?" Reverend Lovejoy glared at his eldest son. "God's opinion is the only one that concerns me. And this"—he gestured in a circle, taking in Fossi and Daniel—"matters naught by any measure. Foster's obsession with mathematics is vanity and pride, at best—"

"Her gift *comes* from God, Father." Will pushed his case.

"No, her proclivity toward numbers is a dangerous distraction that must be carefully controlled. We have had this conversation more times that I can count, boy. And, now, to know she continued correspondence with that *Society* which glorifies man's intellect over God's—"

"Father, you misunderstand the matter." Fossi found her voice. "The Society of Mathematicians certainly does not consider itself above God's intellect—"

"You lied to me, child." Reverend Lovejoy's words hung in the room. "Even if you split hairs and never told an out-an-out falsehood, you knew I considered the matter closed. You deliberately deceived me."

"Father—" she began again. "Things are not quite—"

"Enough!" her father boomed, bushy eyebrows drawn down. "We will discuss this later, when . . . *company* is not present."

Daniel's heart sank. What would this 'discussion' entail? Should he be worried for Fossi's safety?

Mmmm. Granted, he would consider chaining her to a desk, but the thought of anyone else harming her upset him? Such hypocrisy was . . . unhelpful.

Fortunately, Fossi looked distressed but not panic-stricken.

Daniel knew he should leave it alone. Just take his leave and walk out the door, regroup for the next skirmish.

But . . .

Fossi with her sparking wit and rare courage deserved more than this. More than a sheltered half-life where all decisions were taken from her.

"Your daughter is a rare genius, sir. Her mathematical mind knows no equal. She is possessed of a spirit of inventiveness that gives fresh life to her calculations—"

"You are quite through, *Mister* Whitmoor." Reverend Lovejoy had turned an alarming shade of red.

Which truly was unfortunate. The color was quite unbecoming and Daniel had a terrible tendency toward flippancy when faced with outrage and huffy conceit.

"Uh, Ashton, actually. Daniel Ashton, at your service."

He bowed. Polite. Precise.

And possibly with a hint of irony this time around.

"Well, *Mister* Ashton, you will kindly remove your unwelcome personage from my home . . ."

Daniel gave Fossi another apologetic look as her father waxed on and on about Daniel's defective character and the excesses of the aristocracy in general.

Fossi managed a small, hopeless smile in return, her dead eyes telling Daniel all he needed to know.

THE IMAGE OF those dead eyes—lifeless pools of muddy brown—chased Daniel out of the Lovejoy's home and back to the Royal George Inn where Garvis and his carriage awaited.

Daniel would consider the whole affair to have taken a nearly comical turn . . . if his own self-loathing and need for redemption were not so overwhelming. If the hopelessness in Fossi's eyes hadn't tugged at that deeply buried part of him.

Damn.

The woman who could conceptualize Fourier's Nemesis merited, at the very least, a healthy dose of respect.

Would he add to her distress and force her to work for him?

There was no doubt he *could*. If Fossi refused to help him willingly, there were any number of ways Daniel could ensure her *un*willing cooperation.

Empathy and esteem for Miss Foster Lovejoy would only hamper him in doing what had to be done. Ruthlessness, when warranted, had never been a struggle for him.

Daniel rubbed at his forehead as he trudged up the stairs to the suite of rooms he had taken. Garvis was waiting for him, scribbling in one of his endless journals.

Garvis fancied himself something of a writer.

One look at his master's face was all it took. "It went that poorly, eh?" A grin tugged at the man's mouth.

"Not a word." Daniel muttered, trying to fight the throbbing in his head, regretting for about the thousandth time that 1828 was short on ibuprofen.

His tired, hurting brain couldn't think of an ethical solution to his current problem. Guilt pounded through his chest, the anguishing pain that constantly lurked.

Miss Foster Lovejoy was the only one who could work the complicated formulas he needed. He had no other option. She was his only hope.

The portal *had* to be fixed. His very sanity depended on it.

Fossi refused to help of her own accord.

Her family certainly would offer no assistance in persuading her.

He was at an utter impasse.

Was kidnapping the only option left, then?

On that depressing thought, Daniel fell into a dreamless sleep.

He woke after dawn to birds chirping far too cheerfully outside his window.

His headache, fortunately, had abated—sleep and rest providing the necessary medicine.

Daniel got up, washed his face using a washbasin and pitcher in the corner and took advantage of the stowed chamber pot.

It was only as he finished tying his cravat that he noticed the white slip of paper slid underneath his bedroom door.

Even from across the room, her bold handwriting was unmistakable.

> *If you still wish to engage my services, I have decided to accept, provided we can come to a mutually satisfactory agreement. You will find the remains of an old mill a mile up the road toward Bath. I will await you there at noon.*

All the breath rushed from Daniel in a swoosh of relief.

Hallelujah.

So unexpected.

They would come to a satisfactory agreement. On *that* point, he did not worry.

This was a sign. He was on the correct path.

Hope flared bright.

Promise you will keep it for me. Don't forget.

A solution was within his grasp. At last.

Chapter 8

THE OLD MILL
NEAR KILMINSTER, DORSET
AUGUST 8, 1828

Fossi was not surprised to find Lord Whitmoor already waiting for her as she topped a small rise and descended toward the abandoned mill.

He struck her as the kind of man who grasped opportunity the way other lowlier mortals breathed air—his by right of merely existing.

From her vantage point, she could see his fine carriage on the road, horses held by a coachman and groom. Another man rested against the coach, a booted foot propped on the door, arms folded across his chest, hat pushed low.

Lord Whitmoor himself paced beside the crumbling stone walls surrounding the old mill, hands clasped behind his back. His head swung her way as she walked toward him.

Her heart thundered. Was she truly going to do this? It had seemed a sane choice in the dead of night but now felt like walking into the lion's den.

The events of the previous afternoon would not leave her be. She had been up for the better part of the night, assessing, contemplating.

The entire mooring of her life had been swept out to sea in one swooping tidal wave. The only option left her was to decide what to do with the scattered remains.

After Lord Whitmoor took his leave yesterday evening, her father had spent the better part of two hours venting his temper, railing on her deception, Lord Whitmoor's audacity and the failings of the aristocracy in general. Fossi had borne it all without comment. Opening her mouth would merely prolong her father's tirade.

Her father had decided, in the end, that she was a wicked creature for having associated with such a man. And, if given enough time, he allowed that he could forgive her trespasses, provided she cease all correspondence with the Society of Mathematicians and Lord Whitmoor and never mention the matter again.

When he was finished, he sent her to bed.

Without any supper.

Thirty-two years old and she had been banished to her room like a recalcitrant child.

Her family clearly saw her as an eccentric burden—tolerated because she was, after all, their own flesh and blood. A trial to bear. But not someone valued. Not someone needed.

The idea . . . burned, ached. It was a fresh wound, gaping and raw.

Her father did love for her—she was honest with herself in this—cared for in as much as Reverend Lovejoy was capable of love. But his paternal affection was a distant thing.

And now that she *knew* she was a burden to him and her siblings, everything had become tinged with a sense of obligation. The future with her family appeared bleak.

On the opposite hand, Lord Whitmoor needed her.

His purposes might be clandestine and shrouded in mystery, but at least he didn't hide his motives behind a false smile, righteous platitudes and rote familial duty.

He would not tolerate her if she became a burden.

Any relationship between them would be strictly economical in nature—a business transaction. Lord Whitmoor would certainly never view her with fondness. She was simply a tool. He would use her mathematical talents, and she would receive payment for her endeavors—money that would shore up her beleaguered future prospects.

Lord Whitmoor would cast her off as soon as she ceased to be useful.

But . . . as it turned out, so would her family.

More to the point, Fossi would never have expectations of anything *more* from him. It was a black-and-white viewpoint of the world that she easily understood.

There was a reason Fossi loved numbers. They didn't lie. They didn't say one thing and think another.

They were truthful and straightforward.

Lord Whitmoor was hard and unyielding and the world he inhabited frightened her. But he had defended her abilities to her father, which displayed a streak of loyalty within Lord Whitmoor she had not anticipated.

He would not betray those he saw as *his*.

"Miss Lovejoy." Lord Whitmoor tipped his hat and gave her a small bow as she stopped in front of him. "As you can surmise, I received your note."

"Indeed, my lord." Fossi bobbed a curtsy. "I had placed the odds of you appearing here at one out of five point four, but there was a margin of error of seven point three six percent, so I was uncertain, as you can imagine."

To Lord Whitmoor's credit, he only blinked twice at her statement.

"Well, despite the unfavorable odds, it is certainly a pleasure to see you again. Perhaps under more auspicious circumstances this time?" His head angled in question.

"Yes, my lord."

Fossi set her small bag upon the ground. She had packed it in the early morning hours—her computation notebooks and other scribbles, three dresses, a change of underthings—and stowed it away in the woods to be retrieved before meeting Lord Whitmoor.

As for that, it had been a simple thing to slip a note under his door at the Royal George on her return from the woods. There was only one room fine enough for a gentleman of Lord Whitmoor's standing and everyone in Kilminster knew it to be the front bedroom and parlor overlooking the village green.

After leaving a note for Lord Whitmoor, she had returned home and written another tear-stained note for her father which she left on her made bed. The note expressed her love for him and gratitude for his support over the years, ending by stating she did not wish to be a burden upon the family and was seeking to live elsewhere. She did *not* tell him where she was going. Why hand Reverend Lovejoy ammunition?

She then attended family prayer meeting and helped Betsy finish tying herbs in the cold room. At which point, she had foregone lunch to retrieve her bag and meet Lord Whitmoor here.

"I feel compelled to offer my most humble apologies for the scene my arrival provoked yesterday," he said. "I did not mean to cause you distress before your family."

It was a kind observation. Fossi believed him . . . or, at least, he genuinely disliked that he had misstepped.

Lord Whitmoor looked . . . *more* today. His dark coat and trousers were less fussy and tailored than others she had seen him wear, a nod to the long journey ahead perhaps.

Most significantly, his waistcoat was a startling blood-red satin. It was almost impossible to not see the striking splash of unexpected color as symbolic. A small glimpse, perhaps, into the man behind the persona of Lord Whitmoor.

Or, the cynical part of her muttered, a way to make him seem less aristocratic and more approachable.

Here, you can trust me because I am just a simple man trying to hire help.

Lord Whitmoor weighed every decision with cold calculation.

"My father can be quite . . . forceful in his opinions, unfortunately," she said. "He obviously sympathizes with both the American and French Revolutions and does not see much use for the . . . upper classes."

"I see," Lord Whitmoor said. "Had I known the particulars of your situation, I would never have subjected you to the censure of your family. Please accept my apologies."

He said this with a smile so lethal it bordered on criminal. His blue eyes crinkled and his teeth sparkled, alarmingly straight and white in his face. Lines magically appeared around his mouth and eyes, shining outward like sun rays.

It caused an odd stuttering in her chest, that smile. Fossi had never been on the receiving end of such potent charm.

Huh.

She had *vastly* underestimated its effectiveness.

Were he to continue to smile at her like that, she could find herself agreeing to a great many things she oughtn't.

Yes, indeed.

Lord Whitmoor was a master puppeteer. Effortlessly performing a set of actions intended to gain a specific reaction. He clearly understood that knowing how to persuade someone was the first step to controlling them.

Of course, the inverse was to be avoided at all costs. As a master of knowing, he was even more skilled at being *unknown*, sealing his true self deep inside that unassailable fortress.

Fossi hazarded that very, very few people were allowed to see the true Daniel Ashton. But, she suspected, the real man behind the wall would be a fascinating one.

That was the problem with men who hid in iron-willed fortresses.

Such things challenged, begged to be besieged and conquered. She understood better why Alexander had felt compelled to vanquish Tyre, why men went to war at all.

That same energy she had observed before swirled around him, but this time it wasn't contained within a room. Logic—and, quite frankly, all three of Newton's Laws of Motion—would insist that the force of his personality should feel weaker in the open countryside, as nothing confined it.

But trust Lord Whitmoor to defy even the rules of physics themselves.

The vivacity of his person loomed larger, consuming more than his share of space.

All these thoughts pinging around her brain meant it took a moment for his words to sink in.

Had I known the particulars of your situation . . .

Wait. What?

He had violated her privacy and stolen her ideas before they even met. How could he have been ignorant of her circumstances? Of her gender? That did not . . . compute.

He read the confusion on her face.

"Either my presence is upsetting or I have managed to puzzle you?" He flashed another delicious smile, deadly in its calculation.

Her heart pitter-pattered, causing her breath to hitch.

Action. Reaction.

She was merely experiencing Newton's Third Law of Motion in an up-close and personal way.

Nothing more.

Courage, Fossi.

She straightened her shoulders. She was made of sterner stuff than charming smiles. "I am merely trying to understand yet *again*, my lord, how you came to know my own personal notes and yet remained ignorant of the other basic facts of my life, such as my family life and . . . gender? Would you care to enlighten me?"

His mouth twisted, as if her question were . . . troublesome.

Oh dear.

Perhaps this wasn't going to work, after all. Perhaps the kinship and understanding she sensed from him was all a fabrication of her overactive imagination.

He was, after all, a man who dealt in secrets with the highest people in the land. Heavens, he probably had *personal* conversations with the King himself.

Lord Whitmoor's face morphed into etched lines of remorse. The expression had a studied air. As if he had dipped into a trunk of costumes and pulled out his *Regretful Gentleman* guise.

"Unfortunately, Miss Lovejoy, I cannot share how I came to know of your mathematical equations." He sighed. It was a *very* convincing sigh but in an actor-ish sort of way. "Surprising as it may seem, my choices are not always my own. Please know that my inability to offer an explanation in no way reflects contempt for your intellectual abilities nor a lack of trust. The confidence is simply not mine to share."

Oh, *bravo!*

Such a clever little piece of rhetoric that speech was. She resisted the urge to clap.

"Given how wide your eyes just went, Miss Lovejoy, perhaps you do not agree?" He seemed bemused, the wretch.

A pause.

"I was merely admiring your speech, my lord. It was so perfectly . . . practiced. Do you use a mirror when you rehearse?"

"Pardon?" Now *his* were the wide eyes.

"Your explanation was truly a masterpiece. Remorseful and heartfelt with the sigh. The subtle letting down of your guard and sharing a confidence with me. All of which was meant to convey trust, the suggestion that you value my cooperation and opinion but are hopelessly constrained by prior obligations."

Lord Whitmoor darted his eyes left and right. Opened his mouth. Frowned.

"I meant no offense," Fossi hastened to add. "I just couldn't help but admire the calculation that went into it all. It was a remarkable performance."

She extended a hand, as if to touch him in reassurance the way she would one of Prudence's boys.

There, there. I know you are telling me a falsehood, but I forgive you.

But then Fossi remembered who *he* was and who *she* was and how touching Lord Whitmoor in any way would be an unfortunate idea.

Action. Reaction. And so forth.

He glanced back at his waiting carriage and kicked a booted foot against the stone wall. "I am truly sorry that I cannot tell you, Miss Lovejoy. I *can* assure you that no one trespassed upon your father's property to obtain your computations." His sincerity seemed genuine this time. "I am being as honest with you as I can."

How could she read him so easily? She had wondered if London had been a fluke. A mere fanciful perception clouded by a long journey, too little sleep and toxic London smoke.

But it seemed not to be the case.

He snorted and continued, "Though I must say, I fear I am losing my touch if I am so easily seen through."

"It was a very elegant bit of oration." Fossi reassured him. "I was definitely charmed."

He chuckled, low and throaty, a mixture of astonishment and surprise.

"And do you like me more this time?" He met her gaze, a wry grin tugging at his mouth.

"Decidedly. 'Tis much more pleasant than arguing."

That reply got her a genuine laugh. Head back, teeth flashing, honest merriment dancing through his eyes.

Fossi forgot how to breathe.

This was a glimpse of the real man behind the granite wall. The true Daniel Ashton, Lord Whitmoor.

Heavens. He was beautiful.

Beautiful not in the way of a sunset or a flower garden. It wasn't harmony of person or features.

No, he was beautiful like the fury of a storm battered sea. Like lightning snaking across a black sky or winter winds scouring the moor.

Beauty that came from awe . . . from observing something powerful and rare and . . . liberated.

It was an unfortunate observation.

Fossi didn't know much about the relationship between a hirer and hireling, but she was quite sure that finding one's employer beautiful was generally frowned upon.

At the very least, it made one's employment more fraught, if her own current emotional state were to be used as evidence.

To consider employment at all was already bad enough, but to make it *fraught* employment . . .

His smile faded, though a sort of fond mirth remained in his eyes.

"Come now," he said, "let us negotiate in earnest. You stated in your note that you were willing to assist me, provided we could come to a satisfactory understanding. What odds do you place on us doing so?"

Fossi couldn't help her reciprocal smile. "I would say the odds are against it, my lord. Though I did struggle when assigning a numerical weight to your desperation, so my figures include a decided margin of error."

He laughed again, delighted, genuine. "From my vantage point, I will put our odds at nearly one hundred percent."

"Truly?" Fossi was impressed.

"Indeed. My desperation is acute. Pray tell me, Miss Lovejoy, what does your notion of 'satisfactory understanding' encompass?"

Fossi squared her shoulders, pushing back all thoughts of unhandsome men who still managed to be beautiful.

This was the critical moment. Would he agree to her conditions? Could she still call herself a lady after making such demands?

And given the sad state of her life, did she much care?

"I have pondered the matter at length, my lord . . ." She swallowed. "I do not know, after my sojourn in your employ, if I will find welcome again in my father's house."

He . . . sagged at her words.

It wasn't as if his shoulders slumped precisely. There was no outward movement. But she sensed that her words caused something to tumble inside him.

"Miss Lovejoy—"

"Please"—she held out a staying hand—"allow me to finish. Because of the future uncertainty my employ will engender, I fear my demands will be . . . high. Perhaps excessive."

She paused.

He rolled a hand. *Go on.*

Deep breath.

"I require ten thousand pounds, as well as a chaperone, my lord."

She stood still, allowing the words to hang between them.

It was a staggering sum. An heiress' dowry.

She knew it to be an absurd sum which was why she had only packed a small bag of possessions.

The odds were not in her favor. She was quite sure Lord Whitmoor would smile politely and send her back to her father.

But . . . if she was going to be cast off and enter the employ of a master secret-keeper, she wanted to ensure she had a roof over her head and food to eat for the rest of her life. Before throwing off any chance of a future with her family, she needed a guarantee of having a future elsewhere.

The fact that Lord Whitmoor merely regarded her for a long moment, head tilted, did nothing to allay the butterflies currently fighting to escape from her stomach.

DANIEL RAISED HIS eyebrows.

Ten thousand pounds.

He had respected her before now, but that esteem ratcheted up a notch. That would be nearly a million pounds in the twenty-first century.

She had gumption.

Go big or go home? Wasn't that the American phrase?

He approved that she did not value herself cheaply.

The sum she named was high but not exorbitant. Not for a man of his wealth. He would barely notice its loss.

But for her . . . it would mean the difference between a life of penury and one of modest comfort.

And thank *heavens* they had arrived at this point. Negotiation and willing cooperation were so much better than his other options.

He would have paid *anything* she requested.

Redemption and a future were worth everything he owned.

But, he sensed, even *had* she known that fact, she wouldn't have requested more. Miss Fossi Lovejoy was innately honest and fair. She might omit truths but she would not tell an outright lie. She had honor.

And he'd be damned if that didn't make him like her all the more.

Her pulse fluttered in the smooth column of her neck. He admired again the classical perfection of her face. Had he thought her to be a Renaissance Madonna? No, she was more akin to Athena, goddess of wisdom. A Greek statue of serene alabaster.

Pity he found her attractive and interesting. Such things were an unwelcome distraction at this point.

Dark eyes met his with courage from underneath, quite frankly, a hideous bonnet. Shapeless and sun-bleached, the poor thing looked desperate to be put out of its misery.

Had she ever owned anything new? Experienced the fun of having dresses made specifically for her?

He might have to insist she accept some new clothing as part of her employment.

No. He was going to *require* it.

He nodded, slowly. "You drive a hard bargain, Miss Lovejoy. I will agree to your demands on two conditions."

He paused for effect.

Given how her spine straightened and her eyes sparked, it was not an ineffectual pause.

He ticked the items off on his fingers. "One, I require you to have a new wardrobe—"

"My lord—" she began on a shocked gasp.

"No, that point is non-negotiable."

"I *cannot* accept clothing from you, my lord." Her tone so agonized. "It would be . . ."

She stopped right there, voice strained and awkward.

He understood the direction of her thoughts.

Men who purchased clothing for women were either relatives or *not-*relatives purchasing decidedly more than just *clothing* for the woman in question.

"Though I understand your misgivings, Miss Lovejoy, I cannot have someone in my employ dressed as . . ." He stopped, unsure how to continue without being unforgivably rude.

"A poor parson's daughter? An aging spinster?" Fossi offered. "The things that I am?"

How did she turn the tables on him so quickly?

"At the risk of giving offense, I must say you do yourself a disservice. You are much more than those things, Miss Lovejoy."

"Perhaps, but—"

"No. I am quite firm on this matter. I will include a stipend with your payment, allowing you and your chaperone to arrange for new clothing. Would that be satisfactory? Those in my employ must look the respectable part."

A long pause, during which they stared at each other.

An impasse.

Until finally . . . she straightened her spine and bobbed her assent.

Damn but he admired her.

She deserved so much more out of life. Which probably explained why he said what he did next.

"Item two," he said, before she could interrupt again, "I will pay you ten thousand pounds *now*, as a show of good faith and a nod to the personal sacrifices you are making on my behalf, as well as providing you with the requested chaperone. If you stay through the completion of the project, there will be an additional ten thousand pounds for your efforts."

She hissed in a breath, shock clearly jolting her body.

She swallowed. "You are offering me *twenty* thousand pounds and a chaperone, in addition to a new wardrobe?"

"Yes."

A beat.

And then a delighted smile spread across her face. "I vastly underestimated your desperation, my lord. It *is* acute. Had I known, I would have placed our odds at one hundred percent, as well." Her dark eyes danced. "What precisely *am* I to be engaged in doing? Highway robbery?"

That surprised another soft laugh from him.

"The lamentable truth, as with most everything I do, is that I am unable to tell you the *why* behind what I will ask you to do." Honest sincerity laced his tone. "But know the equations you complete will be for a noble cause that will possibly save lives."

A drawn out moment.

"I suppose I must simply accept that?" she said at last.

"Yes. Unfortunately, I cannot offer further explanation at this time."

"I see."

Another pause.

"So . . ." he began.

"I accept your terms, Lord Whitmoor." She nodded. "I assume you will have a legal document drawn up as a contract?"

"Indeed I will, Miss Lovejoy." He smiled, extending her a gloved hand. She shook it. "Welcome to my crew."

Chapter 9

THE ROAD TO BATH
A FEW HOURS LATER
AUGUST 8, 1828

The carriage swayed gently to and fro, the entire apparatus moving as if settled atop down pillows.

Of course, Lord Whitmoor's carriage would never dare do anything so gauche as *rock* or *jolt*.

Fossi sat in the forward facing seat, gloved hands clasped in her lap, trying to quell her nerves. Lord Whitmoor sat to her right and his man, Mr. Garvis Samuelson, slept on the seat opposite, if his rasping snores were any indication.

Countryside scrolled past her window, sheep and stone fences and another small village every three or so miles.

Fossi could scarcely believe how dramatically a mere twenty-four hours had altered her life . . . how far her day had come.

She was to be paid for doing something she loved.

Twenty *thousand* pounds.

She let that number rattle around her brain for a minute, kick up some dust, knock down a few long-held assumptions.

She had spent the past hour dissecting the sum, dividing it, multiplying it, square-rooting it.

How many prime numbers were contained in twenty thousand pounds? How many derivatives?

How many dreams and desires?

One thought kept popping back in:

She would now have sufficient funds to start a girl's school.

Yesterday afternoon, accomplishing even the simplest item on her list had seemed a distant possibility. But now she might be able to achieve one of the points she had deemed *impossible*.

Gracious, if the full twenty thousand pounds materialized, she might even have to *add* to her list.

What a thought.

She had always longed to create a safe haven for girls, children like she had been. Intelligent. Inquisitive. But denied any extensive education due to their gender.

Fossi had been fortunate. Her mother had insisted Fossi sit in on her father's tutoring lessons, broadening her education. Will had then added what he could. Now Fossi would have the chance to pass along that opportunity to other girls. Her mind spun with hopes for her suddenly bright future.

Beside her, Lord Whitmoor stretched his long legs out, careful to avoid Mr. Samuelson's across the carriage.

Fossi tried not to think of her father's reaction to her traveling with not one, but *two*, men who were not relatives. But, again, she was not a young miss and, aside from her own family, no one else would think anything remiss in their travel.

Lord Whitmoor consulted his pocket watch.

"We should reach Bath in time for supper." He tucked the watch back into his waistcoat pocket. "Once there, I suggest we dine while the horses are changed. We can then continue on until sunset and stop for the evening at a coaching inn I prefer outside Bristol. Can I call upon your reserves of fortitude, Miss Lovejoy, to extend the journey that far?"

Heavens. Did the man not remember he was paying her *twenty thousand* pounds?

"Of course, my lord," she said. "This carriage displays at minimum a sixty percent reduction in erratic, jostling motion, resulting in more energy being conserved as forward momentum and giving the horses a twenty percent boost in overall power . . ."

An awkward pause. The kind with which she was all too familiar.

Mind your tongue, Fossi, before Lord Whitmoor finds your company too odd.

He shrugged. "I had hoped the carriage design would result in a seventy-five percent reduction in non-conforming kinetic energy. But even at sixty percent, it still provides comfortable travel." He flashed a wan smile.

Surprise jolted her.

No one *ever* understood her ramblings.

But of course Lord Whitmoor would be educated in the basics of mathematics and energy. He had sought her out, after all.

How unfortunate to find a keen mathematical intellect behind all that attractive exterior.

"Comfortable carriage or no, I appreciate your patience with the journey, Miss Lovejoy." He leaned forward slightly as he said this, gazing out her window.

The smell of bay rum wrapped around her, laced with under-notes of peppermint. It was a particularly masculine scent and, as such, had the unfortunate side-effect of making Fossi hyper-aware of how very *male* he was. Broad-shouldered and deep-chested and coiled energy.

A man in the absolute prime of life.

"I hope to reach Kinningsley by tomorrow evening," he continued.

"Kinningsley?"

"Yes, forgive me for not explaining sooner." He sat back, taking the lovely smell with him. "I have dragged you off into the wild unknown. Kinningsley is the seat of my good friends, Lord and Lady Linwood."

Oh, dear. More aristocrats.

But how odd to hear the phrase *good friends* drop from his lips. Were they truly good friends? The sort of good friends he invited inside his granite fortress?

"You will be able to complete your calculations in peace there," he continued, "and Lady Linwood will provide companionship and any chaperoning you feel necessary."

"And the nature of these calculations, my lord?" She was desperately curious to know what mathematics commanded such a high price.

"I would prefer to wait until we arrive at Kinningsley before diving into that. For now, I think, we shall simply pass the journey. Are you having second thoughts yet?"

"No, my lord."

Not that second thoughts—or even third or fourth thoughts— would do her any good. She didn't have a farthing to her name, as every last penny had been spent on her prior trip to London. Returning home at this juncture wasn't an option unless she wished to walk.

Clearly, she had not carefully thought through this entire chain of events. The odds had been against her ending up in his employ. Granted, twenty thousand pounds had a tendency to cloud even the clearest of thinkers.

Another reason to denounce greed and riches, she supposed.

But something in her reply grabbed Lord Whitmoor's attention. A slight hesitation or wistfulness or . . . *something*.

He turned his head toward her, eyes hooded underneath the brim of his top hat. Bay rum engulfed her again.

"Am I to take you at your word when you say you are not having second thoughts?" he asked.

"Yes, my lord." She swallowed, having trouble meeting his intent gaze.

She wasn't doubting her decision, per se. Just perhaps wishing she had negotiated an escape clause or access to funds should she change her mind.

Or, at the very least, a brushing up on her ladylike manners for interacting with the aristocracy.

But surely she wouldn't have much to do with this Lord and Lady

Linwood. Fossi would simply be another invisible servant in their household.

She might have nibbled on her bottom lip.

"Ah." He sat back, as if that tiny nervous twitch had told him all.

And then he said nothing more for a solid hour.

Maddening man.

He peered out the window beside him, tapping a hand against his thigh, knee bouncing. It seemed an unconscious gesture to her. Which made her . . . wonder. Surely Lord Whitmoor was always too aware of his surroundings for unconscious gestures.

Unless he felt . . . *safe*. Safe with her and Mr. Samuelson in this carriage and, thus, allowed his mind to wander elsewhere.

It was unexpected.

But, again, how could she read him so readily? Perhaps she wished so desperately to humanize Lord Whitmoor the Legend, she was conjuring things that did not exist.

"So, Miss Lovejoy, tell me more about yourself?" he finally asked.

She sensed he posed the question more out of idle curiosity and politeness than any real desire to know her personally.

But still, the small intimacy set her slightly off-kilter.

"What do you wish to know?"

"Tell me about your family, perhaps starting with your unusual names. Foster, for example?"

That was easy enough. "My father, being the clergyman and biblical scholar that he is, wished us to remember God in all things, starting with our names. I was christened Foster Love Among Us Lovejoy."

He continued to tap his hand on his leg, but he did smile. "An unusual name to be sure."

She was unsure of his tone. Did he find her name lacking? And why should she care if he did?

But . . . it seemed a tiny part somewhere behind her third rib *did* care what he thought of her.

That would be . . . ill-advised.

She should let it pass, say nothing.

"Do you consider my name unfortunate, my lord?" She asked anyway.

His hand stilled and he fully turned his head in her direction.

"No. Of course not, Miss Lovejoy." *That* was sincere. "Though you seem unperturbed by the thought."

Fossi suppressed a rather ill-bred shrug. "I avoid feeling embarrassed as a general rule."

Now she had his full attention. "And why is that?" he asked.

"Embarrassment as an emotion usually says more about the embarrass-ee than the embarrass-er." She did *not* twist her fingers together as she said this. Though the urge was decidedly strong. "Embarrassment is simply the polite manifestation of uglier emotions—shame, regret, envy."

All things she refused to sink to.

She was not ashamed of her family, despite their actions toward her.

She did not regret her station in life. Nor did she envy his.

Twenty thousand pounds or no.

"I see," he said. Lord Whitmoor nodded, slow and thoughtful, as if truly seeing her anew.

Silence for a moment.

"And your siblings?" he asked.

"Well, there are ten of us, my lord." That didn't garner a reaction either, beyond another polite tilt of his head.

"And your placement?"

"I am third, behind Will and Prudence."

"Will and Prudence?"

She understood the question. "God's *Will* Be Done and Let *Prudence* Guard your Way."

He chuckled. "And do you? Let Prudence guard your way?"

"Naturally." Fossi smiled gently. "Though there is no 'letting' about it. Will and I consider Prudence to have been quite ironically named."

Another low laugh. "And the rest?"

"Well, after me, there are my brothers—Seek the Lord's *Justice* and Find *Strength* in God."

"Strength and Will I met while speaking with your father, correct?"

"Yes. Then two sisters—Surround Yourself with *Virtue* and Let Your Heart Abound with *Charity*. From there, we have Obey God's *Call*,

~ 93 ~

another brother. My youngest sister, Walk in *Faith* and the last boy, Give and Ye Shall *Receive* but we all call him Reece."

"Fascinating. Let me see if I can name them all . . ." Lord Whitmoor squinted, forehead wrinkling. He ticked off his fingers. "Will, Prudence, Foster, Justice, Strength, Virtue, Charity, Call, Faith and Receive or Reece."

It was an impressive feat of memory.

Something that clearly came in handy as a spy.

Part of Fossi wondered if the spying created the superb memory or if the superb memory led to the spying? Or was she perhaps naive in thinking one to be the causation of the other?

"From what I saw of your family, it appeared most were married?" he continued.

"Yes, everyone is married except myself, obviously, and Reece. He works as a clerk for Will, who is a solicitor in Kilminster."

"Your eldest brother chose *not* to follow in your father's footsteps?"

"Yes. He and my father . . . differ in many ways. Justice, however, has eagerly joined my father's ministry—"

"Justice will inherit the crown, as they say." Most dry, that sentence.

"Something of the like."

"And what about you, Miss Lovejoy . . . though, I remember your family calling you Fossi . . ."

"Yes, though only Will calls me Fossi anymore." She hesitated but then continued. "My mother used to, as well . . . when she was alive."

"Ah." A world of understanding in that sound. "How old were you when your mother passed away?"

"Sixteen."

"A difficult age to lose one's mot"Is there ever an easy age?"

A pause. He tapped his leg again.

"I suppose not."

"Prudence had only just married at the time. Faith and Reece were scarcely out of leading strings . . ."

"So you raised your siblings instead of marrying yourself." He finished the thought for her.

"Yes." Curious how one word could summarize so much.

Though he was kind to assume she would have married if she hadn't had her siblings and father to look after.

Her sisters did have the right of things there—Fossi was far too odd to ever marry.

Marriage had never been part of her future.

Lord Whitmoor sat back, lost in thought for a moment. The carriage rocked and creaked, the wheels grinding on the road. Bay rum reached her again, that unique smell of sandalwood, spices and rum.

She resisted the urge to breathe it in with eager gulps.

Fossi supposed their conversation over. Though, really, it had felt more like a friendly interrogation.

But, as in all things, Lord Whitmoor was two moves ahead of her.

"I lost my mother, too." His voice hushed in the closed carriage. "I lost her before I was really old enough to understand what that meant."

Oh.

His words swept over her like stumbling upon an unexpected vista— the view all the more breathtaking for having been unanticipated.

Had his statement been calculated? Or had he let her inside the fortress, giving her a glimpse of the true Daniel Ashton?

It truly felt as if he had reached out to her in a sense of . . . kinship.

I understand what it is to lose a parent young. I see you.

Fossi blinked. Hard. Her throat developing an ache.

"My older sister, Kit, raised me," he continued. "Our father was . . . distant."

The vision tumbled through her brain.

Lord Whitmoor as a child . . . just Daniel then. Possessed of those same blue eyes, only open and innocent, letting the world see straight through to the soft bits inside that were so easily damaged and hurt. Eager for love and acceptance that was probably in short supply.

"Your sister—Kit was it?—is your only sibling?" She asked this gently, tentatively.

A brief pause. "Yes. There are only the two of us now. My father died shortly after my twentieth birthday."

"Kit must love you very much."

More hesitation and then, "She does." He turned fully back to Fossi, his blue eyes pools of summer sky. "In large part, she is why you are here. I cannot explain it fully—the confidence is not entirely mine to give—but I can say that the work you will do for me . . . it benefits Kit among others."

Oh. She believed him.

Not only was he loved, but he loved in return.

Her heart swelled.

He needed to be loved. Everyone did. But particularly Lord Whitmoor in his granite castle with iron-banded walls.

She was glad he did not inhabit that isolated space alone.

Again, she had to wonder . . . was he messy color inside his fortress? A vibrant red like his current choice of waistcoat? Or was his internal life as structured and rigid as his external seemed to be?

All thoughts that led to her next question.

"Are you married then, my lord?"

It seemed innocuous enough at first. A simple continuation of their conversation.

But he stiffened, head shooting upright. All that life behind his eyes crashed closed—a portcullis slamming shut.

The atmosphere in the carriage instantly morphed from warm to chilly.

Fossi had clearly misstepped.

He turned his rigid spine away, gaze staring out the window.

Oh dear.

She wanted to summon back the question. "I-I am terribly sorry, my lord, I did not mean to pry—"

He held up a gloved hand. *Silence.*

Fossi snapped her jaw shut with a *click.*

The arm went down.

"Yes," he finally said, body still turned away from her. "Yes . . . I was married, Miss Lovejoy."

Was married. Past tense.

A long pause and then so quiet she barely heard him.

"Once upon a time."

His words landed at her feet—a fractured fairy tale. A paradise lost.

He wore no black armband which meant that despite his terse, withdrawn reply, his wife's death could not be recent. Unspoken was the sense that her loss had cut deep.

A reason to encase his heart in granite and retreat into iron-clad numbness where nothing could hurt him.

Ah. Now she understood.

He was a professional plasterer.

Life took a chink out of him and so he plastered it over. With each chink, his plaster became harder, more obdurate. And because making repairs was hard and painful, it was simply easier in the end to become so hard that nothing could ever get through.

Fossi should know.

That tightness in her throat threatened to choke her. The iron and granite would be easier to deal with if it *did* extend to his core.

But she suspected now that it did not. She hated that she had been the cause of his retreat.

She didn't speak again.

Neither did he.

They stared out their respective windows while Mr. Samuelson snored away across from them, oblivious to everything.

Leaving Fossi to her wandering thoughts.

She decided Lord Whitmoor called to mind Mr. John Shakes, the blacksmith in Kilminster.

Mr. Shakes had fought against Napoleon in the Pennisular War and returned a hero. He never spoke much about his experiences in Spain and Portugal, but Fossi had read accounts of the horrifying campaign in the broadsheets and knew enough about the world to understand what was *not* said. When you spoke with Mr. Shakes, his eyes held discerning depths of calm and steadfastness.

Fossi thought she understood. It was how she felt after attending the sick bed of the four Carson girls, helplessly watching as, one-by-one, their little bodies stilled and passed on. Or when she had assisted Dr. Andrews as he cut a living babe from its dead mother's stomach.

Once you had lived unrelenting horror and loss, you would never again confuse those profound emotions with their lesser siblings—irritation, frustration, disappointment. True suffering had a tendency to blow away the chaff of life, leaving only hardened grain.

That was what she saw in Lord Whitmoor's eyes—the gaze of a man who had seen too much, lived too much and was, consequently, tired and worn beyond his years.

A professional plasterer, indeed.

Several hours later, the carriage pulled into the coaching yard of a busy inn. Mr. Samuelson lurched awake.

"Eh, made it to Bath, did we?" he asked, rubbing sleep out of his eyes and leaning forward to peer out Fossi's window.

"Indeed, Garvis." Lord Whitmoor pushed the door ajar, allowing Mr. Samuelson to exit.

Fossi moved to follow, but Lord Whitmoor stopped her with a mild touch on the elbow. She turned to him, staring into his emotionless eyes.

"For you, Miss Lovejoy." He bounced something in his palm, causing her to look down.

He set a coin purse in her hand, heavy with money.

Fossi blinked.

"An advance on your payment," he explained, expression still shuttered.

"My lord, you needn't—"

"No." He silenced her with a subtle squeeze to her arm. "Everyone deserves choices, Miss Lovejoy."

Fossi tried again. "But I cannot—"

"Keep the purse." He folded her gloved fingers around it. The motion oddly gentle, belying the hardness of his gaze. "I want to ensure you never feel trapped in your employment with me. The money will guarantee you always have options. Or, at the very least, a way home."

He touched the brim of his hat and stepped out of the carriage.

Leaving Fossi with the knowledge that she wasn't the only one who saw beyond masks and walls . . . to the person within.

Chapter 10

KINNINGSLEY, SEAT OF VISCOUNT LINWOOD
OUTSIDE THE TOWN OF MARFIELD, HEREFORDSHIRE
AUGUST 9, 1828

They arrived at Kinningsley the next evening, just as the sun dipped to the horizon and flooded the world in hazy, golden light.

Daniel let out a long sigh of relief.

The carriage rattled up Lord Linwood's long lane until, at last, the house came into view, rimmed by the blazing sunset.

Arriving in the town Marfield—and, by extension, the estates of Kinningsley and Haldon Manor—always felt like coming to a second home. And as an added bonus, the Linwood's estate was only a few short miles from Duir Cottage and the haywire time portal in its cellar. Proximity would easily allow him to test any answers Fossi may find through her sums.

"Have we arrived?" Garvis asked from across the carriage.

"Aye."

For her part, Fossi smiled tightly, looking out the window toward the house. Given the tense set of her shoulders, he supposed she felt out of her milieu. But if she were in danger of swooning from fear, she didn't show it.

She had been a courteous traveling companion, speaking little and asking for nothing. Daniel suspected Miss Foster Lovejoy was used to going without and would never dream of troubling others with her modest needs.

The thought, for some reason, nettled him.

Had *no one* ever stood up for her? Why did she value her own company so cheaply?

And was that why he had given her the small bag of money? It had been an impulsive decision on his part. She had appeared so . . . lost. And that emotion tugged at Daniel as nothing had in more time than he could easily remember. Fossi deserved a champion.

Granted, now she had a way to leave him. But freedom of choice was often a powerful psychological motivator, engendering loyalty.

He settled on that as the reason behind his seemingly uncharacteristic actions.

The carriage pulled to a stop in front of the house. Imposing and classical, Kinningsley boasted columns under a pedimented frieze. Two semi-circular staircases swept from left and right up to the front door on the *piano nobile*.

Daniel stepped out and helped Fossi to alight. By the time he turned around, the front door had opened and two dark heads flashed down the steps, taking them three at a time.

"Uncle Daniel, Uncle Daniel!" The two boys practically flung themselves onto his legs. Daniel staggered back but managed to retain his balance. He wasn't precisely their uncle—more like a distant relation via his sister's marriage—but the boys called him that nonetheless.

A smiling Jasmine walked down the stairs behind the boys at a more sedate pace, her eldest daughter, Aurelie, at her heels.

The entire familial scene shot a bolt of anguish through his heart.

Steady, man. There is hope yet.

"Scamps." He knelt down and gathered a boy into each arm for a tight hug which they returned with enthusiasm. "Here is where you show your mother you have some manners." Standing, Daniel turned to Fossi. "Master Charles and Master James, may I present Miss Foster Lovejoy?" Daniel gestured toward her. Fossi curtsied. "Miss Lovejoy, Charles and James Linwood, Lord and Lady Linwood's sons."

The boys bowed politely. But at ages nine and seven respectively, that was all the decorum they could handle.

"Did you bring us sweets?" That was James.

"And a present?" That was Charles.

This was their standard routine. Daniel made a show of looking around and then studying his coach. He scratched his chin. "You might have to talk with Garvis, lads. I'm not sure anything was packed, you see."

"Uncle!" They both howled and then attacked poor Garvis, who now had the task of finding the treats that Daniel had personally wrapped for the boys.

"Jasmine." He pressed a kiss to her cheek as she and Aurelie stopped at the bottom of the stairs. "I near mistook you for your daughter—"

"Uncle Daniel!" Aurelie exclaimed.

"—but then I noted Aurelie has been growing again and has clearly surpassed you in nearly every way."

Aurelie giggled and blushed. At just barely thirteen, she was well on her way to womanhood. She had her mother's dark hair and bright, blue eyes, but as she already stood a solid four inches taller than Jasmine, she had thankfully received her father's height.

"Heavens, Daniel." Jasmine batted his shoulders, the soft twang of her American accent still evident in her speech. "You never change, do you?"

That was only a partial truth.

He *had* changed, as a matter of fact. Quite a lot. He was a long way from the eager, optimistic young man who had slipped through the time portal fifteen years earlier.

But then Jasmine had changed too. Tiny and petite, she had a nearly fey quality about her with dark hair and huge, blue eyes. But laugh lines had set in earnest about her mouth, and the strain of the broken portal had caused traces of gray to thread through her hair. She hadn't had another severe collapse, but she tired easily and her bubbly good cheer often felt forced.

Daniel had met her when she became Lord Linwood's bride nearly fourteen years earlier. He had been employed as Linwood's man of affairs at the time. The position had been a springboard for his dealings in business, as well as the Home Office, which meant he owed the Linwoods a tremendous debt of gratitude.

The Linwoods with their three children had become like family to him—brother, sister and a niece and nephews—with Jasmine as the beating heart of them all.

But now . . . Jasmine tugged at his heartstrings. Her eyes still danced, but there was a fatigue about her. She looked . . . worn.

Fossi couldn't find a solution fast enough. For him. For Jasmine.

Speaking of which . . .

He turned to Fossi standing quietly behind him.

Poor thing. Her eyes kept darting up the enormous facade of Kinningsley, surreptitiously taking in the splendor of the house and estate, twisting her gloved fingers together in a sign of anxiety. Her shapeless bonnet hung low on her forehead, shadowing part of her face.

He nodded encouragingly at her. "Lady Linwood, Aurelie, may I present Miss Foster Lovejoy?"

Fossi, Jasmine and Aurelie made their curtsies to each other and exchanged pleasantries. Say what you would about Foster Lovejoy's economic situation, the lady had exquisite manners.

"Miss Lovejoy has agreed to help us with our . . . problem," Daniel continued.

"Oh!" Jasmine sucked in a breath. And then her face split into a sparkling, delighted smile. She laughed like the Jasmine of old. "How lovely, Daniel. A woman!"

"Indeed."

Daniel had neglected to inform his friends of Fossi's gender. It mattered little, in the end, and Jasmine's breathless surprise was worth the small omission. What fun was it having an adopted older sister if you couldn't tease her from time to time?

"She's wonderful! Look at her, Daniel." Jasmine clasped her hands under her chin and bounced on her tiptoes, surveying Fossi from head to toe. It was an utterly *Jasmine* thing to do. "Such an unassuming woman on the outside, and yet she is one of the most brilliant mathematical minds alive today. Do you think we will be great friends, she and I? Oh, I certainly hope so. Though we will *definitely* need to have the dressmaker from Marfield summoned. Life is far too short to spend it so shabbily dressed—"

Jasmine stopped mid-sentence, shooting Daniel a concerned look.

"Yes," he nodded. "You said that out loud."

She pinched her lips together. Being unable to separate internal and external dialogue was another distinctly *Jasmine* characteristic.

Jasmine gave a strained smile.

"You must excuse my eccentricities, Miss Lovejoy. I meant no offense. We are so happy to have you." She extended a hand to Fossi. "Come, let us get you situated."

THE SOUTH DRAWING ROOM
KINNINGSLEY, HEREFORDSHIRE
LATER ON AUGUST 9, 1828

"THE PORTAL IS much the same, I take it?" Daniel asked, setting down his teacup.

He, Jasmine and Timothy, Lord Linwood, were seated in the south drawing room after supper. Daniel in a wingback chair; Jasmine and Timothy on an opposite couch. A fire crackled between them, warming the cool summer night air.

Fossi had declined to join them for dinner, claiming fatigue and wishing to have a tray sent to her room. Daniel easily read between the lines, understanding that Fossi found Kinningsley and the Linwoods to be overwhelming. Hopefully she would feel more comfortable here after she settled in.

"No change." Jasmine leaned into her husband, resting a head on his shoulder. For his part, Lord Linwood glanced down fondly at his tired wife, wrapping an arm around her.

Tall and trim, Lord Linwood's photo would not be out of place next to a dictionary definition of *British aristocrat*. Dark-haired and gray-eyed, he embodied the English idea of a stiff-upper lip and impassive demeanor. Until he smiled at his wife.

Daniel still marveled at how thoroughly the tiny Jasmine Fleury had altered haughty Timothy Linwood. Timothy laughed now and often, playing with his children and interacting with his tenants. He was still taciturn and reserved in new settings, but contentment and good humor clung to him.

"How are you faring?" Daniel asked Jasmine.

"No change," she repeated.

"She is tired and, yet, will not rest." Timothy shook his head, the topic obviously a sore spot between them.

"You still have warm, fuzzy feelings about Foster Lovejoy?" Daniel crossed a foot over the opposite knee, ignoring the pain festering in his heart.

There will be a solution . . .

He loved Jasmine and Timothy with every last breath. But seeing them together with their children—their happy family life, their easy affection—made his throat ache and his lungs hurt.

That ever-lurking guilt blasted through, escaping with crushing force. The horrid anguish he had inadvertently caused . . .

Some things were impossible to accept. The best you could do was learn to coexist with the pain.

Daniel flinched from the idea, grief heavy in his chest.

There is hope yet.

He had found Fossi and started on the path to redemption.

He *would* fix this. His mistake *would* be corrected.

"I do have warm, fuzzy feelings about Foster Lovejoy," Jasmine chuckled softly. "Though shame on you, Daniel, for keeping her gender a secret—"

Daniel forced a laugh. "You should have seen your wife's face, Timothy. I've rarely seen Jasmine do a double-take on anything."

Timothy smiled, dimples flashing, and cuddled his wife closer, dropping a kiss on top of her head.

"Well, your intuition to pursue the author of Fourier's Nemesis was spot on, I think," Daniel continued.

"Jasmine's intuition is never wrong," Timothy agreed.

That was true. Jasmine, mother of three and Viscountess Linwood, was also the Keeper of the portal—a woman of ancient bloodline gifted with a sixth sense of premonition and bound to the time portal itself.

After Jasmine's collapse and partial recovery, Daniel and Timothy had frantically chased idea after idea for fixing the portal. Jasmine had been the one to sit them both down and work through a more logical approach.

Ironic in the extreme but nonetheless true.

As the Keeper, she could feel and sense things about the portal that were beyond physical understanding. Consequently as they had bounced around possible answers, it had been Jasmine who insisted that a mathematical solution to the portal *felt* correct. After a lot of back and forth and examples, she had intuitively honed in on Fourier's Nemesis as being the correct path to a solution.

"If the problem is to be solved, Fossi will solve it. I feel she is critically important, and I'm never wrong. Timothy will tell you." Jasmine elbowed her husband in the ribs.

"My wife is never wrong," Timothy deadpanned.

Jasmine stuck her tongue out at him. Timothy smiled and kissed her head again.

"Well, we're still going to need some luck," Daniel said. "Fossi has a long road ahead of her. I'm hoping a merger of Fourier's Nemesis with later theorems regarding wormholes will do the trick."

"Are you not concerned about disrupting the space-time continuum?" Timothy's eyes narrowed. "Wormhole theory will not be formulated for . . . quite some time yet, correct?"

Daniel nodded. "True. I have given the matter considerable thought. As far as I understand, the author of Fourier's Nemesis is lost to history, which means Fossi was never well-known."

"That is unfortunate," Jasmine said. "Women never get enough credit."

"Agreed, but it works to our advantage. I will require Fossi to sign what basically amounts to a non-disclosure agreement—she will be forbidden to discuss her work for me with others. Timothy, I have your man of affairs drawing up the contracts even as we speak."

"You think a simple non-disclosure will be sufficient?" Jasmine asked. "We will be giving her nearly a hundred year's worth of mathematical knowledge almost overnight."

"True, but Fossi is an honest person, and I trust she will not publish the theorems we discuss. In the end, math is math. The numbers and variables change, but the processes remain generally the same. Besides, I have no intention of letting her know *what* she is calculating. A computer doesn't need to know why it crunches numbers. It just needs to give us an answer."

"How do you intend to use the numbers Fossi calculates again?" Jasmine asked.

"Numbers form models, my dear, as we've talked about before," Timothy said gently.

"Precisely. And models should tell us where something went wrong," Daniel added. "Perhaps there are orienting stones buried in the ground that the earthquake shifted. Perhaps the portal is now misaligned to ancient star patterns. A model would show us that. It's hard to say what we will find until we dive in and see where the math leads us."

Jasmine scrunched her nose. "It makes a sort of sense, I suppose."

"'Tis an excellent place to start, I believe." Timothy shifted her closer.

Jasmine focused on Daniel with too-seeing eyes.

"What will you do if the outcome is not what you anticipate, Daniel?" she asked. "Fixing the portal is only the first step. As I have said from the beginning—what you seek may not be possible."

He bounced his knee and ran a hand through his hair, his agitation breaking free. "I see no other options, Jasmine. I made an unforgivable mistake that caused this entire predicament. Only I can make it right. End of story."

She heaved a weary sigh. "Yes, but Daniel sometimes we just have to accept—"

"Enough, my love. You and Daniel have covered this ground most thoroughly already. I would not have you quarrel tonight. If nothing else, fixing the portal is critical for returning you to health. Let it be for now." Timothy stood. "Allow me to assist you to your bed. You are far too fatigued for my liking."

Daniel stood and watched Timothy tenderly pull Jasmine to her feet. When she swayed, he effortlessly lifted her into his arms, nodding good-night to Daniel as he carried his wife from the room.

Jasmine's words lingered.

What you seek may not be possible.

That same pain shoved through Daniel's defenses yet again.

The walls suddenly felt too close, his breathing too labored.

Just breathe. In. Out.

You will live through this agony.

Which, in a way, was the greatest irony of all.

Turns out one could *not* actually die of a broken heart.

No matter how hard one tried.

THE BLUE BEDROOM
KINNINGSLEY, HEREFORDSHIRE
EARLY ON AUGUST 10, 1828

FOSSI OFFICIALLY GAVE up on sleep a little after midnight.

The fire had burned low in the grate, casting her bedchamber in dim shadows. Though Fossi didn't need the light to remember how the room had appeared in daylight—washed with sun pouring through not one, but *two* windows. Nestled into a corner of the guest wing, her bedroom had a beautiful dual aspect over the rolling Herefordshire countryside to the north and the rising Welsh hills to the west.

When the sun was up, that was.

In the dim firelight, Fossi could still make out the outline of two wingback chairs flanking the fireplace to the right of the grand four-poster bed. The entire space was elegantly appointed in soothing colors of cream and gold and teal blue.

It was the most beautiful room Fossi had ever seen. And it was to be hers for the duration of her stay.

Her brain reeled with everything that had transpired.

Kinningsley was . . . magnificent. Modern and formed after classical lines. Why, there was even a dressing room and water-closet with running water for her own *personal* use.

The maid who brought her dinner tray up—Sally, by name—had confided that Lord and Lady Linwood had their own bathing chamber with *heated* running water.

Such extravagance boggled the mind.

Even without Lady Linwood's words, Fossi would know that her shabby self didn't belong here. Part of her refused to be intimidated by Lord and Lady Linwood and their obvious wealth. *This* was the sort of excess that her father constantly railed against.

But—and here Fossi collapsed back against the soft goose-feather tick and even softer down pillows—why did luxury have to *feel* so . . . luxurious? It was all too easy to denounce lavish comforts when one didn't have them. But when faced with the reality of fluffy-plush bedding and delightfully clean sheets . . . casting them off seemed the height of insanity.

Vanity and pride and gluttony.

Heavens but she was adding to her sins hourly.

Granted, leaving the sheltering arms of her family and wandering into the wicked world probably topped them all.

I want to ensure you never feel trapped in your employment with me.

Lord Whitmoor's words in the carriage would not leave her be. The feel of his large hand pressing the money bag into her palm.

The money will guarantee you always have options. Or, at the very least, a way home.

He had seen. He had known.

He desperately needed her help and yet had provided her with a way to leave him.

Everyone deserves choices, Miss Lovejoy.

She wasn't sure if she should feel touched at his kind consideration or horrified by his masterful manipulation.

By giving her choices and a sense of freedom, he had engendered her loyalty. He had to know that a woman with so few ties would feel intense allegiance to those who showed genuine care and concern.

Which she now did.

Drat him.

Well-played, Lord Whitmoor. Well-played, indeed.

Fossi sat up with a sigh.

She *did* have choices, thanks to him.

How could she be so suspicious of Lord Whitmoor's motivations and secret-keeping, and yet feel deep within that he was to be trusted? It was a conundrum without logical explanation.

For example . . . why had he invited her to dine with the family? Why not send her to sup with the servants?

Granted, he was paying her an heiress' dowry to work sums, so perhaps he viewed her comfort as a type of security against his investment in her?

Gah! She was driving herself mad with this round and round.

So despite a host of conflicting feelings—concern, unease, excitement, agitation, expectation—she chose to stay the course. She knew what she had left behind and her current situation was decidedly preferable. More to the point, her present course offered her a path into the future.

But what about Lord Whitmoor? From the little she had seen, he clearly doted on the Linwoods and their children, behavior that had caught Fossi off-guard. She would not have considered Lord Whitmoor to be the doting type.

And yet . . . he appeared different here at Kinningsley. Less Lord Whitmoor-ish. More open and genial.

A man she had yet to properly meet.

Well, assuming he ever decided to make a proper introduction, which . . . who knew?

And with all these thoughts rattling around her brain, how was she to sleep?

Fossi threw off the counterpane and found a simple dressing gown laid out for her. She, of course, had never owned anything as dignified or warm as a dressing gown. It was a comfort to draw it on over her worn shift.

Gathering the gown around her, Fossi stirred the fire to life and lit a candle from the embers.

She was eighty-five point nine percent confident she remembered the way back downstairs. Decent odds. And despite the late hour, she wanted to explore the magnificent library she had seen from the enormous entry hall—a soaring, sunlit room with white-washed bookshelves along the walls and tables and chairs stationed throughout the room.

A few minutes later, Fossi was quite sure she had arrived in heaven. Even exploring by candlelight, the library was more than she could have imagined. Books stretched from floor to ceiling and ran full three sides around. Several map tables stood near the doorway, and not one, but two seating areas with comfy chairs.

A large console in the middle of the room held a hodgepodge of mechanical and mathematical objects from automatons to an astrolabe to a selection of tuning forks. Someone in the Linwood household obviously had a love of mathematics and engineering, too.

Everything had the appearance of being well-used and well-loved. Exactly as a library should be.

Yes. She would return here whenever she could.

Fossi lifted her candle high. She had read only a few novels—books lent to her by kind friends and carefully hid from Reverend Lovejoy's censorious eye. How lovely to have an entire library at her disposal.

She spent the better part of thirty minutes scanning book titles in the flickering light. She finally settled on a novel by Mary Shelley,

Frankenstein, or the Modern Prometheus. It sounded scientific and bone-chilling all at once, which she counted as an excellent boon.

Fossi tucked the book against her chest and crept out of the library. She was halfway across the vaulted entry hall when a noise reached her ears. Muffled but distinct.

Having spent so much of her life comforting others, she instantly recognized the sound of sorrow.

Someone wept. Messy. Ugly. Sobbing as if their heart would crumble.

The sound came from a smaller door to the right of the main staircase.

She should just continue on up the stairs. Obviously, whoever was upset did not wish to be disturbed.

But . . .

When you were a connoisseur of pain, it was difficult to ignore it in others.

Fossi set her candle down on a side table and quietly walked forward on tiptoe feet. Carefully, she peeked through the cracked door.

Light from the fire in the hearth cast the room in long, flickering shadows. A large figure sat hunched over a desk in profile to her, fingers threaded through his dark hair, head bowed and cradled in his palms.

Lord Whitmoor.

A simple wooden box rested before him on the desk, the lid opened and bracketed by his elbows, as if to keep the box sheltered and safe. Lord Whitmoor's chest heaved, air leaving him in harsh bursts—the sound of a strong man's heart breaking.

It was not elegantly done.

Clearly, Lord Whitmoor had not much practice.

Those who felt the deepest cracked into the most jagged splinters.

He appeared so shattered. So isolated. A vast sea of emptiness surrounding him.

A Lord Whitmoor without lies or mask.

The man hidden in the iron tower that no one could reach.

So . . . this was the real man, then? This broken person grieving over a wooden box, alone in the dead of night with none to witnesses the moment?

Was it his wife he mourned—the love lost to him?

Fossi felt her own heart constrict in empathy.

She could easily imagine what his wife had been like—beautiful, elegant, charming . . . vibrant color inside and out. A light to illuminate his dark.

Such a loss would be . . . catastrophic.

Maybe all that granite and iron didn't keep the pain out but instead corralled it inside, safe from others' careless prying.

Lord Whitmoor would *not* appreciate her seeing him like this.

Fossi backed away from the door. One step. Two steps. Until she could turn and quietly retrieve her candle, retreating to her room, book clutched to her chest.

"Foster Lovejoy, what have you involved yourself in?" she whispered to her dying fire. "How many secrets does that one man hold?"

When navigating the bewildering landscape that was Fortress Whitmoor, she did indeed need to let prudence guard her way.

Chapter 11

LORD WHITMOOR'S PERSONAL STUDY
KINNINGSLEY, HEREFORDSHIRE
AUGUST 10, 1828

Please be seated, Miss Lovejoy." Lord Whitmoor stood and motioned for Fossi to sit at the desk. "I had Lord Linwood's man of affairs draw up the papers yesterday evening and now have the full contract here for you to review."

Fossi managed a small smile and took a seat behind the enormous oak desk.

Immediately following breakfast, she had been summoned down to the small room off the central staircase. The same room where she had watched him weep the night before.

Odd how daylight thoroughly changed the shape of things.

August sun flooded the room, brightening even the darkest corners, chasing all trace of shadows away.

Lord Whitmoor was Lord Whitmoor again. Urbane in his meticulously tailored coat and trousers—both dove gray today—hair perfectly styled, that distinguished peppered-gray peeking out at his temples.

All traces of the man wracked with sorrow were neatly tucked away. So complete was his disguise she almost wondered if the events of the night before had been a fevered dream.

But, no. The same box sat to one side of the desk. She could not have dreamed that particular detail. It stood as silent testimony to reality.

The box lid was closed today like Lord Whitmoor himself, sequestering away all the emotional messiness of life. Her eyes lingered on it. Did the box hold love letters between him and his wife? Trinkets of their adoration?

And why was she so curious to find out?

Fossi gave herself a mental shake.

It is none of your concern, Foster Lovejoy. Mind your manners.

Lord Whitmoor moved around the desk to stand behind her, one hand on the back of her chair. He reached around her shoulder to pull a stack of papers across the desk.

"Here is where you sign, Miss Lovejoy."

He tapped the bottom of the document and nudged an inkwell and pen toward her.

She couldn't help but admire his hands as he did so. Long fingered, broad palms, elegant yet strong. The heat of his chest radiating against her shoulders. The smell of bay rum and peppermint eddying around her.

Heavens.

Unfortunately, witnessing his distress the night before had created a sense of intimacy. She had seen deep inside him, to the man hidden within, and was now helpless to stop the lure of him.

"I should like to read the document before signing." She was surprised her voice didn't tremble.

"Of course. I would strongly recommend it."

She nodded and proceeded to read. Or, at the very least, put on a credible show of doing so.

The words were stubbornly determined to remain on the page, unable to pound through the thoughts whirlwinding around her brain.

Her gaze kept darting to that box and its closeted secrets, the joy and anguish so irrevocably linked.

From the corner of her eye, she noted Lord Whitmoor pulling over a second chair and seating himself. He leaned back and steepled his fingers, pressing them against his lips.

Was he now staring at her? Just the thought made her heart pound faster.

Fossi bit her lip, ordering her wayward thoughts to focus.

I, Daniel Ashton, Lord Whitmoor, do promise to pay the sum of ten thousand pounds sterling to Miss Foster Love Among Us Lovejoy for the duration . . .

Her mind wandered through the technicalities, while the rest of her remained keenly attuned to his every subtle movement. It was an acute sort of pain, another sense.

Her body hummed, a tightly strung violin string.

She was *not* so naive as to misunderstand what was happening.

She was attracted to Lord Whitmoor.

It wasn't specifically his physical appearance (though she admired that too) or his wealth.

It was his pain.

The sense of another creature recognizing its own kind.

Action. Reaction. Physics in practical application.

Her eyes darted to the mysterious box once again.

Fossi frowned, moving on to the next page.

Attraction was . . . not good. It would only serve to torment her. The man clearly did not, and *would* not, ever return such affection. The very idea was laughable. Her energy would be better spent on longing for the moon than Lord Whitmoor's regard—

He cleared his throat, causing Fossi to jump.

"You will notice the clause for a chaperone is deliberately vague," he murmured. "I was unsure if you still wished me to engage the services of a companion to act as a chaperone. Do you find being under Lady Linwood's watchful eye sufficient for your comfort?"

It was a fair question. Per society's view, staying at Kinningsley with Lady Linwood in residence was sufficient chaperonage.

Fossi pondered it for a moment, imagining an unknown woman sitting in the corner all day, watching her as Lord Whitmoor currently did—

She swallowed. That would be . . . uncomfortable.

"I find the situation sufficient for now," she said.

"Excellent." A pleased smile in his voice.

Fossi risked a glance up, noting for the first time the enormous mirror across from them. The whole room reflected in its surface.

She nearly flinched.

She sat behind the desk, a gray mouse of a person. Worn clothes horridly out of fashion, hair primly pulled back into a simple bun, face plain, skin dull and showing wrinkles at the edges.

A nothing, no one.

Lord Whitmoor rested to her side, one leg elegantly crossed over the other. Clothing expensive and neatly pressed, hair carefully styled. Charismatic, suave, every inch a man of impeccable taste and power.

Clearly a *Someone*.

The tableau was a bucket of ice water over her head.

You are fifty ways a fool, Foster Lovejoy.

This needed to cease. She was to be his employee for the foreseeable future. Unwanted admiration and empathy would only make her life more problematic.

Deep breath.

Twenty thousand pounds. You can do this.

She forced herself to stare in the mirror a moment longer, memorizing the excruciating differences between them.

His urbane polish. Her shabby gentility.

The harsh contrast would be a strong physic for her, an image to pull out time and again to remind her of reality.

Lord Whitmoor shifted beside her, the morning light catching his hair. He raised his head and, finally, noted their joint reflection. His eyes met hers in the mirror, startling cerulean blue. The barest of smiles touched his lips. If he noted the disparity between them, he did not show it.

Was this more acting on his part? A way of ensuring she felt at ease?

Regardless, it was too much . . . his apparent acceptance of her.

Strangers did not just 'accept' Fossi and all her oddness. She was more like a brisk wind—bracing and startling at first, but then more tolerable the longer you experienced it.

Fossi purposefully lowered her head and raised the paper she was holding, blocking the sight of them both.

Lord Whitmoor reached over and tapped the document in her hand, continuing on as if he had seen nothing amiss. "Also note the clause requiring complete confidentiality. Unfortunate as it may seem, I cannot stress enough the importance of keeping everything we do entirely secret. That means never speaking of or demonstrating the mathematics we will utilize."

Ah.

And there it was.

Secrets. That welcome dose of reality.

Apparently, she was to be a secret, too. No one was to know what she did here. Assuming *she* ever managed to figure it out herself. How could she trust a man who couldn't even tell her *why* he had hired her?

And did she find it acceptable to remain silent about the mathematics she did in his employ?

"What if I am asked to do something against my conscience, my lord?" She *had* to ask at least that much.

The question gave him pause. She lifted her eyes to his.

"Nothing I ask you to do should create a crisis of morality, Miss Lovejoy," he said after brief hesitation. "If for some unknown reason it does, please bring it to my attention. I would not have you distressed."

His gaze was sincere. *He* truly believed that.

Did *she* believe him, however?

Her heart insisted he was trustworthy. It dripped from his tone, from the steadfastness in his eyes. Instinct told her he was genuine.

Her mind, however, could see it as a charade. As one more move in this giant chess game they played.

But . . . and here her mind provided its own counter argument, Lord Whitmoor *needed* her cooperation. If she objected to something and refused to work, he could not force her. Not without resorting to fiendish coercion, which she supposed he could do . . .

She hesitated too long.

"Would you like me to have that added as a clause to the contract?" he asked. "That you shall have recourse to redress the contract should something violate your sense of right and wrong?"

Again, he surprised her. Why go to such lengths if he was *not* sincere?

Fossi sighed inwardly. Questioning his every motive was proving exhausting.

"Yes, my lord," she replied. "It would set my mind at ease."

"Then consider it done." He gave a polite smile and nod. "I shall have the clause added and the contract redrawn up."

This was why controlling her attraction to him would be a chore. The innate kindness, the sense of kinship, tugged at her.

Lord Whitmoor went to the door to summon Lord Linwood's man of affairs.

But still her doubts whispered.

You don't know him, she reminded herself, stealing another sideways glance at the box on the desk. *He deals in secrets upon secrets. It could just be another mask he wears.*

Protect yourself.

She held the contrasting image of them in the mirror, clutching it in her mind like a shield. A protective weapon to prevent her foolish heart from being needlessly hurt.

A bustle of noise from the entrance hall interrupted.

Lord Whitmoor looked back at her.

"We will sign the new contract tomorrow, Miss Lovejoy." He nodded to someone outside the door. "But for now, I do believe the dressmaker has arrived."

BY MID-AFTERNOON, FOSSI was quite sure she thoroughly understood how it felt to be a pin cushion.

Who knew that beauty and fashion also came with a hearty side dish of pain?

Madame Beauford and her tapestry of muslins, silks, ribbons and scurrying assistants had been overwhelming.

Fortunately Mrs. Arthur Knight, Lord Linwood's sister, had arrived on the heels of Madame Beauford. Dark and petite, though not quite as small as Lady Linwood, Mrs. Knight radiated a warmth and gentle kindness quite at odds with the stern aspect of her elder brother.

"How wonderful of Daniel to bring you here, Miss Lovejoy," she said after Lady Linwood made the introduction. "Please, you must call me Marianne."

"Yes, indeed," Lady Linwood chimed in, "and I must be Jasmine."

Both woman turned to Fossi with honest hope on their faces.

It was utterly disarming.

Fossi did not know how to respond to such genuine charm. She had been raised to view aristocrats through the narrow lens of her father's prejudices and Sir Phillip Nobly's arrogance.

So far, the upper echelons of the *Beau Monde* had not aligned with her preconceptions.

"Of-of course," Fossi stammered, "and I would be honored if you would call me Foster."

Lady Linwood . . . erhm, Jasmine . . . and Marianne proceeded to follow Madame Beauford *et al.* up to Jasmine's sitting room, dragging Fossi in their wake.

Marianne and Jasmine sat together on a sofa, like spectators at a horse show, watching Madame Beauford fit Fossi for a new wardrobe.

Fossi didn't know whether to be delighted at their kind company or worried about their effrontery. For a woman unused to physical touch and habituated to perpetual privacy, the experience was decidedly rattling.

But such thoughts were soon cast aside as she realized the scope of the wardrobe being ordered for herself.

To Fossi, a wardrobe consisted of two day dresses, a slightly nicer dress for Sunday services, a simple evening gown for the rare occasion when she might be invited to dine out, a few underthings, a pelisse, a cloak, a pair of walking boots and a pair of slippers.

That was her expectation when Lord Whitmoor had suggested the wardrobe clause in their contract.

Clearly, the word *wardrobe* meant something far more vast to Jasmine and Marianne.

Fossi stood in her sole worn shift as Madame Beauford measured and barked notes at one assistant while another pulled fabric samples for the ladies to chirp over.

Fossi couldn't keep up with their talk of morning gowns, walking gowns, carriage dresses, promenade dresses, evening gowns, spencers and pelisses.

And truthfully, how could there even be a difference between a walking gown and a promenade dress? But given how everyone in the room froze and stared at her when she asked the question . . . apparently, there were differences.

"Will the lady wish for French or Italian lace on the blue walking gown?" Madame Beauford asked.

Not to Fossi herself, of course. That question was directed to Marianne.

"Italian, wouldn't you say?" Marianne turned to Jasmine.

"Definitely. The lace out of Venice this year has been stunning." Jasmine spoke without looking up from a Parisian pattern book, simultaneously pointing out a fashionable dress for Marianne. "Corsets are not what they once were. Waistlines have sunk at least an inch a year over the past decade."

Fossi wasn't sure if she wanted to cry or laugh. Her father would have an apoplexy at the sheer vanity of it. Her sisters would claim to be appalled and then borrow the items incessantly.

She could certainly cross *Own a dress that hasn't been turned* off her list.

"I most certainly don't need any silk gowns," Fossi eventually chimed in. "I have lived thirty-two years quite comfortably without owning anything made of silk."

"One can *live* without silk, that is true," Marianne agreed.

"But why should you, if you don't have to?" Jasmine shrugged. "Silk feels lovely against the skin."

That was news to Fossi.

"Regardless, one woman does not need twenty-one gowns made out of seven different fabrics and trimmed with forty-three types of ribbon and lace," Fossi entreated. "Heaven knows how many buttons will need be supplied."

To Jasmine's credit, she scarcely blinked. Instead, she nodded her head.

"You are absolutely correct." Jasmine snapped her fingers. "Madame Beauford, we must consider the buttons, as well. Have you brought samples? Or should we send for the haberdasher?"

Heavens.

"You misunderstand, Jasmine."

"How so?"

Fossi nearly threw her hands up in exasperation. "I want to wear the dress myself, you see. I do not want the dress to wear me."

That got everyone's full attention.

Six sets of eyes turned Fossi's way.

Right.

Fossi pinched the bridge of her nose. "What I mean is . . . when I walk down the street, I do not want people to see a dress approaching first and then realize, oh goodness, there is a person in there, too."

Jasmine angled her head.

"I think I understand, my dear." She reached out and patted Fossi's hand. "Marianne, perhaps we should scale back to just two flounces per dress?"

Oh. That wasn't what Fossi meant at all—

"Please no flounces or ruffles," she pleaded. "I wish to look distinguished and elegant, not frippery-laden."

A beat.

And then Jasmine smiled. Bright and delighted.

"I actually agree. Elegant it is." She raked her gaze up and down Fossi. "Though you do realize that elegant means even more silk, correct?"

Fossi swallowed and closed her eyes, fighting the urge to slowly beat her head against the stone fireplace mantel.

As the afternoon wore on, Fossi became more inured to the entire process and found she really did have opinions about fashion in the end.

Jasmine and Marianne chattered the entire time and talked fondly of Lord Whitmoor—or rather, Daniel.

It jolted Fossi every time his given name dropped from their lips.

Daniel said he will be coming . . .

Did Daniel mention that too?

As Daniel, he seemed so . . . normal. Approachable. Human.

Not the powerful persona of Lord Whitmoor at all, but simply a man among friends.

The flesh-and-blood resident of his granite fortress.

Fossi found herself thinking of him the same way—Daniel. Knocking the king from his throne, as it were.

As they talked of Daniel, Fossi realized that the families—Ashtons, Knights and Linwoods—were all related via marriage.

"It is quite easy to understand, I think." Jasmine said with a grin when Fossi asked. "I am married to Lord Linwood whose younger sister, Marianne"—here she held a hand out to her friend—"is married to Arthur Knight of nearby Haldon Manor. Arthur's brother, James, married Emme Wilde, who in addition to being a dear friend of mine, has a brother, Marc Wilde, who is married to Daniel's older sister, Kit. So we're basically just one big happy family as all our children are cousins of some sort or another."

"That is true," Marianne said. "Even Georgiana is tangled in our web."

"Georgiana?" Fossi asked.

"The younger sister of Arthur and James. She is married to Sebastian Carew, Lord Stratton, and resides in Warwickshire."

Fossi's head spun. She would have to make a chart of their relationships later on in her notebook.

Her mind fixated on Kit, the sister who had raised Daniel. The person that Fossi's theorems were supposed to somehow help.

"Does Lord Whitmoor's sister live nearby?" Fossi asked, lifting an arm so Madame Beauford could pin another panel of fabric.

Jasmine and Marianne exchanged a glance, as if silently debating how to answer the question.

That was . . . interesting.

"Marc is American," Jasmine finally replied, "so they live in the United States. Daniel hasn't seen Kit in nearly two years."

"Oh." That answer seemed oddly . . . deflating.

How could Fossi's mathematics possibly help a woman who lived thousands of miles away? And why the hesitation when discussing where Kit lived?

It made no sense. Had Lord Whitmoor—Daniel—lied to her to protect some other secret? But if that were the case, why did he bring it up at all?

And just when she thought she was starting to unravel him, everything knotted into a tangled ball again.

What *were* all these secrets Daniel kept?

"That will look lovely on you, Foster." Marianne gestured toward the blue gown Madame Beauford had tentatively pinned around her.

Fossi stared at her reflection, the icy-blue silk falling in gentle folds to the ground, the color catching previously unseen highlights in her hair.

The look would not be . . . unsatisfactory.

Jasmine giggled behind her. "I can just see it now. Foster in shimmery water silk sitting down to dinner. An army captain in dashing regimentals looks her way. She says something coy. He responds with open flirtation. She offers a witty rejoinder. He laughs in delight—"

"Oh, please stop!" Fossi pressed palms to her flushed face, meeting Jasmine's gaze in the mirror. Did the woman not *think* before she spoke? "Please. Dress me like a peacock, if you wish, but I shall never learn how to flirt."

A pause.

Jasmine pursed her lips, a blush touching her own cheeks, and then gave a helpless laugh.

"Well, why ever not?" Jasmine sounded genuinely puzzled. "Every person should know how to flirt. If you feel unequal to the challenge, Foster, we should find you a tutor. In fact, Daniel is a most excellent flirt, perhaps he could—"

"Lord Whitmoor mentioned that he had been married?" Fossi blurted out, desperate to change the subject. "His wife passed on?"

Her words landed with all the skill of a poorly aimed arrow.

Jasmine's expression instantly morphed from casual to strained, and Marianne suddenly found a pattern impossibly interesting.

"Yes," Jasmine said after a too long hesitation. "Daniel was married. Alice passed away about five years ago. A hereditary wasting illness, I believe the doctors said." Jasmine sat back, crossing her arms. "Though it is not as if Alice—"

"Jasmine." Quelling censure in Marianne's tone as she darted a quick glance at Fossi.

Neither lady said anything more on the subject.

Silence.

Madame Beauford moved fabric this way and that. Birds chirped outside the open window.

"Ah," Fossi managed to reply as it seemed the ladies were waiting for her to say something.

The topic was clearly taboo.

By the end of the afternoon, Fossi was exhausted both physically and emotionally. The cobbler had been summoned, and Jasmine's own French maid dispatched to trim and style Fossi's hair.

Madame Beauford left after promising the first of the dresses would be delivered in several days.

As usual when dealing with Daniel Ashton, Fossi was left with more questions than answers.

Alice.

The woman had a name.

Her death had . . . altered Daniel, it seemed. And he kept a box that he wept over.

Fossi had scores of follow-up questions she longed to ask.

Were they hopelessly in love? Was she sunshine to his night? How had he managed to survive her loss?

Why did others not wish to speak of it?

She was coming to see him as a labyrinth of a man. A convoluted maze so full of twists and turns, she wondered if anyone could discover his true center. Granted, that meant he had to *allow* someone within his outer perimeter.

Someday though . . . perhaps someday she would understand.

And, hopefully, the answers were ones she could in good conscience live with until she finished the task he had hired her to do.

In the end, however, it wasn't thoughts of Alice that chased her to sleep that night.

It was Jasmine's earlier observation.

Daniel is a most excellent flirt, perhaps he could—

Perhaps Daniel could . . . what?

Chapter 12

DANIEL'S STUDY
KINNINGSLEY, HEREFORDSHIRE
AUGUST 11, 1828

I will ensure you receive a copy of these." Daniel took the papers from Fossi, one-by-one, as she signed them.

They were together again in his small study next to the stairs. She sat before his desk, while he had claimed a chair at her side. This space had been his office when working as Linwood's man of affairs, and Timothy had kept the room for him even after Daniel left his service nearly a decade ago.

Fossi's contract had been amended and now firmly signed. He stacked the papers together, setting them to the side of the desk.

Fossi seemed . . . subdued this morning. It was more than the sad state of her clothing and quiet primness of her mouth.

Something was eating at her.

And why that simple fact pulled at him . . . he refused to examine.

She flashed him a wan smile and braced her hands on the desktop. "Are we to start on equations today, my lord?"

From their brief acquaintance, Daniel understood that Miss Lovejoy hid herself deep inside a shell. Their relationship was not such that he could call her out for her moods. Not yet, in any case.

Though . . . funny that his mind assumed they would reach a point where he *could* do such a thing.

So instead of questioning her, he replied. "Yes. Let us get started."

Reaching across, he opened a workbook, displaying a page of equations he had prepared.

She gasped.

The numbers were complex; ideas poured from them. Not that Fossi would know exactly what the numbers meant. But as any good mathematician, she could easily tell at a glance that treasures were hidden within.

She leaned forward, staring with earnest intent, doldrums abandoned.

Huh. Forget bonnets and dresses for Foster Lovejoy. Cheer her up with a complex equation or two.

"You are a man of secrets indeed, my lord." She continued to study the page, eyes devouring the sums. "This is fascinating."

He settled back into his chair beside her and spent the next hour outlining what she needed to do.

"Basically, you wish me to run this equation"—she pointed to the largest number set—"over and over, moving through numerical iterations as I go, correct?" she asked.

"Precisely."

"The idea is eventually to land on values and a structure that cause these two equations"—here she pointed at another value set—"to match, or at the very least, coalesce."

"Exactly."

They continued on.

She asked questions. He answered them.

Foster Lovejoy was astonishingly intelligent.

Like . . . freakishly, frighteningly smart.

He had intellectually known that—the mind behind Fourier's Nemesis *had* to be brilliant—but it was something else entirely to be faced with it.

She was a nerdy engineer's dream date. Her nimble mind quickly grasped complex wave oscillation theory and instantly moved into innovation and creativity.

Damn. He had forgotten how attractive intelligence could be.

Which most likely explained why he found himself studying her as they talked, the animation in her face, the spark in her eyes.

It was astonishing the difference a simple hairstyle could make. Fossi still wore one of her old dresses (the new ones would begin to arrive later in the week, apparently) but the softer styling of her hair accentuated the elegant loveliness of her face. Clean and pure in its simplicity.

Her skin glowed in the morning light. A comparison to pearls would be perhaps a bit beyond the mark, though—he contemplated for a moment—perhaps not by much. There was truly a graceful courtliness about her.

It was only as their discussion drew to a close that the epiphany hit:

Daniel genuinely wanted to earn this woman's friendship.

She was insightful and clever in a way few people—men or women— ever were. He intuited that her internal life was rich and varied. That once she gave her loyalty, it would be for life.

And he suddenly wanted that loyalty with a longing that surprised him.

How could he want to know her so soon? Such behavior was . . . atypical.

After several hours discussion, they had laid the groundwork for her employment with him.

"I sent a missive to my solicitor yesterday, detailing our contract." He swept a hand over the documents still resting on the desktop as he stood in preparation to leave. "He will be in contact with you within the week to assist in settling your new funds."

It was vitally important to him, he had decided, that she have access to funds almost immediately. She had spent so much of her life without. He wanted her to find some pleasure in having plenty. And he ignored the little pang of guilt that told him he wasn't being entirely honest with himself.

"Thank you, my lord. That is excellent news." Fossi stood as well, stretching slightly.

"Have you decided what you will do with your newfound wealth?" he asked.

"Pardon?" Her eyes shifted to meet his. Pools of liquid chocolate.

"Your twenty thousand pounds. Have you decided what you will do with it?"

A pause.

She blinked. And then blinked again.

What joy would Foster Lovejoy find in riches?

He could practically see the gears of her mind considering and weighing her reply.

"May I suggest truth?" he continued.

"My lord?" More confused, wide eyes.

"You were sorting through answers, trying to decide if you should state the truth of what you intend with your funds, or if polite deflection were the better option."

"I-I am not quite—" She stopped and smoothed her skirts. She looked to the wall behind him, studying something there.

Looking for courage, he supposed.

He was happy to help her along.

"Polite deflection—though by its very definition *polite*—is rarely as interesting as truth," he said. "Particularly, as I imagine, *your* truth would be, Miss Lovejoy."

It was a sudden bold statement.

Again . . . unlike him.

But nonetheless true. He wanted to know how that brilliant mind of hers worked.

A long silence.

He hadn't a clue what her reply would be.

And for a man who had spent the last decade acquiring an advanced degree in Body Language of the Human Race, the anticipation and mystery were novel sensations.

Frowning, she brought her gaze back to his and angled her head, looking slightly like a curious bird.

"Do you mock me, my lord?"

Daniel nearly winced.

Heavens! *That's* where her thoughts landed?

"Why would I ridicule you?" His words hung in the hush.

She began to shrug and then caught herself, stilling her shoulders before finishing such an ill-bred motion. A habitual action, he realized.

She frowned instead.

A thinker, Miss Lovejoy. Thank goodness.

"There is no logical reason for you to ridicule me, my lord," she said after a moment's contemplation, "but I do not suppose mockery has much in common with logic. Your compliment merely struck me as . . . unexpected."

Ah.

His intense curiosity had caught him off-guard, too.

Daniel suppressed a small smile. "I fear I engaged in some slight flirtation, Miss Lovejoy. A rather ill-advised attempt to be charming, perhaps. Forgive me."

Though curious that his interest in her would manifest itself as flirtation.

Her mouth formed a surprised 'O.'

She did *not*, however, smile or blush. Which seemed . . . uncharacteristic.

"Did Lady Linwood urge you to flirt with me?" she asked.

What?

Now the bewilderment was all his.

Of course, Fossi Lovejoy would instantly turn the tables on him.

"Why ever should Jasmine have asked such a thing of me?"

But . . . now that he considered it, he wouldn't be opposed to flirting with Foster Lovejoy. With her quick mind, it would be delightful. When had he last thought to flirt with a woman?

Her eyes narrowed. "Do spies receive training in that, too?"

He blinked. "Flirtation?"

"No." She made an exasperated noise. "Replying to a question by posing yet another question. 'Tis a non-answer that smacks of evasion and secrecy, my lord."

Oh.

True that.

He would know.

"My apologies." He bowed slightly. "Sincerely though, what did Jasmine say?"

Her eyes narrowed further, landing firmly in Annoyed School Marm territory.

Oh. Right.

Daniel scrubbed a hand across his face. Shook his head. "Please pardon me. Some habits are . . . ingrained."

Silence for a moment.

Her shoulders relaxed.

"Lady Linwood spoke of flirtation, and she thought it might be good for me to perhaps learn," Fossi said. "As you can tell, I do not have sufficient experience with flirtation to recognize when it is directed at myself. I am sure she spoke of it to you."

"She did not."

Fossi's gaze said she did not quite believe him.

He didn't press her to believe him. If she thought his flirtation to be at Jasmine's behest, well, that was probably for the best.

"To be honest, I find the subject confusing. It is not clear or precise at all." Fossi pursed her mouth. "For example, I can quite easily identify flirtation when listening in on a conversation. But when in the midst of it myself . . ."

Her voice trailed off, a blush *finally* flooding her cheeks.

Tenderness swept Daniel.

Fossi repeatedly brought the emotion out in him. Why? Was it because she was unlike any woman he had met in . . . forever?

She looked down, fascinated by her hands twisted before her.

No one should be so doubting of their own allures.

Yes. Jasmine's instincts had been correct in this.

Foster Lovejoy deserved a little flirtation in her life.

"I find it curious that you are so surprised by any charm or flirtation sent your way," he said. "Surely gentlemen have drowned you in compliments on occasion?"

A pause.

She swiveled her head away.

"I . . . I-I have always been far too odd, my lord. Flirtation is a language I never learned."

"Are you interested in becoming conversant?" He had to ask the question.

He was suddenly breathless for her answer.

Another beat.

"I don't know." She lifted her head. "Is it commonplace for an employer to flirt with an underling?"

Daniel mentally flinched.

Wow. Talk about a direct hit.

The answer, according to Daniel's more modern point of view, was an emphatic *No.*

No, it was not proper for an employer to flirt with an employee. All the more reason to let her think Jasmine had requested it of him.

"Perhaps not," he admitted, color now touching his own cheeks, "but it is time-honored social banter between men and women. And if Jasmine suggested it . . ."

He let the thought dangle.

"I shall ponder it, my lord," she finally said. "Perhaps it would make me seem less odd in company?"

Odd? He found her refreshingly delightful. How typical of the world to demean the parts of her that he found most interesting.

"I would call you an Original, Miss Lovejoy," he said.

"A clever twisting of perception, to be sure."

Silence hung.

Fossi shook her head, as if mentally dismissing their topic.

"To return to your original question, my lord, I wish to use my new wealth to start a school for girls. A real school," she hastened to clarify, "not a glorified academy for embroidery and bonnet decoration. A place for those of my sex who are intelligent and wish to better their lives through extensive education."

Her eyes dared him to laugh at her.

"That is an excellent use for your wealth, Miss Lovejoy." He nodded solemnly.

Of course, Foster Lovejoy would use her money for a good cause. It was so innate to her, as natural as breathing.

He found himself admiring her even more for it.

Admiration. Warmth. Tenderness.

What had gotten into him today?

"You do not censure my desires, my lord?" She mistook his silence.

"No."

"You do not find them fanciful and silly? An aberration to my sex?"

He was quite sure her father and brothers—perhaps with the exception of Will—would think so.

But not him. "No."

She looked away, as if the dream were too large to contain, and she didn't know how to process it. Her fingers twisted around each other again.

"I think the idea to start a school as lovely and magnificent as its owner."

The compliment dropped from his mouth, startling even him with the depth of its sincerity.

She started and then whirled her head back to him, obviously trying to parse his words into meaning.

"That was more flirting, Miss Lovejoy," he said, attempting to cover the slip.

Apparently, his reply was correct.

"Oh!"

Fossi . . . smiled.

A brilliant, delighted thing that lit her face and captured all the shades of the forest in her eyes—earthy brown with flecks of mossy green and summer gold.

She was quite . . . transformed.

A ferocious blush followed swiftly at its heels.

"It is this, Miss Lovejoy," he said. "You are apprehensive and worried about the scope of your dreams. But I say—"

He paused for effect.

It did not go unappreciated. Her gaze bounced back to his.

"If your dreams do not terrify you, then they are not yet sufficiently grand." He smiled sincerely. "You should be genuinely frightened by the desires of your heart. Only then will you know you are reaching high enough."

Her eyes flared and she sucked in a gasp of air.

It was a good maxim. He remembered reading it on a motivational poster at university years ago.

"And you?" she asked in return. "What dreams could possibly scare you?"

He stiffened. Had she known that question was like an arrow through the chest? Was he so transparent?

He could never maintain the upper hand for long with her. She always found a way to outshine him.

Suddenly, his own skin felt too tight.

He walked over to the window, staring out across the manicured gardens.

Silence.

"Sometimes—" he finally began. Cleared his throat. "Sometimes there is not enough money in the world to purchase what we want most."

Unbidden his eyes drifted toward the wooden box on his desktop.

"Ah." A universe of understanding in one syllable.

He continued, "A wise friend once told me that if money can solve a problem, then it is not truly a problem."

"Ah." Again. Laced with humor this time. "Though I would hazard that only someone who had never known genuine want would say such a thing."

Daniel snorted. "True."

Silence reigned, this time more comfortable.

THE EVENTS IN his study continued to haunt Daniel hours later .

He decided to do whatever it took to draw Fossi out more—flirt, tease, cajole—and blamed this decision on his innate sense of fairness.

Someone as intelligent and honorable as Foster Lovejoy *deserved* to live life fully.

Yes. That was it.

He pondered this as he watched Fossi throughout dinner. She had protested when he asked her to dine with them that evening.

First she cited her lack of appropriate clothing, which he dismissed. Then she pointedly remarked that a servant did not dine with her employer. But as Garvis and Linwood's man of affairs were dining with them too, that argument didn't take either. In the end, she had agreed to join everyone for dinner.

She had changed into what Daniel recognized as her nicest dress. It was somewhat threadbare and dreadfully out of date, but Daniel didn't care. It was Fossi herself who captured his attention.

She asked questions and offered intelligent comments throughout the meal. Over roast beef and creamed peas, Daniel, Timothy and Fossi found themselves in a deep discussion regarding the strength of frequency waves relative to sound in the new locomotive industry. Wherever the conversation went, Daniel found himself watching Fossi.

After dinner, he stared as she followed the other ladies from the room leaving the men to their port. Which basically meant Daniel regarded her backside as she left the room.

Such behavior was . . . unlike him.

Though he had admired the view.

He managed to shake such thoughts until Arthur, Timothy and himself joined the ladies in the drawing room a short while later.

Jasmine and Marianne were laughing over some quip or another, Fossi looking on with a small smile that didn't quite touch her eyes. Daniel sensed Fossi's unease. She didn't feel at home in these surroundings.

He hoped that changed.

And then he spent a solid five minutes wondering *why* he cared so much that Fossi felt at home with his friends.

What was this woman doing to him?

"How are preparations coming at Whitmoor House, Daniel?" Marianne's voice broke through his reverie.

"Pardon?"

"Preparations for your annual harvest festival. I assume your housekeeper has them already underway?" Marianne leaned forward as she spoke. "We received our own invitation just yesterday."

"Heavens, Marianne. The festival must be a full eight weeks off." Arthur Knight sat back in his chair, stretching his legs and nursing a glass of brandy. "Surely Daniel shouldn't have to discuss the festivities for at least another month."

Marianne laughed good-naturedly and patted her husband's knee. "Not everyone is as opposed to celebrations as yourself, my dear."

"Daniel is, I daresay," Arthur muttered behind his glass of brandy, "particularly after everything that transpired—"

"Yes, tell us how the preparations are going, Daniel." Timothy interrupted Arthur, somehow sending the man a quelling look without even glancing in his direction. It was quite the feat of aristocratic breeding.

Of course, it was too little, too late. Tension had flooded Daniel at Arthur's words. Grief and guilt washed in behind in equal measure.

Jasmine, bless her, watched him with eyes that said *I understand.*

Daniel suppressed a grimace and downed his own glass of brandy in one throat-searing shot. "The festival preparations are going ahead as planned. There will be sack races and leg wrestling and a feast for the tenants, followed by a harvest ball in the evening."

"The harvest festival at Whitmoor House is the event of the season in northern Gloucestershire," Marianne said to Fossi by way of explanation. "I, for one, am excited to attend every year."

Arthur opened his mouth as if to say something more. Daniel had a good guess as to what it would be.

None of them wanted to think or talk about Alice tonight.

Marianne noticed too and instantly morphed into management mode.

"Do you play, Miss Lovejoy?" she asked Fossi, gesturing toward the gleaming grand piano in the corner.

Fossi blinked. "I-I play only a little," she stammered.

Silence hung for a moment, awkward and laden.

A crimson blush flooded up Fossi's cheeks. "I could sing, however, if you would like," she murmured into the hush.

"That would be delightful. I should enjoy that." Jasmine sagged against Timothy. She appeared less tired today but still far from her buoyant, animated self.

"Excellent." Marianne bustled to her feet, heading toward the piano. "I will play for you."

"Marianne plays *excessively* well," Timothy said, a wry smile touching his lips, "so it is fortunate that you do *not*, Miss Lovejoy. Nearly all others suffer in comparison."

"*Timothy*." Marianne shot her brother a most aggrieved look.

"Do not look askance at me, sister dearest. 'Tis only the truth."

"Agreed," Jasmine said, suppressing a yawn. And then realized she might have been rude. "Not to say that you don't play well, too, Miss Lovejoy—"

"I play quite ill indeed." Fossi took a fortifying breath as she stood. "I shall do my best to not disappoint with my singing, my lady."

Fossi joined Marianne at the piano, both women rifling through a large stack of music, their bent heads nearly touching.

It struck Daniel how natural it felt to have Fossi here. Almost familiar. Like she belonged with them somehow even despite her apparent unease.

He was hesitant to study the emotion too much. Perhaps it was because, unbeknownst to her, she now shared their burden of maintaining the time portal.

"This one," Fossi murmured after a moment, pulling a book from the pile.

Marianne looked at it, a frown creasing her brow. "Are you certain?"

"Of course."

Marianne raised her eyebrows and then shrugged and sat at the keyboard, the music before her.

Fossi positioned herself in front of the piano, hands clasped at her waist. Her position with the piano at her back announcing that this was a piece she already had memorized.

Marianne studied the music for a moment and then launched into a series of scales and trills. Marianne was truly a gifted pianist. The music sounded vaguely familiar but Daniel struggled to place it.

Mozart, perhaps.

Like everyone else in the room, he reclined casually, an ear angled toward Foster Lovejoy's performance. Hands at the ready to politely clap when she was finished.

It was a standard routine for any informal entertainment among friends.

For Fossi's part, she focused on a point above all their heads.

And then she opened her mouth and began to sing.

Bloody hell!

Daniel was quite sure he would remember the shock of the moment fifty years on.

She was . . . *astonishing.*

He instantly sat up, back rigid.

It was . . . inexpressible. Her voice . . . a coloratura soprano of such clarity and brilliance—

She was . . . no, *he* was transformed.

It *was* Mozart.

The Queen of the Night aria from *The Magic Flute*, to be precise.

It was notoriously difficult . . . legendary, in fact. Most sopranos attempted but failed to master the impossibly high trilling arpeggios.

Fossi sailed through them with the blinding ease of a true virtuoso.

Daniel had heard it performed before . . . on the London stage by opera singers of international renown.

And they all paled in comparison to Foster Lovejoy, spinster mathematician, late of Kilminster, Dorset.

Shabbily dressed . . . looking so much like that little gray mouse he had first supposed her to be.

And yet, the sound coming from inside her . . . she was anything but a mouse. A lioness, perhaps.

Words failed him.

Once again, she had utterly whitmoored him.

She sang with her whole body—

Correction.

She sang with her entire soul.

It was that point in the opera where the Queen of Night, in a fit of vengeful rage, shoves a knife in her daughter's hand and threatens to disown her unless she assassinates a rival.

The German words poured from Fossi, the anger and fury of a denied Queen.

Outcast be forever/Forsaken be forever...

Voice soaring with crystalline purity, breathtaking in sheer *ability*.

How could shy, retiring Fossi be the originator of such exquisite sound?

Shattered be forever...

Like that moment earlier in his study, it was a vision straight to the very center of her. The realization it was a vibrant place of color and emotion and so very ... *alive.*

This was the woman who found magnificence in numbers.

Emotion pricked at the back of Daniel's throat. Raw. Aching.

She drew it from him ... pain, longing, sorrow and wove it into treasured beauty.

She sounded the last note and Marianne finished with a few flourishes.

The silence was deafening.

Jasmine's sobs intruded, face pressed into her husband's chest.

Arthur wiped a tear from his cheek.

Even Timothy appeared moved which ... he was *Lord Linwood,* for heaven's sake. Icebergs had been accused of showing more emotion than Linwood.

"That was truly *exquisite*, Miss Lovejoy." Timothy said, voice gruff as he pulled his crying wife closer. "Thank you."

Jasmine bobbed her head. *Yes.*

"Well." Marianne dabbed at her own wet cheeks with a handkerchief. "I know what *I* am going to request every evening for as long as Miss Lovejoy is here."

Fossi blushed, twisting her fingers together, eyes everywhere but on any of them.

"You are too kind," she murmured.

"No," Timothy snorted. "Jasmine and Marianne, perhaps. But I have never been accused of excessive kindness."

"Indeed." Daniel found his voice. "That was . . . remarkable in every way, Miss Lovejoy."

His praise simply deepened her blush.

"Who was your tutor?" he asked.

It went unsaid that she had to have received training. One was not simply born with the ability to sing the Queen of the Night aria anymore than one was born able to paint the *Mona Lisa* or formulate a theory of gravity. Such a skill required a combination of natural talent and years of dedicated learning.

Fossi knotted her fingers further. "My mother was classically trained, and she taught me. My father"—here she paused, swallowed—"my father does not approve of my *vocal theatrics*, as he calls them. I am allowed to sing in church, but I have missed being able to sing more openly."

"A brilliant mathematician *and* soprano virtuoso." Marianne shook her head in wonder.

"They are quite linked, you know." Fossi hastened to explain. "Music is merely mathematics in practical application."

"If you insist."

"Truly. Harmonics adhere to strict fractional rules. Why Fourier himself was the first to postulate that sound is nothing more than a wave nearly a quarter century ago." Fossi's face opened again, lit with earnest intelligence. Daniel would never tire of seeing her thus. "So much is contained with a single note. For example, when I sing the high B-flat in the Queen of the Night, you can hear the corresponding overtone an octave higher which would result in a wave height—"

"Heavens, Miss Lovejoy. You bury us all with your knowledge," Arthur said, voice strained.

Fossi instantly clamped her lips shut—pulling the plug on all that lovely vivacity—a blush making another appearance.

Damn, Arthur.

Daniel considered the man a friend, but his manners could be offputting at times.

"Your brilliance is a thing of beauty," Daniel countered. "I, for one, thank you profoundly for having shared it with us."

Of course, his words only served to move her blush from simply red to scarlet.

Her eyes flitted to his, showing him another tantalizing glimpse of the beauty that lay within.

"Thank you, my lord."

They insisted she sing more for them. Her glorious voice too rare to *not* be heard. Every song lit Daniel's world in brilliant color, setting his heart thumping.

And again, at the end of the evening, his eyes followed her as she retired from the room.

Chapter 13

THE BLUE BEDROOM
KINNINGSLEY, HEREFORDSHIRE
IN THE EARLY HOURS OF AUGUST 12, 1828

Several hours later, Fossi was quite sure she would never sleep again.

She shut *Frankenstein* with a firm snap and tossed it on the bed beside her.

The coal popped in the fireplace, sending sparks up the flue.

Fossi flinched, gripping the counterpane tightly.

The descriptions of Dr. Frankenstein's monster had her jumping at shadows.

Yes. Sleep would definitely be elusive now.

In her defense, Fossi had only opened *Frankenstein* in an ill-guided effort to banish Daniel from her mind.

Daniel . . .

The image of his shocked face when she first opened her mouth in song. The almost painful burst of joy that washed her in its wake.

His reaction had been unnerving.

Granted, that described nearly her entire day.

I think the idea . . . as lovely and magnificent as its owner.

His words would not leave her.

To think she had achieved another item on her list so soon—*flirt with a gentleman.*

She didn't know whether to bless Jasmine for her insight or curse her for her meddling. It went without saying that Jasmine had asked Daniel to teach her how to flirt.

A man like Daniel Ashton did not just take a fancy to a woman like Foster Lovejoy and flirt with her. It spoke volumes to the level of friendship between Daniel and the Linwoods that he would listen to Jasmine's request.

Thankfully, Daniel had taken pains to help her understand that his flirtation was meant to be instructive—a helpful lesson in expected social behaviors.

The flirtation itself had been . . . distressing.

She would have expected it to feel exciting and daring and . . . confident.

Why she had thought flirtation would be so many things that she herself was not . . . Fossi wasn't sure.

Your brilliance is a thing of beauty.

Had that been more flirtation? The compliment had felt somehow . . . more than mere flirtation. But as she was so new to sincere compliments and flirtation, it was difficult to know.

Regardless, that solitary sentence of his weighed on her thoughts. Her cheeks burned at the memory.

Her sisters would chide her, claiming she was behaving fast and wanton. Her father would be properly horrified and threaten to disown her.

Was that why she had left her family as she had? Disowning them first, in a way, before they could disown her?

Would she have reached such a point of discontentment with her life and her family if Daniel hadn't drawn her out? Or would she have remained quiet and passive in her familial role?

It was an uncomfortable thought.

Would she ever come to regret severing ties with her family?

But regretting leaving them also meant she would regret working for—and by extension being around—Daniel. And she hated the thought of regretting anything about her time with him.

Case in point—the note that had been delivered to her just before she crawled into bed:

Please meet me in the library tomorrow morning right after breakfast.

Her foolish heart pitter-pattered in anticipation.

The man was her employer. Of course, he would want to meet with her; she was his to command.

But the more time they spent together, the greater the chance she and Daniel could become friends, and who knew where that—

Ugh!

She needed to stop.

Fossi dragged the covers over her head and nestled into her pillow.

Firmly trying to banish all fantastical thoughts and dreams.

With only marginal success.

THE LIBRARY
KINNINGSLEY, HEREFORDSHIRE
MID-MORNING ON AUGUST 12, 1828

"WILL THIS BE adequate for you as a work space, Miss Lovejoy?"

Daniel watched as Fossi spun in a circle, eyes wide with wonder. Summer sunlight bounded through the room in gleeful glory.

"Heavens. It's lovely."

The idea had come to Daniel late the previous evening—Fossi needed a beautiful space in which to work her sums.

This corner of Kinningsley's library definitely qualified.

Per Daniel's orders, a large desk had been moved before one of the paned windows, perfectly situated to take advantage of the splendid view to the park lands beyond. But it wasn't the greenery and riot of rose-bushes out the window that drew his eye.

No, it was Fossi herself, spinning round still dressed in her shabby gowns. The dancing sunlight caught the red highlights in her brown hair—which truly looked more chestnut than uninspired brown—and in turn brought out gold flecks in her forest eyes.

She turned those eyes back to him now.

"Thank you." She smiled, shy but less withdrawn. She walked over to the desk, setting her own notebook down, running a hand along the large workbook, foolscap, ledger and cup of pencils he had prepared for her. "This is more than adequate."

He pulled the large ledger toward them, flipping it open and motion-ing for Fossi to look at it with him. There was one small anachronism that Daniel decided to employ.

She studied the headed columns and labeled rows.

"Goodness! What beauty is all this?" Delight lit her eyes and popped a small dimple in her left cheek.

Huh.

Was it only a few short days ago that he had considered her more plain than beautiful? Surely he must have been mistaken.

Foster Lovejoy was decidedly lovely.

Granted, her affinity for equations could also have colored his assess-ment. It took a special type of woman to react to numbers like they were a new dress design from Paris.

He was utterly enchanted.

"What is it?" Fossi asked, still studying the unique pages Daniel opened before her. "It looks like an expanded sort of ledger."

"I would call it a spreadsheet. It is a way for you to catalog your findings. I'll have you enter the number of the equation in this column here, followed by your results here . . ."

Daniel continued, outlining how he wanted her to meticulously track her results. There was no telling what would prove useful in the future.

The more he spoke, the more excited Fossi became.

"Oh my," she finally breathed, voice breathless, "this is truly marvelous, my lord." The woman nearly clasped her hands in glee.

Daniel paused. Was she being sarcastic?

"Are you quite all right, Miss Lovejoy?"

"Yes, it's just so very . . . exhilarating."

A beat.

"You find spreadsheets . . . exhilarating?"

"Of course. Don't you? It is a thing of such beauty in its simplicity. It quite steals my breath."

Right.

Still no sarcasm.

A grin tugged at Daniel's lips.

This woman.

"And here I had been hoping that *I* could be the one to steal your breath away." Daniel pasted a look of deep regret on his face.

Fossi froze in place.

"Flirting, Miss Lovejoy." He raised his eyebrows. "You had said you were interested in becoming more conversant."

She blushed, vibrant and brilliant.

"I-I fear Lady Linwood underestimated my reserves when it comes to flirtation," she stammered.

"Simply consider it exponentially advanced charm."

"I am not sure I am up to the challenge." She pressed her hands to her fiery cheeks. "Is it normal to find flirting so distressing?"

"Once one moves past the novice stage, flirtation is a delightful game." He chuckled. "We shall have to acclimate you by degrees."

Another pause.

"I am not sure if I should thank you or be terrified."

"I assure you, my flirting abilities rarely inspire horror."

That startled a laugh out of her. Giddy and decidedly breathless.

"Flirtation is quite simple," he continued. "One merely indicates through either body language or words—often both simultaneously—a playful interest in a member of the opposite gender. Flirting should always communicate a desire to further the acquaintance of the other person. Shall I give an example?"

"Please."

"Very well." He pushed away from the desk and walked into the center of the room. "Let us say that we have just happened upon each other and you make a comment about the agreeable weather."

Daniel gestured, indicating that Fossi should make such a comment.

She blushed again and said, "The weather is quite lovely today."

Daniel met her gaze and then allowed a small smile to touch his lips, his eyes warming. "Indeed, Miss Lovejoy, it is a *delightfully* lovely day at present."

Everything about his gaze and tone, however, stated that he found *her* lovely.

She smiled, a breathless laugh escaping. Eyes sparkling with life.

Daniel quite forgot to breathe himself—the teacher, again, being schooled by his student.

She clapped.

"That was impressively good," she said. "Your words and behavior were utterly proper, but the tone in which you said them communicated a different message. Bravo, my lord."

"Daniel," was his reply.

"Pardon?"

"Please, call me Daniel. We will be working together after all."

She blinked and abruptly took a step back, flinching as if his words were cold water flicked upon her.

First her eyes shuttered, then her shoulders slumped. Bit by bit, light by light, Fossi extinguished. It was like watching someone close up a house for the night. Every last bit of that lovely excitement and energy doused.

Daniel watched the transformation with something akin to horror.

No! Come back!

She dropped her head and gazed at her hands, twisting her fingers in her habitual way.

"That would hardly be seemly, my lord." Her voice quiet, achingly polite and proper.

"I would consider it an honor, Miss Lovejoy."

"I am an unmarried woman of no station. Flirtation, or exponentially advanced charm as you called it, is fine if sanctioned by Lady Linwood and couched in terms of furthering my social education." Her tone was agitated now. But at least she raised her eyes to his. "However, to call you by your first name . . . it would imply a degree of intimacy—"

"A woman who agrees to enter my employ as my personal mathematician is hardly one who stands on societal ceremony."

"Perhaps, but I still must live within that society."

"Will you at least consider the idea? When we are in private, just you and I? I will be Daniel and you will be Fossi?" His gaze plead with hers.

A long pause.

"Very well," she whispered. "When we are alone, just you and I . . . we can be Fossi and . . . Daniel."

Breathing a sigh of relief, Daniel extended his hand.

She pursed her lips and then settled her much smaller palm against his. Though dainty, her grip was firm as she shook his hand.

"Deal."

KINNINGSLEY, HEREFORDSHIRE
AUGUST 19, 1828

FOSSI HAD MANY opportunities to ponder cause and effect over the following week.

Action. Reaction.

Lord Whitmoor and herself.

Or rather, Fossi and Daniel, as they were now to be to each other.

Calling him by his Christian name . . . as his other friends did . . .

Fossi tried not to dwell too much on what it meant.

Of course, her emotions were a pendulum.

When Daniel smiled and sought her out, his words were a buoyant lifeline of hope and solidarity.

When he retreated to his study or took a long walk with his mysterious box, his words became a painful millstone, dragging her down.

Action. Reaction.

Every evening she would join Daniel and Lord and Lady Linwood for dinner, as if she were part of their little group instead of a decided outsider. After dinner, she would sing and they would listen.

She reminded herself at minimum twenty times a day that Daniel was Lord Whitmoor—the man whose name was synonymous, quite literally, with secrets and espionage.

Every day, she worked her equations in one book and charted her results in another, laboring to find harmony between two different theorems that she did not fully understand.

The reaction of all *that* action was a persistent nagging frustration.

Why was she working these equations? What was their purpose? Why pay a king's ransom for her abilities?

Why, why, why did the dratted man have to be so secretive?

Fortunately, her progress (or lack of it) did not seem to perturb Daniel.

And then the first wave of her new clothing arrived.

The housekeeper informed her of the fact as several footmen passed by, carrying parcels to Fossi's room.

Following them, Fossi carefully unwrapped each package, admiring the fabrics and stitching with Sally, the friendly upstairs maid who waited upon her now.

"Cor, Miss Lovejoy," Sally sighed over a silk evening gown, deep green with moderately puffed sleeves slashed with gold. "You'll be a dream in this, you will."

Fossi fought an odd mix of excitement, mortification and nervousness.

The gown *was* beautiful.

"Shall we get you dressed for dinner then?" Sally practically bounced across to Fossi's dressing table.

Fossi could only nod.

An hour later, she stared at herself in the mirror.

The dress was a work of art.

The mossy green fabric shimmered in the candlelight and cinched tight to her small waist before flaring over her hips.

Drat, Jasmine.

The silk *did* feel lovely against her skin.

Most significantly, the gown made the most delightful swishing sound when she walked.

Sally had styled her hair in a sophisticated sweep atop her head with several loose curls resting beside her face. The look was more mature than that of a debutante but certainly not matronly either.

"You look so lovely, Miss Lovejoy. They'll scarcely recognize you." Sally smiled at her in the mirror.

Fossi barely recognized herself. The woman staring at her from the mirror appeared . . . confident. Refined. Elegant.

A true lady.

She was unsure how to feel about the transformation. Was this person genuinely her? Or was this merely a false mask for a different environment?

And what did it matter if it was? At the end of the day, she would still be odd Foster Lovejoy.

Nothing more. Nothing less.

Well . . . except dressed in velvety silk.

These clothes would be her uniform while she was here. She could continue to feel unequal to the task of wearing them. Or, she could rise to the challenge and accept them.

Notching her chin higher, Fossi gave a strained smile.

Acceptance, it was.

DANIEL STRODE FROM his small study. He had just finished changing for dinner and had stopped to look over several missives which had arrived via the evening post.

As he emerged, a noise from the staircase to his left caught his attention. He glanced up at the pretty young lady descending the stairs and then back at the letter in his hand.

Ah, Aurelie must be joining them for dinner this evening. Jasmine probably felt the girl was old enough to begin practicing dining in company—

It took a moment before the jolting frisson of recognition swept down his spine.

His head rocketed up with whiplash force, staring at the woman on the stairs.

Good heavens!

He was quite sure his jaw literally dropped. Or would have, if shock hadn't rendered him entirely motionless.

Yes. The figure on the stairs was decidedly *not* Aurelie.

It was Fossi.

But not the Fossi he knew.

She wore a mossy green silk gown, expertly cut and hugging surprising curves, showcasing a naturally small waist. Hair prettily framed her chin, highlighting the graceful lines of her face. The whole effect was elegant and refined, matching Fossi's own reserved temperament.

Daniel felt like he was witnessing a . . . metamorphosis. Fossi emerging from her cocoon.

Or was the metamorphosis his own?

She descended in a soft rustle of skirts, stopping a stair above him, nearly eye-level, a tentative smile on her face.

Daniel bowed, low and proper.

Fossi curtsied.

"Miss Lovejoy," Daniel managed to get out, "might I be the first to compliment you on your attire this evening?"

Her smile expanded, touching her eyes with warmth.

A beat.

"You may, my lord," she replied, shooting him a coy glance through her eyelashes.

Daniel paused. And then smiled, wide and delighted.

"Did you just flirt with me, Miss Lovejoy?"

Fossi blushed.

"Did I?" she asked.

"I do believe you did. You are a quick study, I must say." He nodded and offered her his arm. "And you *do* look lovely this evening."

KINNINGSLEY, HEREFORDSHIRE
AUGUST 22, 1828

DESPITE DANIEL'S GRATIFYING reaction to her new clothing, Fossi was still unsure what to think of her new employer and his penchant for secrets.

The numbers she worked on day in and day out were fascinating, each iteration spitting out different values that she carefully charted. Fossi had never had the luxury of devoting most of her day to sums. Hours would pass without her raising her head and, initially, she worked late into the evenings after dinner.

Daniel quickly put a stop to that, insisting she took regular breaks.

"I prefer those in my employ to *not* drop over from exhaustion," he said when she protested.

Of course, the breaks gave her too much time to think about Daniel, the odd equations and what secrets they all held. She was convinced Daniel knew what the variables represented, but he consistently dodged her questions about the matter.

She suspected that g stood for gravity and m stood for mass. But if that were the case, what did c mean?

And given the complexity of the equations, what was Daniel investigating and why? How was this helping Kit in America?

Pondering it led to more frustrating questions, not answers.

So she turned her mind to investigating what she *could* about him.

Namely . . . his wife, Alice.

Who was Alice? What kind of woman would capture the heart of a man like Daniel Ashton? Enough that he still grieved so thoroughly five years on?

And so Fossi, being a woman of methodology, set her mind to discovery.

"I can't rightly say I know who Lady Alice was, ma'am." Sally said when asked. "Whitmoor House is some distance from Kinningsley, and I've only been in service for less than a year."

Mmmm.

"But you say Lady Alice? Not Lady Whitmoor?" Fossi pressed her.

"Well, that's how Mr. Jones refers to her. Lady Alice, he says."

"Mr. Jones . . . the butler?"

"Yes, ma'am."

In retrospect, Fossi realized that if Lady Alice had died five years ago, she would never have been Lady Whitmoor, as Daniel had been elevated to the peerage only recently.

Which meant for Lady Alice to be called Lady Alice, her father had to be a duke, a marquess or an earl.

Heavens.

A woman of impeccable bloodline then.

Why Fossi found that information dispiriting, she chose *not* to examine.

She managed to ask Mr. Jones about it two days later.

"I cannot speak about Lady Alice, Miss Lovejoy. 'Tis not my station," Mr. Jones replied. "Would you like me to summon you some tea in the library?"

The housekeeper, three footmen and a groom all gave similar replies.

Say what you would about Lord and Lady Linwood, their servants thoroughly understood the value of discretion.

Fossi (briefly) considered asking Jasmine about it, but if her servants were close-lipped, the lady of the house would be even more so.

And despite her open manners and aura of kindness, Fossi disliked the thought of appearing impudent to Lady Linwood.

A trip to Whitmoor House would have solved the problem. Surely she could get answers to all her questions there. The house had to be full of Lady Alice's affects—a silent testimony to her passing.

However, Fossi considered it unlikely she would participate in the planned festivities next month. It was not as if Daniel needed his pet mathematician to run triangulations for his harvest festival.

I do believe the angle would be more acute if we were to lower the bower four inches to the left . . .

Such an idea was absurd.

Fossi finally resorted to scouring the well-worn copy of *Debrett's Peerage* in the library, hunting through the daughters of dukes, marquesses and earls looking for an Alice who would be about the correct age.

Unfortunately, Alice proved a fairly popular aristocratic name for a number of years running.

Of course, Fossi could have applied to the man himself for answers to her questions but . . . she remembered that moment in the carriage. How even talking about his wife caused him pain.

And she profoundly disliked the idea of contributing to that pain in any way.

Chapter 14

Two weeks after their arrival at Kinningsley, Daniel happened upon Fossi as she walked across the lawn. Though *happened upon* might be doing it a bit brown.

He had noticed her walking from his window upstairs—twirling something in her hand—and had found himself following in her wake not even ten minutes later.

Granted, she normally took the air each afternoon during her post-luncheon break, walking down to the small, man-made lake beyond the expansive south lawn. And if he found reasons to be along the walk around the same time . . .

He enjoyed Miss Foster Lovejoy's company, that was all. It was delightful to speak with another mathematics enthusiast. And, here he was slightly more honest with himself, he relished watching her blush when she realized he was flirting with her.

Though today, a pucker furrowed her brow as he approached, something tightly clutched in her hand.

"Good afternoon, Fossi." He topped his hat to her. "Though that frown upon your face makes me concerned for how your day is progressing."

She startled and then color washed her cheeks, bold and shockingly red-pink in color.

Did she know how charming her blush was?

Granted, her bonnet was decidedly new and smart and tied beneath her chin in such a way as to showcase that elegant jawline of hers. Her rose-colored pelisse nipped in her waist and lent further color to her complexion.

She looked lovely.

"Good afternoon." She smoothed her creased brow. "I am doing well, I suppose. Just seeking some fresh air and clarity."

He stepped into place beside her, walking toward the house in the distance.

"And are you finding any?"

His comment earned him a small smile.

"Some, I suppose. Fresh air, that is. The clarity is still in short supply."

It was his turn to smile.

"Is this what has clouded you?" He motioned toward the item she held in her hand.

"This?" She held up a tuning fork, metal glinting in the sun. "Somewhat, I suppose. I hit a specific iteration of the first equation today that perhaps hinted at a point of reconciliation with the second theorem."

"Pardon?" Adrenaline jolted his system, pulling him to a stop. Had she solved the problem so soon?

Fossi swung to face him, expression instantly alarmed. "Do not suppose that I have hit upon any real answer." She wagged the tuning fork at him. "It is merely a small conundrum that I struggled to instantly resolve, and so I took it upon myself to walk off my thoughts."

He motioned and they strolled onward together. The sun danced cheerily in the sky around puffy, happy clouds. Birds called merrily.

"I would love to hear the idea that has clouded your way," he said.

"It isn't much. Perhaps it is because I stare at Lord Linwood's collection of tuning forks all day." She slapped said tuning fork against her palm. "Or simply the result of all the singing I have been doing as of late. Regardless, I find myself thinking in terms of pitch and frequency more than normal."

"And that is a problem?"

"No. More of a catalyst. I have begun wondering if pitch—or in other words, wave height and frequency—might be a unifying factor between the equations."

Daniel's head reared back, his mind instantly flitting through the ramifications of pitch as applied to wormhole theory.

"That is . . . fascinating," he murmured. "You were right to explore the idea further."

Fossi gave a small self-deprecating laugh. "Well, thinking about exploring the idea further is about as far as I have come."

"You are far too modest."

"Quite the opposite, I assure you. I merely understand my limitations. But thank you for believing in my capabilities."

"You are the one with the talents, Fossi. I am merely harnessing them for my own good, as any wise person would."

A fraught little pause.

Daniel could practically see her squirming under his praise.

"I am truthfully nobody," she finally said.

He stopped walking, forcing her to halt and meet his gaze. "Well . . . if so, I would say *nobody* is absolutely perfect."

He waited.

It took her a moment to get it.

It was like sunrise . . . surprise and delight sweeping over her features, lighting the landscape as it went.

He would never tire of astonishing her.

Fossi gave an exuberant laugh, eyes dancing in wonder.

"Skillfully done! You are a master flirt, sirrah." She waggled the tuning fork at him again.

He chuckled and bowed before waving for them to continue onward.

Daniel savored the swish of those skirts as she walked with him. He had forgotten how much he enjoyed this . . . a woman at his side, taking support and offering equal measure in return.

It had been far too long, not since Alice—

He paused his thoughts right there. The day was far too delightful and cheery to drag the likes of Alice into it.

"Do you suppose that there will ever come a time when women will have more choices?" she asked, seemingly from out of nowhere. "Where people will simply be judged by their ideas and abilities, rather than their gender?"

It was a valid question.

He could hardly answer with the truth.

Someday, perhaps. Give it about two hundred years and even then things will be difficult—

"I have shocked you?" She darted a look at him.

"No," he replied, "you misunderstand my silence. I agree with you. I believe that birth and gender should not confine a woman to a tiny box of living."

"I have a secret wish to be known as a woman to the Society of Mathematicians."

"It is a good wish . . ."

"But unlikely to happen, I know," she finished for him. "That is part of why I want to start a girl's school. Women must be educated as men if they wish to participate in traditionally male intellectual pursuits."

"True. It is a man's own loss in the end . . . to shun intelligent discourse with a woman such as yourself."

He caught the tiniest glimpse of a smile from underneath her bonnet. "Are you being charming again?"

"Of course. You said you like me better when I am charming."

A pause.

"I am your employee. Why take the trouble to teach me social customs, like flirting?" she asked, genuinely puzzled. "Why do you care if I find you charming?"

And wasn't that the question, in the end?

Why *did* he care if Foster Lovejoy found him charming?

Because as he examined the emotion, he discovered that he *did* care.

How to answer?

"Are you sure you are simply my employee?" he asked.

She shot him her now familiar stop-answering-my-question-with-a-question look.

He grinned.

"I thought we had become friends, haven't we?" He winked.

Another glare.

"We have?" She arched an eyebrow at him.

He laughed in earnest.

They walked in silence for a minute or two.

"Thank you," she said on a sigh.

He shot her a quizzical look.

"We *have* become friends, I think," she explained. "You didn't have to befriend me in addition to employing and housing me. And I thank you for that."

She was correct.

He hadn't needed to make a friend of her. And yet he had.

They *were* friends now. More than employer and employee.

The thought chased him throughout the rest of the day.

It was later in the early morning . . . after staring at the canopy above his bed for several hours that it all sank in . . .

Fossi.

The brightness of her intellect, the charm of her voice, the spark of joy in her beautiful eyes when he flirted with her—

Good heavens above.

He was falling for her . . . Foster Lovejoy.

Hard. Fast.

His stupid heart leapt into his throat at merely the thought.

Which given his past, the current mess with the portal and his own future plans . . . such emotional entanglement was unacceptable. He had decided on his current path nearly two years ago, when the world had figuratively and literally shook.

He rolled over.

Promise you will keep it for me. Don't forget.

As usual, guilt crashed in behind the thought.

He had to fix his mistake. Emotional attachment to Fossi would be a complication to that.

Friend or no.

He would just need to limit the time he spent with her. This inconvenient infatuation would pass soon enough.

He would not deviate from his chosen course.

Not even for a woman full of mesmerizing color.

DANIEL'S STUDY
KINNINGSLEY, HEREFORDSHIRE
SEPTEMBER 2, 1828

THREE TUESDAYS AFTER arriving at Kinningsley, Fossi experienced a true breakthrough of sorts.

She had been working equations all morning and had a minor epiphany regarding how to meld pitch frequency with the second theorem.

To clarify, the epiphany was not her breakthrough, merely its catalyst. She had diligently recorded it in her spreadsheet, but then she wished to share her discovery with Daniel, particularly as he had expressed interest in the idea.

She still struggled to understand his interactions with her.

He had spent the last week being emotionally hot and cold.

Sometimes she sensed true regard from him . . . that she was a genuine friend that he sought out.

Other times, she was quite sure he viewed her as a merely useful person in his employ.

Not that it mattered, she supposed.

In the end, he was Daniel Ashton, Lord Whitmoor.

Keeper of secrets. Spy master to the Crown.

Grieving widower of Lady Alice Ashton.

She was plain Foster Lovejoy, late of Kilminster and nothing to no one. No matter his flirting and kindness.

He had hired her to do a job.

Fossi bundled the ledger under her arm and wandered from her library sanctuary, across the cavernous great hall, around the gilt marble staircase and to his small study. The door was ajar but she still knocked politely.

No answer.

She pushed the door open and quickly surveyed the space.

Empty. Daniel had stepped out.

She turned . . . but stopped before exiting the room, slowly pivoting back around.

She meant to leave. Truly she did. She had no intention of violating his privacy.

It was just . . .

That mysterious box. The one Daniel carried with him on garden strolls and wept over in the dead of night—

It was sitting on his desktop. Open. Rimmed in cheery sunlight.

She stared at it.

All these weeks wondering what it contained. Love letters written when Daniel and Alice were apart? A priceless necklace he had given Alice for her birthday? The gloves she had worn that one memorable evening at the theater?

It had somehow become Pandora's box in her mind. Full of secret emotions that, if unleashed, would reveal him.

Maybe . . .

Fossi's heart drummed in her throat.

She swallowed convulsively.

Her slippers crossed the six feet of space to the edge of the desk without Fossi willfully *telling* them to move.

It was as if the box had its own gravity outside of Newton's Laws, and her body was helpless to obey anything else.

Action. Reaction.

Or . . . that is what Fossi whispered to herself.

Her ledger clutched to her chest . . . she *leeeeeaned* forward.

And peeked inside.

Blinked.

Frowned.

Her shoulders slumped.

She moved to the side to get a better look.

Hmmm.

She made a quick mental catalog.

Three small twigs. Twenty-seven rocks of varying size. A feather of uncertain origin. A bit of rope. A cracked snail shell. Two strands of red yarn. And half a robin's eggshell.

Just so . . . unexpected.

Well, more like anticlimactic.

What on earth could Lady Alice have wanted with twenty-seven rocks of varying size? And a feather?

That will teach you to snoop where you oughtn't, Foster Lovejoy.

A clatter outside the door jerked her upright and sent her feet out the door.

But the box buzzed in her mind for days afterward.

She found herself wanting to talk to him about it. Not because it belonged to him, but because he was sincerely becoming her best friend.

And she would confide important and interesting things in a best friend.

You will not believe what has occurred. My employer has a box he weeps over and yet it contains rocks and other debris. Is that not odd, Daniel? What should we make of it?

That would never do.

Her heart thumped and her throat constricted whenever she thought of it.

Because she was not so naive as to misunderstand the emotions coursing through her.

She *liked* Daniel Ashton. Deeply. Profoundly.

Even though he remained a labyrinth she could not unravel, she found herself fiercely drawn to the respectful way he listened to her and to his easy acceptance of her oddness. To his innate kindness and sense of honor. To the quirky uptick of his mouth when he smiled and the way humor glinted in his blue eyes when he showed her how to flirt.

She *cared* what he thought of her. And that was a . . . problem.

Because caring led to *expectation*.

Expectation as to how he would behave around her.

Anticipation as to when she would see him again.

Hope and desire for their continued friendship.

It would be so easy, she realized, to fall deeply in love with him. To mistake his kindness and goodness for regard and a return of her affections.

But she knew that kindness and genuine devotion were two entirely separate things.

She had learned that bitter lesson nearly a decade previous when Mr. Thomas Young had returned from London following the death of his wife. He had attended Reverend Lovejoy's sermons and politely escorted Fossi home each time, listening attentively as she chattered about the weather or the importance of *pi*. He had even offered her his greatcoat when they had been caught in a rogue cloudburst. She had thought of him for hours at a time, creating grand dreams of Mr. Young offering for her and sweeping her off to far-away London, certain that he had singled her out as the object of his affections.

And then came the fateful day she overheard Mr. Young complaining to Mr. Martin about that 'odd Foster Lovejoy' always lingering around and driving him 'nigh crazy with her nonsense.'

Fossi had cried herself to sleep for two weeks, by which point Mr. Young had betrothed himself to Mary Baker and returned to London.

Lesson learned.

Men declined to indulge in the game of layered artifice most women played.

No, men were simple creatures.

If they adored you, they said so.

If they wanted to marry you, they asked.

If you questioned in any way whether a particular gentleman cared for you, he did not.

And based on those criteria, Daniel had no interest in her beyond simple friendship and their working relationship.

So Fossi focused on having Daniel Ashton as a friend.

Because even his friendship was a gift to be treasured.

THE SOUTH DRAWING ROOM
KINNINGSLEY, HEREFORDSHIRE
SEPTEMBER 10, 1828

"YOU SAY OUR Fossi is making progress then?"

Daniel glanced at Jasmine reclining in a chair opposite him, raising his eyebrows at her question.

"Yes. She has had some brilliant ideas regarding pitch and wave frequency. I have every hope she will solve the problem of the portal."

Jasmine looked beyond him for a moment. She remained pale and weak, the portal's malfunction continuing to affect her. Daniel knew Timothy was beside himself with worry. They all were.

"I am still not sure things will go as you expect, Daniel," Jasmine said. "Perhaps it is time to accept that mistakes happen—"

"No." Daniel shook his head, guilt pounding through him.

"Daniel—"

"No, Jasmine. Please . . . let's not rehash this. I know what *you* think. You know *my* opinion. We have agreed to disagree."

A beat.

"Yes." Voice weary. "But merely consider this—are you willing to spend the rest of your life in this place? In this situation? Waiting for a solution that may never come—"

"There will be a resolution, Jasmine. History demands it. You need it. Fossi will find it." He shook his head. Resolute. "I will accept no other outcome."

KINNINGSLEY DEVOLVED INTO a rush of energy as autumn progressed. Tenants worked to bring in the harvest and servants prepared for the Linwood's departure to Whitmoor House for the harvest festival.

Fossi made more progress with her sums and anticipated the quiet that would follow everyone's departure to Gloucestershire and Whitmoor House.

She had also had some success in banishing thoughts of mysterious rock-filled boxes and the men that wept over them.

Well . . . make that marginal success.

Which made the summons to Jasmine's sitting room all the more unexpected.

Lady Linwood, Madame Beauford, three assistants and fourteen bolts of luxurious silk awaited her.

"Excellent. Thank you for coming, Foster." Jasmine welcomed her with a wan smile. Lady Linwood had seemed even more tired as of late. "Madame Beauford is here to fit you for your gown."

Fossi darted her eyes between all the women in the room.

"My gown, my lady? I do believe Madame Beauford has already done marvelous work with my wardrobe—"

"Of course," Jasmine waved a hand, "but you will need a ball gown for Whitmoor House."

"A ball gown?" *Wait.* "Whitmoor House?"

"Naturally. I insisted you have a new gown for Lord Whitmoor's harvest festival ball. We depart in less than a week."

"All of us?"

"Most definitely. We cannot leave poor Daniel to face everything all alone, now can we?"

Oh.

Well.

It seemed Fossi would be going to Whitmoor House after all.

Chapter 15

What are your thoughts? Do you like my home?"

Fossi turned her head at Daniel's question.

"'Tis marvelous." She tucked a stray wisp of hair back into her bonnet while taking in the view.

She and Daniel stood side-by-side on a small bluff, surveying the valley with Whitmoor House at its center. A gentle breeze tugged at her bonnet and billowed his greatcoat.

They had all traveled together in a merry string of coaches—the Linwoods and their children, Daniel and Fossi. Arthur and Marianne Knight would join them too, right before the festival itself.

As for the journey itself, Fossi had expected to help with the children and be a backdrop to everyone else's entertainment. But Jasmine and Daniel had refused to allow her to retreat, insisting she join in their laughter and cheer.

Fossi couldn't help comparing their interactions with those of her father and siblings. Such geniality was not part of her life in The Old Vicarage. There, strict rules of sober conduct and religious reflection were firmly entrenched.

Fossi had been raised listening to Reverend Lovejoy rail endlessly about the aristocracy and their high-handedness. And certainly such aristocrats existed. But Fossi was coming to realize that members of the peerage were just like everyone else in the world—varied and unique.

Though given the comfort of the coaches and ease of travel, aristocrats certainly did everything with more flare and style.

As their little caravan neared Whitmoor House, the sunny weather convinced them to pile out of the carriages and complete the last mile on foot. They strolled down the tree-lined lane and passed by a crumbling medieval watchtower which the children climbed with laughing delight.

Daniel had pulled Fossi off the main drive and up a small path to the top of a low hill that provided an overlook to the house itself.

Whitmoor House rose out of the forest, a somber memorial to times past. The house had its origins in the Middle Ages but had been added to over the years, lending it a bit of a hodge-podge look. A medieval keep stood in its center, flanked by two Tudor halls that branched into Jacobean wings that eventually enclosed a courtyard area behind the house.

It did not escape Fossi's notice that iron bands wrapped around the granite medieval ramparts.

An unexpected bit of irony that.

"I've always thought Whitmoor House defined the words 'ancestral pile'—a complete mishmash of styles and additions that somehow work together to create a complete building." Daniel tapped a walking stick against the ground, a sort of shy affection in his tone. As if her opinion of his home mattered.

Because we are friends, she reminded herself. *That is why he cares. Nothing more.*

"It has been in your family for generations, then?" she asked.

He paused and then gave a one-shouldered shrug. "Not exactly. I purchased the property about a decade ago. It was named Whitmoor House at the time and, over the years, Whitmoor became associated with me."

"Hence the verb?"

He gave a rueful chuckle. "Among other things. I merely completed the circle by taking Whitmoor as the name for my baronetcy when raised to the peerage."

Unspoken was his intention that Whitmoor House would be the ancestral pile for his descendants.

Daniel looked freer here and yet not.

Fossi hadn't missed the tension in his shoulders as they drew nearer to Whitmoor House. He obviously loved his home, but she could only imagine how bittersweet it must be. All the memories—both good and bad—it held.

Had Lady Alice loved Whitmoor House too? When returning home, would they alight from the carriage and continue on foot as she and Daniel were right now?

He waved his waking stick toward the large house in its picturesque setting. "Will you be able to focus on your work here, do you suppose?"

His question had a slight teasing tone that melted a solid seventy-five percent of the emotional barrier Fossi had constructed to protect her heart from such things.

Drat the man.

He was determined to undermine her *We're Only Friends* position.

Unfortunately, it didn't stop her from replying, "Presumably, as long as I avoid going off on a tangent."

It was, of course, a mathematical joke.

It took him a moment and then his face lit, like sunrays over the ocean, sparkling and delighted.

Blasting his way through the battered remains of her self-preservation.

"Well done!" he laughed. "*Brava.*"

"I have been practicing." Fossi willed herself not to blush. With only marginal success.

It was both a blessing and a curse to feel so comfortable around him, as if she were at home.

"Well, I *have* long considered you to be the square root of two." Daniel doffed his hat and swept her a bow.

She tilted her head, trying to sort through the puzzle.

He leaned in. Close enough that she could see the flecks of gold in his irises. "Because I often feel quite irrational when I think about you."

He winked.

Fossi laughed far too loud.

As an example of mathematical flirting, it was brilliant—the square root of two being an irrational number.

But before she could examine Daniel's face to determine if he were merely teasing her or . . . she wasn't sure what . . . the chatter of the Linwood's children drifted from behind them, Charles and James arguing over treasures they had found in the old watchtower.

Still smiling, Daniel gestured for them to descend the path ahead of the children.

He went first and then turned.

Stretching a hand back to her to steady her down the steep hill.

Fossi stared at his gloved hand. It seemed a . . . portent.

Swallowing, she carefully set her own gloved palm against his.

Strong fingers wrapped around hers, firm and solid, sending an arc of electricity up her arm.

Gracious.

How was she supposed to protect her heart when he behaved like this?

Breathe, Fossi. He is only helping because it is the gentlemanly thing for a friend to do.

"Careful there," he said, looking ahead as they stepped down worn stairs.

Fossi studied the back of his neck as they went, that small strip of skin she could see between the brim of his top hat and the top of his collar.

Dark brown hair threaded with the occasional wiry gray strand. Skin pink from the sun. So vulnerable and humanizing.

Tiny glimpses of the fascinating, kind, generous man she knew lived inside him.

He released her fingers as soon as they exited the narrow path. Fossi's own hand instantly felt cold and lonely.

Naturally, Daniel resumed his place beside her, seemingly unaffected as they approached the front of the house with its imposing medieval central tower.

Friends. Nothing more than friends.

A pair of enormous, wooden doors stretched upward from the center of the tower, flung wide-open to accommodate the arriving guests. Footmen unloaded trunks from the baggage coach, supervised by a rotund, balding man who could only be the butler. When the servants would have paused to bow to Daniel, he waved them off.

Say what you would about aristocrats in general, Lord Whitmoor didn't take his station too seriously.

"Come." Daniel placed a firm hand under her elbow.

Instead of drawing her past the footmen and into the house, Daniel skirted the main entrance and led her to a recessed area to the right of the central tower. A small, age-darkened door emerged from the shadows—an entrance so short Daniel would have to stoop to pass through it.

She raised her eyebrows—a question mark.

"I figured we could beat Charles and James here," was all he said.

Daniel smiled as mischievously as any child and tugged the glove off his right hand. Fossi stared at the tendons flexing across his bare hand as he reached between the door and stone wall, a solitary long finger fitting into a groove carved into the limestone.

"Take off a glove so you can feel this." He jerked a chin toward his hand.

Fossi obliged with almost embarrassing alacrity, pulling her own glove off.

"Here." He placed his opposite hand underneath her elbow, drawing her forward, her shoulder nearly *touching* his chest.

Fossi swallowed. Flirting from across a room was one thing, but holding his hand to descend a path and now this . . .

She had never been this close to him. Touch of any sort was rare in her life. In fact, she couldn't remember a time she had been so near *any* man who was not her father or brother.

He seemed much larger up close. If he wrapped her in his arms, she would see nothing else but him, buried against the heat of his chest.

Which . . . *gracious*. What a thought.

She was already struggling to focus when he did the worst—or was it the best?—thing possible . . .

He took her bare right hand in his. On the path, their hands had been gloved, but now . . .

His palm felt calloused and rough against hers. Warm. Dry.

Heat flared up her arm, a desert sirocco blowing across her brain. Surely her face reflected the heat, a furnace of color.

Oh!

Later, Fossi would wonder how she had managed to keep her gasp silent.

His palm was so . . . warm. And so large. And strong. And so very . . . *alive*.

Daniel gently pulled her hand to the same groove next to the door, fingertips pressing into her palm.

"Feel that?" he asked.

Heavens yes!

Not what he meant, surely.

Fossi managed to wiggle a finger in the groove. There was a chain or loop of some sort buried in it.

"You pull. Like this." He drew her arm downward, her finger taking the chain with it.

She should have been concentrating on the door or the mechanism or *something* other than the whoosh of her pulse in her ears and the radiating power of his body beside her.

It was all just so . . . unexpected.

She longed to lean back into him, to feel his opposite arm come around her, bringing his chest to her back, his voice in her ear.

They both watched him draw her hand down, as if that point of connection between them weren't pulsing with frantic, kinetic energy.

Fossi heard the *snick* of a locking crossbar lifting behind the door.

Daniel pushed the door open.

Which given that he still held her right hand in his and stood behind her . . . meant that his left hand snaked around her left shoulder.

All he would have to do is bring his hands together, and he would be embracing her from behind.

His coat brushed her shoulder blades. Peppermint and bay rum enveloped her.

Careful what you wish for, Foster Lovejoy.

Surely he *had* to have heard her gasp this time.

"I've always found this door to be unique." His voice at her ear. "Such a clever way to provide entrance without needing a key."

Her breath caught, a painful little snag. Such a small detail, but . . . he had wanted her to know this tiny piece of him.

"Clever." She repeated, voice embarrassingly too breathless. "It is action . . . reaction."

She mimed pulling the chain and the bar lifting to clarify, mostly for herself, what she meant.

"Yes." Was his tone extra husky?

Time stretched, sticky molasses taffy . . . delicious and heady but difficult to extract oneself from.

Fossi's eyes threatened to roll into the back of her head. She swallowed. Once. Twice.

Move. You need to move!

It was just . . .

She could *feel* his breath on her neck, brushing in and out softly beside her ear. She had never been so grateful for bonnets and their sun-shading brims. That he couldn't see her shocked expression and flared eyes and violently red cheeks.

No. All he would see was her jaw.

Which . . . was he staring at it? At her?

Her skin prickled with awareness.

He leaned forward, his chest actually touching her shoulder blades in earnest. His breath skimmed up the side of her neck and wrapped around her ear. Warm. Soft. More peppermint and bay rum.

Gooseflesh pebbled in its wake.

Action. Reaction.

Was he breathing her, as she was him? Did he know that their lungs had instantly synchronized?

In. Out.

Two souls inhaling as one.

He leaned farther, surrounding her with his arms and body.

She felt him suck in a deep breath of air.

"Shall we?" His words caused her to jump.

He moved beside her and swept his arm out, indicating she should proceed into the house.

Oh.

Oh, yes.

Of course.

He had just been patiently waiting for her to move forward while she had been thinking . . . other things.

Friends. That's right. We are simply friends.

Fossi's blush moved from violent to molten lava. Never had she been so grateful to duck her head and pass through a doorway, disappearing into the gloom beyond.

Daniel closed the door and reset the crossbar, plunging them into darkness.

"The boys will be disappointed if they can't work the mechanism too," he chuckled, voice loud in the hush.

Was it *too* loud? Did he sound strained?

Unthinking, Fossi shifted her feet in the dark, stumbling against an unseen step. Instinctively, she reached out to him to steady herself.

He caught her hand. Despite everything, her traitorous body reacted, burning at the touch.

"Careful. There's a step there." He chuckled again. "Come this way. The medieval great hall is through here."

He drew her up the dim narrow stone stairs and through another door into the large central hall flooded with daylight.

Fossi blinked. It was a brisk dowsing of cold water, that light.

In the sunlit room, his expression was all polite solicitation, nothing more.

In it, she could clearly see that their *moment* back at the door had been nothing more than Daniel being a kind friend and helping her feel welcome in his home.

For the seven hundred and fourth time, she gave herself a stern mental rattle.

You would build a castle out of cobwebs, Foster Lovejoy.

Daniel laughed as the Linwood boys bounded up the stairs behind them and darted into the soaring great hall with its minstrel gallery and enormous fireplace, fluttering banners and aged beam ceiling.

Everything was a whirlwind of greeting and unpacking after that.

Many hours later, Fossi slowly peeled down the sleeves of her carriage dress and pulled a dressing gown over her shift.

She had been assigned a lovely, Tudor-era bedroom with dark paneling and an intimidating poster bed that called to mind a fortress. Wine-colored velvet hung around the bed and framed the mullioned window with its lovely aspect of the rolling Gloucestershire hills.

She sat at her dressing table and stared into the mirror.

It was always a shock, seeing her face. Inside, she felt so young, so vibrant.

But the mirror didn't reflect that. There she saw a woman with wrinkles starting around her eyes. A plain face that was too round and eyes that lacked anything distinguishing.

What has gotten into you? she asked the pale-faced woman who stared back at her. *You must cease this madness.*

How her father and siblings would contemn her for entertaining romantic thoughts of Lord Whitmoor. They would call her thirty ways a fool and with just reason. No man looked at Foster Lovejoy with interest, particularly not one of the most sought-after gentleman in Britain.

Daniel was a friend. Nothing more.

"Stop being obtuse," she muttered to herself.

It was, of course, another mathematical pun.

But she turned to her bed with a heart too heavy to find even fleeting pleasure at her own cleverness.

THAT FEELING LINGERED with Fossi the next morning when she met Mrs. Evans-Clark, the housekeeper, for a tour of Whitmoor House. Daniel and Lord Linwood had risen early to enjoy a bruising ride. Jasmine was not feeling well and the children had stumbled off to the stables to inspect a new litter of puppies, which left Fossi to Mrs. Evans-Clark's care to orient her to the house.

Fortunately, the lady in question had bonhomie to spare.

"I trust you had a delightful rest, Miss Lovejoy?" she beamed as Fossi joined her in the medieval great hall.

"Yes, thank you."

"Excellent, excellent. I always want guests here to feel like this home is theirs, too." Rosy-cheeked and dumpling-round, Mrs. Evans-Clark was cheer personified in her bustling dress and floppy mobcap.

"I am hardly a guest, Mrs. Evans-Clark. Merely a hired employee—"

"No, no. That I do not believe. His lordship said you were to be treated like a guest and so I shall."

Fossi stomped on the thrill of delight that washed through her at those words. Daniel had thought about her? Enough to mention it to Mrs. Evans-Clark?

A friend. He's a friend.

"Come, then," Mrs. Evans-Clark said. "We'll have you laughing and enjoying yourself in no time. His lordship said you were to have run of the library for your work. Let us start there, shall we?"

Mrs. Evans-Clark kept up a steady stream of commentary as they went. Which truly was a blessing, as Fossi couldn't control the depth of her interest about Daniel's house and surely would have embarrassed herself. Mrs. Evans-Clark did an admirable job of anticipating every possible question.

"His lordship loves this library something fierce," Mrs. Evans-Clark said as she stirred the fire, waving a hand to encompass the dark bookshelves lining the walls and table in the center of the room. "I believe he's read every book here. I find the Tudor wainscoting quite dark myself, but his lordship thinks it cozy."

Surveying the room, Fossi had to agree with Daniel. The age-darkened wood did lend the room an air of warmth and comfort.

Of course, Mrs. Evans-Clark's opinions did not stop at the library.

"As you can see, the former owners of the house were quite dedicated to using weaponry in their decorating." Mrs. Evans-Clark said as they passed a series of lances, pikes and claymores while climbing the wide central stairs.

About the blue drawing room overlooking the drive, she commented, "His lordship was most insistent we keep the original dark paneling and mullioned windows. He says they give the room personality. Can you imagine? A room with personality?"

It didn't take too long for Fossi to see Whitmoor House as an analogy of the man himself—hodgepodge construction, the clever side door, the hidden treasures. Forbidding on the exterior but once you knew the secret mechanism to get inside, it was light and color and unexpected beauty.

Mrs. Evans-Clark obviously adored her employer.

"He's a good man, he is, Lord Whitmoor. Kind and fair. You could not ask for more in a master, I say."

Daniel's hand was everywhere in the house, and Mrs. Evans-Clark delighted in pointing it out.

"His lordship insisted on placing the desk there, as it affords a view to the watchtower when the leaves have gone from the trees."

"His lordship made me promise to never change the color of the drapes in the dining room."

Telling, however, was a complete lack of anything related to Lady Alice.

No paintings of her. No embroidered pillows. Nothing.

If Fossi didn't already know, she would assume the man had never been married.

Finally, Fossi couldn't contain her curiosity.

"Did Lady Alice, his lordship's late wife, approve of his decisions regarding decoration?"

The jovial Mrs. Evans-Clark instantly turned prune-mouthed, eyes shuttering.

Fossi took a step back at the abrupt transformation.

"Lady Alice did not spend much time here. She couldn't abide this house. Called it doom and gloom." Mrs. Evans-Clark waved away the question, as if the presence of a mistress of the house were unimportant.

Oh.

"I wonder why Lord Whitmoor did not build her something more suited to her taste then?" It seemed logical. The man who cried over a box would certainly have spent some of his riches on a home for his beloved wife.

Mrs. Evans-Clark snorted. "I cannot say that his lordship cared one way or another what Lady Alice thought."

Well.

Well, well.

That was . . . unanticipated.

"Indeed." Fossi leaned forward. It was a pose she knew from past experience invited the listener to share a confidence. "I was under the impression that Lord Whitmoor was quite attached to his late wife. In fact, I am quite surprised not to have seen a portrait of her—

"Attached to her? Why on earth would his lordship keep a portrait of *that* woman?" Mrs. Evans-Clark looked well-incensed. "After everything she did?"

Fossi's face surely communicated her surprise. "But she was his wife, correct?"

Another snort. "That woman was never any sort of real wife to his lordship. Refusing to live under the same roof as him. Consorting with other men . . . no, it was deliverance when she ran off to Spain with that Mr. Terrance."

Gracious heavens!

"We all made a cheerful bonfire of her effects when she finally, truly left. Good riddance, I say." Here Mrs. Evans-Clark crossed herself. "Far be it from me to wish ill upon the dead, but suffice it to say, not a soul shed a tear when word reached us that Lady Alice had died. The Lord's justice will be served in the end, I say."

Fossi passed the rest of the tour in a haze of confusion. Follow-up questions flitted through her brain with startling force.

Had Daniel loved his wife then? Just because Mrs. Evans-Clark disliked the woman, it did not necessarily follow that Daniel did, too. Many a man had continued to love a less-than-worthy spouse.

Fossi could see Daniel possessing that sort of devotion.

Granted, the thought of the affections of his enormous heart being bestowed so undeservedly . . .

Fossi had to blink-blink the emotion back down her raw throat.

Was this what had driven him to withdraw behind fortress walls?

Goodness how unfair life could be. If Fossi had the love of such a man, she would cherish and adore him—

She stopped her thoughts right there before they spilled over into sentiment that would make her weep for days.

And so she listened as Mrs. Evans-Clark moved on to talk about the dual aspect of the long gallery, the excellent sound of the pianoforte and Lord Whitmoor's changes to the view over the north lawn.

It was only as they were passing along the corridor back to the central stairs, that Fossi realized they had skipped a room. Nestled into one corner with an impressive double-door entrance, it had to have spectacular views down to the river.

Fossi paused, motioning toward the closed doors.

"What is in that room, Mrs. Evans-Clark?"

The housekeeper paused, brows furrowing.

"It is nothing you need concern yourself about, Miss Lovejoy," she said after a moment. "It's just a room that his lordship keeps locked for himself."

"How . . . singular."

"Even I don't have a key for it," Mrs. Evans-Clark said. "His lordship always tends to the room on his own when he is here."

Mrs. Evans-Clark moved on, but Fossi remained rooted in place, staring at the barred doors.

A locked *room?*

It felt a little as if Fate had said, *I see your mysterious little box, and I raise you a sealed room. Trump that, if you can.*

"Come now." Mrs. Evans-Clark's voice at her elbow startled her. The woman had returned to fetch her. "Let's get you settled in the library with a nice pot of tea and some scones, shall we?"

Fossi nodded, though she was quite sure she would be unable to focus on sums for the rest of the day.

Lady Alice had not been worthy of Daniel's affections.

Daniel had purged his house of every trace of his dead wife but kept a mysterious box *and* a locked room.

Would the room also be full of stones and twine and the occasional feather?

And just when she thought she understood this man, she found herself literally back at the beginning.

It was too fitting for a spy master—the man who was his own personal labyrinth.

Whitmoored, indeed.

She had considered his fortress a monolith—a single, hollow tower. But that was simply not the case. He truly was a maze with unexpected twists and turns.

Who knew when one reached the center? What would one find there?

Such thoughts plagued her, pushing aside her efforts to reconcile *g* and *m* with *c* and the other odd variables in Daniel's equations.

After several hours of ineffectual work, Fossi found herself prowling the confines of his library, studying the most worn volumes, those with cracked spines. She imagined him opening them time and again to read . . . *Sonnets* by William Shakespeare, *Robinson Crusoe, The Iliad, Ivanhoe* . . .

Tales of romance and adventure.

She could see their fascination for him. How reading others' exploits would spur and inspire his own.

She pulled down the slim book of sonnets.

The pages fell open, revealing a pressed lily marking a passage—Sonnet 50.

The words slipped from the page.

How heavy do I journey on the way
When what I seek (my weary travel's end) . . .

A sonnet of sorrow and pain. Of never-ending grief.

For that same groan doth put this in my mind:
My grief lies onward and my joy behind.

Oh, Daniel.

The words caused her throat to ache and next she knew, Fossi found herself sitting on the floor, palms pressed to her eyes, choking back tears.

Because . . .

Because—

She *felt* his pain. Breathed it. Lived it.

An echo of her own loss.

Of a mother gone and a happiness that would never be recovered.

Fosse.

Wouldst that it had been.

She understood that type of grief . . . where only darkness lay along the path ahead—

Kindred soul meeting kindred soul.

And in that moment . . . she *knew.*

Against her better judgment, against her own mental warnings . . .

She loved him.

Daniel Ashton.

Hopelessly. Irrevocably.

It had been entirely too predictable, really.

Her circle of acquaintance was so small and the magnetism of his personality too great—

Naturally, she would be drawn to him, a moth to flame. Complicit in her own fiery demise.

In fact, the thought of throwing herself upon the pyre of her love

. . . sacrificing herself in one glorious blaze of color as a monument to him . . .

It had a certain maudlin appeal.

Particularly if it eased his anguish in any way.

But she doubted even a sacrifice of her entire soul would abate the grief he kept locked deep inside.

FOSSI WOKE THE following day, concerned that her newfound understanding and adoration of Daniel would shine from every pore, revealing her inner emotional state at the slightest glance.

She dreaded and yet longed to see him with equally fierce hope.

But the man made no appearance.

"His lordship is off helping a tenant farmer roof his cottage," was Mrs. Evans-Clark's explanation when Fossi inquired as to his whereabouts.

"Meeting with his land steward," was the next day's excuse.

"Off to Gloucester on business with his solicitor," was the reason the day after that.

On the fourth day, Fossi suspected Daniel was avoiding her.

The idea that Daniel was deliberately avoiding her caused Fossi pain and yet, strangely enough . . . hope.

Well . . . hope in a sad, demented sort of way.

Avoidance required effort.

Avoidance implied that he thought of her and had devised a plan of action.

But why?

Wasn't she a friend?

Why avoid Foster Lovejoy?

Was he like Mr. Young once upon a time? Did he consider her tiresome and an abuser of his kindness?

That thought burned with vicious mortification.

But she was his employee . . . she didn't *require* his kindness. There was no societal reason for him to feel obligated to be amiable towards her. He could send her away at any time if he found her irksome.

So perhaps she was wrong about the deliberate avoidance then.

But . . .

He wasn't gone all day. He *did* return. He just ensured he was never where Fossi was.

She realized this as she strolled the garden in the late afternoon on the fifth day after her arrival at Whitmoor House, trying to calm her emotions and tire her muscles enough that she would find sleep once evening fell.

Daniel had not shown himself all day. Everyone had said he was gone to town (the butler) or out visiting (Mrs. Evans-Clark) or . . . something.

But Fossi chanced to look up at that mysterious corner room with its locked doors that no one entered.

Sunlight poured through one window and out the opposite pane . . . rimming a tall man in silhouette.

A man who looked out to the garden and surely saw her as clearly as she could see him.

For a man who was theoretically *not* avoiding her, Daniel had every appearance of wishing to remain invisible.

And why couldn't she decide if such avoidance—if it *did* exist—was a good or bad thing?

Chapter 16

THE LOCKED ROOM
WHITMOOR HOUSE
SEPTEMBER 26, 1828

Daniel was avoiding her.

Even worse, he was quite sure Fossi *knew* he was avoiding her. She was far too intelligent and observant.

That moment with the entry door . . .

Daniel drew in a deep, fortifying breath.

He had known there was *something* between him and Fossi. But it wasn't until he held her bare hand in his that he realized precisely *how much* chemistry they had.

Sparks. Electricity.

He had lived long enough to understand exactly how rare such a connection really was.

As they had stood in front of the door, her back to his chest, he had nearly caved. Wrapped an arm around her waist, pulled her against him . . . she would have been soft and warm in his arms. The motion felt so natural, an outward expression of what his heart already knew. Even five days on, the tangible feel of her hadn't left him.

And given how her breath had hitched and skin blushed, she had not been unaffected.

So much fire burned just beneath her surface. She would never be a dull companion, her manners easy and unaffected. With her quick wit, she would always match him. Her mind always three steps ahead.

Anyone could be beautiful, Daniel had long ago decided. The world abounded in beautiful women.

But it took something more for a person to be beautiful *and* interesting. A certain spark that captured the mind as well as the heart.

Foster Lovejoy failed to understand her charms. Her complete lack of artifice was one of many traits that drew him. She would never play emotional games, as Alice had.

But after the Door Fiasco, as he mentally dubbed it, distance had seemed . . . wise.

Fossi was an emotional complication he could not afford.

Guilt swept through him with brutal force, crushing from all directions. Regret that Fossi could never be more to him. Shame because she deserved better than his erratic hot-and-cold behavior. Deep-rooted blame for the event two years ago that had brought him to this point.

He had to keep a laser-like focus on his goal. Too much depended on it.

Returning to Whitmoor House had brought home, quite literally, the enormity of the task before him.

He stood in the room he kept under lock and key. It hurt, being here. Guilt threatened to drag him under. Which explained why it had taken him five days to work up the courage to enter. But seeing the space again gave him continued resolve.

He would fix his mistake.

This room was his past and his future. And neither could feature Foster Lovejoy in any permanent way.

Of course, all these thoughts did not prevent him from staring at her as she paced the garden out the window.

She was upset. He could see it in the tense line of her back, the inward slouch of her shoulders.

He had missed her, these past few days.

And his foolish heart decided that it couldn't tolerate the thought of Fossi being hurt. Even if he were the cause.

He relocked the room and was halfway down the stairs before he admitted what he was doing.

He should just continue to avoid her. Listen to all the guilt his conscience shouted his way.

She would finish her work for him and, once he fixed his mistake, she would remember him no more.

But . . .

He was helpless to stay away.

The one person who could possibly solve his situation was also rapidly becoming a source of its potential demise.

Impossible contradictions.

He found her seated on a bench in the rose garden. The air had acquired the subtle crispness of fall, making the warm sun all the more precious.

Consequently, her head was bare—her bonnet nestled beside her on the bench—the caramel highlights in her hair glinting in the sunlight. She had her face tilted up toward the autumn sky. The angle emphasized the graceful beauty of her neck, the alabaster porcelain of her skin.

She stole his breath.

His feet crunched on the gravel walk, startling her.

Her head jerked upright, and she bounded to her feet, bobbing a polite curtsy, head down.

"Lord Whitmoor." A telling flush spread upward from her neck, her gaze fixed on his toes.

Back to that, were they?

"I trust you have settled in well, Fossi?" He had no intention of retreating into formalities, despite his better judgment.

"Yes. Mrs. Evans-Clark has been most accommodating."

She finally lifted her head and pinned him with those midnight eyes of hers.

Had he truly once considered them something so monolithic as plain brown? No, they were pools of warm chocolate, flecked with brandy and moss.

Damn.

A man was in a sad state once his thoughts ran to poetry.

Daniel rubbed the back of his neck.

Fossi straightened her shoulders further.

"I fear I shall be impertinent, my lord—"

"Daniel. Please."

She took in a sizable breath. "Daniel . . . you have had every appearance of avoiding my company. Is that true?"

Naturally she would immediately call him on the carpet.

A long, drawn out pause.

A multitude of answers flitted through his mind. Denial? Truth? Distraction?

He went with, "Would the answer matter?"

Annoyance flitted across her face. She nearly stamped her foot.

"Friends don't let friends answer questions with another question." She folded her arms across her chest.

Ah. Schooled yet again by Fossi Lovejoy.

Damn but he adored this woman.

"I would know if I have offended you in any way," she continued.

"You have not offended me, Fossi." Voice low and quiet.

"But you do not deny you have been avoiding me?"

More silence.

She looked past his shoulder, as if staring at him caused her pain.

Which, in turn, made his heart lurch.

Finally, she shook her head and bravely brought her gaze back to his.

"I am a simple woman, Daniel." Deep breath. "I don't understand how to play the games of the *ton*. Despite a few, perhaps unwise, forays into the realm of flirtation, I do not understand such rules. If you wish a certain behavior from me, please ask for it. If I have been remiss in some way, please correct me."

Curse this woman and her humility. So willing to own every aspect of herself.

How could he state the truth?

You see, Fossi, I find myself wishing for more than mere friendship from you, but given that I have a problem with a time portal to solve that will, in turn, likely negate your presence in my life . . .

"Being home has seemed . . . difficult for you." She spoke softly, placing her words with gentle care. "I would assume that the memories of . . . of—" Here she paused. Swallowed. And then continued. "—of Lady Alice must be overwhelming."

Shock chased Daniel's spine.

It seemed a blasphemy, Alice's name on Fossi's lips.

How had she known—

Servants. It had to be his servants.

Though it was not as if his marriage to Lady Alice Montague were a clandestine thing.

Dark, perhaps. Grim and dismal, certainly.

But not a secret.

Studying Fossi standing before him with her sun-tangled hair and quiet elegance . . . the difference between the two women could not be more pronounced.

Fossi's honesty and goodness and cleverness.

And Alice . . . the exact opposite of all that.

No. There were no memories of Alice here.

Fossi misunderstood his silence. She licked her lips and looked away.

"I must apologize, Lord Whitmoor. I have overstepped—"

"No, you have not—"

"Do you miss her?" Fossi leaned forward, as if she couldn't stop the empathy she felt.

That question landed on his psyche with a dull splat.

Did he *miss* Alice?

"Miss her? That woman? Good heavens, no!" The words poured out of him. "Alice was not much of a wife to me."

"But . . . you have her box." Fossi gazed at him with genuine confusion. "You care about the box. Quite significantly."

Daniel's heart stilled, thoughts instantly winging to the room he had just locked behind himself.

How had Fossi learned about the box? Granted, he was not terribly circumspect in his attachment to it.

"No. No, you are mistaken, Fossi. That box never belonged to Alice."

He couldn't look at her, the weight of guilt and memory and responsibility too heavy. His throat clenched around emotions, tight and raw.

Promise you will keep it for me. Don't forget.

Daniel stared across the lawn and into the surrounding trees beyond. Why was talking about this so hard? But Fossi . . . she pulled these things from him.

"No . . . that box," he said with a slow shake of his head. "That box . . . it belonged to Simon."

A pause.

"Simon?" she prompted so softly he barely heard.

He brought his eyes back to her.

"My son."

My son.

How could one single phrase encompass everything that Simon had been? Daniel's greatest joy. His deepest sorrow. The salvation of his future.

Fossi said nothing.

Her silence came not from discomfort but from understanding.

She *knew.*

Foster Lovejoy with her wisdom and generous heart comprehended what it meant to lose someone so dear.

Tears welled in her eyes but did not fall.

"It was Simon's treasure box." Voice gruff. "He was barely six years old. You have nieces and nephews. You know how children are at that age. Every smallest thing is the greatest prize. A seashell. A sparkling rock. A smooth twig."

"He would give them to you." The quiver in her voice said she understood. That she *saw* what his relationship with Simon had been.

"Yes. We would play at pirates or treasure hunters, and he would come running to me with something new for his box."

"What have you here, Simon?" Daniel squatted down next to the small boy's side.

"Rocks." Simon grinned merrily, his blue eyes lit with mischief. "This rock has sparkles in it, Papa. Look." He held up one of his prizes, turning it until it caught the sunlight and glittered.

"That is a very fine rock, my boy." Only years of practice allowed Daniel to keep his voice grave and serious. "Impressive, even."

Simon nodded earnestly. "It is." He placed the rock in Daniel's hand. "Promise you will keep it for me?"

"Of course."

"Don't forget."

"I won't. But let's put it into the box with all the others just to be sure."

Simon darted to his feet, instantly worming his small hand into Daniel's grasp. He skipped at Daniel's side as they walked toward the house.

"I have lots of treasures."

"That you do, Simon."

"I am a master treasure hunter."

"You are."

"And you are a master secret keeper, aren't you, Papa?"

"Something of the like."

"Good. I know you will keep my treasures safe for me."

Except Daniel hadn't kept the most important treasure safe.

He had made a catastrophic mistake.

"I-I brought him some sweets from a trip. I didn't know . . . I should have thought—" Daniel swallowed back the lump that threatened to choke him. "He had a reaction. His throat swelled shut and he couldn't breathe. I was helpless to do anything. It was all my fault."

IT WAS ALL my fault.

Daniel's words echoed through Fossi's brain. The sheer devastation in that single sentence.

A son. Daniel had lost a child.

Her heart hammered out of her chest, desperately trying to beat its way to him.

Daniel appeared so broken. His face too bleak.

All light and life and color snuffed out.

"The best of me died with him." Daniel turned and looked back over the fields again, expression utterly shuttered, emotions tucked deep within his fortress.

But she *knew*. The deeper he felt, the more iron he would seem.

And in his quiet hours, he would press a lily of remembrance into a Shakespearean passage to mark his grief.

What could Fossi say that would not be inadequate? Words were paltry substitutes.

Her foolish heart pulled her forward, compelling her to *Do Something*.

The one thing no one ever did for her.

Without thinking, she closed the distance between them. Her arms wrapped around his waist of their own volition, her face pressing into his chest, breath jagged.

Take my comfort, her actions whispered. *You do not need to be iron and granite around me. Lean on me.*

Even Lord Whitmoor needed to be held.

Physical contact was probably as scarce in his world as it was in hers.

He froze for only the briefest moments. And then rapidly reciprocated.

His arms clutched her to him, lungs heaving under her cheek—the deep, rasping sounds of a man fighting to hold his broken spirit together.

"It was my fault," he repeated against her hair. "I k-killed my precious, s-sweet boy—" His voice ended on a gasp.

She responded by holding him tighter.

Here. I am here.

I see you.

I stand as witness to your pain.

His lungs a bellow under her cheek. Her own sobs mingling with his.

A chill breeze ruffled her skirts. Sheep bleated in a nearby field.

Little by little, his serrated breathing subsided, his grip loosened. She reined back her own emotions.

And still he held her, cheek resting against the top of her head.

Warmth bloomed between them.

His arms shifted, his hold moving from comfort to something . . . different.

Affection, perhaps?

All the while, Fossi's brain screamed at her.

Daniel is holding *you. You are in his embrace.*

He completely engulfed her. Peppermint. Bay rum. Strong arms and deep chest. Her hands pressed into his back, the thump of his heart beneath her ear.

So many sensations at once . . .

Overwhelming in their force.

The moment extended and stretched.

Fossi knew she should step back. Break the contact.

But it felt so right, being in his arms like this. And once she stepped back . . .

She would never be so close again.

And her foolish, stupid heart would not allow her to relinquish him. He would have to push her away.

Finally, he did just that. Gave a tight squeeze and let her go.

Fossi ignored that pang that accompanied his actions.

She pulled back, fixing a kind smile to her face.

"Thank you," he whispered, running thumbs underneath his eyes, wiping away the evidence of his grief.

He heaved several deep, steadying breaths, looking at a point beyond her head.

This allowed her to study him unfettered. The line of his nose with its small bump in the middle. The sun ray wrinkles beside his eyes. A small spot of whiskers just south of his jaw that had been missed when shaving.

When had his face become so dear?

"Would you like to talk about Simon?" Fossi had to ask it. His gaze swung back to hers. "I think when we trap beautiful things deep inside us, they can fester and cause . . . harm. Beauty is meant to be shared."

The same went for uglier emotions too, but she declined to point that out.

He blew out a heavy gust of air, bowing his head before finally nodding. He lifted his head, eyes so . . . haunted. With a tentative smile, he offered her his arm.

Fossi stared at it for the barest moment before understanding.

With almost sacred reverence, she looped her hand through his elbow, the heat of his arm burning through her gloves.

He motioned for them to walk.

They moved in silence. Across the rose garden, through an arched gate and down the wooded lane.

The quiet should have felt oppressive but, as always with Daniel, it was a companionable thing.

Part of Fossi reeled from the revelation and actions of the last half hour. The other half sighed in amazement that she was strolling with Lord Whitmoor as a debutante might.

She waited.

Finally, Daniel cleared his throat. "He was a terrible scamp, was Simon. Always into mischief."

"Did he favor you?"

"Yes. Dark hair, blue eyes. Terrible curiosity."

Fossi smiled as he shared Simon with her. A little boy who loved outdoors more than sleep. Who constantly dismantled things to discover how they worked. Who specialized in sticky kisses and lisping whispers.

"Say what you will about Alice and her later behavior," Daniel said after a solid hour of telling tales, "she gave me Simon, and for that, I am grateful."

Fossi knew she should let it go, but her mind latched on to Lady Alice. This woman had been his *wife*.

"Was she a good mother, Lady Alice?"

"Heavens, no." He snorted. "I doubt Alice had a maternal bone in her entire body. Our marriage was not . . . cordial."

Ah.

She held her tongue.

He appeased her curiosity. "Before our marriage, I did not take the time to get to know Alice as I should have. I allowed others' opinions and my own vanity to sway me. Yes, she was beautiful externally, but as the poet has said, 'The beauty of my wife is but skin deep.' That was Alice. She pretended affection, but I found her locked in a scandalous embrace with another man soon after our marriage."

"Gracious."

"Do I shock you? Should I cease?"

"No, not at all. Merely sharing your horror."

They passed over a small stream. Sheep baaed in the distance.

"We came to an agreement after that incident. She would provide me with an heir that I knew to be mine, and I would grant her freedom afterward. She kept her part of the bargain, living with me here at Whitmoor House until Simon's birth. Then she . . . left." A pause. "And I let her go."

"Many a man would not have."

"I am not so proud as to force a woman to endure my company unwillingly. She seemed genuinely happy to bid Simon and me goodbye." The hardness of his tone belied the congeniality of his words.

Such loss there, Fossi realized. But even with Alice's perfidy, he had behaved with honor and graciousness.

Traits Daniel Ashton had in abundance, she now knew.

He helped her over a turnstile and offered his arm again, leading her around the upper edge of a field.

Fossi's thoughts tumbled and turned.

It didn't require sleuthing to understand what was in the locked corner room. Simon's nursery, perhaps? A shrine to a lost child?

And would Daniel ever decide to allow his heart to heal? Or would he continue to pound it over and over on the anvil of his guilt?

"Well, that is quite a bit about my family. Have you heard from yours?" Daniel finally asked, shifting the topic from his pain to hers.

Heavens. Had her family spared a thought for her departure? She had thought of them enough, she supposed. But then she had always had greater affection for them than they for her.

"No, but I do not expect to hear from them."

"Why ever not?"

They skirted around a small stream, giving Fossi time to formulate a more positive answer than, *Because I'm quite sure they were content to see me leave.*

"To begin, I didn't tell my father where I was going—"

"Wait—" Daniel came to a stop and faced her. "Your father doesn't know you are here? Working for me?"

"No."

His brows drew down. "Why would you not tell him—"

Fossi looked away, biting her lip. "He wouldn't understand, Daniel. He is a good man but limited in his ability to comprehend the world. I didn't wish to bring any trouble upon you."

He reared back.

"Trouble for me?" The incredulity in his voice clearly communicated how absurd he found the idea.

Reverend Josiah Lovejoy cause problems for the powerful Lord Whitmoor?

Pshaw.

Daniel clearly did not understand her father.

"Obviously, my father could do nothing legally or even physically to harm you. I am of age and free to make my own decisions. But Reverend Lovejoy is decidedly skilled in the art of making himself a consistently felt nuisance." She pointed a finger at him. "*That*, my friend, is something you could do without."

"Ah. But I possess excellent nuisance-busting skills and a high tolerance for aggravation." He smiled easily and motioned for them to continue walking. "Though you were kind to concern yourself."

More silence as they crossed the field.

"Will you attempt a reconciliation with your father? When your task for me is completed?" he asked.

Fossi's heart lurched at the thought of leaving Daniel's employ. But, of course, that day would come . . . perhaps sooner than she would like.

As for the idea of Reverend Lovejoy welcoming her back into the family fold . . .

"I am not sure," she answered truthfully. "As I have stated before, I cannot imagine my father will be so accepting. It is why I wish to start a girl's school. It will not only grant me more permanent employment, but it will give my life purpose."

Daniel was quiet after her pronouncement.

"Is that—" he began. Paused. And then stopped walking again, forcing her to meet his gaze. "Is that what you want most from life then? To own a girl's school? That is your heart's desire?"

Gracious. As if she indulged in such sweeping hopes and dreams. Those were cares for much younger, prettier women.

Fossi controlled her shrug. "I cannot say it is my heart's desire, but it is a good choice and—"

"What *is* your heart's desire then?"

His gaze made her squirm. She found her eyes drifting beyond him, her tongue thick and awkward in her mouth.

She swallowed.

"I . . . I do not allow myself to have such a thing as a *heart's desire*."

"Why not?"

She sighed, defeat settling over her. "Because why wish for the unattainable? It only leads to discouragement and discontent—two emotions I would be happy to live without."

He frowned and turned from her, walking on. He looked . . . disappointed. Which shouldn't have upset her . . . and yet, it did.

She quickened her steps to catch up.

"I *did* make a list," she offered as she drew alongside him again. "A list of things I wanted to do. After our conversation in London, I realized that I could demand more from my life."

He nodded, shooting her a sideways glance. "What are the items on your list?"

She clasped her hands in front of her. "They were silly things, like buying shoes for family members and repairing Faith's cottage."

"But if your family doesn't know your whereabouts, then you haven't sent them money for those items."

"Correct. I was hoping your solicitor could help and perhaps send some money anonymously."

"Of course. That can be easily arranged." He switched at some grass with his walking stick. "Giving to others is admirable, but please tell me there was something on your list for yourself?"

"A few things."

"Like what?"

"Simple things. Taste a pineapple, own a Kashmir shawl, receive a gift, dance at a ball . . ."

"You have never received a gift?" His eyes flared wide.

"You mustn't be so horrified," she smiled. "Gifts were not part of my father's religious beliefs, even if there had been the money for them. I cannot miss what I have never known."

"A gift." He snorted, a gentle puff of a laugh. "Trust you, Foster Lovejoy, to have such manageable dreams."

He came to a full stop and bowed, low and proper.

"Along with that, would you do me the honor of saving me the first waltz at the harvest ball next week?"

"Gracious! N-no, my lo—Daniel." Fossi blinked and then flushed a vividly painful red. "I did not say that to prompt you to ask me—"

"It would be my honor to dance with you, Foster Lovejoy." He smiled a smile that said he found her flustered response delightful.

She bit the inside of her cheek. "I cannot accept, Daniel. I feel ashamed."

"Nonsense. It is settled." He gave a gentle laugh and motioned them along, ignoring her spluttering. "But I'm not going to let you off so easily. Aside from a dance with myself—"

"My lord." Surely her cheeks would ignite the surrounding grass.

"—deep in your soul, what do you want?"

She barely stopped the honest answer from escaping.

You.

She wanted him. The fierce heart that wept over his son's little treasures. His intelligent insights. His gentle humor. The warmth of his smile.

As impossible as walking on the moon, those things.

So she went with, "I simply want what others have."

Vague. A non-answer really.

"Like marriage?" He persisted.

Yes. Exactly like marriage. A best friend. Someone to love, to serve . . . to cherish and be cherished in return.

Silence hung between them, a damning answer in its own right.

She dodged a direct reply.

"As I hinted earlier, sometimes dreams are impossible," she finally said. "So why waste energy wishing for impossibilities?"

He deflated a little. As if her dreams were . . . disappointing.

Which she allowed, in the harsh light of day, they were. Pathetic, dreary things.

So she said the next thing that popped into her head.

"Marriage might be beyond my grasp but"—she paused—"I would like . . . a witness. A witness for my life."

"*Ah.*" Such a deep sound. Profound.

Of course, he understood exactly what she meant. They were two halves of a whole, after all.

A witness. Someone to walk beside her through life. To say, *I see you. I understand you. I want to experience life with you.*

It was a painful acknowledgment. Because life did not always grant one's greatest desires.

It was what made life poignant—that distance between one's current position and where one wished to be. Measured in dreams lost and reality accepted.

Daniel, she was sure, understood this better than most.

"What of you?" she asked. "What is your heart's desire?"

He swung his walking stick again, switching the tops off errant strands of wheat. "That is simple."

He fixed her with bleak eyes that blazed with almost unholy determination.

Voice fierce. "I want Simon back."

Chapter 17

The ferocity of his statement surprised even Daniel.

"I want Simon back," he repeated.

Fossi radiated pity.

"I would give just about anything to see my mother again." She placed a gentle hand on his arm. "Even one day with her."

Daniel nodded but didn't clarify the sincerity of his statement.

"You encouraged me to state more than impossible dreams, so I am now going to press you," she said, shooting him a faint smile. "What is your heart's desire?"

He *had* stated his truth.

He wanted Simon back.

Literally.

Completely.

He had made a mistake. A terrible, anachronistic mistake that set in motion a series of catastrophic events.

He had visited Kit for an afternoon in the twenty-first century and, on a whim, had returned home to Whitmoor House with a small bag of hard candy for Simon to experience.

Just a little taste of Daniel's own upbringing.

But Daniel had forgotten about his own father's allergic sensitivity to synthetic red food dyes. Simon had eaten half the bag one day without a problem. It was only the next day when he ate the rest . . .

Simon went into anaphylactic shock almost instantly, suffocating within precious minutes.

Fossi would restore the portal. Daniel would use it to prevent Simon's premature death.

That was the only answer to their current problem.

"I want a son." He gave her a partial truth.

He wanted Simon.

Simon was his heir. His future.

Daniel truly was his own eighth great-grandfather. As such, he needed to have a son and he had one . . . in Simon.

When Daniel had introduced the twenty-first century candy which caused Simon's untimely death, he had unleashed a series of catastrophic events, perhaps even the earthquake itself.

Daniel *had* to right this wrong.

Simon's death was an aberration that had to be corrected.

Guilt reared its head again . . . whispering that Fossi was a complication and distraction. That his affection for her threatened his goal.

No. Daniel would not deviate from his path. He loved his boy too much.

"So you will remarry?"

No. "Eventually. Perhaps."

She angled her head, as if his answer didn't make much sense.

Which, from her point of view, it obviously didn't.

He was deflecting.

Marriage to Alice had been . . . difficult. Daniel was not eager to embrace the institution again. Besides, once he returned to the past and restored Simon, he would have no need of a wife.

Based on his understanding of the space/time continuum and Einstein's predictions regarding time travel, this current timeline was an aberration.

Daniel had disrupted the timeline when he inadvertently caused Simon's early death. This, in turn, had led to things happening that never should have—namely, the earthquake.

Daniel's father—the seventh Lord Whitmoor—had been a history professor at the University of Gloucester. The man had extensive knowledge of the area and its history.

Nowhere had Daniel ever heard or read about an 1820s-era earthquake.

Certainly earthquakes did happen on occasion—there had been a similar one in the area in 1990, for example—but Daniel was convinced the earthquake of 1826 was a deviation. Something that should never have occurred. An outward manifestation of the cosmic chaos Simon's death had caused.

Simon's death had thrown them on to an incorrect timeline. A world where an earthquake in Hereford *did* occur, breaking the portal, causing Jasmine to fall ill . . . and who knew how many other incorrect things.

Surely Fossi isn't one of those incorrect things, his conscience whispered.

He shook off the thought. No distractions.

The error of Simon's death had to be fixed. Daniel would return to the past and ensure that Simon never touched those damn modern candies. Everything would continue on as it should have from that point.

Simon would live.

The earthquake would never happen.

Jasmine would never become ill.

Daniel and Fossi would never meet—

He shook away the jarring pang that accompanied the thought.

But Fossi . . .

She should marry.

A witness for my life.

That is what she had said. Not marriage. Not a partnership. Nothing so grand for Foster Lovejoy.

She deemed those things . . . impossibilities.

Simply a witness. Someone to testify that you had come and gone. An observer of the trace of your life.

Daniel's throat tightened for about the twentieth time that day. He hated the thought of Fossi settling for merely a witness to her life.

He dreamed too big.

She dreamed *far* too small.

She deserved grand dreams. Enormous dreams. Dreams so large they overwhelmed.

But he couldn't say that to her.

And, worse, would he be the source of her not achieving even the modest dreams she did have, returning her to life in 1826?

The thought . . . hurt. He mentally shied from it, shoving it away.

"Tell me how your research goes," he said, effectively changing the subject. Moving them firmly back into employer and employee.

"Yes!" Her face lit in excitement. "I did have a remarkable insight just yesterday. I overheard Mrs. Evans-Clark asking the footman to stop clinking the silverware as they polished it for the ball. But the tonality of the sound gave me another insight into the tuning forks. I may have landed on a way to meld the two theorems using frequency heights."

She chattered on, outlining her ideas.

It was a brilliant observation. *She* was brilliant.

She burned so bright. So captivating. Part of him retreated in fear. Worried that she would bewitch him into giving up his goal.

He intended to right the mistakes of his own past and forge a different future. A future where they would never meet.

Where Foster Lovejoy would not be a part of his life.

And he had to accept that.

THE NEXT FEW days flew by in a flurry of activity. Footmen hung bows of wheat sheaves and maids polished every surface. The kitchen was a hum of activity.

Daniel left Fossi to her sums as he worked with his housekeeper and steward to coordinate the festivities.

Which meant it wasn't until the afternoon before the ball that he found time to visit Simon's room again.

Daylight drifted through the windows, casting the room in long shadows and highlighting the dust hanging in the air. It was a cheery space, abounding in energy and hope.

Which somehow made its silence all the more terrible.

The rocking horse in the corner stood motionless. The blocks and toy soldiers were stacked in precise formation on shelves. School books rested on the child-size desk. The bed drapes were neatly pressed and stretched tight.

A heaven waiting to be restored.

Shutting the door, Daniel opened the windows and set to dusting the space.

Nothing could be amiss.

He worked for an hour or so and then finally just sat at the tiny desk chair and stared over the landscape. Too many emotions chased him. Too many memories.

Simon racing with his dog across the lawn.

Simon tumbling with laughter into Daniel's arms.

Simon snuggled against his chest, fast asleep.

Ah, Simon. My bright, beautiful boy.

That ever-present guilt reared its ugly head, choking, suffocating.

He *had* to fix his mistake. Find redemption and absolution.

The *snick* of the door opening only registered once Jasmine perched next to him on the desk. She glanced around the room.

"Simon always loved this space." Her voice was tentative, uncertain of her welcome.

Wise woman.

"He did." *No.* "He *does.* He loves his room."

Jasmine did not miss his change in verb tense.

She sighed.

"Daniel . . ." So weary.

"No, Jasmine. I don't want to argue with you—"

"I am the portal's *Keeper*." She placed a caring hand on his shoulder. "I see this situation in ways you cannot."

"You're wrong. I am central to this problem. I caused it. It is mine to solve. This is my *son* we are talking about. My heir. My future in every possible way, both literal and figurative."

"I know. We all loved Simon and miss him but—"

"Imagine if this were Charles or James. You would be singing a different tune."

"No. I wouldn't." Her blue eyes sparked. "I *have* imagined it being one of my children, and I can absolutely empathize with losing a child. But you assume too much—"

"Jasmine—"

"Enough, Daniel." She sliced a hand through the air. "I'm only going to say this one last time. I am nearly certain that the portal—and, by extension, the universe itself—will *not* allow you to do this. Sometimes, we just have to accept that accidents happen."

Daniel shook his head. Guilt pounded. There was no forgiveness for this sin.

"The portal is *broken*, Jas" he said. "So until it's fixed, how can you say that with any certainty?"

A beat.

"You're not accounting for one critical fact: I am a unique member of the cosmic ocean." Daniel pressed his case, angling his body toward her. "I am my own great-whatever grandfather. I form a sort of pivotal loop. I was born in the twentieth century. If I am to be my own grandfather *then*, then I must have a child *here*. Simon was that child and his death broke the loop, throwing us onto a different timeline and causing new events with disastrous consequences. To fix everything, I must restore Simon as my heir—"

"Are you certain?"

"Pardon?"

"Are you *certain* the heir was Simon?"

Daniel paused. He wasn't certain, but any other explanation meant giving *up* Simon. And *that* was simply unacceptable.

"You don't know who your heir is, Daniel," Jasmine continued. "It's a mystery. The universe has never allowed us to see it. Something always happens to interfere when we've tried to look. Which, I might add, is evidence for my case. You're only thirty-seven. That's plenty of time to have a dozen more children."

Daniel lurched to his feet, the walls of the room closing in on him. Blame and regret crushed his lungs with brutal force. He paced to the window and then braced his hands on either side of the open window frame.

He shook his head. Left. Right. "No."

"Daniel, please. Think about this rationally. It is a paradox of such magnitude . . ." Jasmine sighed. "So let's play this forward."

"Jas, we have already been over this—"

"I know but humor me. You fix the portal and it what? Sends you back two years? You know how fickle it can be. The portal might send you back a millennium or forward three months—"

"True, but you are its Keeper and it tends to listen to you when you prompt it to go somewhere."

Another pause.

"Fine. I will grant you that," she shrugged, "but the portal is still more of a cat than a dog. It's not eager to do my bidding, per se. It will do something I ask if it feels it's important or in everyone's best interest."

"Exactly." He turned around, lacing his fingers through his hair. "As I've repeatedly said, I introduced the modern candies which killed Simon. His death was a cosmic aberration which launched a series of new events, like the earthquake which caused the portal to stop working—"

"It's still your assumption that the earthquake is an aberration."

"Jasmine, as I've said, I don't remember any modern mention of it. And given my father's studies, I would have known—"

"That's thin circumstantial evidence at best. Not proof."

She held up a staying hand.

"So returning to my point," she continued. "Let's say you're correct. Fossi fixes the portal, you travel back two years and save Simon's life. Then what? You *still* exist in 1826, which means that there will be two of you, which is an enormous contradiction—"

"I don't think it will go like that, Jasmine. Again, we've talked about this." He shook his head and turned to look out the window again. "I've spent absurd amounts of time mentally reviewing what I know of Einstein's theories of Time. Time doesn't like paradoxes. Therefore, when I return to the past, my two selves will resolve. Once I correct the mistake of Simon's death, the ocean of Time will settle down and oscillate in harmony again. My two selves will merge into one and our current history will cease to exist. Time will revert to what it should have been."

"Are you willing to take the risk?" she asked.

"Pardon?"

"*If* things go down as you seem think they will, none of us will remember that this timeline ever existed. That could include you, as well."

Silence.

"It is entirely likely you will forget Fossi." Jasmine connected the dots for him. "I would not go forward assuming that you will remember her enough to track her down. You might gain Simon only to lose Fossi."

More silence.

Typically Jasmine. She had already understood the depth of his attachment to Fossi.

But . . .

That was the deal, wasn't it?

When he corrected his mistake, this slice of history would cease to exist. The world would turn back to November 1826.

Fossi would forget that she had ever met him. He would revert to being a stranger. He alone would retain the memory of this time.

And, perhaps, not even him. Who knew what would happen when Time realigned itself? If this offshoot of time were truly erased as if it had never existed . . .

It was possible he would forget her too.

He wanted to howl his frustration. Why did this have to be a choice?

"That said, I still stand by my earlier thoughts," Jasmine continued. "The universe has a built in safety valve, like you say. But its protection of the space/time continuum is more stringent than you think. I'm not sure I believe in the concept of deviant timelines. The universe simply won't allow such disruptive things to occur. Despite how much it pains me to say it, I don't think Simon's death is what needs correction."

"You're wrong." Emphatic.

She sighed. "Perhaps. All I can see is that Fossi holds the answer."

"And she's working on our solution. I think she is close."

Daniel turned back to Jasmine. He didn't miss the bags under her eyes, the exhaustion lines beside her mouth.

Jasmine was slipping away from them, the chaos of the portal taking its toll.

He needed absolution.

Jasmine needed a cure.

Fossi's solution couldn't come quickly enough, for everyone's sake.

But what about Fossi herself? That bit of conscience whispered. *Everyone benefits from her efforts except her.*

Daniel pushed the thought away.

He had no answer.

Chapter 18

The night before the harvest festival, Fossi found a package on her bed wrapped in paper and tied with a pretty ribbon.

A note was nestled beside it.

Thank you for lending your acute intellect to my fractious problem. I am exponentially grateful.

She smiled at the puns, turning the card over and back.

There was no signature.

There couldn't be, of course, because it was quite improper for an unmarried man to give a present to an unmarried lady.

Fossi waited for a sense of outraged morality to raise its hand.

Nothing.

Well, then.

She stared at the bold handwriting scrawled across the foolscap for a full three minutes, firmly telling her racing heart to *cease this foolishness.*

But the silly organ would not obey.

It galloped and frolicked and made such a jolly mayhem in her chest, she feared she might burst.

Daniel had . . . cared. He had listened and wanted to give her this. Not just the present itself. But the experience of having received a gift for the first time.

She traced a finger over the silky soft ribbon.

She could see why others found gifts to be so thrilling.

What was contained within?

As this would likely be the only present she ever received, she desperately wanted to savor the sensation.

She gently pulled on the bow, slowly unraveling it.

She parted the paper to reveal another layer of tissue. But beyond the tissue—

"*Oh!*"

A gloriously soft length of Kashmir tumbled onto her bedcovers—a vibrant red and blue paisley border against yards of soft cream. Luxurious and incredibly expensive.

Fossi gathered the length of fabric into her hands, fingers shaking, clutching it to her chest.

The kind man.

I hear you, the gift said. *I witness you.*

She buried her nose into it, breathing deep. Could she detect lingering bay rum?

Would he keep his promise to dance with her tomorrow?

Embarrassment tinged her cheeks.

Part of her hoped he would forget, as she wasn't sure she could bear the mortification of having practically *asked* him to ask her to dance.

Of course, there was another part of her—the part that fully intended to sleep with his shawl wrapped around her—that didn't care how the dance came to be . . . just that it did.

Now how was she supposed to sleep?

DESPITE THE ANTICIPATION for the next day, Fossi did manage to sleep. She credited the heavy warmth of her new shawl.

The shawl stayed with her throughout the day, adorning one shoulder as she cheered on tenant farmers and Daniel in sack races and foot ball. She draped it over her elbows as she and the vicar's wife judged the embroidery contest entries and then wrapped it around her upper body for warmth as dinner was served on groaning tables.

All too soon, Fossi had changed into her ball gown and members of the local gentry arrived at Whitmoor House. Lantern-lit carriages dotted the drive in a patient line, each one waiting to discharge its passengers.

The medieval great hall had been transformed. All the furniture had been removed and chairs installed around the perimeter. Flowers and greenery festooned the chandeliers and sconces. A roaring fire in the enormous hearth added to the cheer. A small orchestra tuned their instruments in the minstrel gallery, violins running scales beneath the hum of conversation.

Fossi surveyed it all with astonished eyes. *Heavens.* She had entered a fairy tale.

She scanned the room, knowing her eyes sought out one person in particular. As master of the house, he stood near the front door, greeting guests by name as they arrived. Dressed in a formal black cutaway coat with crisp white cravat and waistcoat, Daniel was elegance personified. More than one woman stole glances at him.

And *this* was the man who would ask her to dance—

"Foster! You look positively lovely this evening. I knew that color would become you."

Fossi startled and turned to find Marianne Knight at her elbow.

"Thank you." Fossi smoothed her hands down the sides of her red silk gown. "How lovely to see you again. I am glad you arrived safely."

"We did. Jasmine tells me you are to sing tonight. Is that so?"

Butterflies launched a valiant effort to breach the walls of her stomach. Fossi placed a hand over her abdomen to hold them in.

"We shall see."

But, of course, Jasmine was correct. Fossi was to sing. Daniel had asked it of her and Fossi had been helpless to refuse, despite her nerves and shy embarrassment.

How her father would rage over the vanity of her performing before a crowd. Not to mention the lurid reputation opera singers had in the public eye.

No. Her father would consider this performance a disgrace of apoplectic proportions.

But a musical performance was appropriate for a lady and as Daniel had wished it . . .

All too soon, the man himself made his way to the front of the room, standing on a small pedestal placed just for the occasion.

Daniel raised his hands for silence.

"Welcome one and all to Whitmoor House," he said. "It is a delight to see all my dear friends gathered for an evening of dancing and conversation."

Daniel continued on for a few moments, complimenting some and being good-naturedly ribbed by a heckler or two in the crowd. The moment passed too quickly.

"To launch the festivities this evening, I have invited Miss Foster Lovejoy to share her prodigious vocal talents with us. She is a rare delight." Daniel smiled and held out his hand to her. "Miss Lovejoy."

Fossi focused on his gaze, pulling strength from him as she took her place on the small pedestal and faced a room of staring eyes. She had never performed for so many people at one time.

The musicians struck up several cords. Those dratted butterflies choked her, and she missed the first two notes before beginning the song.

Daniel's shawl helped in the end. The warmth of it settled around her shoulders, and she forgot everything but the music.

As usual, she poured her soul into her voice. All the color she typically hid deep inside.

And in that moment, she felt whole. Not simply the shattered fragments of something potentially lovely.

But genuinely beautiful in her own right.

Daniel had done this, she realized. His belief and kindness and acceptance had, in turn, allowed her to fully accept herself.

The song trilled up and down, scales running, her voice ringing true and clear.

It felt glorious.

Thunderous applause met her final note. Fossi flushed and curtsied. And then curtsied again. She raised her head and looked for Daniel but couldn't see him for the crush.

She took the offered hand of a local gentleman and stepped down. Kindly faces surrounded her, offering congratulations and asking questions about her training.

The dancing was well underway before Fossi broke free of her admirers to scan the crowd again for Daniel.

Wasn't the next dance to be their promised waltz?

Later, Fossi would reflect on how quickly everything could change.

Through the crowd she spotted Daniel. His head was bent and a lady—a remarkably pretty woman, expensively dressed with jewels in her blond hair—pressed a hand to his shoulder, standing on tiptoe to whisper something in his ear.

The act of familiarity wasn't necessarily the problem.

However, Daniel smiled at the mysterious woman. It was his true smile, the one that lit his eyes and allowed a person straight inside his walls.

The one Fossi thought maybe he saved just for her.

The orchestra struck the opening strains of the waltz. Daniel didn't budge from his position, laughing and then replying to the woman.

Fossi felt a chasm open beneath her feet. A vast expanse of empty space that served to highlight the enormous gulf between Daniel and herself.

Of course he didn't remember their waltz. She had asked him to forget about it. And he was gracious and would take her at her word. It wasn't as if he genuinely *wanted* to waltz with her for her sake.

That would suppose deeper feelings.

Foster, you would spin a queen's robe out of coarse thread.

She was reliving that moment with Mr. Young all those years ago. The acute mortification. The sinking rock in her stomach.

You will never learn, will you? If a man cares for you, he will say so. Did that note earlier speak of love? Of affection? Of anything beyond polite gratitude?

No.

No, it had not.

Simply an expression of thanks wrapped in some mathematical puns. A generous gift to a *friend*.

Daniel drew the lady's hand through his arm, waving at someone across the room before turning back to smile merrily at the woman. His face utterly delighted.

Fossi's shawl pulled on her arms, a heavy weight. Was the room too warm?

"Miss Lovejoy." A voice at her elbow. "Would you do me the honor of this dance?"

Fossi turned to the middle-aged, stout man smiling beside her. Mr. Thomas. He had been introduced to her after she sang and had said kind things about her performance.

Daniel walked further away.

He didn't look back.

"I would be honored, Mr. Thomas," she said with a small smile.

Fossi turned away from Daniel and allowed Mr. Thomas to lead her into her first waltz, feet remembering the steps her mother had taught her long ago.

She smiled at Mr. Thomas' comments and asked questions. It didn't take much to get him talking about his horses and hunting dogs.

And with every down-up-up of the waltz, she mentally repeated.

Let him go. Let him go. Let him go.

Which was absurd in the extreme.

Daniel had never been hers in the first place.

⟞⟝

213

THE WALTZ WAS nearly over before Daniel realized he had missed it.

Damn.

His heart sank.

How could he have done such a thing?!

Georgiana and Sebastian Carew had arrived quite unexpectedly from Stratton Hall just as Fossi finished singing, surprising them all.

As Arthur Knight's younger sister, Georgiana knew about the time portal and had experienced her own trials with it years ago. She was now happily married to Sebastian Carew, the Earl of Stratton, and had a bevy of children. As some of the few people who knew his complete history, Daniel felt a deep connection with Lord and Lady Stratton and considered them to be an older brother and sister.

"Daniel." Georgiana placed a hand on his arm as he craned his neck, looking for Fossi. "Are you quite all right?"

"Yes, just trying to see Fossi."

Had Fossi remembered that they were to dance? He hadn't reminded her, but then he had every intention of being at her side, so it hadn't seemed necessary.

He couldn't easily spot her head amongst the crowd. Where had she gone?

"Will she fix the portal, do you think?" Georgiana quietly asked, standing on tiptoe to join him in his search.

"Absolutely. She is a true genius."

"She is a remarkable talent." That from Sebastian who stood beside Georgiana. "Her singing . . ." He trailed off into a look of wonder.

Daniel heartily agreed with the man.

His heart had nearly burst from his chest as she sang, voice soaring through the room.

Even in the twenty-first century with instant access to millions of songs and vocal performances, Fossi would have been remarkable.

In the nineteenth century performing before people who had rarely heard a well-trained voice . . . she was a revelation.

Heaven made earth-bound.

Daniel realized, yet again, that any woman could be beautiful from the outside in, but it took much more for a person to be beautiful from the inside out.

Foster Lovejoy was beautiful from the outer tips of her toes to her innermost soul.

Wasn't *that* a humbling thought?

And he had missed their waltz together. A waltz he had been looking forward to with far more anticipation than wisdom.

Finally he saw her. Across the room, she curtsied to Mr. Thomas and excused herself out a side door. One that led to a small corridor that opened into the Tudor-era courtyard.

Was she upset? Or just overwhelmed and wishing to escape the crowded room?

"Excuse me, if you would." He smiled at Georgiana and Sebastian.

Georgiana returned a far too-seeing grin, dazzling and full of mischief.

"Go to your Miss Lovejoy, Daniel," she said with a jerk of her chin. "We shall track down Linwood and torment him."

"Indeed, we shall. I've been practicing my dad jokes," Sebastian chuckled, waggling his eyebrows.

Poor Timothy Linwood.

"But I insist you introduce us to Miss Lovejoy before the evening is out, Daniel." Georgiana beamed at him and gave a little push. "Now, off you go or Sebastian will begin his torment with you."

"You think so little of me, darling." Sebastian placed a hand on his chest, expression mock-pained. "I was simply going to ask Daniel if he knew the difference between roast beef and pea soup?"

Daniel shook his head. "I think that's my cue to leave."

"Run." Georgiana gave a firmer push, but Sebastian's words reached him anyway.

"I believe anyone can *roast* beef, but only a truly talented person can—"

"Sebastian," Georgiana said warningly. "Let's go find Timothy."

Daniel chuckled.

How he had missed his friends.

DANIEL FOUND FOSSI five minutes later, seated on a bench in the small courtyard, her new shawl pulled tight around her shoulders. Music from the great hall drifted out. Braziers flared around the perimeter of the courtyard, sending tendrils of light flickering up the ancient walls and dancing across Fossi's face.

Heaven help him. She was beautiful. Stunning. The classical purity of her jawline and arched brows, the porcelain glow of her skin, the burnished chestnut of her hair.

How had he not seen her thus from the first moment they met?

Though, as he thought about it, he supposed he had. He just hadn't fully appreciated how thoroughly her exterior matched her interior.

The wine-red ball gown hugged her figure, showing her curves to advantage. The red silk gleamed in the firelight, contrasting ribbon of the same color setting off her lovely collarbones and small waist. Jasmine had suggested the shawl as a perfect match to the dress when he had asked her opinion.

He liked seeing Fossi wearing his gift. It was an unexpectedly possessive emotion and gave instant insight as to why it was considered taboo for men to give unwed women gifts of clothing. But the caveman part of him wanted to give her more, to stake his claim.

Such thoughts were not helping his feelings of guilt.

She glanced up as he approached, flashing a wan smile.

Ah.

Her eyes said everything he needed to know.

She *had* remembered his promise to dance with her. This was her first ball and her first dance—both important items on her meager list of dreams—and he . . . hadn't been there for her.

She had danced with a stranger.

His stomach plummeted. Disappointment in himself joining his guilt over Simon.

Typical of Fossi, she was not angry with him.

No. She would never turn her emotions outward and throw them at the feet of others.

The world had let her down and passed her by too often for Foster Lovejoy to feel anger over a missed dance.

Anger would imply *expectation*.

Expectation that someone else would meet her halfway. Expectation that she mattered to others.

By now, he knew Fossi didn't do expectations.

But other emotions were written upon her face—wistfulness, sadness, resignation.

It was the resignation, in particular, that hit him hard.

The expression that said, *This is how life treats me. I expect nothing else. It is why my hopes and dreams are so small. And even then, I cannot reach them.*

He *hated* that he had been the one to put that look on her face.

"There you are." He winced at the banality of his words, his voice sounding far too loud in the gloom.

She sucked in a deep breath. "Here I am." Her tone was light, belying the unhappiness in her eyes.

They were to speak in inanities, he supposed.

But, as usual, she surprised him.

"Thank you for the shawl, my lo—Daniel. It is lovely. " She pulled the shawl tighter around her, wrapping a hand into its softness.

Using the thing to create a barrier between them. To swallow back her sadness and move on.

He didn't want her resignation.

He wanted her anger.

He wanted her to believe in herself enough to be *angry* at him for his behavior. To demand more.

Daniel clenched his jaw.

Dimly, part of him recognized that Fossi felt this way because she cared about him.

Just as he cared for her.

Yes, they were friends. But there was decidedly *more* between them too.

More that could only lead to heartache.

He *would* bring Simon back. Daniel would not give up on his son.

Fossi would forget about him.

Would he forget her too?

And why did just the thought make his chest squeeze and his breathing tight?

He sat beside her on the bench.

She did not look at him, instead focusing on the patterns the braziers were casting on the wall opposite.

"You sang beautifully," he murmured.

"Thank you."

"I am terribly sorry I missed our waltz. No sense dancing around the subject."

He meant it as a joke.

She didn't smile.

Instead, she flinched at his words. Gave her head a tiny shake, as if trying to drive something from her mind.

"There is nothing to apologize for. We had not formally agreed to dance—"

"Oh, but we had."

"—and Mr. Thomas was most kind to ask me." A brazier popped, sending sparks upward into the night. "It was lovely."

He studied her profile with its magnificent edges. "I have disappointed you. I have disappointed myself."

"My lord, there is nothing—"

"Call me Daniel." Pleading in his tone. "Please, Fossi."

Nothing for a moment. And then . . .

"Wouldst that it might have been . . . "

"Pardon?"

"*Fosse,*" she whispered. "Wouldst that it might have been."

He scrambled to catch up with her train of thought.

"My name in Italian," she explained. "Fossi means 'wouldst that I had been' . . . *fossi, fosse, fossimo . . .*"

She whirled through several conjugations and then gave a one-shouldered shrug.

"Wouldst that we might have danced together." She shook herself and then smiled. Soft. Wan. "Sorry. You are seeing me at my most maudlin tonight."

Silence.

"There will be another waltz later this evening. I insist on dancing it with you." Even to Daniel's ears, the promise sounded too little, too late.

"Of course. If you wish. You most certainly should feel no obligation." So polite. So proper.

So Fossi.

Not being a martyr. Just not wanting to make waves. Rock the boat.

"Please tell me there is something else on your list I can help you achieve as a penance."

She plucked at her shawl. "This beautiful shawl is more than enough—"

"No. I insist on being allowed to atone for my sin."

That finally got him a censorious narrowing of her eyes.

"Daniel—"

"I hope your list is actually a spreadsheet. Everything entered and tallied."

"Perhaps." She smiled then. A real smile. Genuine. But still tinged all around with that sadness.

"Who was the woman you were speaking with? The blond one?" she asked.

Bingo.

Suddenly everything made sense, like the sun breaking through on a gloomy day.

Fossi was . . . jealous. She had seen him with Georgiana and was green-eyed of it.

Elation jolted through him.

Which, really, was not the correct emotional reaction. But he couldn't help it.

He liked her feeling possessive of him.

Damn. Talk about a caveman response—

"I appreciate you asking," he replied. "The lady in question is Georgiana Carew, Lady Stratton."

A frown wrinkled her brow. "Arthur's sister?"

"Yes."

He related to her Georgiana and Sebastian's unexpected arrival and the chaos that had ensued. As he spoke, her shoulders relaxed and her expression eased from resignation to understanding.

"Lady Stratton requested that I introduce you to her as soon as we return to the great hall. Would you be amenable to the connection?"

Fossi blinked and then chuckled, low and throaty. "Heavens, such a question. I should be honored to be introduced. As if I would scorn the friendship of a countess."

"Your father would."

"Yes, well. That is my father for you." She swallowed. Pulled her shawl around her again. "My father would disapprove of a great many things I do, I suppose."

Silence again, only less fraught this time.

"So," he began, "are you ready to tell me what other item on your list I can fulfill to appease my poor guilty conscience?"

"Daniel." A heavy, weary sigh. "I was sincere a moment ago. There is nothing for which you need atone."

"No, I insist. If you won't tell me, then I shall be forced to guess."

She pursed her lips and shot him a rather effective glare. If she hadn't been obviously stifling a laugh at the same time, he might have been worried.

But as it was . . .

"Hmmm. What else could be on Foster Lovejoy's spreadsheet of wishes?" He made a show of stroking his chin in thought. "Visit the Royal Menagerie in London?"

She raised an eyebrow at him.

"I take that as a *No*." He thought further. "Own a horse?"

"I am not much for riding."

"Own a penguin, then?"

"You are absurd." But she did grin.

"I will ferret this out." He paused and pointed a finger at her. "It isn't a ferret, is it?"

"Stop." She giggled.

"You wish to keep house for dwarves and are terrified of poisoned apples?"

Fossi laughed in earnest. "You are impossible."

"I have it." He snapped his fingers. "You wish for true love's first kiss."

The words just popped free. It was only after they escaped that he realized how it sounded.

Or, perhaps, it was Fossi's frozen reaction and huge eyes darting a glance at his mouth before instantly looking elsewhere.

Well.

Well, well, well . . .

Bullseye.

A deep, scarlet blush washed up her neck, likely as painful to feel as it was to watch.

Daniel thought to back down, kindly push the remark away—

He *ought* to back down.

It was just . . .

That word hung between them now.

Strung taut. Potential-laden.

Kiss.

And, suddenly, all he could think about was kissing Foster Lovejoy.

Her soft lips on his. The lushness of her body wrapped in his arms. The give and take of breaths as she rose on her tiptoes to brush her mouth across his—

His heart tripled, booming against his ribcage.

It would be so *right*, kissing her. It would feel like home.

A wise man would leave it be. Make some inane comment about the weather and escort her back inside.

But wisdom was not something he embraced when it came to Fossi.

Clearly, he wanted more *literal* embracing.

To that end, he stood up and grasped her gloved hand in his.

"Dance with me?"

"Pardon?" Her eyes flew wide, searching his in the moonlight. "Here? Now?"

"Answering questions with a question is my job." He clicked his tongue. "And yes. Here and now."

He tugged her to her feet. She rose. Not reluctantly, thank goodness.

Music from the great hall wafted to them, the violins carrying bright and clear in the still night. The crisp smell of autumn and wood smoke swirled around the courtyard.

He pulled her forward, drawing her closer.

She stumbled.

He steadied her, taking the excuse to wrap his free hand around her waist, drawing her even nearer. Not quite into a full embrace. But . . . *close.*

He kept her other hand in his, forcing her to place her opposite hand on his shoulder.

He was a thousand ways a fool.

Guilt tried to reason with him.

They had no future together. Nothing beyond this simple moment.

Not if he were to restore Simon.

And yet . . .

She would not remember him. She would forget his slight this evening.

Forget that he held her in his arms while they danced in an ancient torch-lit courtyard under twinkling stars.

Forget the magical beauty of here and now.

The thought tightened his throat. He *adored* Fossi.

He didn't want her to forget him.

Would he remember her? Or would that be taken from him too?

FOSSI STARED UP at Daniel.

His words buzzed and hummed and would Not. Be. Silenced.

True love's first kiss.

Oh!

If only one could *die* of mortification . . .

But he had said it and she had thought it and now it rested between them like a schoolyard taunt—

Kiss! Kiss! Kiss!

She desperately wanted to stop looking at his mouth. But it was proving nearly impossible.

She had never experienced a kiss.

For years, she had wondered if she would even enjoy such a thing. It seemed too . . . personal. Too intimate.

But the thought of kissing *Daniel*—

Heavens.

It made her heart leap and her blood burn and rendered every last inch of her skin so achingly *alive*.

His hand was a delicious weight in the center of her back, his chest a blaze of heat against her front.

He pulled her closer. Which did nothing to assuage her fiery blood and electric skin.

Let this be enough, she whispered to herself. *A dance will suffice.*

But even she could hear the lie in her own thoughts.

He danced with her then. A slow waltz and with each step, he pulled her closer.

Closer. And closer.

Until her skirts jumbled in his legs in earnest, and he had to curtail his waltzing.

He adjusted and spun her in an unhurried circle instead.

Closer, closer, closer until her chest pressed against his.

It was such a *relief,* that contact.

Something so vitally needed.

Finally Fossi could rest her head against his shoulder and sag her weight into him and set every other care free.

His touch soothed an irritant within her that she had never known existed. And when everything clicked back into its proper place, peace and calm and harmony descended in a profound rush.

And still he drew her closer. Until their legs tangled and they merely swayed side-to-side, his cheek resting on her head.

She breathed in deep heady lungfuls of him. His typical scent of peppermint and bay rum, but this close there was something else. An undernote of earthiness and pure male that could only be Daniel himself.

So this is what heaven feels like.

It was a decidedly florid thought but true nonetheless.

This *had* to be what heaven felt like. Which explained her next action.

She snuggled closer, unconsciously nuzzling her nose into his throat.

It simply felt too natural. She was compelled. Her own heart and very nature conspiring against her.

Daniel and she were simply two halves of a separate whole and now that they had joined again, she couldn't get close enough.

His reaction was deliciously gratifying.

He inhaled deeply and clutched her closer, stopping them entirely.

"Fossi." His voice the barest whisper.

Her name a plea. Or perhaps a benediction.

She really didn't care.

All she knew was that she wanted this.

When she was eighty years old and living alone with only cats and knitting for company, she wanted to be able to dust off the memory and relive kissing Daniel Ashton, Lord Whitmoor, on a crisp autumn evening underneath the stars.

To that end, she lifted her head from his shoulder. Wrapped her free hand around the back of his neck, sliding her gloved fingers into his hair.

She arched up on her tiptoes.

He bent his head.

Her arms trembled, her knees shook.

It was her own personal earthquake.

Her eyes drifted closed.

His breath skimmed over her lips, not quite touching.

Close.

So close—

"By all that is unholy, you will unhand my daughter immediately, sir!"

The cry of a thunderous Reverend Josiah Lovejoy rent the night.

Chapter 19

THE LIBRARY
WHITMOOR HOUSE
OCTOBER 2, 1828

"You, sirrah, are a scoundrel." Reverend Lovejoy paced before the fire in the library, pointing an angry finger at Daniel. Fossi winced at her father's words. "A villain of such a degenerate mien—"

"We understood your point the first twenty-three times you stated it." Lord Linwood's dry voice cut her father off. His lordship flicked a speck of fluff from his elbow where it rested against the mantelpiece. "Please say something relevant or cease this tiresome repetition."

Her father shot a baleful look at Lord Linwood—who returned an equally haughty, condescending scorn. Had Fossi not already seen Lord Linwood behaving as a devoted husband and doting father, she would have believed him truly proud and arrogant.

Fossi twisted her fingers in her lap, fighting yet another vicious blush.

They had all retired to the library to 'discuss the matter' after her father, Will and Strength had interrupted her moment with Daniel in the courtyard.

Lords Linwood and Stratton had quickly joined the fracas. Though Fossi was left to wonder if they were there to support Daniel or simply provide droll commentary.

Of course, part of her marveled how quickly one could move from Heaven to Hell. And which part, in the end, was the Heaven? And which the Hell? The almost kissing Daniel? Or the embarrassment of having her father interrupt a private moment between her and her . . .

Mmmm. Here Fossi had to pause. What *was* Daniel to her?

Her employer? Certainly. A friend? Most definitely.

But beyond that?

She couldn't call him a suitor or an admirer. Certainly not her lover.

Her father had made *his* opinion on the matter abundantly clear—

Daniel was a reprobate of the worst sort. Only the good reverend's timely arrival had saved Fossi from certain ruin.

For his part, Daniel stood still and silent beside Lord Linwood, expression utterly unreadable. He had withdrawn deep inside his fortress. Surely reinforcing his battlements and preparing to vigorously defend himself.

Lord Whitmoor at his most formidable.

Lord Stratton sat in a chair opposite Fossi, tapping his fingers on his knees. A look of bemusement on his face.

Between Lord Stratton and Fossi, Reverend Lovejoy paced, raining down fire and brimstone on everyone within the room. Will and Strength stood beside Fossi's chair. Strength reflected his father's outrage. Will remained impassive. If she knew him, Will had come simply to keep his father and brother in check and ensure that Fossi made decisions of her own free choice.

Reverend Lovejoy jabbed a finger at Daniel. "I will not cease shouting my opinions of *this* man—"

"Daniel is taking this quite well, I do say." Lord Stratton looked up at Lord Linwood.

"Indeed," was Lord Linwood's reply. "Though I do not expect him to remain so calm for long. I predict an impressive eruption of temper."

Daniel shot the two men a quelling look.

They ignored him.

"One can always hope." Lord Stratton nodded toward the bell pull. "Do you think we could ring for some popcorn?"

Reverend Lovejoy was not amused. "This man is a scoundrel—"

"Father!" Fossi could not remain silent. "Please stop. I beg of you."

Her words had the effect she intended. Her father whirled on her.

"You will be silent, woman! You have brought shame upon our entire family through your thoughtless, wanton behavior—"

"Come now." That from Lord Stratton.

"Father!" That from Will.

"Enough." Daniel sliced a hand through the air, the suppressed fury and force in his voice instantly silencing the room.

He was Lord Whitmoor. A man of authority. Radiating command and power.

Reverend Lovejoy glared daggers at him.

"You have said enough, sir." Daniel held her father's gaze. "Fos— Miss Lovejoy has been welcome in my employ—"

"Employ as what, sirrah? Your doxy?"

Oh!

"Drat. This really does need popcorn," Lord Stratton whispered to Lord Linwood.

"*Father.*" Will again, voice pained. He turned to Daniel. "You must forgive him, my lord. He did not mean to imply that—"

"I most certainly *did* mean to imply what I did. Her behavior was already suspect when she ran off. But once we realized she had visited *Mister* Ashton's townhouse in London . . . well, that's when I knew. As further proof, he has dressed her as his strumpet and we all saw them engaged in that carnal embrace."

"Hear, hear." Strength added his opinion, shooting Will an angry glower.

"Carnal embrace? Hardly." Lord Linwood sounded amused.

"The good reverend clearly doesn't get out much." Lord Stratton leaned toward his friend. "Perhaps someone should break down the differences between carnal versus non-carnal embracing for him."

Fossi clutched a hand to her stomach and pressed the other against her fiery cheek.

Would that she could pass two minutes without her skin going up in flames.

Daniel didn't respond instantly. Instead, he clenched his jaw, pinched the bridge of his nose and appeared to be saying a silent prayer.

The sounds of music and chatter and gaiety drifted in. The harvest ball was still underway.

"Miss Lovejoy has been a model of virtue and decorum in her time in my employ," Daniel said. "What you witnessed this evening was an extension of the regard in which I hold her—"

"Hah! We most certainly did see how you hold her!" Reverend Lovejoy retorted. "Has it not always been thus with the aristocracy?"

"Lord Whitmoor should offer marriage to her. It is the honorable thing to do." That was Will. His voice so reasonable and calm.

Fossi's heart nearly stopped at his words.

Of course Will would see marriage as the correct option here. It *was* the honorable thing to do, when one was caught in a compromising situation with a genteel woman of marriageable age.

"Marry her?!" Reverend Lovejoy whirled on his eldest son. "Why should I wish for any of my progeny to be connected with the worst of our degenerate aristocracy?"

"Degenerate?" Lord Linwood sniffed.

"Well, I grant that we can be quite boisterous on occasion," Lord Stratton sighed, "but that hardly qualifies as true degeneracy. Again, I don't think the good reverend gets out as much as he should."

Fossi's heart sank.

Oh that one could truly die of embarrassment.

Daniel said nothing about the thought of marriage. He did not seize the idea nor dismiss it. He merely ignored it, as if it were so ludicrous . . .

Fossi bit her inner cheek, using the pain to keep her tears from falling.

Instead, Daniel said, "I would ask you to apologize to your daughter." His voice so frightfully calm. A chill chased Fossi's spine.

"The whole world knows how Lord Whitmoor treats a wife." Reverend Lovejoy jabbed a finger at Daniel. "I heard what transpired with your wife and the man she ran off with, sir. That little scandal even reached my ears—"

Lord Linwood loudly sniffed. "I do believe the room suddenly smells of impudent mushroom."

Lord Stratton joined him in sampling the air. "Why, I daresay you are correct, my dear man."

Daniel's eyes flashed, nostrils flaring.

"You. Will. Apologize." Daniel enunciated each word with distinct precision.

"I will not apologize for speaking so of your wife—"

"Miss Lovejoy!" Daniel roared. "I don't care about my damn wife. She *was* the sort of woman you have accused your daughter of being. But Fossi . . ." Here Daniel heaved in a deep breath, taming a tempest. "*Fossi* is not. You will apologize to her at once."

Despite the tension in the room, Fossi's heart soared.

No one had ever defended her like this.

He may not wish to marry her, but how incredible to not feel alone in this trial. To *know* a friend would stand by your side.

Reverend Lovejoy narrowed his eyes and thrust his jaw out stubbornly.

"No." He all but hissed the word. "She has acted the whore and she knows it!"

It all came crashing down.

All the years of caring for her brothers and sisters, assisting her father, jumping to answer every beck and call, denying even the modest wishes of her heart for the greater good. Never once giving her father a moment's doubt as to her virtue and goodness.

And *this* was what he thought of her?

Daniel lunged toward her father, intent on *making* him apologize.

Fossi jumped between them, placing a staying hand out to stop Daniel. Which, to his credit, he did.

She whirled on her father, fists shaking in rage.

"How. Dare. You!" She could hiss words too. "How dare you spend *decades* ignoring me and neglecting me and *using* me. And then the second

I make a decision that does not conform to your ideals for me, you accuse me of being a-a—" Fossi paused, as she couldn't bring herself to actually say the word *whore* to her father, even though he had not shrunk from calling her one. "—of being a woman of loose morals. And, worse, you have now accused Lord Whitmoor of base behavior, when his lordship has been nothing other than kind and proper with me—"

"Foster Love Among Us Lovejoy, you will march yourself out of this room and await my displeasure—"

"No." She lifted her chin.

"No?!"

"I am thirty-two years old, Father. A woman grown. I await *no* man's displeasure."

"You go girl," Lord Stratton encouraged.

Lord Linwood rolled his eyes. "You're far too old to say that, Stratton."

Inexplicably, Lord Stratton snapped his fingers in a 'Z' shape instead of replying.

"Jasmine has been *such* a poor influence on you." Lord Linwood rolled his eyes a second time.

Lord Stratton grinned.

Fossi shook her head. Getting back to the point at hand—

"I chose to come into Lord Whitmoor's employ," she said, "and I will remain in his employ until I finish the task he has assigned me."

"You would spit thus on your mother's memory? She would be horrified—"

"That, sir, was beneath you." Fossi's chest heaved. "My mother loved and cherished me. Things you have *never* done. She would be ashamed of your behavior today. If anyone has spit upon her memory, it has been you."

Reverend Lovejoy flinched.

She pressed her advantage. "You should have more faith in me, Father. I have been a good daughter to you. I would like to be a good daughter to you in the future—"

"We've come to bring you home," Strength said, jumping into the conversation. He shot a sideways glance at the lords in the room. "You belong with your own kind. Not here with these . . . people."

"I will gladly return home once I have completed the work Lord Whitmoor has requested of me."

"No." Reverend Lovejoy straightened his shoulders. "You will come home now or not at all, Foster. How can you choose to stay with this man? He is a keeper of secrets. Do you even *know* what you do for him?"

Fossi winced before she could control her expression. That little barb had struck true.

Daniel *did* keep too many secrets. It seemed she uncovered one simply to find another dozen buried underneath. Would she be whitmoored in the end?

"Father—"

"This is your only chance, Foster." Reverend Lovejoy pressed his advantage. "You will quit this den of iniquity, renounce your wayward ways and come home with me at once."

"I cannot, Father. I have an obligation to Lord Whitmoor at present."

"Return or I will consider you dead to me!"

"I, for one, am heartily glad this hasn't taken a melodramatic turn," Lord Linwood drawled.

"Hear, hear." Lord Stratton nodded to his friend. "Though I still say we should have rung for popcorn."

Reverend Lovejoy did *not* appreciate their wry humor. "Consider carefully, Foster. I *will* disown you. 'Twas not an idle threat."

All eyes turned to her.

From the beginning, Fossi *knew* this was how things would end with her father. She had just assumed they would never have an official conversation about it.

"I am sorry, but I cannot return with you, Father." A decidedly wistful smile touched her lips. "You say I will be dead to you. But such an opinion assumes I was once alive in your eyes." She shrugged. "And we both know I have never been alive to you."

Reverend Lovejoy and Strength gasped.

Will and Lord Stratton whistled.

Fossi curtsied. First to her father and brothers. Then to Lords Whitmoor, Linwood and Stratton.

"Good evening, gentleman," she murmured. "Goodbye, Father."

Holding her head high and Lord Whitmoor's shawl around her arms, Fossi exited the room.

Chapter 20

Daniel stared into the dying fire.

The house was finally quiet. All his guests had left, both the invited *and* uninvited ones. The Lovejoy men had taken themselves off willingly, though Daniel had been half-tempted to toss them out anyway.

Will, at least, had the decency to apologize for his father's behavior.

"Please send me word if Fossi ever needs help," he had murmured on his way out. "I do love her and want her happiness." Will fixed him with a steely gaze. "Why *haven't* you offered for her? Your embrace earlier certainly implied some affection between you."

It was a fair question. Daniel answered truthfully.

"I am not at liberty, currently, to take a wife. Were my situation to change, I would happily offer marriage to your sister."

Will let that sink in. "I see. Fossi is intelligent and more than capable of making decisions for her own life, but I am glad she seems to have a good friend in you."

"That she does," Daniel had agreed.

Will nodded once, a knowing smile on his lips. "She is the best of women. Treat her well."

"I will."

Will left with a handshake and tip of his hat.

Reverend Lovejoy, on the other hand, had stomped out without a backward glance.

How a man such as Josiah Lovejoy could have sired a woman as remarkable as Fossi . . . it boggled the mind.

Though Daniel supposed many a husband had thought something similar about his in-laws.

Not that he considered himself a husband for Fossi.

Though . . .

The words he had spoken to Will were utterly true. Were things different with Simon, were he not determined to change the trajectory of Time . . .

Daniel blinked and sank further back into the leather wingback chair. The fire flickered, bravely fighting for life.

Images danced through his brain.

Fossi holding the hand of a child with Simon's eyes and her oval face, both smiling as Daniel entering the room.

Fossi wrapping an arm around his waist as they gazed at their sleeping children in the nursery.

Fossi cuddling next to him on the sofa, twining her fingers with his and resting her head on his shoulder—

Longing swept in behind, nearly pulling him under with its strength.

The sheer *pain* of it. Wanting something with such ferocity, but knowing that to have it, you would have to give up something equally precious—

Daniel gasped, trying to quell his tight chest and rough breathing.

Simon's face danced before his eyes . . . or rather . . . almost.

He was forgetting the exact shape of Simon's nose, the precise cadence of his voice.

Daniel swallowed and sat forward, tipping his head into his palms, elbows resting on his knees, fingers threaded through his hair.

Wouldst that it had been . . .

Ah, Fossi.

In a different universe with a different life trajectory for himself . . . would they have met and married? Would Simon have been her child instead of Alice's? Of a certainty, they would have been happy together.

But this slice of Time . . . this place where they knew each other would soon cease to exist.

She wouldn't remember him.

And he . . .

. . . he would likely forget her too.

That was why he was staring into the fire at four in the morning.

Up until recently, he hadn't really cared whether he remembered or forgot. The idea that he might not retain a memory of the agony and sadness of these past two years hadn't troubled him. He would have Simon and they would continue through Time, everything restored. Anything he forgot would be re-experienced anyway, so it hadn't concerned him.

But to forget Fossi . . .

It was extremely unlikely that in a new timeline, he would meet Fossi.

And that was surprisingly . . . devastating.

The *click* of the door opening startled him.

He lifted his head from his hands and peered around the flared sides of the wingback chair.

Somehow, he had summoned her.

Fossi carefully set her candle down on a side table and drifted across the room to him. She wore a dressing gown and hugged his shawl tightly around her shoulders, hands clasped to her chest. Her chestnut hair tumbled in a thick braid down her back, the fading firelight catching gold highlights.

She sat in the chair next to him, perching on the edge.

"I assume you found sleep elusive, as well?" he asked.

She nodded.

"Settle in." He jerked a chin toward the back of her chair. "Might as well keep me company then."

She sank back into the chair, tucking her feet underneath her. Leaning her head against the wing of the chair, she joined him in staring into the fire.

"Do you want to talk about what happened with your father earlier?" he asked.

"No." Her voice barely a whisper but still loud in the way sounds are in the dead of night. "I do believe my father and I discussed all the salient points."

"You are not the things he said."

"I know."

"You will always have a home within our little clan. Stratton, Linwood and I discussed it afterward."

"Thank you."

Silence rang between them. Laden with so many things that remained unspoken.

Finally, Fossi sighed.

"I need to know, Daniel." Her voice slipped through the hush, laced with gentle gloom.

Daniel froze.

Damn. There were far too many things that could be attached to that question.

Why don't you want to marry me?

Why are you holding on to Simon so fiercely?

Why am I here with you?

This was the problem with being a master secret-keeper. Sometimes, there were too many secrets to choose from.

He needed specificity.

He *hated* asking the question. "What precisely would you like to know?"

"The theorems."

"Ah." Unexpected that. A relief and, yet, with her usual acumen, she had drilled down to the question that answered all the others.

She shifted in her seat. "How did you know about my work, but knew nothing about me specifically?" she asked. "What am I working on and why? What are your goals with it? I need to know I am not being whitmoored. Your reputation does proceed you."

That it did.

"Who is Daniel Ashton?" he clarified.

"Precisely. The man behind the iron curtain."

He laughed at that. Iron curtain.

If only she knew.

He inhaled deeply. Pondering.

He could tell her about the time portal. After she fixed it and he corrected Time, she would cease to remember. So it wasn't a large risk. And the others would understand why he did it.

But . . .

"Are you sure, Fossi?" he had to ask it. "I keep these secrets more to protect you than myself."

She twisted her head to meet his gaze, face a question mark.

"That seems . . . convenient," she finally said.

He shrugged. "It does not, however, make it untrue."

"I would know."

A pause.

"Even if knowing will alter you?"

DANIEL'S WORDS lingered.

Knowing will alter you.

But wasn't she already altered? Hadn't her transformation begun the second she saw his posting in *Scriptis Mathematicis?*

"I need to know why I have given everything up, Daniel. Has it been worth the cost?"

That took him aback. His bloodshot eyes gazed into hers, pools of murky blue in the low light.

There was little of Lord Whitmoor about him now. Gone was the elegant coat and embroidered waistcoat, the sense of leashed power.

Instead, he was in shirtsleeves, trousers and slippers, a loose banyan thrown over as a nod to decorum.

Simply Daniel.

Her heart lurched.

She *adored* Simply Daniel.

"You said at the beginning that I would be helping Kit, but I understand she currently lives in America." She pressed her case. "How are my equations *here* helping her *there?*"

He scrubbed a hand over his face and then kept on going, raking it over his hair too, leaving it standing deliciously askew.

How she wanted to follow those fingers with her own. She had evening gloves on earlier during their almost kiss in the courtyard and hadn't been able actually *feel* the texture of his hair. Would it be soft and silky? Springy and slightly coarse?

She gave herself a firm mental shake.

Solving the mystery of Daniel's hair was *not* why she had entered the room when she saw him here.

"Daniel?"

He dropped his hand and tapped his fingers on a leg and then sighed.

"Last chance," he said, turning his eyes to hers. "Last warning before I alter your perception of reality."

She smiled. "Are you always so melodramatic in the early morning hours?"

He shrugged. "When the situation merits it."

"You do realize that the statistical chances of actually altering my reality are improbably high, correct?"

"About one in eleven million point three four five."

Fossi chuckled despite herself. *How* she loved this man.

"I believe I am prepared." She placed her palms on her thighs, bracing herself. "Do your worst."

It was a dare.

And she knew Lord Whitmoor would never back down from a dare.

"Fine. But you were warned."

He shook his head. Deep breath.

"I was born at Whitmoor House to the seventh Lord Whitmoor," he said.

He looked at her and paused.

Fossi blinked. Thought through what she knew of his history and then cocked her head at him.

His words made no sense.

"That's not . . . possible," she said. "You said yourself that you purchased Whitmoor House a decade ago. You were born here?"

"Yes. My father was the seventh Lord Whitmoor."

"Oh." She thought further, frown deepening. "No. That can't be right. *You* are the first Lord Whitmoor. There were *no* Lord Whitmoors before you. You are the first to hold the title."

"That is also true. I am."

His eyes dared her to arrive at some logical conclusion.

But the 'logical' conclusion was absurd.

Fossi sighed.

"Are you attempting a joke? Daniel, please be serious."

"I am serious," he said. "Completely and utterly so."

He looked serious. There was no trace of humor or anything in his eyes.

Fossi pursed her mouth. "The only way you could be the first Lord Whitmoor and your father the seventh is if—" Here she broke off, her puzzled brain trying to put together a possible answer. "You were born at some ludicrously far off point in the future and then traveled backward in time and somehow became the first Lord Whitmoor and purchased the house . . ."

Fossi laughed at the absurdity of what she was saying.

"Honestly, Daniel," she continued, "it's a clever logic puzzle, but as reality it is so ridiculous, I don't know—"

She stopped.

Right there.

In the middle of her sentence.

Because Daniel wasn't laughing or smiling or acting . . . surprised. He was just staring at her, face impassive.

"So . . . if I were born in say the year 1991," he said into the quiet, "and realized due to our family history that I was actually my own eighth great-grandfather. And then decided when I was in my early twenties to use—shall we say a time portal on Arthur Knight's estate in Hereford-shire?—to travel two hundred years into the past to ensure that I took up my title as the first Lord Whitmoor . . ."

Fossi literally forgot how to breathe.

The *shock* of that moment . . .

Which could be the only explanation for the inanity of her reply:

"Does Arthur Knight *know* he possesses a time portal on his estate?"

That got her a glimmer of a smile.

"He does. As does Marianne."

Sweet, gentle Marianne Knight knew that Daniel was from another century?

Wait.

Was she truthfully considering this?

No. It was ludicrous.

It figured Daniel would be mad in the end.

She shook her head. Refusing to believe.

"It's impossible," she repeated.

Compassion tinged Daniel's gaze.

"I know it is fantastical, but it *is* truth," he said.

More head shaking. "I cannot believe it."

"It will take time and more proof, but you will understand it to be true in the end."

"That seems . . . unlikely."

"You do realize this isn't like a religious conversion, right?" A smile touched his lips. "I am not asking you to have *faith* in my words. I expect you to doubt and wonder until presented with overwhelming empirical evidence."

She supposed that was meant to be comforting.

"Do other's believe?" she asked.

"Yes."

She rolled her hand. *Elaborate, please.*

"Georgiana and Sebastian. Timothy and Jasmine. Jasmine is from another time as well. She is the Keeper of the portal and mystically tied to it."

Fossi sat back, surely her eyes as glazed and startled as she felt.

"Do you need a moment?" he asked.

She shook her head. *No.*

"Are you certain?"

"Yes."

"You've gone pale."

"Well, I suppose that is allowed when one meets a time traveler. I can't say I have consulted an etiquette book on the matter."

"Quite right."

A long pause.

"Why?" Fossi asked.

Why do you need me? Why am I part of this?

The fire popped, making a last desperate bid for life. Daniel stood and grabbed a poker, jabbing at the smoldering coals and throwing another log on. Flames eagerly caught it, lapping bright warmth.

He set the poker down and turned back to Fossi, hands on his hips.

"The problem is this. In order to be my own eighth great-grandfather, I need to have a son—"

"Simon," she breathed.

"Exactly. He was my heir."

That made sense, she supposed.

But . . . Daniel could have more children, couldn't he?

"Do you remember the earthquake that occurred in Herefordshire?"

She nodded. "Yes. I remember reading about it. We didn't feel it down in Dorset, of course."

"The earthquake happened just a day after Simon's death and was centered directly under the portal . . ."

Fossi listened in amazement as he explained about anachronistic mistakes, the time portal, oscillating waves on the ocean of Time, deviating timelines of history and a genius mathematician lost in the annals of history who would conjure up Fourier's Nemesis.

Fossi wasn't sure how to feel about her theorems being known two hundred years into the future.

"So you see, my dear Fossi, I tracked you down based on what I remembered from my university studies in the twenty-first century. That is why I knew your theorems but nothing more about yourself or your situation."

Her mind pointed out that his explanation actually made perfect sense, provided she accept the idea he was a time traveler.

Again, was she honestly ready to accept his bizarre explanation?

And if she did?

All this time, she had considered him a spy of extraordinary ability. Which, she supposed, he still was. Just different than she had expected.

"So once I fix the time portal, you will be reunited with Kit and other friends you have in the future?" she asked.

"Yes, that is part of it."

Fossi frowned and then it hit her in a breathtaking blast of understanding.

"Oh, Daniel." She lifted a stunned hand to her mouth. "You truly do want Simon back, don't you?"

A long pause.

"I do. I absolutely do." Voice ringing with conviction. "I made a terrible mistake that must be fixed."

Her mind whirled, moving through all the possibilities—

No. All the *impossibilities* of his desires.

"So . . ." She swallowed. "You will use the portal to go back in time and what? Bring Simon to our time, so as to save his life? Use medicine in the future to save him?"

"No. He is my heir, so there cannot be any doubt that he lived two years ago. My own anachronistic actions caused his death. I will simply prevent him from dying in 1826."

"But you already exist in 1826."

"Yes. However, the universe doesn't like paradoxes. So when Simon lives and the timeline changes, I will simply reabsorb into one person. It's like a kinked rope, looped back around itself and creating a mess.

Everything right now is convoluted and wrong. I intend to straighten the rope. Once it straightens, things will snap back into place."

Fossi followed his logic. She wasn't sure she agreed with it, as it felt fundamentally wrong on some levels.

Who was Daniel to judge what God intended for their lives?

But if his vision came to pass . . .

"We will never meet." She said the words almost to herself. A horrified realization. "You will never know me. I will never know you."

Fossi pressed her palm to her mouth, as if to hold her dismay inside.

She swallowed back a raw tightness in her throat, but it didn't stop the world from going blurry and unfocused.

She would never know him. He would never know her.

Never draw her out of her shell.

Never converse and laugh and *flirt* with her.

She would never know what she had . . . known.

Never grow. Never change.

She would just remain . . . Fossi.

Trapped forever in that wishful state of wanting to be something more . . .

"Fossi . . ."

He moved toward her, a blurry, Daniel-shaped blob.

She held out both hands, palms out. *Stop.*

"We will never know each other . . . in your 'correct' timeline?" Surely her eyes begged him for truth.

She wiped her tears away. She wanted to *see* his reply.

His shoulders sagged.

"Yes. That is true."

Silence.

What more was there to say?

Of course he loved his son. He was a devoted father. It was one of the things she adored about him—the way he loved those who were *his.*

How could she be angry over his desire to prevent Simon from dying?

And yet . . .

She *was* angry.

Furious.

How could Fate do this to her? How could she finally find the courage and a path to *life*, only to have it ripped from her again?

It was so . . . cruel.

And Fossi was so tired of being the whipping boy for other's dreams.

Such a selfish thought for her.

But she finally admitted it as such.

She *could* be selfish. She could demand more from her life.

Selflessness, after all when taken too far, became a sort of pride too. Didn't it?

"Fossi?" Daniel's voice held a question now.

Are you all right? it said.

No. No she was not all right.

She—no!—*they* had never had a chance. Fossi and Daniel . . . doomed before it even began.

Fossimo . . . wouldst that we had been.

And he had *known*.

This was why he hadn't offered for her. Marriage was simply . . . pointless.

It explained why he flirted with her and behaved in unguarded ways.

There were no consequences for his behavior. So why not?

She swiped at her cheeks.

Tears seemed the most manageable place for her anger and frustration and disappointment and hopelessness to go. Otherwise, she was likely to start shattering crockery against the wall and screeching.

She brushed tears away for a few more moments.

"Fossi—" Daniel started one more time.

She held up a finger. *No. Stop.*

Wiped more tears on his shawl. The beautiful, soft, luxurious gift that he would Never. Give. To. Her.

That thought deserved a few more tears.

"Hey." Daniel squatted down in front of her. "Talk to me."

She swallowed.

"All the clothing, the promised money, our friendship . . . all l-lies," she hiccupped.

"No!" Emphatic. "Never that. That is why I gave you the ten thousand pounds up front. I wanted to be as honest as I could, to allow you to use your funds as soon as possible. To live as you never had."

"And our friendship?" She had to ask it.

He bent his head and leaned closer, trying to get her to meet his gaze.

"I have been my most genuine self with you, Foster Lovejoy. Please. You must believe that."

It was a non-answer.

She dabbed at her cheeks again with his shawl.

"We are in unsure territory. The end outcome is still conjecture," he continued.

"But you suspect that all will revert to 1826? Me. You. Simon."

A beat.

"Yes." His voice so final, drifting through the nighttime hush.

She gritted her teeth, anger warring with shattered sadness.

Words clogged her throat.

She stuffed them back, but they burst forth anyway.

"How could you do this to me?" Soft. Not hissing or furious. Simply tinged all around with devastation. "I thought you were my f-friend. I will fix the portal for you and then you will abandon me to my dead life, living without living. You will have joy and I will have"—a hiccuppy sigh—"n-nothing."

Daniel flinched. Hard.

She had struck true.

She could leave now. Take her ten thousand pounds and high away, absconding. Start a girl's school far away from here.

Leave the portal broken.

Abandon Daniel to his grief and guilt.

But even as the thought flitted through her mind, she cast it out again.

No.

She was not that sort of person. Her honor would not allow her to behave in such a manner.

Besides, she loved him too much. Even *knowing* the outcome, knowing what it would do to her and her own future . . . she would help him.

"Talk to me," he repeated.

He placed a tentative hand on her knee, shaking her slightly.

It was an absurd method of comfort.

When what she really wanted was—

Yes. She knew what she wanted.

She wanted a repeat of what had *almost* happened earlier . . . before her father had interrupted.

Foster gave her cheeks one last swipe. Opened her eyes and met Daniel's gaze.

If they both would forget all this anyway . . . if there truly were no consequences.

The thought gave her courage. More than she ever imagined having.

She leaned forward and fisted the front of his shirt in one hand. Pulled him forward. Hard.

His balance tipped toward her and his hands landed on her hips to keep from crashing into her.

Action. Reaction.

Perfect.

His mouth was only inches from hers.

She closed the gap.

And kissed him.

Her mouth pressed against his.

It was a graceless bump of lips. More a peck than anything else.

Hmmmm.

No. That wasn't quite how she had envisioned it.

When she did new things, she liked to do them well.

She tried again.

She pressed her mouth to his, lingering more this time.

It was . . . better.

Odd how lips seemed so solid when merely observed, but when touched, they became clouds of softness and sensation.

She broke the kiss again and was contemplating a third-go, when Daniel wrested all control from her.

His strong hands grasped her hips and pulled her upright to her feet. And then he kept right on reeling her in, until her entire body was flush against his.

He bent his head . . .

And that's when Foster Lovejoy learned what a kiss *really* could be.

Daniel didn't just kiss her.

He devoured.

He savored.

He feasted.

He was a man lost in a desert and she the only water he could find.

Fossi wrapped her hands into the soft lawn of his shirt and held on.

His large hands were on her back—one at her waist, the other between her shoulder blades—pressing her closer.

"You are utterly magnificent when you are angry," he whispered against her mouth.

"How *dare* you forget me!" She shook the fists of shirt she held.

He chuckled.

The. Nerve.

She kissed him for that.

Arched up on her tiptoes and partook of his mouth like she owned it. As if his kisses belonged to her and he, true to his nature, had whitmoored them from her.

She wanted them *all* returned. With interest.

Dimly, sounds intruded.

Shouting. Was someone shouting?

The door to the study burst open.

Fossi and Daniel flew apart. For the *second* time that night.

Lord Linwood stood in the doorway, completely disheveled, face ashen.

"Daniel," he gasped, "you must come."

"Whatever is the matter?"

"Jasmine. She had a seizure in her sleep and now will not wake. Something has gone terribly wrong!"

Chapter 21

Jasmine was delirious.

Daniel watched her head tossing to and fro in Timothy's arms.

The carriage hit a rut in the road, jolting them all.

Timothy simply held his wife closer, face grimly determined.

"We'll solve this problem, Timothy. I'm here for you," Daniel said, forcing Timothy to meet his gaze. "Fossi is here for you."

At his side, Fossi nodded without lifting her head from the equations she feverishly worked.

They were racing for the portal. Jasmine had collapsed into a raving delirium. She wasn't fevered, per se, just unhinged somehow.

"Home. Father," she murmured. "Broken. Portal. Must return . . ." The rest was lost in a mumble.

Timothy kissed his wife's forehead.

This had been their routine for the past five hours. The coachman driving hell-for-leather for Duir Cottage. The four of them tensely riding inside. Fossi desperately working toward an answer. Timothy caring for his wife. Daniel providing moral support for them all.

They had to fix the portal. Jasmine's health depended on it.

They hit another bump. The coach rocked along. They had stopped twice now to switch horses. At their current pace, they would arrive at Duir Cottage before noon.

"I have it!" Fossi lifted her head, eyes feverishly animated.

Daniel whipped his head her way.

"Truly?"

"Yes." A fervent nod. "I really think I do."

Hallelujah!

"Though it is . . . interesting," she continued.

Daniel and Timothy fixed her with intent eyes.

Fossi's face was excitement personified.

"Knowing *what* I was solving for helped immensely. I was able to quickly hone in on numerical values that were most appropriate. I think it is related to pitch, in the end"Pitch?"

"Yes. Once I knew that this was a problem related to wave oscillation, it was easier to focus in on the concept of frequency resonance as a solution." She held out her workbook, angling it so both men could see her calculations. "I derived the frequency here with the equations here. When the two are solved together, you arrive at this height calculation which if placed back into the equation, gives you infinity as the answer."

A beat.

Daniel stared at her answer.

Fossi noticed his noticing.

"Well, almost infinity," she amended. "There is a remainder."

Indeed there was.

"One." Daniel read the number.

"Exactly. That's the problem and the snag I've been hitting over and over. I get infinity plus a remainder. This particular iteration comes the closest to solving the entire problem—"

"But you still have a remainder."

"I do. And it's plus one or minus one. But it is always one."

"May I?" Daniel extended a hand for her notebook.

They rocked along for a few minutes in silence, Daniel skimming over her numbers.

Damn.

The woman was an absolute genius. Awe-inspiring, really.

Her solution was typical of the best mathematical minds of history—staggeringly simple and breathtakingly insightful.

It gave them a specific wave frequency and height, which Fossi had noted as a distinct pitch—D-flat.

But when plugged into the framework, the remainder was the same—infinity . . . plus or minus one.

Which didn't make sense, did it? He would need to think it through more.

But for now . . .

"How will we sort this into a plan of action?" Timothy asked.

Wasn't *that* the question of the hour?

"We are dealing with guesswork at this point, my lords." Fossi nodded at them both. "However, I have an idea that may work. But it does mean quickly stopping by Kinningsley before continuing on to Duir Cottage."

THEY ARRIVED AT Duir Cottage two hours later after a brief detour to Kinningsley.

The picturesque cottage emerged from the autumnal trees at the end of a short lane. Ivy had claimed the front of the house, as well as the stone fence surrounding it. A young oak tree grew to the right, though more a teenager now than a sapling.

Daniel rushed out of the carriage almost before it stopped, waving at the exhausted coachman to stay on his perch. Poor man had worn his heart out to get them here so quickly.

Timothy climbed out, Jasmine's limp form in his arms. Fossi followed after, carrying the small bundle she had retrieved from Kinningsley.

Daniel led the way up the front walk and through the carved front door. Down the central hallway and into a closet under the staircase. He lifted a large trapdoor in the closet floor. Stairs dropped away, disappearing into the murky darkness below.

"Need a candle?" Daniel asked, turning to Timothy.

"I can manage. There's not much to see down there."

Daniel moved aside, letting Timothy pass by and descend the stairs. Daniel followed behind and then held up a hand for Fossi, helping her down into the cellar.

They stood for a moment in the semi-darkness, allowing their eyes to adjust. Slowly, the familiar features of the small room came into focus. Stone walls, dirt floor, a carved granite slab directly opposite the stairs, the dark, circular depression of the portal in front of it.

The space pulsed—a dark morass of energy.

Normally the power of the portal hummed like an electrical wire. Orderly. Organized. A conduit.

But at present . . . the portal was chaos. Frenzied. Disorganized. Kinetic pandemonium.

"Heavens," Fossi gasped as the energy whirled around them. "It is . . . intense."

That it was.

Even in the dim light, he could see her wide, surprised eyes.

It was one thing to learn of the portal's existence. It was something entirely else to be faced with its potency.

If Fossi had any doubts, they were rapidly evaporating.

Jasmine moaned in Timothy's arms, twisting as if in agony.

"Hurry." Timothy's eyes pleaded with Daniel's. "Being this close to the portal when it is in such disarray . . ."

"Yes." Fossi dropped into a crouch and unwrapped her bundle. A series of tuning forks and rubber mallet tumbled out.

Quickly, she sorted through them, grabbing the mallet and tuning fork labeled D-flat.

Daniel's hand sought hers as she stood upright. She gave his fingers a quick squeeze.

"Ready?" he asked.

He felt her nod. "This has to work."

Timothy took a step and stood in the depression of the portal, turning to face them. Jasmine's head lolled against his shoulder with another anguished gasp, her dark hair spilling over her shoulder.

"Good luck." Daniel gave him a standard guy chin lift.

Timothy responded in kind.

Fossi moved to face Linwood and Jasmine, not touching the portal but close.

Lifting the tuning fork, she struck it with mallet.

The chime of a pure note vibrated through the space.

Daniel could feel the frequency wave oscillate with the portal, spinning through the chaotic energy in the room.

C'mon, he mentally begged. *Please work.*

The sound petered out.

Timothy gazed at Fossi with fierce intensity.

The muscles in her jaw tensed in determination. Fossi hit the fork again and the chime filled the space. This time she kept rapping the tuning forking, sustaining the tone.

Nothing happened for a moment and then, the portal . . . softened.

The wild kinetic energy calmed slightly, moving a bit with the sound.

The portal obviously liked the tone.

But it felt like spraying a bonfire with a squirt gun—too little to make a difference.

Timothy shifted Jasmine in his arms. "Try holding the tuning fork at the base of the tines. There are octave overtones that might be causing problems."

"Of course. I should have thought of that." Fossi adjusted her grip and rapped the tuning fork again.

To no avail.

After fifteen minutes of trying different iterations of the tuning fork, the stubborn portal wouldn't budge. The frantic electricity responded fractionally to the sound, but not enough to change the portal's state.

Fossi's face was a mask of frustration.

"There is a one in two point six chance that this is the correct answer." She brushed hair out of her face. "Those are decent odds."

Timothy looked up from where he had sat down in the portal, his wife in his lap.

"Would it help if you stood in the portal too, Fossi?" Daniel asked.

She paused, obviously thinking about it and probably running some mental calculations.

"No." She shook her head. "If the source of the wave realignment is at the epicenter of the portal, it would likely tear the source apart in the process of realigning. It has to be done from without."

"And from without, it's just not enough." Daniel rubbed his forehead. "We can't get the resonant frequency to be accurate or strong enough."

Timothy smoothed hair off Jasmine's face and pressed a kiss to her forehead. She continued to writhe, occasionally moaning and mumbling.

With an exasperated huff, Fossi tossed the tuning fork back onto the bundle on the floor.

"The D-flat tone *has* to be the solution," she muttered. "It's the only thing that makes sense with the equations. I'm just missing something."

She tapped her foot for a moment. And then shrugged.

"Well, I suppose I can always try this."

Sucking in a deep breath, she straightened her shoulders and closed her eyes.

Opening her mouth, Fossi sang.

Her voice filled the room, powerful and strong. She sang higher and higher until she hit the D-flat.

She held it, a piercing note of absolute crystal clarity.

The potent sound wave bounced against the oscillations swirling around the room, this time a fire hose not just a squirt gun.

The sound resonated with the oscillation. Wavering. Tugging. Pulling.

Until suddenly—

Pop!

Everything snapped into uniformity.

In a heartbeat, the portal clicked back into alignment. Electrical energy thrummed in harmony.

Timothy's eyes flashed with relief.

And then he and Jasmine disappeared.

Fossi screamed in surprise, breaking the sustained pitch.

She stumbled back, Daniel catching her before she tumbled to the ground.

"Th-they just vanished!" Her hand flew to her mouth. She turned wild eyes to Daniel. "I mean, obviously, that is what we've been trying to accomplish here—make the portal work—but . . ."

"It's one thing to intellectually know the portal exists, but something entirely more profound to see it in action," Daniel finished the thought for her.

Fossi nodded, eyes still flared in shock. "Where did they go?"

Daniel shrugged. It had caught him off-guard too. "I am not entirely sure, to be honest. Though if I were to hazard a guess, perhaps the time period of Jasmine's birth?"

They both stared at the innocuous-seeming depression in the earth.

The portal continued to hum.

Thank goodness.

Elation swamped Daniel.

They had done it!

They had fixed the portal. Fossi's singing had realigned it, forcing the portal back into its correct frequency.

Jasmine's health would be mended.

He could return to the past and prevent the anachronism that caused Simon's death. All would be restored to how it should have been.

At last!

He would have his happy, shiny boy back.

What about Fossi? his soul whispered. *What will happen to her?*

He pushed the thought aside. Who was to say they wouldn't find each other?

His actions had initiated this aberrant timeline with its catastrophic earthquake. Who was to say that he and Fossi weren't destined to find each other in the proper timeline? He would just have to return to 1826 and live that life and find out.

So . . . why did that thought make him feel panicky?

"Well." Daniel turned to Fossi with a strained smile.

She met his smile with a one of her own. It didn't touch her eyes.

"Well," she whispered.

They stared for a heartbeat.

"This is where I fix my mistake and set Time down the correct path. I just need to collect some medicines from the twenty-first century and then return to 1826."

"Yes. I hope all goes well with Simon."

"Me, too."

It hung between them. The knowledge of their fevered kisses only a few hours before.

She had been magic in his arms. Soft, eager.

She fit him. In every imaginable way.

The moment stretched until it was tissue thin.

As if the entire Universe held its breath.

Waiting for . . . what?

He couldn't say, afterwards, which of them moved first.

Perhaps she reached for him. Or he took a step toward her.

But suddenly, she was in his arms again. Chest rising to meet his, mouth finding his with such . . . ease.

As if they had done this a thousand times before and not just once.

He kissed her as he had earlier. Hungry, desperate.

It was *hello* and *goodbye.*

Wonder at having arrived at this beautiful place.

Anguish over being forced to leave it so soon.

You don't have go, that same voice murmured. *You could stay for a while. Simon will wait. What's another day? Or week?*

But . . .

Every day he delayed was one more reason to delay another day. And another. And another.

Until he had delayed his life away and Time fractured because it was on an incorrect trajectory.

No.

He adored Fossi.

But a relationship just was not . . . possible. It had been a tiny green start of an idea, crushed by the harsh winter of reality. Dead before it even began.

And so he kissed her once more.

Who was he kidding? He kissed her ten more times, each more urgent than the last.

And then . . . he released her, stepping back, chest heaving, eyes surely as wild as hers.

Fossi canted forward.

He steadied her, hands on her upper arms.

"Goodbye." He pressed a final kiss into her forehead.

"Goodbye, Daniel." A pause. "Thank you."

It caused something within him to crack, that *thank you*. Of course, Foster Lovejoy would thank *him* for this.

He should be the one groveling at her feet in gratitude. She had given him back his son. Restored his future.

She had given him redemption.

He would be giving her precisely . . . nothing.

He owed her a debt he could never repay.

There were a thousand things he could say, that he *wanted* to say.

But in the end, this whole world was temporary. In a matter of hours, all would go back to how it had been.

He would have Simon again.

He nodded at her and turned to go.

That fissure in his soul stretched wider, pain choking him.

He raised his foot to step forward into the circular depression in the earth—

Crack!

The portal splintered back into disorder.

Frenetic power crashed through the room. Furious. Untamed.

Daniel staggered backward, knocking into Fossi. She wrapped her arms around him, holding him upright.

A pillar of strength.

Fossi's breath came in short bursts against his back. She pushed him away and filled her lungs with air.

Her voice instantly resounded through the room, climbing higher and higher as she sang. Until that glorious D-flat resonated throughout the space.

The portal energy whirled and spun around the room.

Daniel stepped into the depression of the portal and turned to face Fossi as she sang.

Electrical currents swirled and tumbled, not quite moving in alignment.

Damn.

Were things to go like this then?

Fossi altered the pitch slightly.

A thought occurred to him. He frowned.

Wait.

There was a problem—

The portal pulsed around him, tumbling into harmony.

Daniel felt the licking sense of vertigo, that swooping sensation of falling, falling, falling through time.

It wanted to take him . . . home.

But not before Daniel reached out a hand and grabbed Fossi, pulling her into the portal with him.

The problem?

She was his ticket to getting the portal to work.

If he left her behind, he might not be able to return to 1826 so easily.

At least, that's the lie he told himself.

And . . .

And—

He just *couldn't* leave without her.

Fossi's singing abruptly stopped as she tumbled beside him in the portal.

This, in turn, caused the portal to collapse back into chaos.

The portal rumbled to a stop, tossing them out of the wormhole.

Daniel staggered backwards, holding Fossi against his chest. His shoulders hit the carved granite slab that stood as sentinel over the portal.

Darkness shrouded the space. Not even a slice of light.

"Wh-why did you do that?" Fossi twisted in his arms, facing him in the dark, hands pressed against his shoulders.

Daniel winced at the tentative hope in her voice.

"Uh . . . I realized that without you, I may not be able to make the portal function again."

A pause.

He felt her literally deflate.

"Oh," she whispered.

That was it.

No anger. No surprise. Just a sad little, *Oh*.

He was *such* a cad.

"That makes sense, I suppose." Her voice hushed in the dark. "Where are we? No. Scratch that. *When* are we?"

That, Daniel realized, was the critical question.

Chapter 22

DUIR COTTAGE
OCTOBER 3, 2017

Fossi struggled to draw air into her lungs, the cellar inky black.

She certainly hadn't anticipated being . . . wherever she was . . . when she awoke yesterday morning.

Had it really only been less than twenty-four hours since the start of the harvest festival?

"Hold on." Daniel still had a hand around her waist, his warm chest a solid presence under her palms. "Let me see if this time period has light."

He pushed away from her and fumbled along the wall.

Something clicked and light abruptly flooded the space. There appeared to be a type of instant lantern dangling from the ceiling.

She stared.

"A light bulb." Daniel pointed at the lantern, noting her amazement. "It uses an alternating electrical current to generate light."

Oh.

Other than the addition of the light bulb, the space looked generally the same. Packed dirt floor, granite slab, stone walls . . . time portal running amok.

Daniel was already climbing the wooden steps in front of her, pushing open the trapdoor.

Hesitantly, Fossi followed Daniel up the stairs, out the trapdoor and small closet. Entering the house proper.

She hadn't seen much of the house in 1828. Just an impression of a central hallway with a parlor off each side and a door to the kitchen beyond the staircase.

The house appeared the same and yet . . . not.

Standing in the hallway, she noted the same wood paneling on the walls. The same number of doors off the hallway.

But . . . everything was more askew. The floors more worn, the walls less plumb. As if the house had ended up foxed, deep in its cups and tipsy.

Daniel stepped to the rear of the house, where the kitchen would be in 1828.

Fossi walked in behind him, staring at the space.

Now this room . . . *this* looked nothing like the world she knew.

Up until that moment, it hadn't sunk in. She had generally believed Daniel's tale about a time portal and being from the future.

It was one thing to intellectually consider such a reality.

It was entirely something else to be confronted with it.

First Lord and Lady Linwood disappearing.

Then the vertigo-inducing trip through the portal.

And now this odd . . . place.

Her chest felt tight, the air in the room so thick she struggled to breath it in.

Stay calm, Fossi. Hysterics will not improve this situation.

Sunlight filtered weakly through a bank of windows along the far wall. The right half of the room gleamed in steel and glossy stone. A large pale marble-topped cabinet sat in the center of the space, and there seemed to be some sort of spigot over a sunken basin, but everything else was unknown and baffling. Large metal cupboards and strange objects.

An enormous rustic table stood directly ahead of her, its sides ringed with upholstered chairs. To her left, there appeared to be a seating area with a large sofa and wingback chairs facing an enormous fireplace.

And everywhere more of those light bulbs. Nestled into little holes in the ceiling. Tucked into dangling lamps and wall sconces.

Her mind fixated on them. Counting. Cataloging.

There were sixteen alone above the dining table. Ten more in sconces on the wall opposite.

Fossi was quite sure she was somewhere between shock and panic.

Daniel spun in a circle, taking in the space.

Finally, he looked at her properly, clearly reading the alarm and dismay in her gaze.

Sympathy flooded his blue eyes.

"Come here." He opened his arms.

Fossi practically ran to him, desperately needing a firm anchor, to be wrapped up in him.

Her body trembled against his chest, face buried in his shoulder.

"All will be well, Fossi." He rubbed his hands up and down her back, long comforting strokes. "I will ensure it."

He held her for a long time.

Even pressed a kiss or two atop her head.

Held her until her breathing settled, and she felt she could talk without devolving into hysterics.

How she wished he could hold her forever.

Finally, she took a deep breath and pulled away, looking up into his fathomless eyes.

"So . . . ?" Fossi's voice drifted into a question mark.

"When are we?" Daniel supplied. "The portal usually just tethers between the exact same date two hundred years apart."

"So today would be the same day in two thousand twenty-eight?"

"Exactly." He scrunched up his mouth and looked around. "Though this doesn't quite look like the house in two thousand twenty-eight."

Fossi chewed on her bottom lip.

"Ah-ha." He pointed.

Walking over to the large marble counter, he picked up what appeared to be a white envelope.

"Mmmm. Look at this."

He turned the letter toward her, his finger pointing to some printed numbers inside a stamped circle.

01 OCT 2017

It took Fossi a solid ten seconds to decipher it.

"October first, two thousand seventeen."

"Precisely."

A pause.

"So did the portal tether to two hundred years, in the end?" Fossi pointed at the letter in question.

Daniel grimaced, turning the envelope around. "It's an advert for life insurance. Junk mail—"

"Junk mail?"

"Mail that is trying to sell you something unwanted and, therefore, usually ends up in the rubbish bin."

Fossi stared past his head, trying to comprehend his sentence. It took a minute.

"Basically, it's the kind of thing that wouldn't be left on the kitchen counter for over a decade," he clarified.

Ah.

Daniel tossed the letter back onto the cabinet. "When I pulled you into the portal, it abruptly stopped working and simply spit us out into the time it was cycling through. That's the only explanation I can think of for why—"

A rumbling noise and the crunch of gravel came from behind the house.

Fossi looked out the back window in time to see a shiny, black carriage roll to a stop.

There were no horses attached to it.

That panicky breathlessness returned.

"Well, that certainly simplified things." Daniel's voice at her ear made her jump. "Don't have to figure out how to call her now."

Daniel walked around Fossi and threw open the back door, just as a tall woman exited the carriage. Beautiful with auburn hair, she was wearing trousers, boots and a loose shirt. She removed a pair of dark glasses, revealing blue eyes and a face shape that announced she *had* to be related to Daniel in some way.

"Kit," Daniel called, a smile in his voice as he jogged down the short walk to greet her.

Of course.

Daniel's older sister.

The one who had raised him.

Clearly they weren't quite in the correct time, as Kit looked decidedly younger than Daniel.

For her part, Kit stared at her brother, mouth open.

"Daniel?" Her tone utterly quizzical. "Is that you?"

"It is indeed, sister dearest."

"Wha—?" Kit looked beyond him to Fossi standing on the back stoop and then whirled her gaze back to Daniel. "Wow. You gave me quite the start. For a second, I thought you were Dad in one of his cosplay getups."

Daniel laughed. "Figures I would look like him as I age." He wrapped his sister in an enormous hug. "It's good to see you."

"Yeah." Kit hugged him back with fierce strength before pulling back. "I'm glad I decided to stop in and check up on Duir Cottage today. I saw you last month, but that was with the portal time line being tethered to precisely two hundred years in the past, so you were in your late twenties." She pointed a finger at him. "You're not that guy. What's going on Future Daniel?"

"Long story." Daniel peered past Kit to the carriage. "Marc with you?"

"No. He's shooting in the Maldives right now. *Croc-quake.*"

Daniel chuckled. "I remember *Croc-quake.*"

"Last month you said it sounded terribly derivative." Kit glared at him.

"It is. That doesn't mean it isn't good."

Kit shook her head. And then stepped forward, giving her brother kiss on the cheek. "It's wonderful every time I see you, Daniel."

"You too, Kit."

"Now." Kit looked around Daniel to Fossi. "Introduce me, if you would, please."

SEVERAL HOURS LATER, Fossi had learned many things.

One, food in the twenty-first century could be ordered using a flat, rectangular glass slab called a phone, and a half an hour later, a man would arrive with the food in stiff paper boxes. Hot and ready to eat.

Two, women would be given significantly more opportunities in the future. Kit owned her own company and was the current Lady Whitmoor in her own right.

Three, there were things called computers which could do sums on their own. Fossi wasn't sure if she was elated by the idea or horrified at having been 'outsourced,' as Kit labeled it.

Four, mankind flew through the air and swam under the ocean and had even walked on the moon.

And, lastly, Kit loved Daniel with a lioness' ferocity.

They talked for hours and the entire time, Kit sat next to Daniel. A hand on his arm, light in her eyes. She wept over Simon, raged over Alice's perfidy and gracefully thanked Fossi for her help.

Fossi loved her for how she loved Daniel.

But the more they talked, the more Fossi sensed Daniel withdrawing from her. He was focused on his family and the task that needed to be done with saving Simon. And Fossi was an absolute anachronism in his world.

Case in point, during a lull in the conversation, Fossi had asked if people still grew pineapples. Kit and Daniel froze, staring at her. And then, without replying, Daniel had stood, retrieved a tin-can from the cupboard and proceeded to open it with a strange, geared device. Finding a fork in another drawer, he had set the tin-can in front of her.

Pineapple, Fossi decided, was sweet and tart and absolutely delicious. Though given how Kit and Daniel had stared at her as she savored every bite, she didn't dare ask her multiple follow-up questions. Namely, how did the pineapple come to be in the can? Why did it not spoil? And could she have more?

Of course, Daniel would retreat from her. Fossi didn't even understand something as simple as pineapple.

"You really believe that you will be able to stop Simon's death then?" Kit asked, pushing back her dinner plate after finishing eating.

They were all seated around the large kitchen table.

"Absolutely. I inadvertently caused it." Daniel set down his own fork and stretched, lacing his fingers behind his head. He had removed his coat and cravat and was in waistcoat and shirtsleeves, looking utterly at home.

"But . . ." Kit paused, brow furrowed in thought. "You just said that you saw me before taking the candy back to Simon. That's still several years into the future from now for me. Why didn't I ever say anything about it? I could easily have stopped you from taking the candy, preventing this entire mess. Wait . . . did I say something?"

"No, you didn't."

"Okay, but why—"

"It's proof, don't you see?" Daniel didn't miss a beat. "Your silence is further evidence that this timeline is an aberration and will be forgotten. In the correct timeline, we never meet in 2017 like this. So you have no memory of this and that's why you said nothing."

Kit continued to frown.

Daniel sat forward on his elbows. "Think about it, Kit. You'll see I'm right. Even Fossi's answer to the equation proves my theory."

"It does?" That was news to Fossi.

"Of course. The answer is infinity plus or minus one." He said it like that explained everything.

A pause.

"You're going to have to spell it out a bit more for me, Daniel." Kit pointed to her head. "Math idiot, remember?"

"It's like this—infinity is the number of human lives that exist in this vast cosmic ocean. Our answer is infinity plus or minus one. My actions caused Simon's death far too early, causing him to become the missing one. So we restore him and everything settles back to normal."

Kit tapped her fingers against the tabletop. "Hmmm. I'm going to have to think about all of this, Daniel. I'm not sure that's how it works, to be honest."

"How else *would* it work, Kit?"

"I don't know. That's why I need to think about it."

They talked and planned until the hour was late.

Tomorrow, Daniel and Kit would retrieve some medicine that would save Simon if Daniel didn't arrive in time to stop him from eating the candy. Fossi would sing to correct the portal, and Daniel would disappear through to fix what had gone wrong.

Fossi would then continue singing and return to her own time.

As a plan, it was . . . acceptable.

But after the others had sought their beds, Fossi lay awake for hours, staring up at the ceiling.

Funny . . . turned out ceilings were the one thing that *hadn't* changed much over the years.

And in the dead of night, they all looked remarkably the same.

She lay there, feeling somehow like a passenger in a runaway carriage watching the approaching edge of a cliff.

That wasn't quite true.

She *did* know why she felt that way.

There was no room in Daniel's plan for her.

She wasn't part of Simon or Kit and, as such, she would not be part of his future.

He would change their timeline.

She would go back to being Foster Lovejoy in 1826, as she had been. She would never meet him.

And perhaps even worse—

Fossi would never change.

The timid Foster Lovejoy who had ridden the night mail coach to confront Daniel in London was long gone.

Fossi wasn't that person anymore.

She was a Foster Lovejoy who had weathered her sisters' scorn and faced down Reverend Lovejoy's wrath and bravely forged a path for herself in the world.

She was a Foster Lovejoy who had flirted and danced and—heavens!—kissed a lord.

A woman who ate pineapple out of a tin-can and reached for what she wanted in life.

She hated that the Foster Lovejoy she had become would, now, never be.

Fossi.

Wouldst that I had been.

Ugh!

She rolled over and punched her pillow.

Now . . . once Daniel restored everything to how it should have been . . .

She would be forgotten. Quite literally.

No witness for her life.

Without a broken portal, Daniel would not goad her to London.

Instead, she would remain anonymous. The unknown originator of Fourier's Nemesis.

She would age with her father and move in with her unwilling sisters when he passed on. And in between darning socks and scrubbing dishes, she would eke out meager spurts of living through her numbers.

And Daniel would not even know she existed.

Oh.

The thought . . . scorched.

But . . .

How could she have expected more?

There had been no repeated kisses.

Not that Fossi anticipated there necessarily would be more. She was starting to wonder if Daniel had just taken pity on her with them. Kissed her because he was a kind man and wanted Fossi to have something special and they would both forget it happened anyway, so why not?

And even if that *were* the case, Fossi would still kiss him again.

Pathetic, but true.

After hours of tossing and turning in an incredibly comfortable bed, Fossi finally managed to find sleep.

But not before the most depressing thought of all flitted through her mind—

With everything that humankind had achieved in the future, she was three hundred point five percent *more* likely to walk on the moon than keep Daniel in her life.

It just figured those would be her odds with men in the end.

THE NEXT MORNING arrived too soon.

Daniel with medicine and a plan to save Simon.

Fossi standing in the cellar beside him, ready to sing the correct frequency note to get the portal humming in harmony.

Kit sat on the stairs behind them. She and Daniel had already said their goodbyes.

Daniel's goodbye to Fossi had been gruff and quick. An expression of thanks. A sincere hug. He was clearly already thinking ahead to what needed to happen.

He and Fossi were just never fated to be.

"Ready?" Daniel asked her.

Fossi nodded. "Take care." She *had* to say something. "I would say I will never forget your kindness and belief in me but . . ."

Fossi let her words dangle off.

They all knew how the sentence ended.

Daniel smiled at her, tight and withdrawn.

Sucking in a deep breath, Fossi began to sing. She increased her pitch by the tiniest degrees, searching for the perfect tone.

The portal fought her this time.

The energy bounced around the room, stubbornly resisting the resonant frequency.

The correct note was harder to find.

But after several minutes of coaxing, she hit upon it and the portal energies aligned, humming in harmony. Fossi could hear the cadences resonating in the higher registers as she sang.

Giving her one last smile and a tip of his head, Daniel stepped forward into the portal depression.

Nothing happened.

He turned around, confusion on his face.

Fossi took in a quick breath and kept singing.

The portal hummed.

But nothing happened.

They tried for another ten minutes.

She could *feel* the resistance in the portal. It was aligned, but just not . . . interested in cooperating.

Oddly, it was almost sentient. Not quite alive—it certainly didn't have feelings, per se—but it definitely had a sense of which actions were valid and which were not.

Daniel's actions were not valid.

At least, that was Fossi's perception.

Eventually, she had to stop, her voice cracking from the strain.

The portal crashed back into chaos almost immediately.

Daniel stepped out of the depression, eyes bleak.

He stared back at it, running a shaking hand through his hair.

"This is ridiculous. Why won't it let me back?" Voice gruff with frustration. "I have to fix my mistake."

"Daniel," Kit began, "much as it pains me to say—"

He turned to her. "Don't, Kit!"

"—I'm not sure this is the correct path. The portal is telling you so."

He shook a finger at her.

"This *is* the correct path. It has to be. I screwed up and wrecked the timeline. It's my job to fix it. We're just missing something here."

Daniel stomped past his sister and up the stairs.

Kit shot Fossi an apologetic look. And then followed him.

Fossi walked into the kitchen area behind them. Daniel was already pacing beside the kitchen island (she had remembered the name of it), a hand still in his hair.

"We know how this goes, Daniel," Kit sighed. "The portal has ideas about how things should be. It won't let you travel if it doesn't think it's right."

"It makes no sense, Kit." He threw up his hands at her. "I introduced something into 1826 that should have never been in that time period."

"Are you so sure about that, Daniel? The universe protects itself. It won't allow information or people to move in ways that disrupt the space/time continuum. The fact that you were able to give the candies to Simon at all—"

"My innocent son and *heir* died! Saving Simon *is* the answer. That's when everything fell apart. I'm not giving up on him."

Kit sagged against one of the dining table chairs. "I think we're not considering everything here."

"What am I missing?"

"I've been thinking about it. You say Simon is the plus one missing from the cosmic sea of life. But here's the problem, Daniel. Simon *did* exist at one point. The cosmic pool is an infinite number of people who have lived and will ever live. Simon's death at age six or sixty doesn't matter, in the end. He's still part of the pool."

Daniel stopped pacing and faced his sister, chest heaving.

"No." Emphatic. Denial.

"Yes." Kit. Compassionate. Heartbreaking. "Simon cannot be your plus or minus one, Daniel. It was a good thought, but it's not the answer. The universe allowed that candy to be taken to him—"

"No!"

Daniel turned away, bracing his hands on the marble counter top. His entire body shook, violent breaths seesawing in and out.

Kit's shoulders crumpled. She swiped away a tear.

"I am so sorry, Daniel." She lifted a hand to comfort him, but Daniel pushed away.

"No." He whirled on his sister, jaw clenched. "You would never give up on your children. *I* will never give up on mine. There has to be another answer we're missing."

Daniel slammed out of the house.

He didn't look back.

FOSSI STARED AT Daniel from the kitchen window.

He had been pacing in the back garden for the past three hours. She had sat watching him for most of them, eating her way through another tin-can of pineapple.

It tore her apart, seeing him so distraught.

The time portal's stubbornness was weighing on them all. Kit said the portal being fickle was, "kinda its MO." Which apparently meant it was the portal's *modus operandi.*

They were at an impasse. Unable to move forward or backward, quite literally.

Fossi had spent the last two days working sums and plugging in new aspects to the theorems, trying to find another answer. But everything kept landing the same.

Infinity.

Plus or minus one.

How could you *add* someone to infinity?

Daniel had stopped pacing and now braced his hands on the stone fence around the old kitchen garden.

He was dressed as a man from this century—jeans, a black t-shirt and leather shoes. Again, words she had learned from Kit.

The clothing was not . . . unattractive.

The t-shirt hugged his shoulders and molded to his chest. October sun shone on his hair, catching the copper highlights in it.

Fossi crossed her arms, pulling her sweater tighter around her. Kit had found her some clothing—a maxi skirt, t-shirt and cardigan sweater.

Fossi's vocabulary was growing hourly.

Perhaps it was time to use some of her new words on Daniel.

She pulled open the back door and walked down the path. The autumn air had just the right mix of crisp cool and warm sun, all wrapped in the humid smells of damp soil and green things.

Daniel turned at the sound, watching her approach with silent eyes. Every emotion firmly locked down behind the buttresses of Fortress Whitmoor.

"I simply wanted to get some sunlight." Fossi gave a strained smile and tilted her head toward the weak sun.

"No answers?" His question obviously referred to her work.

"No answers."

She stared into the trees for a moment, catching glimpses of green grass through them. A golf course, Kit had said it was.

"I want you to stay." His unexpected words knocked all the air out of her lungs.

What?! What did he mean by—

"Stay here in this century," he continued, oblivious.

Oh.

Fossi's chest deflated. A leaden rock plummeting through her stomach.

Right.

This had nothing to do with *them*—Foster and Daniel.

"Kit and Marc could easily help you get established," he added.

"Why do you assume that Time and the portal would allow me to stay?" she asked. "Once you go back, won't I be returned to 1826 too? Whether I return to 1828 initially first or not?"

He folded his arms across his chest. "I don't . . . I honestly don't know, at this point, Fossi." He turned his blue eyes to her. Bloodshot and so . . . lost.

Her own eyes stung.

She rubbed her forehead. "These time travel paradoxes are giving me a headache."

"Confusion is understandable." He nodded. "This whole situation is unprecedented. Theories on time travel involve ideas of parallel multiverses—" He waved a hand. "I'll spare you details. Basically, you might be allowed to remain."

"Even so, why would I stay?" It seemed baffling to her. This century was too confusing. Too fast.

"There are opportunities here," he replied. "You could be recognized for your mathematical genius. I consider it a crime that your ideas are lost to history. No one here today knows who the author of Fourier's Nemesis was. It isn't right."

Fossi sighed and leaned against the stone fence with him. An errant breeze tugged at her hair in its loose bun. She tucked a strand of hair behind her ear.

"I'm not eager to be renowned, Daniel. You know my dreams."

A beat.

"A witness," he said "Yes."

A boulder of emotion lodged in her throat.

How could something so simple be so impossibly difficult to obtain?

Most of humanity had someone in their life. Someone to love. Someone to love them in return.

If not a spouse, at least a child. Or even an adopted child.

"You could have that here. Societal customs are more open—"

"Daniel, no."

"—and you could find men and women who share your same brilliance and love of numbers."

"I'm not certain that is what I wish."

"Why not?"

"Well . . ."

Because you wouldn't be here.

Those were the words stuck around that aching lump.

I can't stay here *because you will be* there.

Daniel misread her silence.

He turned to her eagerly. "You should stay, Fossi. I know it seems frightening, but you would like it eventually. You would make new friends

❧ 273 ❧

and go to university and . . . and have a life that is of your own choosing." He grasped her hands. "Think about it."

Fossi *had* thought about it. She pulled her hands from his.

"Listen to your own words, Daniel. *Eventually. New.* How is that comforting to me? Yes, there seem to be advantages here, but this isn't me." She waved her arms to encompass the surrounding landscape. "Besides, it's a moot point. If everything reverts back to how it was in 1826, I will never *be* here. This isn't where I belong. I don't want *here.*"

"Fossi . . . please."

"No. A wise man once told me that everyone deserves choices. Well, I have made my choice. I choose to stand by you and see this entire situation through. I'm not going to promise to stay here to soothe your conscience. You have chosen Simon. I understand that. I cannot fault you for choosing your child; it is what any good parent would do. But in making that choice, you negate everything else. You cannot have one without the other."

"B-but I'm hurting you."

Well . . . obviously.

"Of course this hurts." She couldn't stop the words escaping. "It hurts because I feel you were less than truthful to me. It hurts because my dreams will never be realized. It hurts because I will regress to my unhappy life of two years ago."

It hurts because I will lose the only man I've ever loved.

Silence.

Daniel braced his hands on the stone fence, head hanging between his arms.

She didn't want to say it.

She did anyway.

"It hurts because I dared to dream." Her voice drifted through the quiet. "Only to see that dream shatter into a million jagged pieces. I should have known better than to reach too high."

He noticeably flinched, head sagging.

She turned to leave. She needed a quiet corner to cry her eyes out.

His hand on her arm halted her.

"You can't—" He started and then came to a gasping halt. "You can't do this."

She turned her head his way. Noted the terrible desperation in his gaze.

"Do what?"

"Force me to watch you suffer. Reject my help. "

"I am not rejecting you, Daniel." She touched his elbow. "I'm just doing what I have always done."

She applied pressure to his arm. *Please let me go.*

He released her.

"And what's that?"

She smiled then. A sad, forlorn thing. "Making the best of the paltry choices life gives me."

Chapter 23

Daniel sat in his room, staring out the window into the autumn gloom. Rainy with low hanging clouds, the day fit his mood. Rivulets streaked the glass, turning the outside world into blobs of distorted color.

The world viewed through a lens of sadness and desolation.

It was a fitting metaphor for the last five days.

What was the solution to be?

Giving up Simon, as Jasmine asserted and Kit hinted?

How would that solve the problem of the portal anyway? The earthquake and deviant timeline were the problem here.

Simon *had* to be key to it all.

He would not give up on his shiny, happy boy.

But . . . restoring Simon was currently denied him.

Which left . . . what? There was no path to pursue.

He was lost in a fog shrouded wilderness.

The door behind him *snicked* open. Kit's perfume wafted in.

She had called her office manager and put everything else in her life on hold to stay here with him and Fossi.

You need emotional support, was all she had said.

That was true. But at a certain point, there was nothing more to say.

"I don't want to talk about it." Heaven knew he and Kit had more than covered this territory the past couple days.

The sound of wood scraping across the floor and then Kit appeared beside him, sitting on a stool.

"I like your Fossi."

"She's not my Fossi."

Kit snorted. "Uh, yeah. She is. You're just being your usual stubborn self about it all."

What was it about hanging around Kit that made him five-years-old?

Even knowing it would make him feel infantile, he said it anyway.

"I'm *not* stubborn."

His sister smiled. One of those all-too-knowing smiles women specialized in.

Great.

"Fossi cares deeply for you."

"I care deeply for Fossi."

Daniel shifted in his chair. Thinking about Fossi . . . hurt. It was a constant, unyielding ache.

She had been subdued in 2017. Not terrified or upset or concerned or anxious or anything . . .

Just muted.

Bleached color.

She worked equations day after day, trying to find another answer. Something that resulted in infinity *without* the remainder.

And she avoided Daniel. Just as he avoided her.

Kit sighed next to him. "You need to let Simon go, Daniel."

He said nothing.

"That's my tough love statement for the year. Probably the decade, truth be told."

He still said nothing.

"Sometimes . . . even the best of things are not meant to be, little brother. This is your path."

Nothing.

"It's hard, I know—"

"No." Voice dead. "You don't know. You've never lost a child. It's not *hard*." His voice raised with the word. "Losing your job is hard. Recovering from surgery is hard. This"—he tapped his chest, right over his heart—"this is *hell*. This is agony that is fathomless and vast and it Never. *Freaking*. Ends."

It was Kit's turn to remain silent.

"Don't patronize me, Kit."

More silence.

Kit shook her head. "You say I didn't try to stop you from taking the candy back to Simon. I didn't say or do anything. Which means . . . something prevented me. I'm betting every time I tried to bring it up, the universe shut me down somehow." A long, rasping breath. "I *watched* you leave, knowing the end result. Don't you *dare* tell me I don't know hard."

A clock ticked in the corner. Daniel drummed his fingers against his thigh, the motion becoming more agitated with each passing second.

He shook his head. Left. Right.

"Why did I give him that damn candy, Kit?" Tone harsh. "How could I have been so bloody stupid?!"

"It was an honest mistake—"

"I had to watch Simon . . . *d-die*—" His voice broke, ending the phrase on a hiccupping gasp.

"I am so desperately sorry this happened to you, Daniel-mine."

Silence.

Rain pattered against the window. The house creaked in the wind.

"You *have* to forgive yourself, Daniel." Kit's voice drifted in the hush.

A serrated sob broke from his throat.

"I *k-killed* him—"

"No. No, you didn't. It was an accident."

Air lurched from his lungs in gulping gasps.

How could he ever forgive himself for doing the unforgivable?

He buried his fists in his eyes, shoulders heaving. Chest so tight he could hardly breathe.

"I was s-supposed to keep him safe. It was my one job. The s-simplest thing in the world and I *k-killed* him—"

"Daniel—"

"No!" He managed to bring his razored breathing under control.

"Accidents happen. Sometimes children die." Kit swiped a tear off her cheek. "It's what gives us empathy."

He shifted, shaking his head. "I refuse to accept that this pain will be the rest of my life. And don't you dare give me that favorite Princess Bride quote—"

"'Life *is* pain, Highness. Anyone who says differently is selling something,'" Kit recited with a watery chuckle. "That one?"

"Yep. I'm not buying it."

He studied a droplet trailing down the windowpane, air bellowing in and out of his lungs.

"I've realized over the years that the quote is wrong. Life isn't pain, Daniel." Her voice hushed. "Life is *joy*."

Daniel's throat was too raw for words.

Life is joy.

Kit continued, "Pain and Joy are opposite sides of the same coin. You can't understand joy unless you've felt pain. The pain of losing Simon is tied to the joy of being his father. You can't know one without knowing the other."

She wiped more tears away. "The cost of loving someone is the pain of losing them. That's the deal. Joy is *always* Pain on borrowed time."

A pause.

"Who said that?" he asked.

"Lots of people, probably. But right now, it's me."

"You've grown wise."

"So have you, Daniel."

"No. I haven't. I don't want joy at that price—"

"Yes . . . you do. It's what life is for. Imagine the joy of a life with Fossi."

Daniel inhaled sharply.

He *had* imagined that. And he had stopped imagining it because it was . . . compelling. Tempting.

Kit pressed her case. "You can't have the joy of being with Fossi without the pain of losing Simon."

He knew that. It was a choice he couldn't make.

"I can't give up on Simon. I *have* to fix my mistake."

Kit said nothing for a moment and then, "I think that's your excuse, Daniel."

"Pardon?!"

"This isn't about Simon. He's in a happy place, Daniel. Probably romping through angel clouds with Dad. This is about you."

"Me?" Daniel whirled on her, eyes stormy, brows drawn down. "Stop, Kit! This has *never* been about me—"

"You're wrong. This is entirely about you and your need for absolution." The compassion in her eyes belied her stern tone. "You're desperate to avoid the pain of Simon's death. Of having to face your own shortcomings and letting go of your guilt. You don't want the anguish of missing his presence in your life."

Daniel hissed, agony crashing through his chest. A precision bullet strike.

That wasn't true. That couldn't be true—

"You cling to him because letting him go is too hard. The pain and guilt too great. That's not the brother I know. My brother, Daniel Ashton, is the bravest, most courageous person I have ever met. He deliberately chose to make a life for himself in the nineteenth century. He has fought pirates across the high seas and been wounded for his actions. He has braved dark alleys at night to bring truth to light. He has even lasted through years of Lady Ballard's musical evenings and we all know what courage that takes. The Daniel I know would meet the pain with the same aplomb and mettle that he uses to face down organized crime rings."

Daniel bit his lip, fighting against that raw, wet knot in his throat trying to escape.

"Don't deny yourself the joy because you're afraid of the pain." Kit sniffed and rubbed her damp cheek with her shirt sleeve.

"I d-don't know—"

"You do know, Daniel." Kit turned and fixed him with pooling eyes. "Mourn him. Love him. Own your mistakes. And then Set. Him. Free."

She leaned forward and clutched his arm.

"Embrace your Fossi and the joyous future you can have with her. You love her. She loves you. You are brilliant together. You will have more children. You will have an heir, Daniel. It just won't be Simon." She wiped her wet cheeks. "And that's okay."

It was too much. Daniel tipped forward, holding his face in his hands. Sobs tore at him.

Dimly, he felt Kit gather him into her arms. Just as she had when they were children.

"I love you, Daniel mine." She brushed a kiss against his hair. "I want your happiness. Fossi wants your happiness. And Simon"—a gasp—"Simon would want you to be happy, too."

Chapter 24

Fossi sat in the front parlor, listening to the hum of Daniel and Kit talking upstairs.

When they first started their conversation, she had been in the kitchen. Their voices had been distinct there, drifting down to Fossi with brutal clarity.

"I like your Fossi." Kit's voice.

"She's not my Fossi." Daniel's rebuttal.

The words, though utterly true, had stung.

Their discussion descended to murmurs for a moment.

Then Kit again.

"You need to let Simon go, Daniel . . . It's hard, I know—"

More murmuring.

"No." Daniel's voice carried throughout the house. "You don't know. You've never lost a child. It's not hard. Losing your job is hard. Recovering from surgery is hard. This . . . this is hell." So much torment. "This is agony that is fathomless and vast and it Never. Freaking. Ends."

Fossi clapped her hands over her ears and darted out of the kitchen and into the front parlor before she heard any more.

Tears slipped helplessly down her cheeks.

Oh Daniel.

His pain . . . it ripped through her with all the subtlety of scatter shot.

What was the answer here?

They were all at an impasse.

The equations wouldn't budge, spitting out the same answer over and over.

Their timeline needed to be fixed.

Daniel could not give up on saving his son. How could he?

Fossi couldn't fault him for it. It just emphasized the size of his loving heart.

One thing was certain, however.

No matter the decision anyone made, there was *one* answer that remained the same—

Fossi would be left . . . alone.

That fact would not change.

If Daniel did restore Simon, Fossi would go back to where she had been. Living with her family, never knowing Daniel, always a burden to those she loved.

All the growth and understanding and joy she had found with him.

She would not be able to keep it.

If Daniel didn't restore Simon . . . what then?

He would never stop trying. Would they eventually be able to return to 1828 and work from there?

Would she spend her days at his side, watching him suffer over being unable to reset his past? Or would Daniel simply wither away too, as without an heir, he would never be born?

Regardless, there was no future for her with him.

No path. Just like with her family.

She understood Daniel's pain. Well . . . not entirely. She was sure losing a child was a different sort of grief.

But she knew how a broken heart felt.

To want someone in your life with such ferocity, the thought of not having him there made your lungs seize and your breath come in short puffs and a panic threaten to choke you—

Fossi stopped right there, her chest heaving, throat tight.

How could she live without Daniel?

How could Daniel live without Simon?

How could she live without being the Fossi she had become?

She retired to her room for the evening and finally tried to find sleep.

After tossing and turning for hours, she sat up at three in the morning, the answer pulsing through her brain.

Of course.

She switched on a light, snagged her notebook and began to do some frantic calculations.

After thirty minutes, she wanted to smack her forehead.

Gah! She had been such an idiot!

The answer was so . . . obvious.

The best answers always were.

Simple. Straightforward.

This one rang as Truth.

How could you add a soul to the vast Ocean of Time?

You couldn't.

But subtracting a soul . . . *that* might be possible.

She reviewed her calculations again.

Yes. This had to be the correct answer.

The resonant frequency pitch *could* originate from the portal epicenter, but the harmonics would tear the source apart.

Before that had seemed like a negative.

But . . . considering it a positive and plugging it back into the equations . . .

If someone stood *in the portal* and sang the D-flat frequency pitch, the resulting convulsion of waves would tear that person apart at the most fundamental level.

Basically, the person would *become* the frequency stabilizing pitch.

Effectively removing them from existence.

And if that one person were removed from the infinite equation, then the numbers would align.

The math would resolve into harmony.

With the person added to the oscillations, everything would move in unison again. Which meant the portal would be restored.

Daniel could return to save Simon.

Everyone would get what they wanted.

Well . . . except for the person unraveled, of course.

But what awaited her here? Or in 1828?

She couldn't bear watching Daniel mourn Simon year after year. She loved him too much. His suffering, in the end, was her own.

But . . . she didn't want to return to the Fossi of 1826. Or any of the Fossi's before Daniel Ashton, really.

There was truly *no* path forward for her that did not involve significant emotional pain.

She had no husband or children. No one needed her help. No one relied upon her.

She was free.

And the freedom that had always felt isolating and lonely . . . suddenly seemed a gift.

She could leave and no one's life would be altered.

Moreover, being unraveled from Time itself would be more thorough than mere death. Everything would continue on as if she had never existed.

She would never be born. Daniel wouldn't even remember her. Time would snap back to where it had been.

No one would be hurt and Daniel would have Simon.

She tapped her pencil against her notebook, staring at the dark window, considering.

He had asked her. *What is your heart's desire?*

She had thought she wanted him.

And that was true.

But even more than that, she wanted Daniel's joy. She wanted him to be happy.

That was her heart's desire.

He would try to stop her. He was too noble to allow her to sacrifice herself for his cause.

So she wouldn't present the idea for a vote.

Whether it worked or not, no one would be the wiser anyway.

Before she could out-think it, Fossi tossed off the bedcovers and tiptoed down the stairs.

A light glimmered from the great room. She peeked around the corner.

Daniel was asleep on the couch, a lamp turned low on the table opposite him.

Just the sight of his dear face made her heart lurch and her chest ache and her lips tingle.

She loved him. Completely. Utterly.

She truly would do anything for him.

Crossing silently to the couch, she pressed a soft kiss to his mouth.

He snored in response.

Dear man.

He had been sleeping so poorly lately.

"Goodbye, my Daniel," she whispered, more air than sound. "I love you. More than life. More than anything. You will forget my existence. But somehow, I hope I will remember yours."

She kissed him again. And then stood back, drinking in one last look of him sleeping, expression relaxed. Boyish even.

Her throat burned; her eyes stung.

Shaking the emotion away, she turned and walked quietly back out of the room.

The door to the portal was open. She ducked down the steep stairs, not needing a light to find her way in the gloom.

The portal was kinetic chaos. Currents swirled through the room, dissonant and frantic.

Was she truly going to do this? Could she do anything less?

She swiped at her wet cheeks.

For Daniel . . .

Letting out a deep breath, Fossi closed her eyes, swallowing back her tears. Inviting the turbulent energy to engulf her.

The portal seemed to know that she was there. That she alone could solve its problem.

A stray whipping strand of energy latched on to her and urged her forward.

It wasn't a powerful tug. Fossi could break it. But she didn't want to. She *wanted* to be the solution.

Eyes still closed, she stepped forward. Placing her bare feet into the depression of the portal itself. The damp earth chilled beneath her toes.

Electricity and power thrummed around her—a wild, frenzied mess.

Breathing in deeply, Fossi sang, voice seeking the correct note.

She started with the D-flat, but instantly sensed that it wasn't quite the correct pitch anymore. The oscillations had shifted. She moved higher.

D. D-Sharp. E.

The portal liked the E note. Fossi pitched it the tiniest bit higher. Not quite an F, not quite an E.

Eureka.

The portal snapped into alignment, the resonant pitch matching the cosmic sea oscillation frequency.

She felt it then.

A sense of lightness. Of air whistling through her. Tugging. Pulling. Unraveling.

As if she were made of a million miles of thread and someone plucked one end and ran off with it, unwinding the whole.

Faintly, a sound drifted in. Something beyond the hum of the portal and the swoosh of her lungs.

A thumping, scrambling noise—

"NO!"

Arms engulfed her, wrapping around. Bands of iron determined to hold everything together.

"No!"

Fossi whimpered and stopped singing. But the portal kept thrumming, the unraveling continued.

"No. Don't you dare do this." *Daniel.* "Don't you dare leave me, Foster Lovejoy."

Oh, Daniel.

She wanted to open her mouth. To tell him that it was all right. This was her gift to him. To Simon. To them all.

He would not remember her. No one would—

"I love you." His words shook the foundations of her world. "I love you . . . you maddening, intelligent, beautiful, courageous woman. You cannot do this."

She gasped. An agony of sound.

He *loved* her.

That was . . . impossible.

"Please. Don't leave me." His voice a sobbing breath against her neck.

I'll stay, she wanted to cry. *I will be with you.*

But she was a ball of yarn tumbling down a hill.

And nothing could stop her unraveling until she reached the bottom.

DANIEL CLUTCHED FOSSI tighter. He pressed kiss after kiss against her throat, her jaw, her cheek.

He had been asleep.

And in his dream, Fossi had come to him, whispering.

I love you.

You will forget my existence.

The sound of Fossi singing had jerked him fully awake, quickly shaking off his disorientation.

And he *knew.*

Could feel it with a soul-shattering intensity—

She was doing something terrible.

Something final and irreversible.

And in that moment . . . he finally understood.

Finally accepted.

A life without Fossi . . . that was a life he *could not* live.

She *was* his life.

And so he held her with his entire soul. A vice-like grip.

"I love you. IloveyouIloveyouIloveyou," a constant stream from his mouth.

She continued to slip away. He went with her.

The room spun and that familiar vertigo of falling, falling, falling.

But then . . . nothing.

Daniel opened his eyes.

He held Fossi. And she held him.

She looked up at him, an enormous smile on her face.

Wonder. Delight. Adoration.

And then, he glanced around to where they were.

Heavens above!

Quite literally, it seemed.

They stood on a shimmery disk, floating aloft a vast ocean under a pale azure-blue sky, the far-off horizon glowing in the reds and golds and pinks of sunset. As far as he could see, concentric rings rippled, bobbing up and down. Some in harmony, other's in chaotic dissonance.

Wow.

The Ocean of Time itself.

He clutched Fossi closer, pressing a kiss to her forehead.

Love overwhelmed him.

Not his love for Fossi or Fossi for him.

It originated outside them both. Encompassing the entire universe. Suffocating love. Fathomless and endless and full of such . . . *joy.*

A love that said, *I know your heart. I forgive you. Have faith in me. All will be well.*

Something wet his hand.

Daniel looked down at Fossi.

He gently wiped another tear off her soft cheek. She managed a wobbly smile.

"I love you." Her voice carried in the hush. "I l-love you so much."

Daniel smiled then. Huge. Life-altering.

He bent and kissed her.

Perhaps not the thing most would choose to do when surrounded by the Ocean of Time, but he was helpless to resist. Eager to express his new-found convictions.

She welcomed him, kissing him back with eager enthusiasm.

"In case you missed it, I love you, too," he murmured against her lips. "My darling, dearest Fossi."

She hiccupped and then laughed.

"Marry me?" The words slipped from him. The deepest desire of his heart.

But . . .

He *had* to ask. It felt urgent. He *needed* to know that she would be his. That they would walk together through life.

She gasped, an awe-struck sound.

"P-pardon?!" She stared, eyes so hopeful. Another tear tumbled free. "You . . . you sincerely mean it?"

"Of course, my love." He brushed her cheek with his fingers. "More than I have ever meant anything."

"B-but what about Simon—"

His body froze.

Simon.

What about Simon?

His beautiful, shining boy.

He couldn't have both. Fossi and Simon.

He pressed his forehead to hers. Breaths labored.

Simon would want you to be happy, too.

A sob burst from him.

Then another.

Until the dam broke and he keened his sorrow in painful, hiccupping gasps.

Fossi's arms came around him, her own tears joining his.

But even as he wept, he recognized that this time . . . this was different.

His weeping before had been the pain of a wrenched soul. Lost. Helpless.

These tears, however . . .

These were goodbye.

A farewell. A decision.

He mourned Simon. Profoundly. Deeply.

But in his soul, he recognized that Kit was right.

Sometimes life was simply hard.

Bad things happened.

Wives absconded. Fathers made mistakes.

Sons died.

Having a time portal would not shield him from the harsh pain of life.

Of course, that did not make the decision easy. He would never stop mourning his son.

But sometimes, no matter how badly you wanted to go backward, you could only move forward.

And he'd be damned if he let Fossi go on without him.

"W-why?" Fossi whispered after a moment, voice watery.

Why did you stop me? Why did you come?

He forced his shuddery breaths to calm down. "S-sometimes we have to just let go and accept what Fate has decreed. Simon is in a better place. And as for me, I want nothing more than to be with you."

"Truly?"

"Yes."

She sniffled. He wrapped her close.

"Marry me?" He murmured again. "Be my wife, my best friend, my confidant. Be my love."

Joy lit her face, a slow sunrise of glowing happiness.

"Y-yes!!" She threw her arms around his neck, kissing him soundly.

They broke apart, foreheads touching, each laughing through their tears.

Abruptly, Daniel felt something tug on his hand.

And given how Fossi jerked, something pulled on her too.

They both turned. In amazement, Daniel watched a thread reel out from his fingertips. A matching thread spooled off of Fossi's hand.

The threads broke free and twined together. Glimmering gold, the strands swirled around each other. Faster and faster until they merged into one.

The combined string darted away and then, with a dramatic swoosh, *plinked* down into the ocean.

Creating a new ripple. A new ring.

The new ring instantly expanded to connect with other ripples, harmony cascading throughout the ocean in a giant wave.

Until the entire ocean sighed up and down as one whole.

"Oh!" Fossi's wondrous gasp had him bending to kiss her temple.

Out of the corner of his eye, he noted a small strand dart out of the ocean. Silvery-gold, it sailed right to him and wrapped around Daniel's shoulders.

Quick. Delighted. Excited.

Simon's laughter trilled through Daniel's mind.

Happiness. Healing. Love. Joy.

But most importantly . . .

Forgiveness.

A benediction of sorts.

And then it was gone. Spinning away. The silvery-gold thread sank back into its place.

Something wet hit his hand again.

Only this time, it was Fossi's turn to wipe away his tears.

BETWEEN ONE BLINK and the next, the world swooped and vertigo clutched at Fossi's stomach.

The vast ocean dissolved away and Fossi found herself standing in Daniel's embrace in the dark cellar of Duir Cottage.

The portal hummed beneath their feet. Harmonious and whole.

"Did that really just happen?" she whispered into the dark.

"I think it did." Even in the dim light, she could see Daniel's weary face.

He looked . . . open. As if all the walls of Fortress Whitmoor had been bombarded to dust, leaving simply Daniel. Tired. Worn.

Heartsick and heart-full.

"Are you sure about this, Daniel?" She had to ask him.

He closed his eyes with a faint smile. Pulled her into an even tighter hug.

"As sure as I've ever been about anything."

"But, Daniel . . ."

"No, Foster Lovejoy. You just agreed to become Mrs. Ashton. You cannot renege. I will not allow myself to be whitmoored in this."

Joy bubbled through her veins. On a laugh, she popped onto her tiptoes and kissed him.

Daniel flexed his arms around her, returning the embrace with delicious enthusiasm.

A few minutes later, Fossi pulled her head back. "Are we concerned at all about when we are?"

"Right. There is that, I suppose."

They stepped out of the portal, Fossi stumbling on a pile of tuning forks on the ground.

"Interesting." Daniel nudged his chin at the tuning forks. "Back where we started, I'm going to guess. Shall we?"

He motioned for her to head up the stairs.

Once there, he dragged her into the front parlor with its sofa and chairs. Not the same furniture that had existed in 2017 but still comfortable.

"Are you well?" Daniel sat facing her, holding both her hands in his.

Fossi was quite sure her smile was foolishly radiant. The happiness beating through her heart threatened to choke her.

She cupped his beloved face. The bliss shining in her eyes spilled out and tumbled down her cheeks. "I n-never dreamed such joy existed."

He smiled and leaned in for a kiss. His lips warm and impossibly soft. Heavens but she would never tire of kissing him.

Her Daniel.

I would take her a lifetime of kisses to adequately express her love for him.

The sound of voices drifted up from the cellar.

Fossi pulled back just before Jasmine and Timothy walked into the parlor, a giddy grin on her face.

Jasmine's face was radiant, glowing with health. Timothy Linwood simply appeared relieved with his wife's recovery.

Jasmine clearly didn't miss the implications of Fossi and Daniel sitting together on the sofa.

"Hallelujah!" she said. "Please tell me you two have decided to marry?"

"Jasmine—" Timothy began, voice strained.

"No, it is what was meant to happen, Timothy." She turned to her husband. "I always know these things."

A beat.

"What did you know, Jas?" Daniel asked.

She smiled at him, angling her head. "Why, that you and Miss Lovejoy were destined for each other, of course."

Another pause.

"And you didn't tell me this . . . why?" he asked.

Jasmine met Fossi's eyes. And then looked back at Daniel.

As if to say, *Is he serious?*

A smile tugged at Fossi's lips.

How she adored these people.

"I'm pretty sure I did, Daniel," Jasmine finally said. "You just weren't interested in listening. So . . . now that this is all sorted, let's walk down to Haldon Manor and call on Arthur and Marianne. I would prefer not to walk home."

Jasmine twirled to leave the room.

"Whoa there, Jas." Daniel's voice stopped her. "You need to do some more explaining."

She turned around.

Daniel rolled his hand. *Go on.*

Jasmine's eyes softened, moving from mischievous to empathetic. "Simon's death was never a random accident, Daniel. It was your path. Not an easy one, but necessary for you to find Fossi. It was *your* refusal to accept your future that caused the portal to malfunction. The earthquake was simply a random coincidence in the end."

That made sense, Fossi supposed.

But . . .

She frowned. She still had questions.

"I can understand that," she said, "but the math did not change. There still needed to be a plus or minus one to infinity. Something happened when we . . . well—"

Fossi explained about seeing the Ocean of Time and the thread that had spooled off her and Daniel to merge into another concentric ring.

"So what was added?" Fossi asked. "Can you tell us?"

Jasmine laughed, a delighted bell of sound.

"Tell you? And spoil the surprise?" Jasmine winked at them. "Oh no. This is one you two need to figure out yourselves. Together."

Daniel sighed.

Fossi grabbed his coat lapels and pulled him down for another kiss.

Together.

She liked the sound of that.

"You're going to have to come up with an equation for that, you know." Daniel chuckled against her lips.

"Equation?"

"Yes. Explain how one plus one will equal one."

"Me and you together?"

"Mm-hm," Daniel hummed, kissing her temple.

Fossi laughed, breathless and carefree. "We will just have to take a lifetime to find the answer.

Epilogue

"I'm sorry I haven't been by to visit lately." Daniel held his hat in his hands. "Much has happened, as I'm sure you already know."

A wind rustled in the trees. A sparrow trilled overhead. Far off, a cow lowed.

Daniel looked around the peaceful church graveyard. Headstones tilted this way and that. Some shiny. Some weathered.

He looked down at the grave before him:

Simon Daniel George Ashton
B. May 14, 1820
D. November 11, 1826
Beloved son.
My blessed light, gone too soon.

It still hurt to be here. To think on Simon and what would never be.

Daniel was quite sure the pain would never cease. He would never stop missing his bright, sunny boy.

Kit had been correct. The pain was part and parcel of the joy of being a parent.

He would never have wished for this heartrending loss, but the pain *did* make the rest of life sweeter.

Daniel Ashton knew the full worth of what he presently possessed.

And his current life brought him immense joy.

"It looks lovely with the flowers planted round."

Daniel whirled around, smiling as Fossi crossed the grass to him. "It does."

Beloved, beautiful, sparkling Fossi.

How he *loved* her.

She had brought him such happiness. Every day with her was one of delight. Laughter. Sunshine.

That intense bone-deep joy that comes from knowing and being known to the innermost core of yourself.

The bundle in Fossi's arms squirmed and then fussed.

"Here. I'm quite sure he's asking for me." Daniel grinned.

Shaking her head, Fossi gently placed their swaddled son into Daniel's arms.

As it turned out, one plus one currently equaled three.

Daniel smiled down at little George who waved an angry tiny fist back. Daniel offered him a finger to clutch, which seemed to soothe him for now.

Jasmine had been right.

They had needed to understand for themselves.

This was the new ripple he had seen when Fossi had tried to unravel herself from Time almost a year ago.

He had seen George.

Instead of removing herself, they had agreed to marry and metaphorically (and now literally) added baby George to the Ocean of Time.

After returning to 1828 and finding everything restored, Daniel had wasted no time. Their bans had been read, and he and Fossi wed three weeks later at Whitmoor House.

That part was idyllic.

Fossi's father had *not* taken kindly to his daughter marrying into the aristocracy.

Her sisters and Will, however, were delighted.

Her sisters, because Fossi was now in a financial position to advance the fortunes of her nieces and nephews. Will, because he genuinely loved his sister and wished her happiness.

As a wedding gift, Daniel had made a generous donation to the Society of Mathematicians upon the condition that they accept his new wife as a member. The Society easily did the math on that one and readily agreed. Fossi had delighted in exchanging ideas more openly with her peers. Even better, she had established a charity which had already opened two schools for girls with plans for five more.

The past year with Fossi had been the most blissful of Daniel's life. They had only grown closer, the quickness of her mind and inventiveness of her creativity never ceased to amaze him.

At Daniel's side, Fossi bent over and gave George a light kiss on the forehead.

"He does love his daddy."

George gurgled in agreement.

Daniel's heart threatened to burst.

Fossi sighed. It was a deliriously contented sound. She rested her head on his shoulder.

"You do realize that the odds of us marrying and finding such blissful happiness were approximately one in seven point five three two million, right?" She offered George a finger for his other hand.

"Well, I'm glad I risked it then," Daniel chuckled. "It's was all worth it to find such endless happiness. Infinity."

Fossi laughed and kissed George again.

"Plus one."

Author's Note

As usual, when writing a story set in the past, I have incorporated select aspects of history and then blatantly made up others. Allow me to separate out the fact from the fiction. Though, be warned, there are major spoilers in here if you haven't finished *Outshine* yet.

Earthquakes do happen in England. Not often and never too strong, but they do occur. In fact, the largest recorded land earthquake in England was centered around Hereford in 1896 and was similar in strength to the one described in the book.

As mentioned in the book, Joseph Fourier was a French mathematician and physicist (1768-1830) renowned for his pioneering work on waves, heat transfer and vibrations. He did indeed originate the concept of a Fourier Series. That said, Fourier's Nemesis was completely my own fabrication.

Also, I am not a math person. So to that math whiz who read this book and wanted to shout at me for my mathematical stupidity, I am *so* sorry. If it makes you feel better, please email me with your concerns and suggestions. I'd love to improve my math faux-science justifications and learning from my mistakes is a great way to do so. I appreciate any and all insight.

The Queen of the Night aria that Fossi sings is, of course, very real. It is intense and amazing and still one of the most difficult arias for any soprano to sing. Look it up on YouTube or a music listening service. I recommend any version sung by Sumi Jo. It's well worth a listen.

Though rare, individuals have been known to experience a life-threatening allergic reaction to modern, synthetic food dyes.

As usual, I made up a good many things: the town of Marfield and all house names.

For each of my books, I create a Pinterest board of all the visual references I used when writing. So if you would like to see how fashion changed in the late 1820s or my inspiration for Daniel and Fossi, don't hesitate to look me up over there. Just search NicholeVan.

As with all books, this one couldn't have been written without help and support from those around me. I know I am going to leave someone out with all these thanks. So to that person, know that I totally love you and am so deeply grateful for your help!

First of all, thank you to all those who read the earlier books in this series and sent me excited emails, asking if Daniel Ashton would ever get a story. Your encouragement and enthusiasm means more than I can say.

To my beta readers—you know who you are—thank you for your helpful ideas and support. And, again, an extra large thank you to Annette Evans and Norma Melzer for their fantastic copy editing skills and insights.

A huge thank you goes to Lois Brown, Jen Jenkins and Amy Beatty for their always helpful plot suggestions and insights.

And I cannot even begin to thank my brilliant editor, Erin Rodabough. She has the amazing gift of being able to hone in on problems and provide solutions. Not to mention being an awesome friend and travel buddy. Being drenched in Scottish highland rain and braving hurricane force winds is always more fun with you!

Thanks to Andrew, Austenne and Kian for your patience during this time of our life. I uprooted you from friends and family and moved you to Scotland while writing this book. Thank you for always remaining upbeat and positive. And wearing headphones. I definitely appreciate that too.

And finally, no words can express my love and appreciation for Dave. Thank you for being my rock.

Reading Group Questions

Oh yes, this book has reading group questions.
You're welcome.

1. Why do you feel the author named the book *Outshine*?

2. This book hits on a lot of major themes that people face in mid-life. One of these is loneliness. Did the author's description of Fossi's loneliness resonate with you? Have there been times in your own life where you felt a similar sense of separation from friends and family?

3. Masks are another theme of the book. Both Fossi and Daniel wear masks that they present to the outside world. Most of us don masks to a certain extent. Social customs require it. That said, at what point does wearing a mask become a problem? Did you like how Fossi slowly unraveled Daniel's mask as the book progressed? Why or why not?

4. Ideas of love run throughout the book, specifically romantic love and familial love. But as the book progresses, we also start to see threads of self love, too. In what ways did both Fossi and Daniel have to show self-love in order to find their happily-ever-after?

5. The author does not specifically mention God or cite religious ideals in the book. However, Fossi is named by religion, raised by religion and at her core has obvious faith in religion. How does this come through in her decisions throughout the book? What symbolism do you see in Fossi's decision to sacrifice herself for Daniel at the end?

6. When reading Outshine, we don't find out about Daniel's true intentions with the portal until about 60% through. Up until that point, what did you think his grief was about? Did you suspect that Daniel was upset over a child?

7. Both Daniel and Fossi are dealing with heavy weights of grief. Daniel in particular is wracked with intense guilt, regret and sorrow. Did you relate to both their pain? Did you like the heavier themes of the book or did it weigh you down?

8. The author has included a deleted prologue and deleted scene in the appendices here. Why do you think that author decided to use the prologue she did? Why did she remove the scene with James and Emme?

9. Alright, let's cast the movie of the book. (Cause hey, we can dream big, right?) Who plays Daniel? Fossi? etc. How should some of the scenes be filmed? In the movie version, what aspects of the book should be thrown out, condensed or altered? Also, what should the theme love song be?

Alternate Prologue

I swear, I never get my prologue right. This book went through three, entirely separate prologues. I eventually settled on having an argument between Jasmine and Daniel. But here is an earlier version, placing the earthquake at the moment Daniel arrives at Duir Cottage, intent on saving Simon.

All was dark.

The sun may have danced cheerfully in a diamond-blue sky, ricocheting off the yellow and gold and red leaves of autumn that rushed past.

Daniel Ashton didn't notice. He didn't care. He simply pushed his stallion to gallop faster down the rutted, narrow road.

To him, the world was plunged into the murkiest midnight, devoid of stars or moon. A devastated wasteland.

Hope. There must be hope. Because without hope, only madness and despair existed.

Daniel was used to living in shadows. But this time . . . this time was different. If he couldn't fix this, the darkness would never leave, never lift. Boundless in its breadth. Fathomless in its depth.

At last! The lane appeared from the left. Without breaking stride, he turned his horse onto it. The saddlebag bumped his leg, swinging with the curve. A box inside rattled.

Promise you will keep it for me. Don't forget.

Daniel gasped, a deep rasping hiccup of sound. His chest tightened, panic acrid and burning in his throat.

Guilt crushed his lungs in a destructive vise.

He would. He would keep it safe. Safeguarding things was one of his many talents.

Daniel kept secrets and solved problems for the most powerful men in the world. He was considered by some to *be* one of those powerful men.

The world never said 'No' to him.

This was one problem he *had* to solve.

Some wounds were too deep to ever heal. Without a solution, this pain would never cease. The best he could hope for was an uneasy coexistence.

Breathe in and out. One day at a time.

He rounded the final turn and the house came into view. He pulled on the reins and threw himself off the horse, hitting the ground at a run. Past the front gate, up the walkway and through the front door.

A deep rumble sounded from far off, drawing nearer. Like a steam locomotive. Or a vast mining explosion. Or an airplane during takeoff.

He paused in the entrance hallway, hand on a wall, breathing hard.

The sound reverberated, almost like a sonic boom—

No! It was a—

Daniel braced himself, catching a nearby vase before it could tumble to the floor.

The windows rattled. The floor shook. Items danced across tabletops.

He had experienced earthquakes before. One on a rare family trip to Disneyland California as a child. His sister, Kit, had clung to the motel bed as the TV rattled and car alarms blared, her eyes wide and terrified.

That had been before the time portal here in Duir Cottage had forever altered the trajectory of his life.

The rumble turned into a roar. A jet engine of sound.

Daniel turned, ready to dart back outside before walls started tumbling inward, when the shaking suddenly stopped.

He paused, mid-lunge. Dimly, he noted the surprised *baas* of sheep, the frenzied barking of farm dogs.

The earthquake had been . . . distracting.

For ten seconds he had forgotten. Ten seconds without the crushing pain.

It avalanched back over him, driving him to his knees.

Breathe in and out. One day at a time.

There was a solution to this.

And he would have it . . . even if he had to destroy time itself.

Deleted Scene

In Outshine, *I wanted to give all the characters from the previous four books little cameos. Unfortunately, that proved too difficult, particularly with James and Emme from* Intertwine. *Initially, I had all the characters who were outside their original time periods (like James) suffering the same effects as Jasmine. But that angle on the story fell by the wayside and so this small glimpse of James and Emme was cut. This scene occurs toward the end of the book when the characters are gathered in the cellar of Duir Cottage, right after Jasmine and Timothy disappear through the portal but before Daniel and Fossi leave 1828.*

The air over the portal shimmered.

Emme appeared holding a barely conscious James against her body, his blond head lolling to the side.

"Daniel!" she gasped. "Help me!"

Fossi stopped singing. The portal crashed, energy running amok.

Daniel leaped forward, helping Emme pull James out of the depression and gently easing him down to lean against the wall. James' breathing was shallow, skin chilled.

"What on earth." Daniel crouched beside his friend.

Emme was half holding James in her arms.

"He's been fading over the past several months." Emme brushed her husband's hair off his forehead. "At first, we thought it might be cancer or something—"

"It's the portal," James mumbled, nuzzling his head into Emme's hand. A puppy looking for more affection. "I could feel my body out of alignment with the time period. But being back here . . ." James lifted his head on a sigh. Color was already returning to his cheeks. He took in a deep breath. "Wow. It's like everything suddenly snapped back together."

Emme nodded. "It's what we thought. Those who have been out of the time periods of their birth the longest were suffering." She looked around. "Where's Jas?"

"She collapsed completely. Timothy vanished with her."

Emme nodded. "Probably off to her correct time period then." She helped James to his feet. Only then noticing Fossi standing behind Daniel.

"Oh. Hello." Emme smiled at Fossi. "Who is this?"

Daniel made introductions.

"What happened to make the portal stop working?" James asked, pushing himself more upright. "It's been nearly two years since we saw each other."

"It's been too long, my friend."

Daniel explained everything, starting with his mistake and Simon's death, the subsequent earthquake, Daniel's hunt for the author of Fourier's Nemesis, and how Fossi had found a solution, at least temporarily, for the portal.

Given how Emme was staring between Fossi and himself as he talked, she perhaps saw much more than the simple narrative he related.

"Daniel, how awful." Emme clutched a hand over her stomach, eyes bright. "Poor, sweet Simon."

"All will be well, Emme. We'll get him back."

She nodded.

"Shall I sing to restore you to your proper time?" Fossi asked Emme in her polite, direct way.

Emme looked to James and pondered for a moment. "I feel fine. I think it's a slow, cumulative effect of misalignment for those who have been out of the time of their birth. I'm content to stay here for now. Perhaps we can sneak in a visit to Georgiana." She turned to Daniel. "Frankly, I'm surprised you're doing so well, Daniel."

Daniel shrugged. Who knew why he was all right? Maybe because he was the cause of Simon's death and the subsequent timeline fracture? The fulcrum, so to speak? Or because he was the one who had to fix it?

Which thinking of that . . .

"The sooner I restore the timeline to how it should have been, the better."

OTHER BOOKS BY NICHOLE VAN

THE BROTHERS MALEDETTI

Gladly Beyond (Dante and Claire)
Love's Shadow (Branwell and Lucy)
Chiara and Jack (coming mid-2017)
Tennyson and Ainsley (coming late 2017)

THE HOUSE OF OAK

Intertwine
Divine
Clandestine
Refine
Outshine
An Invisible Heiress (a novella in *Spring in Hyde Park*)

Turn the page to read previews of *Gladly Beyond,* first book in the Brothers Maledetti series and *Intertwine,* first book in the House of Oak series.

Gladly Beyond

BROTHERS MALEDETTI, BOOK ONE

FLORENCE, ITALY 2015
CLAIRE RAYTHORN

I've always thought Italian cities are like guys I knew in college:

Rome—the hot frat boy I was dying to go out with (and I did, and it was awesome). But, turns out, *everyone* dated Rome.

Naples—Rome's frat house roommate. The guy on no sleep and his tenth can of Red Bull. No one messed with him cause he knew people who knew people . . . catch my drift . . .

Venice—the dreamily gorgeous philosophy major. Brilliantly eccentric but exotic enough that no one quite knew what to make of him.

Milan—the second-year MBA student who was big on power-ties and power-lunches. Basically, the organized guy who held everyone else together.

And then there was Florence.

Firenze, to those who knew him.

Quiet and unassuming. When we first met, I wondered what all the fuss was about.

But Firenze . . . he was a subtle seducer. If I asked, he could talk for hours about art and history. But, generally, Firenze simply listened. Peaceful. Steady. Ready to shoulder my sorrows.

Firenze is the guy I never got out of my system.

Truth.

I took a sip of my hotel coffee and studied the huge Piazza della Signoria around me.

Classic Firenze.

Stately buildings squished around the perimeter, arched green shutters pushed open, looking out like so many eyes. Across from me, golden April sunlight cheerily danced across the ancient stone of the town hall—the Palazzo Vecchio. (Thirteenth century. Crenelated clock tower.)

Though still early, people filled the piazza. Retired couples nose-deep in Frommers. Rowdy school kids waiting in line for the Uffizi museum. African street vendors offering selfie-sticks for purchase. A line of Japanese tourists cut through, their guide holding a red umbrella aloft like a war banner.

My Grandma Adelaide had loved this city to distraction.

I did too.

In my mind's eye, I could still see Grammy giggling with excitement over being in Florence for the first time. I had been fourteen then, convinced I would have her with me forever.

Grandmas are stodgy and old, she would say. *Grammys are awards. Guess which one I am?*

I blinked, biting hard on my bottom lip.

Why is death like this? It's not enough to face loss once.

No. You have to bury your loved one over and over. Confront each place where she still feels so vibrantly *alive.*

I hadn't known to mentally prepare myself for this pain before leaving my hotel today. To anticipate the pounding waves of raw grief. Grammy's death was still new, and I was a novice to this form of sorrow. I had yet to learn its valleys and cliffs, its ebb and flow . . .

I had simply thought to enjoy a leisurely stroll through downtown Florence, become reacquainted with my long-time-no-see boyfriend city. Let Firenze soothe away my nerves before my hopefully career-resuscitating meeting in an hour.

But, of course, I couldn't escape my problems so easily.

Instead of comfort, Florence had ripped the Band-Aid off my heartache.

I stared at the Palazzo Vecchio, memories swamping me. Grammy had marched over to its massive front doors and pretended to swoon in front of Michelangelo's *David.* (Replica. Victorian.) And then she had snagged some poor guy to take a photo of us both, waving our arms like idiots. Looking as if we could embrace the whole world.

It was a talisman, that photo. I took a copy of it with me everywhere. A reminder that, at one point, I had been thoroughly loved just as I was.

Something I needed, now more than ever. What with the harassing texts at all hours and that scathing, mega-viral video. All due to Pierce, my former fiancé, who I was going to see this morning for the first time since becoming spectacularly *dis*-engaged.

For the record, Grammy had never liked Pierce.

I drained the last of my coffee and tossed the empty cup in a nearby garbage can. Checked the time on my phone. Just under an hour before my potentially life altering meeting.

Suddenly, my neck prickled with awareness. That jungle-sense of being invisibly watched. My nerves flared to high alert.

Please. Not today. Not now.

Carefully, I turned in a circle. Looking for the tell-tale glare of a camera lens aimed my way. People talking and pointing.

What I saw instead was a wrinkled gypsy woman, staring intently. Ragged loose skirt, head scarf, wooden cane. Completely anachronistic.

We locked eyes. Her dark gaze drilled me, wispy strands of gray hair escaping to flutter in the slight wind.

My breath hitched. I instinctively wrapped a firm hand around my purse, pulling it tight against my body. I had seen too many tourists robbed over the years.

"It begins again," the gypsy called in heavily accented English. She regarded me with unnerving directness.

I blinked.

"It will repeat." She smiled, maniacal and toothless. "*Ripetere.*"

What?!

The gypsy lady winked and waved a gnarled hand my way. Before I could react, she turned and hobbled off, swallowed up by a group of Indian tourists.

Okay.

That was . . . weird.

Somewhere on the scale between 'Beware the Ides of March' and a movie trailer for *Borat*.

I stood, frozen. Still clutching my bag across my chest. I thawed my spine enough to scan the people around me, half expecting another gypsy to make a grab for my purse.

Nothing.

I swallowed. Told the pulse in my throat to settle down.

My parents—Lisabet and my step-dad, John-Baptista—are flamboyant installation artists and former stars of their own reality TV show on IFC. (Canceled after one season. Producers said they were too 'nutty.' I repeat: My parents were deemed *too* crazy for reality TV.)

Basically, *weird* and *out-there* have always been par for the course in my life. So an old gypsy lady yelling nonsense at me in the middle of Florence?

Usually, I would just file that under 'quirky.'

But given the hell of the last six months, it was hard to brush things off anymore.

Courage isn't a lack of fear, Grammy had always said. *It's hefting Fear onto your back and trudging forward into the dark.*

I was *so* tired of Fear.

I would *live* my life.

To that end, I lifted my chin and walked farther into the sun-drenched piazza. One more scan for gypsies. Seeing nothing unusual, I pulled out my phone. Framed my face. And took a selfie.

Me. The Palazzo Vecchio. Michelangelo's *David*.

Just to be clear, I'm not usually into selfies. I find them a bit fratgirl-narcissistic.

Grammy, on the other hand, had *loved* them. I've decided selfies move from vain to awesome once you're over fifty.

Today, selfies in our boyfriend-city felt like a fitting homage to my grandmother.

Some people build memorials or start charitable foundations to commemorate a loved one.

I take selfies.

Phone in hand, I walked across the Piazza della Signoria and onto Via dei Cerchi heading toward the Duomo. The medieval streets closed in, buildings rising four and five stories above me.

I paused now and again to take a selfie. The act of taking photos calming me. Allowing me to leash my grief (Grammy), my anxiety (weird gypsy ladies) and my nerves (code-red-critical meeting).

Which was good. I would need deep reserves of serenity today. I had to keep my cool during this meeting. Remain professional no matter how much Pierce taunted me.

Only the combination of a career meltdown and impending financial disaster could force me to deal with my former fiancé in any capacity. But this meeting could result in a job—an extremely well-paying, career-resuscitating job.

I kept walking, moving through the narrow, pedestrian-only streets, a tight hand on my phone and my purse. Heaven knew, I couldn't afford to replace either if they were stolen.

I've always been poor and struggling. Famous parents do not equal moneyed parents—infamous parents even less so. Mine are both and, therefore, eternally one foot ahead of bankruptcy (or behind, depending on the year).

I work as a fine art appraiser and authenticator. Out of grad school, I got a job with Whitman Auction Services, met Pierce Whitman and finally felt like things were on track. I was the appraisal wonder-kid, building a strong professional reputation.

But six months ago, Grammy died of cancer.

It happened so fast. She was with me one week and then gone the next. Cancer does that sometimes. *Devastated* doesn't begin to describe the blackness of my grief.

I had lived with Grammy through most of high school and college, as my parents didn't have the time or money to deal with me. Grammy's arthritis made housework difficult, so I did the cooking and cleaning. We thrifted and budgeted and laughed and somehow made it on her small pension.

Grammy taught me the art of rich-slumming—you know, shopping sales and outlets, cultivating style over expensive couture . . . basically, maintaining a facade of having cash. It's critical in my line of work. Rich clients prefer to work with stylish peers, not charity cases.

But after Grammy died and Pierce . . . did what he did . . . money evaporated right along with my professional credibility.

The meeting this morning was my hail-Mary pass. The last-minute buzzer basket. I was pinned to the mat and about to be counted down-and-out.

I paused, trying to think of another cheesy sports metaphor.

Basically, I needed this job or I was benched.

Reaching the edge of the Piazza del Duomo, I spent a moment drinking in the enormous white-marble cathedral and its distinctive red dome. (Renaissance. Victorian facade.) It never failed to impress. I took a few more selfies and kept walking.

Ten minutes later, I arrived in the Piazza della Santissima Annuziata, stopping short of the palazzo that was the location of my potentially life altering meeting.

The piazza was all charming Firenze, with overhanging arched loggias running the length of the buildings on three sides. A fountain and small gated monument decorated the middle.

I'm one of those people who would rather be a half hour early than two minutes late. But there is such a thing as *too early* and that currently described me.

In an attempt to calm my nerves while I waited, I flipped into my phone's camera roll and opened my first selfie of the day.

Me, across the street from my hotel. Standing on the bridge Ponte Santa Trinitá with the Ponte Vecchio and its precariously clinging medieval houses behind me.

I stared at the photo. Surprised.

And then gave a much-needed smile.

A man stood smack in the middle of my selfie.

The best part? He was dressed like Mr. Darcy from *Pride and Prejudice.* Completely legit.

Top hat, olive-green tail coat, fawn-colored breeches, waistcoat, snowy cravat, tasseled knee-high boots, gloved hands holding a polished walking stick.

His hat sat low, shadowing his face and eyes. I got the impression of dark hair, long nose and full lips.

Okay. Score one for awesome randomness.

Was there some sort of Jane Austen festival going on today?

Or was this a little gift from Grammy?

No one would have appreciated a guy dressed up like something from BBC central casting more than her.

I chuckled and sent a mental *thank you* heavenward. I had desperately needed this boost.

What is it about guys in Regency era costume? It's like insta-toe-curling hotness.

I'm not going to lie; I spent a solid thirty seconds staring at those tight breeches. Because *da-yum*.

And whywhywhy hadn't I seen him when I first took the picture?

I would have taken a second, third and, let's face it, fourth photo.

And then walked across the street and asked if I could take a selfie snuggled up close. Would he smell as good as he looked?

This mysterious Mr. Darcy felt . . . electric. Thrilling.

Which was too bad.

I had sworn off thrilling and exciting men many years ago.

And in the last six months, I had given up the steady, boring ones too.

Cold sober. That was me.

No men.

Not just a temporary boy*cott*, as Grammy would have called it. Nope.

You have a man*agement crisis.* I could hear her laugh. *Time to become officially* e*man*c*ipated. Write yourself a proclamation, sweetheart.*

I had vowed to never trust men again, especially after Pierce—

I swallowed. I still had twenty minutes before scurrying down that rabbit hole. No need to jump into it voluntarily beforehand.

I gave Mr. Darcy one last longing look (and maybe even blew him a kiss . . . from Grammy, of course, not me.)

And then swiped to the next photo.

Stared.

Swiped to the next.

The next.

And the next.

Breathe. Just breathe.

He was *there.*

Mr. Darcy.

In Every. Single. Photo.

Walking toward me along a medieval street, sun streaming behind.

Standing in the middle of Piazza della Signoria, tourists eddying around him.

Paused beside a boutique storefront, head angled my way.

Resting a shoulder into the white marble facade of the Duomo, hand on his walking stick.

It was this *zing* with each image. Something about the man seemed . . . monumental.

As if he could *see* me. As if he knew me, to my very inner self.

My hands shook, heartbeat pounding in my ears.

How had I not noticed someone following me?

I whirled around, scanning the piazza—the hum of passing tourists, the roar of a motorcycle, the occasional voice yelling in staccato Italian.

No historical romance novel models in sight.

I closed my eyes.

Breathe. Calm down. Reason your way through this.

I was simply paranoid. Trauma does that to you. Turns you into someone who sees danger in the innocuous. First an old gypsy lady yelling bizarre things. Now a costume-inclined man with a fetish for photo bombing.

Weird, sure. But hardly threatening, per se.

Besides, what idiot would stalk someone in plain sight dressed like a Regency era nobleman? No one, right? That was nutty even by my skewed standards.

Most likely, Mr. Darcy had just been heading my direction and thought it amusing to pop into my photos.

The reality? This meeting was too critical for me to lose focus; I *needed* this job.

If Mr. Darcy had an issue with me, he could take a number and get in line.

Visit www.NicholeVan.com to buy your copy of
Gladly Beyond today and continue the story.

Intertwine
HOUSE OF OAK, BOOK 1

PROLOGUE

The obsession began on June 12, 2008 around 11:23 a.m.

Though secretly Emme Wilde considered it more of a 'spiritual connection' than an actual full-blown neurosis.

Of course, her brother, Marc, her mother and a series of therapists all begged to disagree.

Thankfully her best friend, Jasmine, regularly validated the connection and considered herself to be Emme's guide through this divinely mystical union of predestined souls (her words, not Emme's). Marc asserted that Jasmine was not so much a guide as an incense-addled enabler (again, his words, not Emme's). Emme was just grateful that anyone considered the whole affair normal—even if it was only Jasmine's loose sense of 'normal.'

Jasmine always insisted Emme come with her to estate sales, and this one outside Portland, Oregon proved no exception. Though Jasmine contended *this* particular estate sale would be significant for Emme, rambling on about circles colliding in the vast cosmic ocean creating necessary links between lives—blah, blah. All typical Jasmine-speak.

Emme brushed it off, assuming that Jasmine really just wanted someone to organize the trip: plan the best route to avoid traffic, find a quirky restaurant for lunch, entertain her on the long drive from Seattle.

At the estate sale, Emme roamed through the stifling tents, touching the cool wood of old furniture, the air heavy with that mix of dust, moth balls and disuse that marks aged things. Jasmine predictably disappeared into a corner piled with antique quilts, hunting yet again for that elusive log cabin design with black centers instead of the traditional red.

But Emme drifted deeper, something pulling her farther and farther into the debris of lives past and spent. To the trace of human passing, like fingerprints left in the paint of a pioneer cupboard door. Stark and clear.

Usually Emme would have stopped to listen to the stories around her, the history grad student in her analyzing each detail. Yet that day she didn't. She just wandered, looking for something. Something specific.

If only she could remember what.

Skirting around a low settee in a back corner, Emme first saw the antique trunk. A typical mid-nineteenth century traveling chest, solid with mellow aged wood. It did not call attention to itself. But it stood apart somehow, almost as if the air were a little lighter around it.

She first opened the lid out of curiosity, expecting the trunk to be empty. Instead, she found it full. Carefully shifting old books and papers, Emme found nothing of real interest.

Until she reached the bottom right corner.

There she found a small object tucked inside a brittle cotton handkerchief. Gently unwrapping the aged fabric, she pulled out an oval locket. Untouched and expectant.

Filigree covered the front, its gilt frame still bright and untarnished, as if nearly new.

Emme turned the locket over, feeling its heft in her hand, the metal cool against her palm. It hummed with an almost electric pulse. How long had the locket lain wrapped in the trunk?

Transparent crystal partially covered the back. Under the crystal, two locks of hair were woven into an intricate pattern—one bright and fair, the other a dark chocolate brown. Gilded on top of the crystal, two initials nestled together into a stylized gold symbol.

She touched the initials, trying to make them out. One was clearly an F. But she puzzled over the other for a moment, tracing the design with her eyes. And then she saw it. Emme sucked in a sharp breath. An E. The other initial was an E.

She opened the locket, hearing the small pop of the catch.

A gasp.

Her hands tingled.

A sizzling shock started at the back of her neck and then spread.

Him.

There are moments in life that sear into the soul. Brief glimpses of some larger force. When so many threads collapse into one. Coalesce into a single truth.

Seeing *him* for the first time was one of those moments.

He gazed intently out from within the right side of the locket: blond, blue-eyed, chiseled with a mouth hinting at shared laughter. Emme's historian mind quickly dated his blue-green, high collared jacket and crisp, white shirt and neckcloth to the mid-Regency era, probably around 1812, give or take a year.

Emme continued to look at the man—well, stare actually. His golden hair finger-combed and deliciously disheveled. Broad shoulders angled slightly toward the viewer. Perhaps his face a shade too long and his nose a little too sharp for true beauty. But striking. Handsome even.

Looking expectant, as if he had been waiting for her.

Emme would forever remember the jolt of it.

Surprise and recognition.

She knew him. Had known him.

Somehow, somewhere, in some place.

He felt agonizingly familiar. That phantom part of her she had never realized was lost.

The sensation wasn't quite deja vu.

More like memory.

Like suddenly finding that vital thing you didn't realize had been misplaced. Like coming up, gasping for air, after nearly drowning and seeing the world bright and sparkling and new.

She stood mesmerized by *him* until Jasmine joined her.

"Oooh, you found him." The hushed respect in her voice was remarkable. This was Jasmine after all.

Emme nodded mutely.

"Your circles are so closely intertwined. Amazing."

Jasmine turned the locket in Emme's hand.

"What does this inscription say?" she asked.

Emme hadn't noticed the engraved words on the inside left of the locket case. But now she read them. Her sudden sharp inhalation seared, painfully clenching.

Oh. *Oh!*

The words reverberated through her soul, shattering and profound.

Emme didn't recall much more of that day—Jasmine purchasing the locket or even the little restaurant where they ate lunch. Instead, she only remembered the endless blur of passing trees on the drive home, the inscription echoing over and over:

To E
throughout all time
heart of my soul
your F

———

Visit www.NicholeVan.com to buy your copy of
Intertwine today and continue the story.

About the Author

An international bestselling author, Nichole Van is an artist who feels life is too short to only have one obsession. In former lives, she has been a contemporary dancer, pianist, art historian, choreographer, culinary artist and English professor.

Most notably, however, Nichole is an acclaimed photographer, winning over thirty international accolades for her work, including Portrait of the Year from WPPI in 2007. (Think Oscars for wedding and portrait photographers.) Her unique photography style has been featured in many magazines, including Rangefinder and Professional Photographer. She is also the creative mind behind the popular website Flourish Emporium which provides resources for photographers.

All that said, Nichole has always been a writer at heart. With an MA in English, she taught technical writing at Brigham Young University for ten years and has written more technical manuals than she can quickly count. She decided in late 2013 to start writing fiction and has since become an Amazon #1 bestselling author. Additionally, her late 2016 release, *Love's Shadow*, was selected as a Whitney Award finalist.

In February 2017, Nichole, her husband and three crazy children moved from the Rocky Mountains in the USA to Bridge of Weir, Scotland. They currently live in a former Victorian orphanage nestled against the Scottish highlands and enjoy walks through the countryside and along the lochs.

She is known as NicholeVan all over the web: Facebook, Instagram, Pinterest, etc. Visit http://www.NicholeVan.com to sign up for her author newsletter and be notified of new book releases. Additionally, you can see her photographic work at http://photography.nicholeV.com and http://www.nicholeV.com

If you enjoyed this book, please leave a short review on Amazon. com. Wonderful reviews are the elixir of life for authors. Even better than dark chocolate.